CALEB GRINNED

When he'd first seen Rebecca, she'd been crouched on the floor hemming a gown, a pair of wire-rimmed spectacles teetering on the tip of her nose. Pins stuck out of her mouth in every direction, and she'd pricked herself trying to hurriedly remove them. He still remembered the curse she'd muttered, thinking she'd said it too quietly for her unexpected visitors to hear. Caleb had heard, though, and he'd had a hard time biting back a laugh.

She was a scrawny, homely thing, her brown hair pulled back in a too-tight bun at the base of her neck, her faded calico dress hanging like a rag doll's.

But Rebecca hadn't looked homely today.

Caleb had hardly recognized her without the spectacles, her cheeks rosy with anger, her hair still in a bun but looser this time and piled atop her head.

Caleb suddenly wondered what it would be like to remove the pins from her chestnut hair. To feel the long, silky tresses running over his warm fingertips.

At the startling thought, Caleb's stomach muscles tightened . . . and his smug smile disappeared. . . .

Cinnamon and Roses

Heidi Betts

LEISURE BOOKS NEW YORK CITY

A LEISURE BOOK®

January 2000

Published by

Dorchester Publishing Co., Inc.
276 Fifth Avenue
New York, NY 10001

ISBN 0-8439-4668-7

To Mom and Dad

Thank you for twenty-seven years of food, shelter, and clothing; for conference fees, trip after trip to the post office, and rides to all of my many meetings. For your unwavering support these past several years, and for not letting your initial concern over my choice of career show too much. When people asked how long I was going to mooch off you, you answered with a staunch, "As long as we let her." Here's hoping you'll soon be able to mooch off me.

And to Toby, who—for a little brother—doesn't seem overly embarrassed by the fact that his sister writes romance. Thanks for all the help with my multitude of computer woes. (And, by the way, I can work a mouse . . . just not a printer, scanner, or webpage.)

And a very special thank you to Linda Shertzer. When I was at a very low point with this story, convinced by unkind spirits that it was useless to continue, you quietly took my synopsis, read it during a conference workshop, and told me it was fine. "Go home and finish it," you said. I did, and look what happened. A simple thank you will never be thanks enough.

ACKNOWLEDGMENTS

Special thanks to Ann Marie Wishard, owner of Sweet Annie Herbs in Centre Hall, PA and author of *Sweet Annie's Healing Herbs*. Not only for teaching me more about herbs than I ever hoped to know, but for helping me with the research for this story by telling me exactly how much of which herbs to use when.

Cinnamon
and Roses

Chapter One

Leavenworth, Kansas, 1880

If that arrogant pig thinks he can get away with this, he's sadly mistaken. Rebecca's hand tightened around the bill that had been returned to her several minutes ago, along with only half the payment due. Not that Caleb Adams couldn't afford to pay. The man's father owned the Adams Express stagecoach company, Leavenworth's only form of public transportation. It was bad enough that Caleb Adams had come to town three weeks earlier with his mistress in tow, but now he refused to pay Rebecca for the elaborate gown the woman had ordered. He'd sent what he thought "the gown was truly worth."

The gown was worth a small fortune in labor alone! Sabrina Leslie had taken nearly an hour to look at all the fashion plates, then decided that not one of them really appealed to her. Rebecca had spent the next three hours drawing sketch after sketch until Sabrina declared it was "Perfect!" Rebecca thought it just plain tawdry.

11

The gown was blood-red with a nearly nonexistent bodice, the sleeves mere threads of silk covered by matching feathers.

Feathers! Contrary to Sabrina's beliefs, not every seamstress had red feathers just floating around in case some man's mistress wanted them on a dress. Rebecca had been forced to buy a chicken from a farmer outside of town. Thank God he'd killed it for her before she had to pluck it and dye the feathers to match the gown's material.

If that isn't worth a few measly dollars of Caleb Adams's family fortune, Rebecca thought, *I'll eat my shoe!* Which was now getting very dusty as she stomped down the main street of town toward the Adams Express office.

For a Saturday afternoon, Leavenworth was fairly busy. Most days there were no more than half-a-dozen people on the sidewalks. But in mid-June, the local ranchers sent their cattle to be sold. That left the small town crowded with herds being brought in every day by men who needed a good night's rest and a hot meal before moving on to Kansas City, where they would ship the cattle east by railroad. The cattle drives would continue throughout the summer, making Leavenworth a bit of a boomtown.

Rebecca's mind was not on the visiting cowboys, however, but on the man she was about to see. *Don't let his wealth intimidate you. Remember, you've seen richer men than Caleb Adams with their britches down around their ankles. He's no better than you are. You not only need that money, you deserve it.*

Rebecca's quick footsteps echoed on the boardwalk as she stormed into the Adams Express office, letting the door slam open and swing back on well-oiled hinges. Built all of oak, the walls were covered with maps, stagecoach designs, and schedules. A marred but freshly polished counter stretched the length of the room, separating the ticket seller from those waiting on the available bench for their stage.

Holbrook Adams, a gentle-looking, gray-haired man in his fifties, stood behind the counter, his black waistcoat pulling tightly across his thick middle. He had always been very amiable, and Rebecca thought that if she could choose a father, it would be someone as gracious and good-natured as Holbrook Adams. She was sorry he would be witness to the tongue-lashing she intended to give his less impressive son.

"May I help you?" he asked, bushy salt-and-pepper eyebrows lifted curiously.

Rebecca swept the room with a glance, spotting the dark figure of Caleb Adams sitting behind a desk in the small back office. "I'm here to see him," she said and started forward. Holbrook made no move to stop her.

Caleb's tall form was bent over the table, scrutinizing the work in front of him. His suit coat was slung haphazardly across the back of one of the extra chairs in the room, leaving him in a wrinkled white shirt. A loosened black string tie hung miserably around the collar as if it was about to give up all hope of surviving and plunge to its death. A tuft of his pitch-black hair fell forward, covering one of his dark-lashed eyes.

She was sure he heard her entrance, but Caleb Adams had yet to look up. Rebecca stopped in front of the cluttered mahogany desk and waited. She thought about slamming the office door for emphasis but decided against it; she wanted his attention, she wanted her money, but she did not want him to think she was addlepated.

Taking this opportunity to study him, she wondered how she ever could have found him the least bit attractive. When he had brought Sabrina to her shop to be fitted, Rebecca's first impression of him was that he resembled an Arabian stallion. He stood half a foot taller than she, and in her mind she could easily place him

13

running wild across a night desert, his dark coloring mixing with the shadows, his deep brown eyes flashing, reflecting the glow of the moon and his desire to be free. But whether or not Rebecca found him handsome was a moot point. She had no intention of ever getting involved with a man.

"Mr. Adams?" Rebecca forced through clenched teeth.

Long seconds passed as he finished what he was writing and, with aggravating slowness, set the pen aside and lifted his head. "Yes?"

"Mr. Adams," she said again in a calm, businesslike voice, holding the bill out for him to see. "You brought Miss Leslie to my home two weeks ago to be fitted for a gown, instructing me to send you the bill. I did that. But in this morning's mail I received only half payment. Would you mind paying me the rest of what you owe?"

Caleb Adams reached across the desk and took the crumpled papers from her hand. "Did you read the letter I enclosed?" he asked with cool diplomacy.

"Yes, I did, and I must tell you that the gown I made was worth every penny I charged."

"I beg to differ, Miss . . . uh, what was it again?"

"Rebecca."

"Well, Rebecca," he said, smiling lazily, his eyes glittering. "I've bought many gowns for Miss Leslie—some even more extravagant than the one you made—and you must understand that I won't pay more for a gown out here than I would in New York City."

Rebecca pressed clenched fists into her hips, stifling the urge to throttle the arrogantly handsome man who stared up at her as if she were the one who didn't understand the value of a dollar. "Mr. Adams, may I remind you that in Kansas things cost a bit more, because supplies have to be transported from larger cities. The silk used for Miss Leslie's gown, for instance, I ordered from New York. So, you see, it most likely *would* cost less if you had the dress made there."

"Still, the price you're asking is outrageous. I won't pay."

"You will," Rebecca said calmly, though her blood was boiling.

"I will not," he repeated, smiling that maddeningly complacent smile once again.

"Oh, but you will," Rebecca insisted, stepping forward until the edge of the desk pressed against the front of her thighs. "If I have to be your shadow every day for the rest of your life, if I have to haunt you, even after death, you will pay me for that dress."

"Be my shadow? Haunt me?" A deep, sardonic laugh filled the room. "Would you really go that far, Miss Rebecca?"

"Mr. Adams," Rebecca said, tilting her head forward a bit, "you have no idea how far I would go to collect what is owed me."

Caleb leaned back in his chair, ease radiating from every pore of his body. "That could be very amusing. You haunting me through all eternity over a silly gown Sabrina will probably wear only once."

Rebecca bit the inside of her cheek, expecting to taste blood. She tried to breathe evenly, waiting until the urge to kill Caleb Adams passed. "Do you have any idea how long I worked on that gown or what I had to do to please your Miss Leslie?" She could feel her body turning hotter with every word. "I had to pluck a chicken. Do you hear me? *A chicken!*"

"Why would you want to do something like that?"

Rebecca gave in to her fury and kicked the foot of his desk, succeeding only in redirecting her anger from Caleb Adams to his equally despicable furniture. "I did not *want* to pluck the damn chicken! I did it because Miss Leslie guaranteed me that you would pay generously for my trouble. Otherwise, I assure you, she could have gone without those blasted feathers!"

Not waiting for a response, Rebecca swung around and stormed out of the office and through the front door—a little less gracefully than she had entered. Without a glance, she passed people on the street she normally would have stopped to talk to and brushed off their concerns over her noticeable limp.

How dare he refuse to pay her! She had slaved day and night over that dress, sewed until her fingers bled. And for what? Half of what the wretched thing was really worth.

Rebecca didn't slow her pace until she reached the peace and solitude of her home. She slammed the door behind her as hard as she could and went directly to the stove to put on a pot of water for tea. Now what would she do? How would she ever break even? Rebecca mumbled a curse under her breath, damning Caleb Adams to eternal hell.

Caleb watched the angry sway of Rebecca's skirts as she left. Then he turned to stare at the crumpled papers in his hand, noticing that his letter was much more wrinkled than the bill. She must have given it quite a beating. His eyes scanned the numbers written in a neat female hand as he tried to recall the many dressmaker bills he'd paid back in the city. When he calculated the difference between some of those and the one Rebecca had sent, he realized she wasn't really asking that much more. And he doubted any of those city seamstresses had ever plucked a chicken.

His mouth curled up on one side. A chicken! Good Lord, he'd never met *any* woman who would do that.

He tried to envision Sabrina with a dead chicken in her hands, pulling feathers for a dress. With an amused chuckle, he realized Sabrina would never dirty her hands with anything so lowly, not even if she was starving.

He could, however, clearly see Rebecca bent over a

lifeless fowl, strands of her brown hair coming loose from her chignon, her nose crinkled in distaste, plucking for all she was worth, just to satisfy a customer. Of course, a woman like Rebecca wouldn't let anything go to waste. She had probably eaten chicken for a week.

Caleb grinned. When he'd first seen Rebecca, she had been crouched on the floor behind a mannequin, hemming a gown, a pair of wire-rimmed spectacles teetering on the tip of her nose. Pins stuck out of her mouth in every direction, and she'd pricked herself trying to hurriedly remove them. He still remembered the curse she'd muttered, thinking she'd said it too quietly for her unexpected visitors to hear. Sabrina hadn't heard. She had been too preoccupied, frowning over Rebecca's tiny shack of a house, which was also her seamstress shop. Caleb had heard, though, and he'd had a hard time biting back a laugh.

She was a scrawny, homely thing, her light brown hair pulled back in a too-tight bun at the base of her neck, the faded calico day dress hanging from her shoulders like a well-worn rag doll's. He remembered thinking she ought to wear more attractive clothes if she expected people to order gowns from her.

But she hadn't looked homely today. He had hardly recognized her when she first burst into the station, not without those spectacles teetering on the tip of her nose. When he realized who she was and what she had most certainly come for, he'd kept his head down, implying he had far more important things to do than deal with an irate dressmaker. It was a tactic he had used often in New York while running his maternal grandparents' newspaper.

Caleb could still see her in his mind's eye when he'd finally deemed it appropriate to acknowledge her presence. He had to smile. He could tell she was trying to stay calm; though her cheeks were rosy with anger, her teeth remained clenched when she spoke. Her hair was still in a bun, but looser this time, and piled atop her head. Caleb wondered what it would be like to remove the pins from her chestnut hair. He could almost feel the long, silky tresses running over his warm fingertips. At this thought, his stomach muscles tightened suddenly, and the smile disappeared.

The woman who had stormed into his office was quite pretty, if the truth be known. Her peach-and-white gingham dress fit nicely—maybe a bit too nicely. It had been snug enough to accentuate the firm roundness of her breasts and the tapering curve of her waist.

Caleb's fist closed around the bill as he pushed back his chair and stood. It was only fair that he pay her, he decided. He would just have to make it clear to Sabrina that she was not to order such extravagant dresses any longer. He strode out of the cramped office toward the ticket counter, where his father stood.

"Is there a problem, son?" Holbrook asked solemnly, his crooked grin giving away his amusement.

"You couldn't help but hear the lady's tirade," Caleb said in answer to his father's question. He straightened his collar and tried to fix his uncooperative tie. "I suppose she's right. I think I'll go over there and pay her."

His father nodded. "Good idea, son. A very good idea." Holbrook's stomach jiggled as he laughed and then broke into a fit of harsh coughing.

Caleb frowned in concern and waited for his father to regain his breath. Finally Holbrook waved him off, and he left the Express office, heading down the sidewalk toward the opposite end of town where Rebecca's house was located.

As he passed the Wilkes Hotel, he glanced up at the second-story window farthest to the right. Sabrina was probably there now, napping. All that simpering and pouting must be exhausting, Caleb thought with a shake of his head. Sabrina was beginning to get bored with Leavenworth. She had told Caleb, after their first week in town, that she tried to make friends with some of the local ladies, but they all sniffed rudely and ignored her, wanting nothing to do with a fallen woman.

Caleb had planned to return to New York at the first opportunity, but now it looked as if he would be staying in Leavenworth a while longer. His father's recovery from the illness that remained a mystery to Doc Meade seemed slow. Maybe he ought to send Sabrina back to her apartments in the city. She would be happier there, and he would no longer have to listen to her complaints about being so far from "polite company." He could give her enough money to keep her occupied until his return—if he returned.

Caleb had just passed the post office, which doubled as a telegraph office, when he heard someone calling his name. He turned to see a tall, reed-thin young man coming toward him.

"Oh, Mr. Adams, am I glad to catch you." The man wiped his forehead with his shirtsleeve, disturbing his adequately greased and combed blond hair. "This just came over the wire from New York. It's for your father, but it sounds mighty important. I thought maybe you could take it to him."

Caleb took the paper the man held out and read it. "Damn!" he swore, instantly turning and starting back across the dusty street toward the Express office. Once there, he smacked the telegram onto the counter. "She's missing," he told his father.

"Who?" Holbrook asked.

"Megan, that's who. Mother says she disappeared two nights ago."

"Dear God," Holbrook whispered, picking up the paper. "What are we going to do?"

"I'll tell you what I'm going to do," Caleb said. "When I find her, I'm going to—"

"How are you going to find her when we don't even know where she went?"

Caleb had already been thinking about that. Why would his sister have run away in the first place? She was only sixteen, not interested in any young man that Caleb knew of, so she hadn't run off to get married. So where could she have gone? Her only family was Mother in New York and he and Holbrook here in Leavenworth.

Caleb nodded decisively. "She's on her way here."

"What?" his father asked, obviously confused.

"When Megan found out I was leaving, she cried for days. She begged me to bring her along, but I wouldn't."

"Whyever not? I'd love for her to come here and live."

"She has school, Dad. Besides that, Mother insists the city is a better place for a girl her age. She'll make friends and, with Mother's influence, be right in the heart of society."

Holbrook's face fell. "True," he said. "Not that I wouldn't rather she were here."

"If I'm right, she will be. Probably today or tomorrow." He stepped outside, waiting for his father to join him. "I'd better telegraph Mother. She'll be worried sick. When does the next stage pull in?"

Holbrook took out his watch and checked the time. "Any minute now."

"I won't be surprised if Megan just happens to be on it." Caleb took a few steps, then turned back to face his father. "If you decide to thrash her, don't be too harsh." He started away, muttering, "Leave some skin for me."

Rebecca stood at an open window with a cup of tea in her hands. She watched Caleb Adams walking down the main street of town in her direction. Her heart leapt as she realized he might be coming to pay the rest of her bill. She flushed, taking back every mean, nasty name she had called him only minutes earlier.

And then, as she saw him stop, speak to the telegraph

operator, and turn to walk back across town, she called him all the names again—adding some new ones and even inventing a few. She stomped her foot, sloshing tea over the rim of the cup and burning her stomach through the material of her dress.

"Now look what you've done, Caleb Adams," she said, brushing at the hot stain. She looked up and saw the afternoon stage barreling into town, stirring up a great cloud of dust. "I hope that thing runs you over. You deserve it."

The Kansas sun beat down on the roof of the Concord coach, baking its tired, dusty passengers. Between the heat and the ruts the stage kept hitting, Megan Adams didn't think she had a chance in Hades of making it to Leavenworth alive. Trying to keep her hair from matting to her sweat-dampened forehead, she ran her fingertips through the dark strands. She would surprise her father and brother, all right—when they were forced to drag her lifeless body out of the stagecoach.

Megan shifted slightly on the hard seat, tugging at the front of her blouse to pull the silk away from her sticky skin. She forced herself to smile at the couple in the seat across from her. They had been staring at her, not saying a word, since they all boarded the stage together. It was like traveling with two corpses.

If she didn't get out of this oven soon, Megan knew she would go mad. Her body felt on fire, every layer of her expensive clothing like another log thrown on to build the blaze. Her mother had always filled her closets with dresses, skirts, and blouses made of the finest materials, but she would rather wear a flour sack for a trip halfway across the country. She smiled secretly, reveling in the knowledge that she had thrown her frilly, annoying hat from the train as soon as they'd pulled away from the depot.

"Leavenworth!" the driver yelled. "Comin' up on Leavenworth, folks!"

Finally, Megan thought, mentally preparing herself for coming face-to-face with her father and brother. It wasn't her father she was worried about so much as Caleb. Papa would be too glad that she was safe to scold her, but Caleb would ream her up one side and down the other—and then threaten to send her home.

Well, she wouldn't go. She just wouldn't. She might be only sixteen years old, but she was certainly mature enough to know she didn't want to live in New York City with Mother any longer. Megan was tired of being treated like her mother's favorite china doll, dressed up and dragged to society parties.

Megan's fingers clenched into a fist around the drawstring of her silken purse. This was all Mother's own fault. If she had been faithful to Papa, Megan and Caleb and their parents could still be living together as one big, happy family.

Megan looked out the stagecoach window at the flat, never-ending horizon. But now Mother lived the life she adored in New York City—and she could do that without Megan—while Papa was happy in Leavenworth, running his stagecoach company. His life seemed infinitely more appealing.

The coach came to a rough halt, and Megan heard the driver jump to the ground. She took a deep breath, hoping she could at least get a little acquainted with the Kansas town before Caleb tied her to the back of the next outgoing stage and sent her home.

Chapter Two

The minute she stepped down from the stage, Megan saw her father and Caleb waiting on the sidewalk. Her father's face seemed calm, but Caleb's was set in a deep scowl, his arms folded across his chest, legs apart in a firm stance. She smiled and tried to pretend he wasn't about to skin her alive.

"Papa!" Megan said, dropping her valise to the ground and running into Holbrook's arms. "Oh, Papa, I missed you so much."

"I missed you, too, Pumpkin. But if you ever scare us like that again—"

"I think this is where I come in," Caleb interrupted. He hugged Megan tightly, then drew back to look at her intently. "You had Mother in near hysterics, young lady. What do you have to say for yourself?"

"Did I have you in near hysterics, too?" she asked cheekily. Caleb took a deep breath, and Megan saw his nostrils flare. She slanted her eyes away from him, wondering if she had pushed too far.

"I am not amused by your antics or your attitude,

23

young lady. You took off without leaving a note or telling anybody where you were going. For someone who wants to be treated like an adult, that was very irresponsible of you, Megan."

She knew she was in trouble any time her brother called her "young lady." Megan stared down at the ground, knowing Caleb was right. "Oh, I just couldn't stand it anymore. When you left, there was no one for me to talk to."

Any passerby who happened to hear their discussion might wonder why Caleb was chastising Megan while Holbrook stood by and watched, saying nothing. But it was Caleb who felt responsible for Megan's upbringing. Their mother did her best but was usually more concerned with social functions. And Holbrook could hardly raise his children from six states away. So Caleb had taken it upon himself to make sure Megan turned out properly.

"What about your schooling?"

"I'm off for the summer. You know that," Megan answered.

"What about next year?" Caleb asked through tightly clenched teeth.

Megan shuffled her feet, her head down. "I thought maybe I could go to school out here next year."

"You want to walk three miles into town every morning for school, then turn around and walk back every afternoon?" Caleb asked in a dissuading tone.

"Of course not," she answered. "I'll just come into town with you and Papa each morning."

They both turned at the sound of their father clearing his throat. "She has a point there," Holbrook said.

Caleb could tell his father was trying hard to keep from smiling. Caleb stood even straighter and turned his attention back to the matter at hand. "Megan, think about this. What future could there possibly be this far west for a young lady like yourself? There are no fine schools, no society functions, and certainly no decent young men would come this far looking for a wife."

Megan put her hands on her hips and threw Caleb a glare. "Who said I wanted to be a belle of society or catch myself a rich husband? If I wanted any of those silly, superficial things, I would have stayed home with Mother. God knows she's already started a list of guests to invite to my wedding—provided she finds the proper husband for me soon."

She twisted one foot back and forth on its heel. "I'm only sixteen, Caleb. I don't want to marry and start a family. I want a chance to see the rest of the world; I know it can't all be like New York. I want to see what Papa does. It must be big and important if he asked you to come out here to help him." Tears gathered in her eyes. "Most of all," she sniffed, "I want to be where my family is."

Caleb looked at Holbrook, whose own eyes had clouded. He wanted to argue with Megan that Leavenworth was no place for a gently reared girl like her, but he knew it would do no good. And besides that, several people had started to gather, listening to Megan's theatrical speech.

Caleb put a gentle hand on Megan's arm and led her into the Adams Express office. When they were all inside the back office, away from curious onlookers, he turned to his sister once more. A smile lit her face, and he knew she was thinking she'd won the battle.

"This isn't over, Megan. We'll discuss it further when we get home tonight." She nodded, but Caleb could tell she wasn't concerned. It was difficult for Caleb to admit he really had no intention of making Megan go back to New York. Oh, he would argue with her, try to convince her that it was best, but he knew Megan would stick to her convictions. He was counting on it. Neither he nor his father could bear to send her away if this was truly where she wanted to live. She might be young, but Megan knew what she wanted; she always had. And once she set her heart on something, she went after it with a passion few people possessed.

Caleb shook his head and gestured for Megan to have a seat until the office closed.

It was just getting dark outside when Rebecca dropped a cinnamon stick into the teapot, removed it from the stove, and carried it to the kitchen table. She let it steep while she brought lamps to set around the rocking chair she usually sat in to sew. She had a lot of work to do before the Wednesday Group came to call.

With all the lamps lit, the area around her chair was quite bright. She brought the tea and a cup and saucer to the table beside the rocker and sat down, putting on her spectacles and picking up the pink calico dress she was trying to finish for Anabelle Archer.

Outside, the noises of the town crept through her closed windows. Friday and Saturday nights were Leavenworth's busiest, and Rebecca's most unsettling. The playful—and sometimes not so playful—gunfire, the tinny music filtering out of the Dog Tick Saloon, the raucous laughter of drunken cowboys and the girls they hired for an hour or the night all made Rebecca sickly uncomfortable. That was why, even on the hottest of evenings, like tonight, Rebecca kept all her doors and windows closed.

Memories, that's all they are, Rebecca tried to tell herself. But it didn't matter. They were bad memories, things she couldn't seem to forget, things she had a hard time putting behind her.

A woman's scream ripped through the air. Rebecca jumped, stabbing herself with her needle. She stuck the bleeding finger into her mouth, cursing silently before pushing the spectacles back up the bridge of her nose with the back of her wrist. A series of shorter, more frantic screams followed, taking Rebecca back to a night long ago. A night she would give anything to forget.

She had been only ten years old, desperately trying to fall asleep on the small, hard cot that passed as her bed, but the noise was too loud, too distracting, as usual. Her bedroom was nothing more than a back storage room in the Scarlet Garter, the most prosperous whorehouse in Kansas City.

Rebecca had just turned over, hoping a new position might help, when the first scream tore through the darkness. She sat up straight, tilting her head to hear better. She heard it again and knew it was her mother. Jumping out of bed, still dressed in the shirt and trousers she always wore, she ran out of the room toward the screams.

She came to a halt at the corner of the hallway when she saw a crowd of onlookers gathering. Slowly, on her hands and knees, she crawled forward, slipping between pairs of booted and bare feet. She got to the doorway and peered around its edge.

The sight that met her far-from-innocent eyes made bile rise in her throat. Her mother was lying on her back, a big, bearded man on top of her. Both were naked. Her mother was still trying to scream, even though the man had one hand locked around her throat. He raised his fist over and over again, bringing it down with a sickening thump on her mother's face. "Goddamn bitch!" he bellowed.

Lilah, the house's proprietress, stood next to the bed, hitting the man on the back with his own cane. "Let go of her, you bastard! Let go of my girl!" Every few seconds Lilah would holler for one of the bouncers.

Finally one came. Dexter, a huge, red-haired seventeen-year-old pushed his way through the crowd and stomped into the room. He grabbed Kate's abuser by the scruff of the neck and tossed him off the bed. Dex stood, feet apart, hands on hips, over the customer's still form, waiting for him to fight back. The man didn't move.

Lilah went to Kate, holding her and trying to wipe away a little of the blood covering her face. Laying Kate back against a pillow, Lilah signaled one of her other girls to come sit with Rebecca's battered mother.

Lilah grabbed up every article of the bearded man's clothing, including his cane, and went to where he was slumped on the floor. She threw the things at him violently. "Take your clothes and your money and get your fat ass out of my place." She gave him a kick in the side for good measure. "And don't ever come back." Turning to Dex, she said, "Get that worthless bastard out of here."

Dex grabbed the man's arm, hauling him to his feet. The man tried desperately to cover his lower body, but to no avail. Dexter pushed through the crowd. "The show's over," he said in a thick Irish brogue. "Get yer butts back ta work, girlies. Yer not makin' any money standin' out here."

Rebecca could still see her mother. Her face was clean of blood now, but she was moaning, and Rebecca could tell she was in pain. She wanted to help her, so she inched into the room. "Mama?" she said softly.

Kate finally glanced her way and said, "Get the hell out of here, kid."

"You'll be a mess in the morning, Katie," one of the girls said, squeezing a cloth over the water basin. The water turned dark red.

Rebecca didn't move, frightened and confused and wishing both to comfort and be comforted. Again Kate glanced her way but only to snarl, "Didn't I tell you to get lost? Christ, you're always in the way, you dumb little bastard."

A gunshot sounded, snapping Rebecca out of her daze. She jumped out of her chair and closed the curtains, as if that would miraculously keep out the horrible memories Leavenworth's night sounds evoked. Back in her chair, she resumed stitching a piece of white lace on the almost finished day dress.

A strained sound came from Rebecca's throat as memories continued to flood her mind. She'd crept back to her room, lying awake the rest of the night thinking about what she had seen. Rebecca swore to herself that she wouldn't stay in the Scarlet Garter, in her mother's way, a minute longer than she had to. And she would never turn into a woman like Kate, so used to unfeeling whoring that she hadn't an emotion to spare for her very own child.

The next morning, her mother's entire face was covered with ugly, dark-blue bruises, her eyes swelled almost completely shut, her mouth so abused that she could barely talk, except, of course, to periodically chastise her "little bastard." Rebecca swore again that she would get out as soon as she could.

And she had. The very night she overheard Lilah telling Kate that Rebecca was old enough to start working—and heard Kate agreeing without compunction. Three years after her mother had been beaten so badly, Rebecca had stowed away with the baggage on the back of a stagecoach, and she hadn't gotten off until it stopped. She had heard the driver announce that they had arrived in Leavenworth, and she had lived there ever since.

Only because Octavia Fitzgerald had found her and taken her in, though. Widow Fitzgerald was about the kindest person Rebecca had ever known, even if she had been a bit stuck in her ways. She'd given Rebecca a warm, comfortable bed for the first time in her life, and she hadn't let her young guest go to sleep dirty or hungry, either. For that, Rebecca would always be grateful.

But the widow had done more than put a roof over Rebecca's head. Octavia had practically adopted her, walking Rebecca around town as if she were her very own daughter, allowing her to use the name Fitzgerald whenever necessary. And the widow had taught her to sew, little by little preparing her to take over the seamstress shop Octavia ran out of her front room. When Widow Fitzgerald died, Rebecca had done just that.

She took a sip of tea, smiling as the spicy aroma of cinnamon permeated her senses. The house was small and simple—the parlor and kitchen all one, distinguishable only by the furniture, with a curtain sectioning off the bedroom at the back—but Rebecca loved the little building. Octavia had made this small house a home for Rebecca. In return, Rebecca had helped Octavia any way she could, including brightening up the cabin. She had sewn new curtains with tiny pink roses for the four windows, including a longer one to make the bedroom more private and cozy.

Rebecca stood and stretched. She'd finally finished attaching the lace to the bodice of Anabelle's dress, and it was well past midnight. She lay the dress over the back of the rocking chair and her spectacles on the table. She would press the dress tomorrow and remeasure the hem on Wednesday when Anabelle came. Stifling a yawn, she blew out all but one lamp, carrying it with her into the bedroom. She got into her nightdress, climbed into bed, and turned down the light, so tired now that not even Saturday night's noises could keep her awake.

"That man is a sinner! And he thinks nothing of flaunting it."

Rebecca stuck another pin into the hem of Anabelle Archer's dress, listening with only half an ear to the other three ladies discussing Caleb Adams.

The Wednesday Group, Rebecca liked to call them, because they came every Wednesday without fail, partly for Rebecca's sewing, partly for the camaraderie, and partly to ensure that Rebecca had customers even if no one else came the entire week. The ladies had all been friends of Octavia Fitzgerald and wanted to support Rebecca in carrying on with Octavia's business.

"That woman who's always with him is his *mistress*," Hariette Pickins continued, as if the entire town weren't already aware of that fact.

Thelma Wilkes, who, along with her husband, owned the local hotel, leaned forward to whisper, "That's right. He goes up to her room and stays there for hours. Well, it's just awful, I tell you."

"At least he had the decency to get her a room at the hotel. Why, poor Holbrook would have apoplexy if his son brought that woman into his home. He told me he downright hates the idea of Caleb keeping that woman, but he's been trying to get his son to come to Leavenworth for so long, I imagine he's willing to put up with just about anything from the boy."

"I think Mr. Caleb Adams is delightful," Anabelle chimed in from her perch on a tiny stool in the middle of the parlor, clasping her hands over her heart. Rebecca pulled them back down to her sides so the dress's hem would hang evenly for pinning. Anabelle didn't let that deter her enthusiasm. "He's tall and handsome and—"

"Anabelle," her mother interrupted sternly. "Stand still or Rebecca will never get that hem done. And as for Mr. Adams, you are not to discuss him in public. Is that understood? He is a sinful, immoral man."

Rebecca remained silent, done pinning the new hem of Anabelle's pink calico day dress. All it needed was a half inch taken in at the hem and the monogram Anabelle insisted be embroidered on every piece of clothing she owned—three A's for Anabelle Amelia Archer.

"But, Mother," the sixteen-year-old protested, as if reading Rebecca's mind, "he's the only man in town whose last name starts with an A." Anabelle was terrified that when she married her initials would change.

"I said that's enough, Anabelle," Mary said with a

31

weary sigh. Anabelle dropped her head in defeat.

"All right," Rebecca said to the girl, motioning for her to step down from the stool. "Let's go into the bedroom, and I'll help you take the dress off without getting pricked by one of the pins."

When they returned a few minutes later, it was to the same conversation as before. The ladies stood up, preparing to leave in a group, just as they always arrived.

"What do you think of him, Rebecca?" Mrs. Pickins asked, her hand on the doorknob.

"Him?" Rebecca brushed an imaginary piece of lint from her skirt, pretending inattention to the man under discussion.

"Caleb Adams," Hariette provided. "Holbrook Adams's son. The man who came to town last week with his mistress." She whispered the last word.

"I saw him come here with that . . . that kept woman," Thelma Wilkes said. "What did you think of him?"

Rebecca privately thought he was the most arrogant, pig-headed man she'd ever had the displeasure of meeting. "He seemed nice enough," she answered diplomatically, reluctant, as always, to gossip.

"Oh, tell us," Anabelle begged, bobbing up and down in excitement. "You've been closer to him than any of the rest of us. We've only seen him in the street; you've had him in your house. Tell us what you thought of him. Is he as handsome up close as he looks? And, for heaven's sake, what did that woman of his order?"

Rebecca put her hands on her hips, angry at the memory. She actually opened her mouth to confide that Sabrina Leslie had ordered a very expensive gown and that Caleb Adams had yet to pay for it, when the front door opened, pushing Hariette back a few steps.

Rebecca felt her heart do a little flip when she looked up into Caleb Adams's coffee-brown eyes. He stood at least six feet tall, towering over her in his black suit, the string at his neck tied neatly this time. Rebecca straightened her spine, chastising herself for noticing anything good about this man, even his strong, fine looks, when she was still furious with him.

"That's him," she heard Anabelle whisper to her mother, followed by Mary's harsh hushing.

Rebecca swallowed but didn't smile. "May I help you?" she asked. If the room hadn't been filled with women who were bound to relay all happenings to anyone who would listen, Rebecca would have told Caleb to get the hell off her property. She had no time for the infuriating man.

But maybe he's here to pay you. Hope sprouted in her breast. It was then that Rebecca noticed a young woman standing behind Caleb. Her dark hair, nearly black with hints of red where the sun caught it, was pulled back from her face and held with ivory combs. She wore a white blouse with lace at the throat and a forest-green silk skirt.

He's found himself another mistress, she thought with disgust. This one was much prettier, much younger than Sabrina Leslie. Much *too* young. The bastard was amusing himself with a child, for God's sake!

Wearing an arrogant half-smile, Caleb put his hand on the girl's back, urging her forward. "Miss Rebecca, this is Megan. She'll be needing a few things. If you're not too busy," he added, glancing at the other four women.

"No, no," Hariette said quickly, bustling out the door and onto the tiny front porch. "We were just leaving, Mr. Adams." Mrs. Pickins looked warily at Megan but smiled brightly at Caleb as she passed him, followed by the other ladies, all beaming up at the dark, impressive man. "Be sure to tell Holbrook we said hello," Hariette called over her shoulder. "Oh, yes . . . good-bye, Rebecca."

Rebecca tried not to roll her eyes at the older woman's animation. One minute she was complaining about this man's scruples, the next she was batting her lashes like a smitten schoolgirl. Why was it that women so often let men dictate their emotions? The smallest hint of a smile from a handsome man and most women started to swoon.

Well, not Rebecca. She had been around all kinds of men most of her young life, and none had ever impressed her. Men were self-centered, arrogant, and domineering. The one standing right in front of her was ample proof of that!

Rebecca smiled at the young woman and led her to the farthest chair in the parlor, offering a book of fashions for her to look through. Then she went back to where Caleb stood by the door and in a harsh whisper demanded, "Are you crazy? Bringing another woman for dresses when you haven't paid me for the last one I made!"

Caleb shifted his weight, looking down at the mousy little woman who once again had her hair in a tight bun at the nape of her neck. And she was wearing those bloody spectacles that never stayed up. "Listen, Miss Rebecca, I've considered what you said the other day, and—"

Rebecca shook her head and interrupted. "It's bad enough that you have one mistress, but to drag this sweet young girl down to your despicable, immoral level is truly a sin. You're a devil to take that poor soul to bed with you."

Caleb stared at Rebecca in disbelief. Had she just implied that his baby sister was a trollop? And he had been about to pay her the money he supposedly owed her.

"I don't think you should comment on things you know nothing about," he said. He didn't know whether to be amused or insulted by her tirade. She had as much as accused his sister of being his mistress. But then, she had also defended the "poor soul."

He glanced in Megan's direction, hoping she couldn't

hear their conversation. She was immersed in the fashion plates on her lap, seemingly unconcerned with their loud whispers.

"Oh, I've known plenty of men like you, Mr. Adams. Your foremost priority is pleasure—your own—and to hell with who gets hurt. Well, you may be rich enough to get away with it, but I will not be a part of that girl's fall from grace. Get someone else to supply gowns for your whores!"

Caleb thought about gently correcting her mistake—until he registered that remark about his wealth. He was well aware that most women were obsessed with material possessions, but despite her demands for the money he owed her, somehow he hadn't thought this petite little seamstress would be among their ranks. He had thought—since she *had* actually plucked a chicken—that Rebecca was different from so many of the other women he had known.

Caleb let the past and his resentment of women in general linger in his mind and decided to go about enlightening Rebecca in a very different way. "Megan, could you come here, please?"

Rebecca took a step away from him, relieved that Caleb Adams and his new mistress would be leaving. Instead, Caleb held the girl's arm as she stood beside him.

"Megan, I'd like you to meet Leavenworth's finest seamstress, Rebecca. Rebecca, this is Megan Adams. My sister."

Chapter Three

Rebecca's heart stopped. Her mouth fell open. "Excuse me?" she gasped, not believing she'd heard him correctly.

"This is my sister, Megan. She arrived from New York a few days ago without much luggage and will be needing some new dresses to fill her wardrobe. I was hoping you could help."

Caleb smiled arrogantly and continued, making Rebecca weaker and more embarrassed with every word. "There is the matter of that last bill, of course." He tapped his chin with an index finger, as though he were considering. "Not to worry, things will even out nicely, I'm sure."

She was sure, too. He would never pay her for Sabrina Leslie's dress now, not after she had so rudely—and so wrongly—insulted his sister. Oh, Lord, things had been much simpler before this man had come to town.

Rebecca acknowledged Megan's polite greeting in numb shock, feeling she had to make some sort of retribution for her ghastly mistake. "I'm sure Megan will find some patterns she likes. We'll have a new wardrobe started before the end of the week." She smiled at Megan, then turned to look at Caleb. "I would like to apologize for any misunderstanding. I sometimes do and say things without thinking them through first."

"We all do at times, I believe," Caleb answered graciously.

But Rebecca could tell he reveled in her embarrassing predicament. His lofty attitude set her nerves on edge, and her earlier mortification fled. She straightened her spine, pushed the spectacles higher onto her nose, and walked across the parlor, picking up the fashion plates Megan had set aside. Megan quickly followed and sat next to Rebecca on the sofa to look through the patterns.

"Now," Rebecca said to Megan. "If you want something that will be comfortable to wear for almost any activity, you should probably look at these day dress designs." She pointed to four simple sketches. "I have some fabrics I think you'll like that will keep you cool during the day. Cooler than those silks, I imagine." She fingered Megan's heavy skirt.

They continued discussing different materials and designs for several minutes before Rebecca noticed that Caleb still stood where they had left him, his arms crossed over his chest. When he brought Miss Leslie, he'd stayed only long enough to instruct Rebecca to give Sabrina whatever she wanted, and then he had gone across town to the Dog Tick Saloon.

She held his gaze for a moment. "This may take a while. If you'd like, you could come back for your sister in a few hours."

Caleb walked past them and sank into an armchair. "I think I'll stay. To make sure I get what I'm paying for this time," he added pointedly.

Rebecca tensed. "If I remember correctly, you got much more than you paid for the last time. You still owe me—"

37

"And I intend to pay." Caleb was enjoying the confrontation. He liked the way Rebecca's eyes narrowed and her face flushed when she fought to control her temper. He could tell she was itching to tell him to go to hell and she'd buy the ticket. But enough was enough. He had already decided—last week, after she'd stormed out of his office—to settle the bill. He simply hadn't had a chance to do so since Megan's arrival.

His declaration obviously shocked Rebecca. She sat starch still, staring at him as if he'd just sprouted wings and was about to fly out her window. Caleb grinned at her speechlessness.

"As I said, I have every intention of giving you the money." He refrained from mentioning what the bill was for in front of Megan. "Add what I owe you to this bill." Caleb saw her wariness and quickly tried to allay her fears. "I promise to pay whatever you say I owe. Within reason, of course."

Rebecca bristled at his comment, her shoulders rising a notch. "The last bill I sent was within reason, but you seemed to disagree."

"I realize that now, but Megan's order couldn't possibly be too high. She only wants a few day dresses—isn't that right, Meg?"

Megan nodded. "I only brought two dresses with me from New York. It was all I could fit in my bag. Papa says I need more appropriate clothes if I'm going to stay in Leavenworth. I can't go around wearing silk gowns, now can I?" She grabbed a handful of her green silk skirt, holding it out for emphasis. "Not with all the dust and heat you have out here."

Rebecca sat back and blinked in surprise as the initially quiet Megan began talking a mile a minute. "It must seem very rural here compared to what you're used to. I'm surprised anyone from a big city like New York would want to live in Leavenworth."

That wasn't exactly true. Rebecca would rather live

here than anyplace else in the world. Not that Leavenworth was special as cow towns went, but it was the first place that had ever felt like home.

"Oh, the city's not as wonderful as you may think." Megan wrinkled her nose and frowned. "It's crowded and dirty and often wet, and everyone thinks they're so much more important than anyone else."

Yes, that sounded like Caleb Adams, all right. Rebecca slanted him a glance. His eyes were locked on her, as if he were reading her mind, and she felt her face grow suddenly hot.

She cleared her throat and turned her attention back to Megan. "Well, we could be here all day if we don't get serious about this wardrobe. Did you see anything you like?"

"Oh, yes." Megan's face lit up with excitement. "This one," she pointed. "This one. Oh, this one. And that one, too."

"Let's stick with three for now, all right, Meg? Maybe you can come back later for more."

Caleb's cultured voice made Rebecca's skin tingle. She reprimanded herself immediately, knowing she had no business even thinking about a man like Caleb Adams, let alone allowing herself to admit an attraction toward him. *He's like all the others*, she reminded herself. *Just wrapped in a prettier package.*

Caleb pushed open the swinging doors of the Dog Tick Saloon and stepped into the noisy, smoke-filled room. He wasn't sure why he felt the need for a drink, except that he knew he had to go see Sabrina, and he couldn't quite bring himself to do it stone-cold sober.

A tall blonde latched onto his arm almost immediately. Caleb gave her a once-over, taking in her long, stockinged legs and the short red dress that covered little of her upper thighs. Her breasts were small but nice.

For a scant second, Caleb considered taking this

woman upstairs and forgetting about Sabrina over at the Wilkes Hotel. But he had already been away from his demanding mistress for the three days and two nights since Megan's arrival. He might have to send Sabrina back over to Rebecca's for something new and pretty just to assuage her hurt feelings.

Caleb cocked his head toward the blonde, whispered in her ear, and sent her away with a smile. He made his way over to the bar to order a bottle of whiskey, taking it and a glass to an empty corner table far from the loud group of cowboys and saloon girls at the base of the staircase. For long minutes he sat thinking, sipping at the brown liquor. It burned a path down his throat, but he enjoyed the warming sensation it caused in his gut.

He had spent more than three hours in Rebecca's presence, listening to her discuss fashions and styles with his sister. After pulling out his timepiece every few minutes for the first half hour, Caleb had found that he actually enjoyed sitting back and listening to the female conversation and frequent singsong laughter. And now he couldn't seem to get Rebecca's image out of his head. Her bright brown eyes and smooth complexion had somehow gotten stuck in his memory. He could still see the way her head tilted back when she laughed. The rippling sound seemed to echo in his ears.

Damn! Caleb threw back two shots of whiskey in quick succession. Rebecca had said she would haunt him, and she was doing a damn good job of it. But this haunting had nothing to do with claiming money owed.

Caleb's imagination was running riot on him. He couldn't seem to keep himself from wondering what it would be like to take the pins out of Rebecca's hair and let it fall in long rivulets down her back. It would brush her hips and be soft to the touch. Her skin would be pale but sparkle in the dim lamplight like morning dew.

Rebecca would be as passionate in the bedroom as she had been in his office only a few days earlier. Caleb didn't know how he knew this, but his instincts told him it was true. He felt himself grow hard just thinking of her standing naked before him. Caleb couldn't let his mind wander farther down that erotic path or he knew he would explode.

With a muffled curse, he pushed back the rickety saloon chair, grabbed the half-empty bottle, and made a beeline for the Wilkes Hotel, trying not to let his eyes stray to the small house at the end of the street with yellow light shining through its gaily curtained windows. Rebecca would be inside, probably starting one of Megan's dresses. Caleb's pace quickened, and he took the hotel steps two at a time. He opened the door to Sabrina's room without knocking. A gust of thick, sickly-sweet perfume washed over him, nearly making his eyes water.

The Wilkes Hotel was one of only two lodging houses Leavenworth could offer, and this corner room was the best they had, though small by city standards. It boasted two windows draped with thick white curtains, one overlooking the town's busy thoroughfare, the other facing the farther, more deserted end of town—where Rebecca lived. A dark, intricately designed dresser lined one wall, with a full-length cheval glass in the corner. Matching nightstands and oil lamps decorated each side of the large canopy bed at the opposite end of the room. The carpet was still deep cherry red but worn and slightly faded around the dresser and bed.

Sabrina was beneath the canopy, reclining against a pile of fat, fluffy pillows. She let out a small cry of pleasure at Caleb's sudden appearance but seemed otherwise undisturbed, as if she was used to men barging into her room at all hours of the night. She wore a filmy pink nightdress covered by a nearly translucent robe of the same color. Neither left much to the imagination.

Caleb wondered briefly if he or some other man had bought the garments, then decided it didn't really matter.

He wanted one thing from Sabrina, and one thing only.

Sabrina sat up, displaying a generous amount of cleavage and a pout she had perfected over the years. "You frightened me, darling. I haven't seen you in so long, I thought you had forgotten me."

Caleb knew she was fishing for a compliment. Something like, "I could never forget you, Sabrina." He said it without emotion, meaning it, but not the way she would think. Caleb suspected he wouldn't easily erase Sabrina from his mind, no matter how hard he tried. Her maple-syrup voice, her liberal use of cosmetics and colognes, and her overly bright yellow hair doubtless would stick in his memory for some time to come.

"Where have you been, then?"

"I've been busy," Caleb answered.

Sabrina continued speaking, and he nodded, pretending to listen to her list of complaints as he made his way to the window facing Rebecca's house. He pushed the white draperies out of the way and stared for a minute at the small, plain cabin, taking a long swallow of whiskey.

Caleb knew nearly every inch of Rebecca's home. He knew the sewing mannequin stood before the fireplace, knew where she kept her fashion plates and sewing supplies, her china and cutlery. And he knew that if he went behind the pink and white rose-covered curtain at the back of the makeshift parlor, he would find Rebecca's bedroom. Caleb suddenly wanted to be in it, to know that room intimately as well.

With that thought came images of Rebecca, the dress she had been wearing that afternoon, and how she would look out of it. Caleb turned his head toward Sabrina, cringing inwardly at the sight. Despite Sabrina's artificial beauty and practiced charms, Caleb wanted to make love to the small, mousy, passionate woman in the cabin below.

The thought of staying with Sabrina became suddenly unbearable. He moved for the door. "I have to go."

"Where?" Sabrina cried, coming to her knees on the bed.

"I have some business to take care of. It can't wait."

Her mouth turned down in a pout. "When are we going back to New York? You said it wouldn't be long, Caleb. I want to go home. I hate it here," she whined. "It's hot and lonely, and nobody likes me. Maybe if I bought some new dresses . . ."

Sabrina's voice hurt his head. He looked at her in stunned realization, as if seeing her for the first time.

"Don't buy anything else on my credit, Sabrina."

Her eyes widened to the size of saucers. "But, Caleb—"

He shook his head and let his eyes fall closed, trying to keep a headache from forming between his temples. "Use your monthly allowance for a train ticket back to New York. There should be plenty of money left." Caleb ran a hand through his disheveled hair and turned toward the door.

"Oh, no, Caleb. I don't mind staying a few more weeks. Really. I know you want to make sure your father is well before going back." Her nervous voice belied the calm of her words.

Caleb tried to be as polite as his liquor-laden mind would permit. "I don't think I'll be returning to New York for quite a while, Sabrina. I can't leave while my father is still under the weather, and you are obviously unhappy here. I'm sorry, but I think we should go our separate ways." His hand curled around the brass knob.

"You can't do this!" Sabrina shrieked, jumping from the bed.

Caleb turned back to her slowly, gritting his teeth against the pain her grating voice caused in his head. "You should have more than enough money to reach New York and live well until you secure a new . . . livelihood, but if you need more for your travel expenses, let me know. I wouldn't dream of sending you back penniless."

"No! I won't let you leave me like this, like some common whore."

He gave her a wry grin and touched her cheek with a fingertip. "*Common* is not a word I would ever use to describe you, Sabrina."

"Oh!" She lunged at him, screaming.

Caleb caught her wrists with ease, holding them in one hand. "Let's not make more of this than there has to be, Sabrina. We both know ours was a temporary arrangement. I'm sorry, but it's over now." Caleb let go of her. "Good-bye, Sabrina."

He closed the door behind him, flinching at the sound of glass shattering against the other side of the thick wood. He made his way down the length of the hallway and stairs, hoping Sabrina's fit wouldn't awaken anyone.

It was only when he stood in the livery stable, waiting for his mount to be saddled, that Caleb remembered he had left his whiskey in Sabrina's room. Just as well. He was drunk enough. The only sensible thing he had done all night was telling Sabrina to go back to New York.

Caleb mounted his horse with some difficulty. As he rode out of the stable, his eyes flew to the dark cabin at the end of the street. His head began to throb anew, and he made himself think of anything other than Rebecca asleep in her bed. He reined the spirited gelding in the opposite direction and headed for home.

A large wicker basket hanging on her arm, Rebecca took the long route to the Adams house, walking far behind the town's main buildings. It was easier than having to stop every few minutes to talk with another acquaintance.

Rebecca had no desire to come face-to-face with the handsome but arrogant Caleb Adams again, either. But she did need to see his sweet young sister, Megan. So she decided to make her trip in the middle of the work-day to ensure that Caleb would be in the Adams Express office with his father.

The pieces for all three dresses were together, and Rebecca wanted Megan to try them on to see how they fit. It would be easier to get precise measurements and sew once than to estimate and end up sewing twice.

For ten in the morning, it was quite warm as the sun's rays beat down on Rebecca, but the wide brim of her straw hat protected her face and kept the bright light out of her eyes. Several times on the three-mile walk, Re-becca stopped to pick wildflowers. Even though she knew they would most likely wilt and die by the time she made it to Megan's house and back, Rebecca couldn't resist grabbing handfuls of the colorful blossoms and holding them up to her nose. The sweet fragrances of four-o'clocks, bladder campions, thimbleweed, and but-tercups aroused her senses, sending her mind into a whirl of idyllic summer images. She would get more on the way home to decorate her parlor with small bouquets.

Rebecca loved summer above all other seasons. It was hot, certainly, sometimes to the point of being quite overbearing, but summer had a way of bringing out the best in people. The season was filled with sunny days, prospering fields and farms, brightly colored wildflow-ers, and cool, starry nights.

Almost before she knew it, Rebecca could see the two-story white house at the end of the long lane and the waist-high picket fence that surrounded the yard. She smiled and brushed a lock of loose hair out of her eyes, looking forward to spending more time with sweet, chatty Megan Adams.

Rebecca set the basket on the ground for a moment while she worked to unlatch the gate. Then, holding the basket in one hand and the hem of her skirt in the other, she walked through and let the gate swing closed behind her, its lock catching by itself.

She made her way up the sturdy porch steps, the urge to hum bubbling inside her for the first time in months. Smiling brightly, Rebecca lifted the brass knocker high on the door and rapped several times, expecting Megan to answer.

Rebecca's smile immediately faded when Caleb Adams opened the door instead.

Chapter Four

Rebecca took a deep breath and straightened her shoulders, readying herself for any barbs Caleb Adams might toss her way this time. In place of his usual black suit and string tie, he wore faded dungaree trousers and a loose-fitting light-blue shirt, open at the neck. On his feet were not his usual half-gaiters but a pair of brown leather boots dusty enough to compete with those of any professional cowboy. His casual appearance warmed Rebecca's opinion of him slightly. Maybe he wasn't quite as stiff and haughty as she had assumed.

Though he had been more cooperative in her shop the week before, Rebecca had no silly illusions about this man. Doubtless he had been on his best behavior only because his sister was in the room. Otherwise, he would have been just as arrogant and rude as usual.

While Rebecca stood on the wide porch in a heavy green walking skirt and high-necked blouse, Caleb's mouth curved up at one side in a grin—that same irritating smile she always seemed to induce.

"Well, Rebecca," he drawled, resting his weight

against the doorjamb rather than asking her in, "what can I do for you?" He leaned forward a bit, quizzically regarding the large front lawn and road beyond. "I don't see a buggy or horse," he commented before she could answer his question. "What did you do, walk all the way from town?"

"As a matter of fact, I did."

Caleb's eyes widened in obvious surprise. "But that's more than three miles. When did you leave town, six this morning?"

"Hardly, Mr. Adams. I enjoyed the walk. And it wouldn't have taken me quite so long if I hadn't stopped every few feet to pick these." She held up her large bouquet of wildflowers.

Caleb stepped back, pushing the door open as far as it would go. He bowed gallantly and ushered her in with the wave of an arm. "Please. Allow me to bid you enter before you—and your lovely flowers—wilt."

Rebecca bit her tongue to stop a smile from spreading across her face. She reluctantly admitted that Caleb Adams could be charming when he wanted to be. Not that that made up for his egotistical attitude the rest of the time.

"I came to see Megan. Is she here?"

Caleb turned from shutting the door. His large hand closed over the handle of her basket, and she had to give over and allow him to take it from her. "Megan is in the kitchen with Nina. I'll let her know you're here."

He took several steps into what looked to be the parlor, though it was much larger and more luxuriously decorated than her own. Caleb set the basket on the nearest wing chair and motioned for Rebecca to have a seat.

Rebecca's skirts brushed against a knee-high table as she lowered herself gently onto the edge of the velvet-covered sofa, expecting to wait while Caleb went for Megan. She toyed with the flowers in her hand, trying to keep her attention averted from Caleb's overwhelming presence. Instead of leaving the room, however, he folded his tall frame into a chair opposite her and smiled. Rebecca felt a blush creeping up her neck and turned away from his intense gaze.

"Megan!"

Caleb's bellow made Rebecca jump. She looked up into eyes sparkling with humor.

"Hey, Megan!" he yelled again, making the delicate crystal teardrops of the room's lamps vibrate. "You've got a visitor."

"Well, you don't need to shout." Megan bustled into the hall, drying her hands on a dishcloth. A flush tinted her porcelain skin, and the dark hair that had most likely been perfectly coifed earlier in the day hung in damp tendrils against her oval face. "Really, Caleb, a person would think you'd have better manners after being raised in the heart of genteel society."

Rebecca grinned, thinking Megan looked and sounded more like an overtaxed wife than a sixteen-year-old girl. For being so young, Megan had a sophisticated beauty about her. Even her full, lacy gown, so out of place in a town like Leavenworth, seemed almost a second skin. Only the gaiety in her eyes gave away her youthfulness.

"Oh, Rebecca," Megan gasped, coming more fully into the room. "Forgive our shouting. We would never dare if Papa were here. He doesn't approve of such behavior." She shook her head, the corners of her mouth turning up. "I didn't expect you to come all the way out here. I was going to ride into town with Papa and Caleb tomorrow and stop to see you."

"I wanted to show you what I've done so far. I'd like you to try them on so I can finalize the measurements."

"Oh." Megan's naturally bright features seemed to dim.

Rebecca could sense something amiss. "Did I come at a bad time?" She started to rise, reaching for her sewing basket. "I can return later if it would be more convenient."

"Nonsense." Megan's body fairly bounced with the word. "We weren't planning anything that can't wait, were we, Caleb?"

"Of course not," Caleb said impartially, rising and starting out of the room. "Let me know when you're done, Meg. I'll be out at the paddock."

As the front door thudded shut after Caleb's exit, a young girl came to the doorway to the parlor. "Are we finished, Miss Adams?"

Megan smiled and took the girl's arm, bringing her into the room. "Rebecca, this is Nina. She's such a wonderful help, especially in the kitchen, since I can hardly boil water. Nina, this is Rebecca, the seamstress from town."

With the introductions out of the way, Megan sent Nina back to the kitchen, asking that she add an extra serving of everything to the basket they had packed.

"We really don't have to do your dresses now, Megan," Rebecca said. "I'd much rather you went on with whatever you were doing. I should have sent a note home with your father to find out when would be a good time for me to stop by. I apologize."

"Oh, posh," Megan said, fluttering a hand in the air, effectively dismissing the subject.

"If you're sure," Rebecca offered one last time. She looked around for someplace to set her bouquet. Her hands were sweaty and turning green from holding the stems for so long.

"Where did you get those?" Megan asked, taking them from Rebecca to study the blossoms.

"I picked them on the way. I just couldn't resist."

"They're lovely. But if we don't get them into water soon, they'll surely die. I'll be right back." Megan followed the path Nina had taken to the kitchen, returning several moments later with the wildflowers in a beautiful etched vase.

"Now, where should we start?" Megan asked, setting the arrangement on the low table in front of the settee and plopping herself down in the nearest chair.

"I'd like you to try on the dresses before I finish them to see how well they fit. It's easier and faster to make alterations before they're sewn."

Rebecca stood to pull the three carefully folded day dresses out of her basket and laid them over the back of the sofa. "Do you want to go up to your room to put these on?" she asked, thinking Megan would not want to undress in the parlor in the middle of the day.

"No. I'll just shut this door and pull the drapes, and no one ever need know." Megan slid the large partition into place and went around to each of the three windows to draw the thick maroon curtains closed.

While Megan did that, Rebecca reached into her basket and retrieved her spectacles, unfolding them and putting them on.

Megan came back and crinkled her nose at Rebecca. "If you can't see, why don't you wear those all the time?"

Rebecca pushed the eyeglasses farther up the bridge of her nose and turned Megan to face the other way. "I can see most of the time. It's only when I'm sewing that I have to wear them."

"Well, that's good because you're much prettier without them," Megan said with conviction.

Rebecca's hands paused for a moment in brushing Megan's loose hair out of the way. Megan was the first person Rebecca could ever remember complimenting her, and she was positive no one had ever told her she was pretty. Rebecca had always thought herself quite plain, with an average-looking face and dull brown hair. She swallowed, forcing her mind to concentrate on what she was doing to stop the sharp prickling behind her eyes.

As Rebecca started slipping the tiny pearl buttons at the back of Megan's fancy pink gown out of their holes, Megan began to giggle. "What's so funny?" she asked, finding the laughter contagious.

Megan covered her mouth with a hand, waiting to catch her breath. "I was thinking about how indecent I'm being, stripping down to my underclothes in the parlor at high noon. Lord, my mother would faint dead away if she knew."

"Then we won't tell her," Rebecca vowed, chuckling along with Megan as she helped remove layer upon layer of heavy, bulky material. "How can you stand to wear all this?"

"I can't," Megan said, screwing up her face to show her distaste. "Why do you think I'm so eager for you to get these dresses finished?"

"I will never understand why women torture themselves with silly contraptions like the corset, only to add twenty pounds by stepping into these gowns. But I probably shouldn't complain, since I make my living by sewing the abominable things."

"That's one way to look at it," Megan said. She struggled into the first dress, trying to keep from being pricked with the few pins still stuck at the seams.

"I think women ought to be allowed to wear pants. And big cotton shirts like men do," Rebecca continued.

Megan gasped and turned around to stare at Rebecca with wide brown eyes. "Why would you want to do something like that?"

Rebecca shrugged and smiled conspiratorially. "Because they're a far cry more comfortable than these blasted things." She pulled at her pine-green skirt, faded almost gray with wear.

"Well, how would you know that?" Megan asked, placing her hands on her hips, then drawing them back immediately when a sharp point dug into her tender flesh.

"I wore them all the time when I was young."

"Your mother *let* you?" Megan asked, awe in her voice.

Rebecca breathed deeply for a moment to keep herself from feeling any pain. Imagine Kate giving a damn about her daughter's clothes. Or anything else about the little girl, for that matter. Her own clothes—now, that was another matter. No expense was spared there. She shrugged again. "She didn't pay much attention to what I wore." That was true enough. Kate had seldom paid attention to Rebecca, except to scold her for being such a burden.

To change the subject, Rebecca tugged at the waist of the yellow dress. "How does it feel?"

"Cool. I can already tell I won't melt inside this material."

"Good," Rebecca said, happy that she had fulfilled Megan's foremost requirement.

All the dresses fit almost perfectly, needing only minor alterations before they would be finished. Megan loved the three colors—bright yellow, emerald green, and deep plum—each meant to bring out the auburn highlights in her otherwise black hair.

"How did you get them done so quickly? I expected them to take much longer than a week."

"I haven't really had that much business lately," Rebecca said as she refolded the dresses and set them in her white wicker basket. She removed her spectacles and laid them on top for the long walk home. "I have three or four regular customers—the ladies who were leaving just as you arrived Wednesday." She looked at Megan to see if the girl remembered. "Thelma, Hariette, and Mary are sweet souls, even if they do sometimes drive me nearly batty," Rebecca confessed. "They were Octavia Fitzgerald's friends. When she died, I took over her dressmaking business." Rebecca didn't go into detail about her past or how she had come to know Widow Fitzgerald. "Now they come every Wednesday to make sure I always have something to sew, even if business is slow. There's been more than one lean time when their loyalty was a godsend. But they understood perfectly when I told them I had to work on your dresses right away."

"I didn't mean for you to take time away from your other customers, Rebecca."

"Oh, I didn't." Rebecca smiled and helped Megan open the drapes. "It's nice to have a chance to work on something brand-new rather than patching the same dresses two dozen times or listening to Mary and her daughter Anabelle arguing about how low I should make a bodice."

Rebecca went back to the wing chair and slipped the handle of the big basket over her arm, ready to go.

"You aren't leaving, are you? I was hoping you would stay for lunch."

Megan sounded almost distraught, and Rebecca's brow wrinkled in a frown. "If I get started on these dresses right away, I can probably have them to you by Saturday or Sunday."

"Oh, what's the hurry?" Megan said in complete contrast to all her earlier statements about wanting some cool dresses for Leavenworth's hot summer days.

"Megan, you said you needed these as soon as possible. Do you want to wear those heavy silk gowns for the rest of the summer?" Rebecca waved a hand at the fancy pink dress Megan had donned again after the fittings.

"Well, they can wait one more day, can't they?"

Rebecca pressed her fists to her waist, the basket thumping against her hip. She was becoming a bit suspicious of Megan's insistence that she stay for the afternoon meal. "I suppose they could wait, but there's no reason I can't go home and fix myself lunch."

Megan went to the parlor door, sliding it open. "Wouldn't you much rather go for a picnic? I've been planning it all week. You must come."

Before Rebecca could protest, Megan threaded their arms together and dragged her through the house to the kitchen, not letting go of her captive even when she picked up the basket Nina had filled. They went out the back door and around the house to the barn.

"Caleb!" Megan called. "Caleb?"

Her handsome brother appeared from behind the barn, his clothes clearly rumpled from outdoor work. "Finished already?" he asked, tucking his thumbs into the front pockets of his pants.

"Oh, yes, the dresses are coming along wonderfully. The best news, though, is that Rebecca has agreed to join us for our picnic. I'll tell Frank to hitch up the wagon." With that, Megan skipped into the barn, leaving Rebecca and Caleb alone outside.

The heavy basket slid down Rebecca's arm and thudded to the ground, and it took her a moment to catch her breath. She raised her head to see Caleb staring at her. She tried to read his expression but found it impossible. His face revealed nothing.

Clearing her throat, she tried to protest. "I didn't actually say I'd go, Megan just assumed—"

Caleb nodded. "If Megan wants you on her picnic, she'll find a way to get you there. She did the same with me."

He sounded almost amused. His strong baritone tickled down Rebecca's spine, making her shiver involuntarily. Her gaze dropped to the ground. "I don't want to intrude," she said softly, berating herself for letting this man intimidate her.

"You aren't."

She raised her head and nearly jolted back a step from the sparks she saw dancing in Caleb's dark eyes. Suddenly she wanted to run as fast and as far as her feet could carry her—before she started to feel things for this man that a woman with her background had no business feeling. For in that instant Rebecca somehow knew that she could easily fall in love with a man like Caleb Adams.

She tried to think of something to say to fill the unbearable silence. "I . . . uh, expected you to be at the Express today."

Caleb shifted his weight and took a step back to lean against the side of the barn. "I would be, but I promised Megan I would take her on this damn—" He had heard the same word pass from Rebecca's rosy lips, but that didn't give him an excuse to forget his manners in front of a lady. He cleared his throat. "Sorry about that. I promised Megan I'd take her on this picnic." And he was none too pleased about it. "The last stage isn't supposed to arrive until ten, so I'll go in later to relieve Dad and stay the night in town."

"Oh, yes, your father keeps a room at the Wilkes Hotel so he won't have to travel home after a late night, doesn't he?"

"How did you know that?" His eyebrows drew together in a suspicious frown. What was Rebecca, the town snoop?

"Leavenworth is a small town, Mr. Adams. Word gets around," Rebecca answered. "Besides, Mrs. Wilkes comes to see me weekly and loves to talk about whatever's going on. I've known about your father's room at the hotel for quite some time. Was it supposed to be a secret?" She diplomatically refrained from mentioning the other room kept for an Adams man, which the whole town also knew about.

"No, I guess not."

"Your father is a very personable man. Everyone likes him. He doesn't seem like the kind of person to have a closet full of skeletons."

"Well," Caleb said, shifting his feet and lowering his voice dramatically, "there might be a few. Like demented Aunt Frances. We have to keep her locked in the attic." He pointed toward the topmost window of the house. When Rebecca looked in that direction, he gave an eerie howl to frighten her. To Rebecca's credit, she didn't even flinch.

She tilted her head and turned to face him, clucking her tongue. "Thought you could scare me that easily, huh? Shame on you, Mr. Adams."

Caleb crossed his arms over his chest and gazed at the woman before him. Her clothes were drab and made her look older than he suspected her to be. The dark green skirt, though lightened with wear, had probably accentuated her dark hair and eyes at one time. Caleb thought he would like, just once, to see Rebecca dressed in fine clothes. He was sure she would shine brighter than any star in the heavens.

Rebecca shifted nervously, taking a step away from him. Caleb noticed and fought the urge to close the distance between.

"You've been calling me Mr. Adams ever since we met," he said, keeping his voice low and friendly. "I keep thinking my father's around. You'd better start calling me Caleb, or I'll get so confused that they'll have to lock me in the attic with Aunt Frances and throw away the key. And it will be all your fault."

"But, Mr. Adams, you don't even have an Aunt Frances."

Caleb drew back, a hand over his heart, acting wounded. "Caleb. Please."

Rebecca sighed and surrendered. "Caleb."

Megan stood just inside the barn, her ear plastered to the rough wood, trying to hear every word of the exchange between her brother and Rebecca. She just

57

knew Caleb was attracted to the seamstress. It hadn't escaped Megan's notice that he had watched Rebecca the entire time they'd been at her house the week before. Nor did Megan misunderstand his disappearance later that night or the gruff humor Caleb had displayed ever since.

If only he could put the past behind him and realize that not all women were like Josephine or that Sabrina Leslie he was keeping at the hotel in town—the one he didn't think she knew about. Rebecca was sweet and kind and would never make a man fall in love with her only to betray him. Rebecca would treasure a man as a husband, companion, and friend—if only she could let down her own protective armor.

"Megan! Is that wagon ready yet?"

Megan jumped at the sound of Caleb's voice, much nearer than she expected, and the sound of his heavy footsteps bringing him closer still. She ran to the other end of the barn, where the horses and buckboard had been standing ready for the past ten minutes. She stopped at the head of one of the matching sorrels, pretending that it was she who had been waiting for them. "All set," she said, slightly out of breath. "What a lovely day for a picnic."

Chapter Five

Megan scraped the last of the baked beans from her plate with a slice of cornbread. "Mmm, that was delicious," she said, standing to pat her belly. "Now I think I need a nice, long walk."

"I'll go with you," Rebecca offered, moving to set her plate down on the blanket.

"No, no. You're not finished eating yet. I'll be fine."

Megan took off toward the tall trees that bordered the daisy-strewn field they had chosen as the spot for their picnic, leaving Rebecca alone with Caleb. Rebecca wanted desperately to go after her, but within seconds Megan had disappeared into the density of the forest.

Rebecca turned to find Caleb looking at her, his lips quirked into a grin while he chewed a bite of chicken. Rebecca's mouth turned suddenly dry, and she pushed the remaining food around on the dish with her fork, unable to bring herself to eat another morsel.

Caleb swallowed, reclining against the trunk of the wide oak they sat beneath, and stretched his long legs out in front of him. As he did, his leg brushed Rebecca's skirt. She inched away, tucking the hem more tightly around her ankles.

"So," Caleb said, leaning forward to choose another drumstick from the platter of fried chicken. "Tell me a little about yourself."

Rebecca stiffened. Her eyes darted to the spot where Megan had entered the woods, her mind scrambling for a story to pacify his curiosity.

"Any deep, dark family secrets?" he asked.

One or two, Rebecca thought wryly. "I don't have any mad relatives in my attic, if that's what you mean."

"Ah, but you don't have an attic. Perhaps you keep your Aunt Frances in the root cellar."

Caleb wiggled his eyebrows, and Rebecca couldn't help but find his conversation amusing. "I don't have a root cellar, either."

"Well, then, the only remaining possibility is that *you're* the lunatic in your family."

Rebecca laughed. "You've discovered my secret, sir. Send me off to the asylum." She set her plate aside and held out her arms as if for him to bind her wrists.

He smiled. "Not quite yet. I still have a few questions for the inmate."

Rebecca lowered her hands to her lap and turned away, wishing her joke had kept him from being so inquisitive.

"Dad told me you've only been in Leavenworth for the past ten years or so. Where did you live before you came here? And where's the rest of your family?"

"I don't have a family," she answered as honestly as she dared. Besides, it was awfully hard to consider Kate "family" in any conventional way. "I lost both my parents when I was little." Rebecca kept her eyes averted, hoping that Caleb wouldn't be able to see through her white lie. "I came to Leavenworth when I was thirteen, and Widow Fitzgerald was nice enough to take me in."

"Who took care of you before that? You certainly

couldn't fend for yourself at such an early age."

Oh, but I did, Rebecca wanted to tell him. *I lived by myself in the back room of a whorehouse.* Instead she said, "I don't really remember. Different folks took care of me when they could." That was true enough. Sometimes, when she was sick, one of the girls or Lilah would look after her a little bit.

A breeze ruffled her skirt and loosened some hair from her bun, blowing it into her eyes. She tucked the strands behind her ear.

"You must have been very lonely," Caleb offered quietly.

She raised her head and met his gaze, stunned by the understanding she saw there. "It . . . wasn't so bad," she answered, looking away.

"Megan adores you, you know."

Rebecca smiled, thankful for the change of subject, "I like her, too."

"Dad and I blame you for her determination to stay here rather than go back to New York."

"Me? Why blame me?" Rebecca's heart fluttered in her breast. All she needed was one more thing for this man to hold against her. "I didn't tell her not to go back. We never even discussed it. You can't possibly fault me."

Caleb chuckled. "Well, Megan insists that if you can live in Leavenworth by yourself, then she should certainly be allowed to stay here with her father and brother. So you see? It's by your example that you're to blame."

Rebecca gave a relieved sigh. "That may be, but I don't see any reason she can't go where she chooses. And if she chooses to live in Leavenworth with her family, all the better."

"How's that?" Caleb asked.

"Megan is a confident young woman more than capable of making up her own mind. Deciding that she wants to live in Kansas with her family is surely better than deciding she wants to live in the wilds like a mountain man—or with a mountain man, for that matter."

"Praise the Lord for small favors!" Caleb slapped his hand, drumstick and all, against his leg with a hoot of laughter. "I can see her doing something like that, though. The girl is headstrong and sometimes doesn't show the sense God gave a garden slug."

"Unlike you?" Rebecca challenged.

"I know better than to run across the country without telling someone where I'm going or considering the problems that might arise once I get there."

"So does Megan. Obviously she knew you and your father would expect her and would meet her when she stepped off the stage. And evidently if Megan had told anyone what she planned to do, they only would have tried to stop her."

"Did you ever think that maybe she *should* have been stopped?" Caleb asked.

"Why? Megan obviously needed to come here or she never would have risked so much—your anger, the possibility that you might send her home. And she seems happy. Isn't Megan's happiness the most important thing in this situation?"

"So you're saying I should let her stay for as long as she wants?" Caleb sounded astounded.

Rebecca shook her head. "No. I'm saying you need to let Megan make the decision of where she stays and for how long."

Caleb huffed a bit, but he knew she was right. He'd pretty much come to the same conclusion himself. Besides, he had to admit that he liked having Megan around and didn't really want her to leave. Perhaps she would go back with him when he went, but until then it wouldn't hurt to let her be a member of the Leavenworth community.

He turned his head and saw Megan appear from behind a clump of fir trees, her arms full of pine cones and leaves and other woodland treasures, gold and fuchsia flowers decorating her hair, her pink gown smudged and wrinkled. "How was your walk?" he asked as she closed the distance between them.

"Just wonderful," she answered, dropping to her knees and letting the contents of her hands roll onto the blanket. "Look at all of this. I don't even know what half of it is."

"Dad will know." Caleb pulled a gold watch from a small front pocket of his pants and clicked it open. "Time to go, Megan. I need to get to town so Dad can start home before it gets dark."

"All right." Megan began repacking the plates and platters with Rebecca's help.

When they finished, Caleb carried the basket to the buckboard. Collecting the odds and ends in the skirt of her gown, Megan followed, stopping every few feet to retrieve something that had dropped.

Caleb helped Megan into the wagon, then turned to assist Rebecca.

"I'll just walk home from here," she said, backing away when he reached out to grasp her waist. "It's not very far. Could you hand me my sewing basket, please, Megan?"

"It's not here."

"It has to be." Rebecca whirled around and stood on tiptoe to look over the sideboard. "I could swear I put it in before we left."

"Well, it's not there now," Caleb said, checking for himself. "You must have left it at the house." He grasped her waist before she had the chance to resist and lifted her onto the seat, stepping over her skirt as he followed her up. He headed the horses home.

Megan remained surprisingly quiet, busy investigating her treasures, until the wagon started up the long, sloping drive toward the Adams house. "Look!" Megan cried. "There's your basket, Rebecca."

And, indeed, Rebecca's wicker basket sat lopsidedly in the front yard.

Caleb tightened the reins and brought the two sorrel mares to a stop beside the picket fence. He leapt to the ground and went to help Megan down.

Without waiting for Caleb's assistance, Rebecca lifted the hem of her skirt, found her footing on the spoked wheel, and carefully lowered herself until her toes met the hard earth below. Straightening her skirts, she walked past the horses and slipped the handle of her basket into the crook of her elbow. She turned around and stopped short as she saw Caleb and Megan standing next to each other, watching her.

"Thank you for inviting me along for your picnic. I had a very nice time." She started past them, hoping to get away as soon as possible. "I really have to go now. I should have been home hours ago."

"Caleb will take you back," Megan quickly interjected. "Won't you, Caleb?"

"Sure." He took a step toward Rebecca, holding out a hand.

She took a step back, clutching her basket all the more tightly. "No, thank you. I'll be fine."

"Posh," Megan said, taking Rebecca's arm and drawing her forward. "Caleb is going into town, and there's just no sense in your walking all that way when he can give you a ride."

She took her brother's wrist and put his hand on Rebecca's arm in place of her own. "You make sure she gets home safe and sound now, Caleb. Tell Papa dinner will be ready by the time he gets here." She turned without another word and hurried across the yard and into the house.

Rebecca moved away from Caleb, breaking his superficial hold on her arm. "I'd rather walk. Really."

"Sorry," he said, taking a step closer. "I can't let you do that. Megan would have my hide if I didn't see you to your door. Besides, I can get you home in half the time it would take you to walk."

Rebecca gritted her teeth and let him put his hands about her waist for what seemed like the hundredth time that day. She scooted to the very edge of the seat, setting her basket between them as a makeshift barrier. Caleb threw her a sidelong glance but refrained from commenting.

Less than half a mile outside of town, Caleb slowed the horses and brought the wagon to a halt in the middle of the road. Rebecca flinched and slid even farther away from him until the corner of the hard wood seat pressed painfully against her hip.

"Why are we stopping?" she asked, forcing a note of bravery into her voice that she certainly didn't feel. Was he going to make advances toward her? Even though he didn't much like her, it was no less than she should expect from a man. Especially one like Caleb Adams, obviously a sensualist used to getting what he wanted when he wanted and answering to no one for his actions.

Rather than moving toward her, Caleb turned away and jumped to the ground. "I thought you might like to pick some flowers."

He came around the front of the team and held out his arms for her. Not sure how to react to his offer, Rebecca slowly reached out to put her hands on his shoulders.

Caleb smiled and let his palms rest on her waist until she found her footing beneath the tangle of skirts and petticoats. "There's quite a variety over there, I noticed," he said, pointing. "I don't know what any of them are, but they look pretty enough."

Her earlier panic washed away, replaced by a slight warming in the region of her heart for the second time in one day. Rebecca smiled. How could she not when

Caleb was being so kind? Imagine his interrupting his drive into town to let her retrieve more wildflowers. He had heard her say she wanted some for her house, and, more important, he had remembered.

The contentment she was experiencing would soon pass, Rebecca was sure, but for once in her life she decided to stop worrying and enjoy a moment of happiness being offered.

"Come on," Caleb said, holding a palm out.

Rebecca held her breath for a moment before relaxing enough to put her hand in his. Caleb's warm fingers grasped hers securely but not tightly enough to make her uneasy. He led her to where a kaleidoscope of wildflowers grew in profusion beside the road.

Rebecca slipped her hand from his somewhat reluctantly and stooped to select her blossoms.

"May I help?" he asked.

"I'd love some of those," she pointed out. "The blue ones. But they're too far for me to reach."

Caleb looked skeptically at the pretty blue flowers growing at the top of the sloping roadside, but he manfully stepped forward.

Rebecca started choosing wild roses closer by, careful of their thorns. When she noticed Caleb had been gone for a while, she glanced up to see him standing at the top of the small hill holding two huge armfuls of turquoise chicories like a warrior returning, home from battle with the armor of his enemy. "Are you happy now?" he said.

"They're beautiful. Thank you."

"Do you want anything else while I'm up here?"

She laughed. "No, I think you have enough there to brighten every kitchen in Kansas."

Rebecca reached for a few tall strands of buttercups as Caleb began his descent. She heard a curse, the sound of rustling leaves, and, as she turned, she saw Caleb's feet slip out from under him before he fell headfirst down the incline, landing in the middle of the road.

The horses whinnied and stepped back from his prone form. Rebecca picked up her skirts, the forgotten roses and buttercups dropping to the ground as she ran to his side.

"Caleb?"

No answer. No movement. She brushed the hair out of his face, looking for cuts or bruises. Pulling at his arm, she gently levered a knee beneath his weight and pushed with all her might until Caleb rolled to his back. She collapsed atop his chest and, pressing two fingers against his neck, checked for a pulse, finding it a bit erratic but strong.

"Caleb?" She shook him, trying to bring him around. "Come on, Caleb, wake up. You didn't fall that far. You couldn't possibly be this badly hurt."

Rebecca's blood pounded in her ears when he still didn't move. She sat back on her heels, leaning over him, grabbing the front of his shirt. "Caleb! Dammit, get up!"

Nothing.

"If you don't get up right this minute, I'll walk the rest of the way into town and leave you here to rot. Do you hear me?"

A low moan and slight movement of his head caught her attention. "Can you hear me? Caleb, answer me." She patted his cheek, her slaps becoming stronger the longer he refused to respond.

"I hear you. Now stop hitting me," Caleb said, grabbing her wrist.

She pulled away and sat back on her heels. "I was not hitting you. I was trying to wake you up." She became suspicious. "Were you really unconscious?"

Caleb sat up slowly, propping his elbow on his bent knee. "Would you really have left me here?" he countered, a sly grin lifting one side of his mouth.

Rebecca straightened her spine and leaned away from

him, crossing her arms over her chest. "So you *were* awake. That's a cruel trick, Caleb Adams. It would serve you right to be left here. It's no better than you deserve."

Caleb touched her arm, unlocking it from the other and bringing her hand to his lips. "Were you frightened, Rebecca?"

"Of course not," she scoffed.

"Then why did you look so worried?"

"Because I . . ." She lifted her head and saw how very near she was to Caleb. His lips were only inches from hers, coming ever closer.

Panic seized her heart, and she jumped to her feet, hurrying to the buckboard. "I think we should go now." She heard Caleb sigh as he, too, rose and made his way to the wagon. He put a hand under her arm and helped her up.

"My flowers!" Rebecca moved to step down from the seat.

"I'll get them," Caleb said, winking and gesturing for her to stay put. He went to collect the scattered blossoms, passing them to Rebecca before he climbed up next to her.

Riding in silence, Rebecca surveyed Caleb's profile out of the corner of her eye. The smooth plane of his jawline, darkened by a touch of new whiskers. The blackness of his windblown hair as it fell across his forehead. As she looked more closely, Rebecca noticed for the first time a slight crinkling of skin around his eyes and mouth. Her close examination trailed along his lean cheek to his neck and shoulder, then down the length of his arm to the strong, tan hands holding the reins.

When her eyes returned to Caleb's face, she found him staring back at her. Rebecca felt an overwhelming urge to turn away but took a deep breath and held his gaze.

Caleb turned away first, regarding the road ahead. Rebecca sighed and looked at the flowers in her lap. A tiny black bug crawled along one of the petals. She watched it for a moment before holding the cluster over the side of the wagon and shaking vigorously, hoping to dislodge any remaining residents of the insect persuasion.

As Caleb drove down the main street of town, Rebecca kept her eyes closed, praying for the fewest number of people possible to spot her in the presence of Leavenworth's wealthiest—and most notorious—bachelor.

She let out a breath when they reached her house. Feeling finally safe, Rebecca let Caleb escort her onto the porch, expecting him to say a polite farewell and leave. Instead, as she reached for the doorknob, Caleb took her wrist, his thumb stroking the palm of her hand. Rebecca watched the circular motion, not daring to breathe.

"I hope you enjoyed yourself this afternoon."

Rebecca nodded, her mouth too cottony for speech.

"I had a nice time, too."

She stood silently, mesmerized by his soft voice and touch. Caleb brought a finger up under her chin, forcing her face up to his. Without word or warning, his mouth lowered, brushing her lips tenderly. His warm breath caressed her cheek, causing her to moan low in her throat.

Rebecca felt Caleb's hand travel along her arm to the nape of her neck, his fingers twisting in her hair. Of its own accord, her body swayed toward his, one palm pressed against the wall of his chest. He nudged her upper lip, urging her mouth open. The feel of his hot, moist tongue against her own shot shock waves of indescribable pleasure through her limbs.

Not wanting it to stop, yet knowing she couldn't allow it to continue, Rebecca reached out a hand, fumbling for the door handle. She leaned back and turned the knob, effectively breaking Caleb's embrace by practically falling into the house.

For a moment, Rebecca simply stood looking at

Caleb. Surprise widened his hazel eyes, his broad chest heaving as he tried to catch his breath. Rebecca opened her mouth to say something, but no words came to mind. She pushed the door closed, leaning against it for support as her weakened body slid to the floor.

Chapter Six

Caleb blinked at the thick wooden portal as it swung closed in his face, wishing he could see through the pink-and-white flowered curtain that decorated the glass from the inside. He thought about pounding on the door and insisting Rebecca let him in but decided he would get further if he flapped his arms to fly across town.

"Of all the . . ." Caleb's words tangled together as he stomped down Rebecca's porch steps to the wagon. He took up the reins and clucked the horses into motion.

"Miss Leslie." Rebecca stepped back to allow entrance to Sabrina and her layers of fluffy skirts and petticoats.

"I hope you don't mind my dropping in. I know it's late, but I must have a new gown immediately."

"Of course."

When Rebecca first heard the knock, she thought that Caleb might have returned. The possibility both frightened and excited her. Instead, she opened the door to find his mistress on her porch.

A pinch of pain tightened her belly. After the picnic,

Caleb's pleasant joking, and that kiss, Rebecca had let her mind wander. Obviously it had wandered far enough for her to forget that Caleb had another woman on hand to fulfill all his wants and needs.

She should have known that the kiss meant much less to Caleb than it had to her. Not that she'd had any silly illusions. A kiss was a kiss, and no matter who happened to be behind it—even the darkly handsome Caleb Adams—it did not change Rebecca's mind about men. She still had no intention of ever getting involved with one.

Rebecca felt her cheeks warm with embarrassment, remembering her intense physical reaction to Caleb's touch. His mouth had made her forget herself, and she didn't think the tingling in her breasts or other extremities had been imagined. If a kiss could cause those kinds of sensations, she wondered what additional touches and tastes might do.

She'd known the facts of life for a very long time and had never been the least interested in participating.

Until this afternoon.

Something about the way Caleb's tongue had brushed her own had made her intensely curious about the rest. What would it feel like to let Caleb run his hands over her naked flesh?

She shivered and shook herself back to reality. She knew better than to start imagining such things. Those thoughts would only lead her astray and further down the path of her mother.

"Could I offer you a cup of tea?" Rebecca asked, moving away from Sabrina to regain her composure.

"That would be lovely. But none of that wretched cinnamon swill."

Rebecca stopped in her tracks, reminding herself that business was business and not everyone was as fond of her cinnamon-stick tea as she. Tastes differed. *And some people have no taste at all*, she thought with a glance at Sabrina's indecently low-cut bodice.

"What kind of gown do you have in mind this time?" she inquired, setting two cups and saucers on the table in front of the settee.

After Sabrina's narration, Rebecca cleared her throat. She didn't want to step on anyone's toes, but she was certain Caleb would not appreciate paying for the gown Sabrina had just described, which would cost even more than the last.

"Miss Leslie, I may be out of place by saying this, but I'm not sure Mr. Adams will pay for such an elaborate outfit. He argued over the cost of the last gown, and I really have no desire to go another round with him. Have you cleared this with him?"

Sabrina's face turned red, her cheeks puffing up in indignation. "You're right, Rebecca, you have overstepped your bounds. It's not necessary for me to ask Caleb's permission for anything. Caleb takes care of *all* of my needs. And in return"—Sabrina's lips curved up in a smile, and she said the words very slowly—"*I* take care of *his.*"

Rebecca understood Sabrina's point perfectly. "I apologize. I'll start on the gown right away."

"Good."

"What happened to Caleb this afternoon?"

Megan lifted her head and set her fork alongside her plate. "What do you mean?" she asked her father.

"He stomped into the Express in an even fouler mood than he's been in since we got word you'd run away. I thought it would have passed by now." Holbrook took a bite of roast beef smothered in thick gravy.

"Oh, Caleb's realized I'll be staying for a while. But I don't think my behavior is the cause of his dark mood."

"If it's not, then what is?"

Megan smiled, twisting the brown cloth napkin in her hands. "Not what, Papa, *who.*"

"Who, then? Megan, what in tarnation is going on?"

"You know Rebecca, don't you? The seamstress in town?"

"Know her? Why, I'm the fellow who found her when she stowed away on one of my stages. Lucky thing Octavia Fitzgerald was there, or I'd have turned her in to the law."

"Rebecca stowed away on one of your stagecoaches?"

"Of course. That's how she came to live in Leavenworth. Nobody knows where she came from—girl doesn't talk much about her past. I don't think even Widow Fitzgerald ever knew the whole of it, and she was like a mother to that child. More than ten years, it's been now. Curse it, Megan, you got me all off track. What does Rebecca have to do with anything?"

"I think Caleb is in love with her."

"In love with her? Why, that's the most ridiculous thing I've ever heard. You've got to stop reading those penny dreadfuls, child. Caleb has never been in love with a woman in his life. I'd sure like to see that boy settle down, but I doubt it will happen before I'm dead and buried. And that woman he's keeping in town, why—" Holbrook's face flushed, and he cleared his throat.

Megan chuckled at his obvious discomfort. "It's all right, Papa. I'm sixteen, remember? I know all about Sabrina."

"When did you find out? If Caleb's been filling your head with ideas . . . I'm still big enough to take him out back of the woodshed, even if he has seen purty near thirty-one summers. About time I had a word with him about that kept woman, too."

"Don't get yourself all worked up, Papa. Caleb hasn't been telling me anything. I just know, that's all. People talk, and it's amazing what you can hear when you eavesdrop."

"Megan Beatrice Adams, who brought you up to listen in on private conversations?"

Megan's nose crinkled at the sound of her middle name being used. "Mother. Now, hush, Papa, and let me finish."

Megan pushed the wrinkled napkin aside and took a sip of water before starting her story. "When Caleb took me to Rebecca for dresses, he stayed the whole time—three hours. And you know how easily Caleb gets bored. I paid close attention to the way he smiled every time Rebecca laughed. And, Papa, he was polite. After three hours of listening to women talk about fashions and measurements, Caleb was still polite. Well, that did it. I'm just positive that he's in love with her.

"So when Rebecca showed up this afternoon for a last-minute fitting of the dresses she's making for me, I took it as a sign from God. Don't laugh, Papa." Megan stuck out her bottom lip in a slight pout. "How else would you explain the fact that Rebecca came the exact morning Caleb stayed home from work to take me on a picnic? It was meant to be, Papa, there's no denying it."

She shifted anxiously in her seat. "Anyway, I talked Rebecca into going with us. It was rather difficult. I practically had to drag her. Then, while I was in the barn watching Frank hitch up the team, I overheard Caleb and Rebecca's conversation. They were dreadfully sharp-tongued. Isn't it wonderful?"

"What's so wonderful about it? It sounds like neither of them can stand the other's company."

"Oh, posh." Megan waved a hand at the ludicrous idea. "They love to argue—that's the one thing they have in common. It's when they fight that they're most attracted."

Holbrook's cheeks reddened. "You're just a child. How do you know of such things?"

"Papa, please." Megan rolled her eyes. "These are the eighties. Women are becoming more independent and knowledgeable at a much earlier age."

Holbrook shifted uncomfortably in his chair. "What else should I know about?"

"Well, I left them alone together during the picnic. I went for a walk and got all those pine cones and leaves and things I showed you. They seemed to be getting along well enough when I returned. Then Rebecca *had* to come all the way home with us because she'd forgotten her sewing basket."

Megan lowered her head, pulling at the lace trim of the tablecloth. "All right, she didn't forget it," she said quietly. "She put it in the back of the wagon, and I tossed it out when she wasn't looking."

"Good Lord, deliver me," Holbrook muttered, raising his eyes heavenward.

"I know it was deceitful of me, but it worked. Rebecca had to come back for her basket, and then Caleb drove her home, since he had to go into town anyway. I'm just dying to know what happened on the ride." Megan bounced on her chair in excitement.

"If Caleb knew what you were doing, he would tan your hide."

"Oh, Papa, you mustn't tell him. Besides, it's not as if I'm doing anything wrong. Caleb and Rebecca are bound to get together. I'm simply helping things along."

"Yes, I'm sure you think so."

Holbrook and Megan returned to their meal. After several moments of heavy silence, Megan tilted her head and said softly, "Papa?"

"Yes?"

"Are you feeling better? I haven't heard you cough once all evening."

Holbrook instantly went into convulsions, hacking until his chest heaved. When the fit passed, he wiped his mouth with his napkin and turned a hard eye toward Megan. "I'm still not well."

"No, but you're getting better. I'm so glad. Caleb will be, too."

"Hush, child," Holbrook said sternly. "Not a word."

Megan smiled at her father's well-planned farce. "Yes, Papa."

Sabrina ignored the delivery boy's outstretched hand, grabbing the brown-paper–wrapped package from him. The door slammed closed as she crossed to the large canopy bed. She tore the strings and wrapping away, revealing thick folds of bright material.

She quickly shed her robe and nightgown, changing into the newest addition to her wardrobe. It was exquisite, she admitted—grudgingly, and only to herself—as she stared at her image in the cheval glass. The scallop-edged bodice covered the better part of her bosom. Much too much for Sabrina's liking. But the waistline and full, voluptuous skirts were quite beautiful. Silver threads sparkled, intricately woven into a rich shade of rose gossamer. Beneath the layers of whisper-thin material lay thick, textured red velvet.

The gown was truly a work of art. But it needed a little something. Sabrina shed the dress, tossing it onto the bed while she went to the bureau for a needle, thread, and some shears.

An hour later, Sabrina once again admired her figure in the full-length mirror. Her alterations were perfect. The scooped neckline now left nothing to the imagination, stitched so low that the blushed tips of her breasts nearly popped from their confines.

And the skirt . . . why, the angled edging up the side of the skirt had been pure genius. Not just a line cut in the fabric to reveal a glimpse of feminine ankle and calf when she walked, but a long slit from floor to waist. Her knee was left bare at all times, her entire thigh visible with each step.

It was time to put her plan into action. A plan she'd been concocting since she saw Caleb kiss that little trollop of a seamstress. It had taken all her will not to scratch the bitch's eyes out when she'd gone to order this dress.

But now she would show Caleb just what he was missing. And what a mistake it would be to become involved with that other woman. She would show him the gown and, with a few female waterworks, blame its disgraceful design on Rebecca. Caleb would, of course, be furious and have the seamstress run out of town in the blink of an eye, her reputation tarnished beyond repair.

Then Sabrina would be the only woman in his life again. And he would never leave her side again.

With a wicked smile on her lips, she wrapped a heavy black cloak about her shoulders and left the hotel room.

"All right, all right. I'm coming," Caleb growled, slamming down his pencil as he rose from the desk. His footsteps echoed through the empty hall as he headed for the front door. He didn't know where everyone was, but he would have to speak to somebody about answering the damn door when he was closeted in the study with paperwork.

He yanked the door open none too gently. Then wished he hadn't answered the summons at all when he saw Sabrina standing on the porch. Her brassy blond hair was piled high atop her head, a long red feather adorning it. As for the rest, she'd covered her entire form with a long black velvet cape—one he had undoubtedly paid for. He could honestly say he didn't miss seeing her hourglass shape. Wouldn't have missed it even if Sabrina were in New York, where he'd supposedly sent her.

"What are you doing here?" he asked.

"Visiting you, you ninny," she said in a high, overly friendly voice. She slipped past him, moving down the hall until she came to the parlor. Without invitation, she strutted across the room and perched upon the nearest wing chair.

"What do you want, Sabrina?" Caleb asked, crossing his arms over his chest. He stood in the doorway, hoping to convince her of her unwelcomeness. "I thought I told you to go back to New York."

"Well, now, what kind of mistress would I be if I didn't know your moods?" she asked rhetorically. "I knew you didn't mean a word of that nonsense. You were simply upset."

"I may have been upset, Sabrina, but I also meant what I said. It's time for you to return to New York."

She apparently missed his order—or pretended not to hear—as she looked around the richly decorated room. "Caleb, darling, I have a terrible dilemma," she said, her gaze moving back to his. "I do hope you'll help me."

He released a breath. He could just imagine her "dilemma." Tardy service at the hotel, perhaps. Or, God forbid, a broken fingernail.

Sabrina pulled a tissue from somewhere beneath the voluminous cape to dab at her heavily made-up eyes. "I'm so mortified, Caleb. You cannot imagine the horror I have suffered at that woman's hands."

His brow creased. "What woman?" he asked. And then he wondered why he even bothered, for he didn't really care to hear her answer.

"That woman!" she said vehemently, coming to her feet. "That . . . that . . . heathen dressmaker." She flung the cloak from her shoulders, revealing the gown beneath. "Just look what she's done to me!"

For a moment, Caleb stared in stunned silence. Then he promptly burst into uncontrolled laughter. He laughed until his sides hurt, until every breath became a struggle. And then he laughed some more.

When his vision once again cleared, he noticed that Sabrina's face was at least three shades darker than the red of her dress. He supposed his reaction wasn't quite what she'd expected.

"How can you laugh?" she asked bitterly. "How could she think I would wear such an abhorrent piece?"

"Looks like Rebecca knows you better than you thought," he said, fighting back a chuckle. He admitted that the bodice was cut a tad low, even for Sabrina. But something about Rebecca's choice in showing that much skin, not only at the chest but also at the leg, struck him as funny. And extremely interesting. Maybe Rebecca wasn't as much of a stodgy old maid as he'd first thought. After all, any woman who would design such a revealing dress had to possess some small depth of sensuality.

Or, in this case, perhaps simply a desire to show Sabrina in her true light.

"I cannot believe you find this amusing!" Sabrina railed, breaking into his thoughts. "That woman is trying to ruin me. I'll be a laughingstock in town if anyone sees me in this atrocity."

"Then don't wear it until you get back to New York," he suggested. "I'm sure your acquaintances there will find it quite attractive."

"New York?" she gasped. "Why, you don't truly mean to send me back, do you? Oh, Caleb," she cried, hurrying to his side. "I can't return without you."

"On the contrary, Sabrina." His tone hardened as he straightened, moving away from her clawing fingertips. "I still expect you to be on the next train East. I thought I made that clear the last time we spoke. In fact, my only question is why you're still in Leavenworth at all. You should be as far as St. Louis by now."

"You can't tell me to go back," she stated.

"I believe I just did." He walked to the door, opening it in a sweeping gesture. "Good-bye, Sabrina."

He didn't bother making sure she left. Once he saw her onto the front porch and locked the door for good measure, he made his way back to the study, Sabrina's "dilemma" already forgotten.

Rebecca's antics were not, however. He found himself chuckling again as he scooped up the pile of correspondence resting on the corner of his father's desk.

What gall it took to do such a thing. To sew a dress that no woman, including Sabrina Leslie, could wear outside the bedroom. Rebecca must sleep on a mattress filled with brass tacks, he thought as he opened the top envelope. No woman could be so bold otherwise, he was sure.

His eyes scanned the paper in his hand. He blinked, then read the figures again.

Damn! Brass tacks was right. And she must battle grizzly bears for fun to have *that* much gall. The thin stationery floated to the floor as Caleb moved to write a scathing reply to Rebecca's latest bill.

When Rebecca finally looked up from her stitching, it was well past ten o'clock. She took off her spectacles and set them on the table beside her rocking chair, then pulled the pins from her straggling hair. Brushing her fingers through it, she let her nails scratch at her tired scalp while rotating her head, trying to loosen the stiff muscles of her neck.

She stood up slowly, giving her body time to acclimate itself to movement. Picking up her teacup, she walked across the room to the kitchen. On the round wooden table lay the newest book of fashions she had picked up at the Pony Express office early that morning. She'd come home and tossed it onto the table, needing to get right to work on the dress Megan was to pick up at noon the next day.

Rebecca lifted the magazine by its corner, thinking to flip through the pages and get a quick look at the newest patterns. Anabelle Archer would surely pick one, if not more, the next time she came in.

Just as she started to open the book, something floated to the floor. Rebecca stooped down and picked up the square, off-white envelope. She slid her thumb under the triangular flap and worked it loose, sliding the crisp, perfectly folded, paper out. She opened the letter and read the short, scrawled note.

Rebecca,

I have no intention of paying for such an expensive gown, especially now that Miss Leslie and I are no longer associated. If you want your money, I suggest you meet her at the Express office, as she is leaving town in the morning.

There was no signature, but Rebecca knew darn good and well who had sent it. Her hand clenched into a fist, the envelope crackling between her fingers. Of all the nerve, she thought. *Mr. Adams and his not-so-attractively aging mistress have a falling out, and I'm the one to suffer*. Well, she needed that money. Rebecca had put all of her own into her business—except what she used for food, of course—and she couldn't afford not to be reimbursed for what she'd spent on that last elaborate gown.

Rebecca threw the book of fashions across the table. Her foot tapped angrily, the beat echoing through the small house. She had fought with Caleb once about Sabrina's bill and won. She would just have to go back and fight with him again. How dare he refuse to pay her!

Completely forgetting her earlier fatigue, Rebecca marched to the door, slamming it behind her as she ran down the porch steps and stalked across town. The street was empty except for a few horses tethered in front of the saloon. She headed directly for the Adams Express, hoping Caleb was working late.

All was dark when she reached the office, upping Rebecca's rage yet another notch. She studied the week's stage schedule that always occupied the lower right corner of the window glass. The last stage had pulled in at nine-thirty. Which probably meant Mr. Adams was staying at the hotel. The problem was, which Mr. Adams had worked this evening?

Rebecca made her way to the Wilkes Hotel, quieting her footsteps the closer she got to the main doors. She opened one and poked her head in, thankful no one was about. Mr. and Mrs. Wilkes were most likely asleep and would only awaken if someone rang the bell on the counter.

Rebecca slipped into the lobby and went to the hotel's register. She knew Mrs. Wilkes required everyone to sign in, no matter how frequently they stayed. Rebecca quickly scanned the signatures. At the very bottom of the page was the name she had been hoping to find. Caleb Z. Adams. Room E.

Looking around one last time to make sure she remained unseen, Rebecca smiled secretly and started up the stairs to the second floor. She would give that insufferable man a piece of her mind and get her money if it killed her!

Her breath caught when she came to the room marked E. A thread of doubt niggled at her mind, but her anger quickly pushed it aside. She rapped her fist on the door three times in agitated succession.

"Come in."

The words were muffled, drowsy-sounding, but plainly masculine. With a slight pang of guilt, Rebecca became aware of the fact that Caleb Adams might have already gone to sleep. *Well, too bad. He's awake now. Go in and give him what for!*

Rebecca turned the silver handle and entered the room, shutting the door behind her. She'd expected the Wilkes Hotel to be nice, but not this nice. She'd had no idea there were sitting rooms between hall and bedroom.

83

What an extravagance for a little town like Leavenworth.

But then, she reminded herself, some people could afford the luxury. Men like Caleb Adams. If he could afford to rent this room for the night when his house was no more than three miles from town, then he could most certainly afford the bill she'd sent.

She took a deep breath and steeled herself to confront him, moving farther into the room. Her steps made a board squeak beneath the carpeting.

"I'm in here," she heard him call. "Just close the door behind you."

Well, surely if he was inviting her in, he couldn't be abed already. He was probably reading or working on some figures for the Express.

She stepped into the adjacent room, her eyes coming to rest on a large mahogany roll-top desk stacked with papers and leather-bound volumes. Low, flickering lamplight emanated from the desk, casting the surroundings into pools of luminous yellow or shadowy gray.

A lump rose in her throat when her eyes fell upon the large four-poster bed in the center of the room. She had never been in a man's room before and wasn't sure she should be now. But she needed that money. Without it, her business would go under faster than a sinking steamship. If need be, she would walk through the fires of hell to exact payment.

She turned her gaze to the other side of the room, where her prey was no doubt sitting up with a good book.

My God! Rebecca's mouth dropped open as she stood stock-still, staring with wide eyes at Caleb Adams—naked. His long body was folded into a tub filled with steaming water, clear but for a thin layer of soap suds.

In an instant, Rebecca took in every detail of the sensual picture he created dozing in the porcelain bath, his head lolling comfortably on one shoulder. She knew it was shameful, but of their own accord her eyes traveled from the damp hair of Caleb's head to that of his chest, glistening with delicate drops of water.

She whirled around—mortified clear down to her toes—and reached for the doorknob. If she didn't get out of here now, her mind would end up where it had no business wandering. She could wait until tomorrow to confront him. At the moment, that certainly seemed the smartest thing to do.

"Just set the towels down over here." With his eyes still closed, Caleb reached out an arm and patted the seat of a nearby chair, freezing Rebecca's blood in her veins. "Hand me the washcloth, please."

If only he would keep his eyes closed until she escaped. Rebecca started to gently pull at the door, grimacing when it squeaked in protest.

At the low moan of ungreased hinges, Caleb's eyes popped open, searching through the dim light for the source of the noise. Startled to find a stranger in his room—and not the young man in charge of his bath—he quickly looked around for something to cover himself, finding nothing within reach. His clothes lay crumpled at the foot of the four-poster bed, and the towels he'd requested apparently had yet to be delivered.

Caleb's gaze returned to the petite girl trying unsuccessfully to sneak out, wondering what the little vagrant had pocketed. Her dress was worn and faded, its hem a bit frayed. Funny, he hadn't noticed any beggars in town before. The only person he'd seen with clothes even resembling those on this young woman was . . . Rebecca.

Caleb's eyes narrowed, traveling up the frail form to light brown hair piled high in a loose bun. Little of her face was visible, only a fraction of her profile, but enough for Caleb to note the smoothness of her skin, cheeks flushed a handsome hue, and her entire person devoid of even a smudge of dirt.

What the hell was Rebecca doing in his room? Come to steal him blind, had she? Or maybe she'd just wanted to get a glimpse of a gentleman sitting stark naked in the middle of a porcelain tub.

Caleb's lips curled in a salacious smile. Right now he was feeling more man than gentle, as was usually the case when he regarded Rebecca.

"Well, well, if it isn't Miss Rebecca. Looking for something, my dear?" he asked with obvious innuendo.

Rebecca kept her back turned, head down, eyes focused on what seemed to be a particularly interesting design in the carpeting. "I wished to discuss Miss Leslie's bill with you, but it can wait until a more appropriate time."

"This is as appropriate a time as any. Let's discuss the matter, shall we? Then we can get on to what you really came for."

Rebecca's head snapped up. She forgot all about modesty and whipped around to face him. "Excuse me?"

"There's only one reason a lady comes to a man's room this late at night. So first we'll talk, then we'll go to bed. Unless you'd like to go to bed now and talk later." Caleb lifted an eyebrow and cocked his head in the direction of the four-poster.

He was trying to shock her. Well, it wasn't going to work. Rebecca had seen a fair share of naked men in her lifetime, and this one in particular was not going to intimidate her. She took a step forward and raised her voice. "You arrogant, self-righteous swine! What makes you think I'd ever want to share a bed with you? Besides, you have Sabrina Leslie for that. But then, you pay *her* generously for her trouble. I—"

A knock at the door interrupted Rebecca's tirade. Caleb smiled at the panic in her eyes. God forbid she be found in his room this late at night, especially with him as naked as the day he was born. Caleb sank lower in the tub, folding his arms behind his head in a relaxed pose. "Those are my towels. Get them for me, will you, sweet?"

Sweet? Rebecca pursed her lips to hold back the string of curses she wanted to throw at him.

"All right, I'll get them," Caleb said casually, taking hold of either side of the tub and beginning to rise.

Rebecca's eyes widened. "I'll get them," she said quickly, holding out a hand to stop him from standing up. If only the knock had sounded from the sitting room door, her situation would not be quite so grim. But whoever was delivering the towels had come through to the bedroom.

She could not be found here, alone with a naked man. Opening the door but a fraction, she stuck an arm through and grabbed the stack of fluffy white towels. Then she pressed her hip against the mahogany panel until she heard the latch catch.

"You can put them here," Caleb said, once again patting the chair's crewel seat.

Rebecca held the pile of thick cotton towels protectively against her chest, locking her teeth together as tightly as a steel trap. Taking a deep breath, she composed herself. After all she'd been through this night, she vowed not to leave until she got what she'd come for.

"I came, Mr. Adams, to collect the money you owe me for Miss Leslie's gown. If you pay me, I'll go and leave you in peace."

"I'm afraid I can't do that. Sabrina and I are no longer acquainted, so to speak. Our relationship has been dissolved for more than a fortnight. And though I had the immense pleasure of seeing your handiwork with a needle, I cannot be held responsible for any orders Sabrina may have placed since the end of our involvement."

"I wouldn't have made the gown if I didn't think you would pay for it. Miss Leslie assured me that you approved of the purchase."

"Apparently, she lied. You really should have checked with me first."

"And just what am I supposed to do now? The dress has already been delivered, so I can't try to sell it to someone else. Not that any respectable woman in this town would wear such a humiliating item," she said with an unladylike snort. "But since it is no longer in my possession, I can't even rip it apart and reuse the materials."

"As I said, I'm sorry for your dilemma, but there's really nothing I can do. You made a mistake in taking Sabrina's word over mine."

Rebecca reached for the straight-backed chair next to the tub, dragging it a distance from Caleb. She put the linens on the seat and walked to his suit, thrown haphazardly across the bed. Rebecca lifted the jacket and pants.

"What do you think you're doing?" Caleb asked in a hard tone, sitting up a little straighter.

Rebecca smiled. "Do you suppose there's enough money in here to make good on your debt?" she asked rhetorically, digging into a trouser pocket.

"Nothing there." Rebecca continued searching. "What about the suitcoat?"

"Get your hands off my clothes. Just who the hell do you think you are, going through my things?"

Rebecca cast him a complacent look. "I am a very distraught seamstress who feels unjustly punished by a wealthy businessman for nothing more than making a dress for his paramour. And since you are somewhat indisposed at the moment, Mr. Adams, I am taking the liberty of exacting rightful payment."

"Rebecca." Caleb's hands clutched the sides of the bathtub so hard, she expected the fragile ceramic to shatter. "If you don't put those down right this minute, I am going to get out of this tub, come over there, and tan your pretty little backside."

Rebecca chuckled, feeling brave with Caleb waist-deep in bath water. "You have never had the pleasure of seeing my posterior, Mr. Adams, so you cannot possibly comment on its appearance."

Holding her hand up so Caleb could see the thick wad of bills she'd found, Rebecca counted out the amount of Sabrina's gown. She tucked the money securely into the square-cut bodice of her comfortable old day dress.

"I'll leave you to your bath now, sir. Furthermore," she said, feeling boldness pumping through her veins as she moved to the door, "you're not hiding anything under that water that I haven't seen before. Good-night."

"Rebecca?"

Caleb's voice was so quiet, so calm, that Rebecca turned back to look at him without conscious thought. When she did, he leaned forward and pushed himself up from the tub. The soapy water lapped against the porcelain sides in waves, spilling over to darken the burgundy carpet. Long trails ran down the length of Caleb's bronzed body, capturing Rebecca's attention.

She swallowed hard. "Oh, my."

Chapter Seven

"I thought your said you've seen naked men before."

Rebecca nodded. "M-Many." Her response sounded strangled even to her own ears. *Just none quite as . . . as . . . Well, none quite like Caleb.*

Caleb kept his gaze on Rebecca, watching as her eyes roamed the expanse of his body. A flush began at the bodice of her faded indigo dress, progressively climbing up her throat all the way to her hairline.

His mouth curved up as he noticed her especially noticing the area below his belt . . . so to speak. His physique must be impressive compared to the other men she'd seen; otherwise she wouldn't look so shocked.

But his smile became a frown as the meaning of Rebecca's words hit him. She had seen "many" naked men. So she wasn't a straitlaced virgin. Far from it!

Caleb didn't know what he'd expected, but the idea of Rebecca being with another man—many men—froze his blood. After seeing her with Megan, spending time with her on their picnic and flower hunt, he had begun to hope she was different from the women he'd known back in New York. Unlike the snooty, aloof ladies he'd had the misfortune to be involved with, Rebecca was warm and personable, with a lively sense of humor. Or so he'd thought.

But really, she was no different than any of the others. She had probably used her body innumerable times to bend men to her will. Her lifestyle didn't show it, of course. She had most likely made bad decisions along the way and lost her illicit earnings, leaving her practically destitute. Now she was on the lookout for another man to lure into her web.

Well, he would not be her next victim, Caleb thought as he stared intently at Rebecca. Her mouth was open, and she swayed slightly as if a sneeze could blow her over. Caleb hadn't noticed before how round and full her breasts looked beneath the faded blue dress. The material tightened provocatively across her chest, tapering down to a waist Caleb could span with his hands. As he had several times on the day of the picnic.

No, he would not be her next victim. . . .

But he *would* be her next lover.

"So tell me, Rebecca, how do I compare to the others?"

Rebecca's head jolted up at the coldness of Caleb's voice. Only then did she realize where her sights had been. Heat flooded her body, and she began to pray that the floor would open up to swallow her whole.

It took a moment for Caleb's question to burrow its way through the fog that surrounded her brain. *How did he compare?* Compare to whom? What did he mean?

Oh, yes. She'd made that flippant remark about his not hiding anything she hadn't seen before. While it was true, she probably would have been wiser to keep her mouth shut. Octavia Fitzgerald had warned Rebecca that her outspoken comments would someday get her in trouble.

It looked as if the widow's prediction had just come true.

Rebecca straightened her spine and took a deep breath. She had never backed down from a confrontation before; she wasn't going to begin now. Caleb Adams acted a bit too high and mighty for her tastes. He needed to be put in his place, and she was just the seamstress to do it.

Tapping her chin with an index finger, she pretended to seriously contemplate the question. Swallowing hard, she let her eyes move boldly, slowly, over Caleb's broad shoulders and chest, following the curly black hair of his "pleasure path"—as the girls at Lilah's used to joke—to the finely chiseled male organ between his legs.

So her presence affected him. Well, she knew how to remedy that.

"Well . . ." Rebecca stretched the word out until Caleb shifted uncomfortably. "I've seen better."

Caleb's body tensed, and he crossed his arms over his chest.

She held her breath to see if her comment produced the desired result. "Now don't feel bad," Rebecca said in a soothing voice. "What you've got is nothing to be ashamed of. I'm sure it suits your purposes well enough."

"And just how do you know so much about the male anatomy?"

Rebecca shrugged one shoulder and smiled secretly.

"Would you say you're an authority on the subject?"

She shrugged her other shoulder, pretending to find the whole topic rather boring.

"Would you care to put your expertise to the test?"

Rebecca didn't move. What was he suggesting? Her voice wobbled as she spoke. "What-what do you have in mind?"

"Oh, simply a chance to sample the goods. An opportunity to compare me with your other conquests."

Rebecca laughed, trying to sound brave and confident. "It sounds delightful, but I really must be going." She turned toward the door, hoping for a quick escape.

"Mind handing me a towel?"

Rebecca flushed guiltily. It was the least she could do after insulting his manhood—literally. She walked back to the chair, plucking one off the pile. She stared at a spot a good three inches above his head and held the towel at arm's length, waggling it by one corner.

Like a striking rattlesnake, Caleb's hand darted out to snag her wrist. Crying out in surprise, Rebecca found herself being pulled to the damp, unyielding wall of his chest and clamped between the steel bands of his arms.

"Let go of me," she hissed, grappling against his iron grip.

"You weren't going to walk off with my money, now were you, Miss Rebecca?"

"It's my money," Rebecca insisted, redoubling her efforts to get free.

"Hardly, my dear."

Caleb stepped from the tub gracefully, as if he wasn't fighting to keep hold of the struggling woman in his arms. He pressed his lips to her ear, her cheek.

Rebecca stilled her protests, remaining like a block of ice in his embrace. When Caleb moved to cover her mouth and kiss her, she dug her nails into his chest, trying to push him away.

He tickled and teased the outline of her lips, eliciting a moan from deep in her throat. Rebecca squeezed her eyes shut, embarrassed by her response to his touch. Was this what her mother experienced each night when she took the patrons of the Scarlet Garter upstairs?

"You are beautiful, you know," he said, dissolving any lucid thought she tried to form. "Even in that ratty old dress."

Caleb's warm tongue pressed against Rebecca's lips,

and she opened to him, no longer thinking to deny the flames that licked at her insides, driving her nearly mad. If what her mother did felt this good, she could almost understand Kate's taking the job. But that didn't excuse her neglectful parenting—or the fact that she had been willing to put her thirteen-year-old daughter to work doing the same thing.

Rebecca leaned into Caleb's body as his left hand traveled down her side to clutch the roundness of her buttocks. His right found one breast, the thumb doing delightfully wicked things through the fabric of her bodice.

Rebecca knew a moment of panic as she felt Caleb's stiff member straining upward against her abdomen. But she forced the fear aside. In her haze of desire, she had actually begun considering allowing Caleb to take her to bed. After all, she was already twenty-three years old, a spinster in most people's minds, and no man was likely to come asking for her hand in marriage. If she ever wanted intimate knowledge of a man, this might be her only chance. And she had to admit that she had recently became terribly curious to see what all the hullabaloo was about.

She could put the experience behind her when it was over and go on with her life, Rebecca told herself. Just as Caleb would. He was used to taking women to bed with no thought of the future. She could do the same. Couldn't she?

Rebecca's back came in contact with a tall wooden column. How they had gotten from the middle of the room to the bed, she had no idea. Startled, she didn't think to struggle as Caleb put an arm under her legs to lift her, following her down onto the softness of the wide mattress.

Caleb fumbled with the long row of tiny pearl-drop buttons at the front of Rebecca's dress as well as the ribbon of her camisole. His fingers brushed the folded bills tucked securely between her breasts. Getting his money back now seemed an infinitesimal matter compared to his need to be close to Rebecca.

He tossed the cash over his shoulder without a second thought, pressing his face against the pulse of her neck, breathing in her scent. She smelled like . . . cinnamon. He smiled. It was a far cry from those fancy city perfumes that could end up stinking like a whorehouse. Rebecca's fragrance was sensually simple. In his most erotic fantasies, Caleb had never dreamed she would smell this delicious.

He began kissing his way across Rebecca's collarbone, pushing material from his path, feeling her quiver beneath his erotic touch. As his tongue flicked out, leaving a wet trail down to the underside of Rebecca's breast, she jolted, and Caleb knew he must be imagining the spicy taste of her skin. No one could possibly smell and taste and feel so damn good.

He yanked at her dress, fighting to untangle it from her arms. With a very improper expletive, he ceased his efforts, sealing Rebecca's mouth with his, kissing her until they were both breathless. Though he wanted Rebecca to be as unclothed as he when they made love, his endurance was nearing an end.

When his hands drew her skirts up so he could touch her bare, slender limbs, he felt Rebecca tense beneath him. He kissed her into compliance once more. His hand stroked her warm inner thigh, his fingers roving higher and higher. "Does that feel good?" He smiled when she gasped and moaned.

He didn't really know why he was bothering with preliminaries. By her own admission, Rebecca had been with many men. But for some reason, Caleb wanted to take it slow, make it satisfying for both of them. He wanted Rebecca to remember this night. He wanted Rebecca to remember *him* above all the others.

With uncommon tenderness, Caleb untied the strings

of her coarse, bleached flour-sack drawers, sliding them down the silky smoothness of her legs, letting them fall to the floor. He was glad to discover that Rebecca hadn't bothered with extra underthings this evening, like a corset or stockings that would only take more time to remove.

Rolling a taut nipple with his thumb and index finger, he kissed her again, drawing her tongue into an intimate duel with his own. His other hand lingered at her thighs. He slid two fingers through her soft, springy curls, between her delicate folds. She arched so abruptly that she almost knocked him off the bed, and Caleb groaned, nearly erupting from the mere thought of pressing himself into her. She was hot and wet and . . . so damn tight. He could hardly fit one finger inside her narrow sheath, let alone two. How had she gone through so many lovers and still remained as tight as a virgin?

Caleb pushed the question aside and nudged her legs apart with his knee, his mouth still on hers. He lowered his body until he felt her moistness upon the tip of his hard length. With one finger, he touched the swollen nub of pleasure hidden within her feminine flesh. Rebecca gasped and arched off the mattress, causing his shaft to enter her even more deeply.

"God." He strived for control, concentrating on inhaling and exhaling lest he forget to breathe. It was too much. "I can't wait. I can't." Caleb hugged Rebecca fiercely and thrust forward, burying himself as deeply as possible. He held still, knowing that if he moved, he would explode.

Through a haze of intense pleasure, Caleb heard Rebecca's cry and looked up. Her eyes were wide with fear as she fought to break his hold. He frowned. Only when her struggles increased and her body moved against him did he realize why she was so small.

"My God." He laid his face on her chest for a moment, counting along with the beat of her heart. His arms tightened and clasped her close. "Don't move." When she didn't heed his warning, Caleb lifted his head. "Dammit, I said don't move." He grabbed Rebecca's wrists and braced them on the mattress, using all his strength to halt her movements. "The pain will pass if you hold still for a minute."

At this promise, Rebecca let herself go limp.

"There, you see?" Caleb asked after several long seconds.

Rebecca nodded.

"Why didn't you tell me?"

She didn't answer. Rebecca remained unmoving, staring up into Caleb's accusing eyes.

"I guess it doesn't matter now. The damage is already done," Caleb said, apparently deciding the matter.

Rebecca watched his eyelashes flutter closed as his hand began stroking her, making her sob with the sheer ecstasy of his touch.

"I'll make it good for you," she heard him say in a ragged whisper.

For a moment, she considered fighting him. But then his fingers began making the most wonderful circular motions, and he pulled out of her only to enter again more powerfully than before.

She gripped his shoulders tightly, afraid of the things she was feeling. Afraid that, at any moment, the blackness that hovered just beyond her vision would reach out and steal her away.

Caleb's motions accelerated. Rebecca dug her nails into his back, instinctively straining to meet his fevered thrusts. Her body tingled and burned. She closed her eyes and felt herself being swallowed alive by the dark, only to scream with shock and pleasure when a burst of light streaked across the horizon. Her body quaked, contracting around Caleb as he drove into her one last time with a tortured moan. She felt a wetness flood within her as he stiffened and collapsed, covering her like a warm winter quilt.

It wasn't until Caleb had rolled away that Rebecca opened her eyes. Her surroundings surprised her. She was still in Caleb's hotel room, the oil lamps burning bright. For some reason, she had expected to awake in some faraway land or a field of colorful wildflowers beneath a blue, cloudless sky.

Somehow she found the strength to lift an arm and rub her eyes. Letting her head fall to the side, she watched the even rise and fall of Caleb's chest. His eyes were closed, and he might have been sleeping. A fine sheen of perspiration dappled his body. His usually neat black hair was tousled.

Caleb groaned and rolled to his side, running a hand through the unruly locks. "I'm sorry."

Rebecca's breath caught, and she closed her eyes, pulling at her bodice to belatedly cover her nudity. Her fingers shakily tied the ribbon of her camisole and re-buttoned the dress.

"Did you hear me? I said I'm sorry."

"Yes, I heard." She reached down to smooth her crumpled skirts. Rebecca wished there were some way to get out of the room without having to look at him. His apology was humiliating enough, but to meet his eyes would surely make her burst into tears.

"If I had known you were . . . well, after you said you'd seen . . . I just assumed . . ." He ran his fingers through his hair again and sat up. "I'm sorry, is all. I never should have touched you."

Rebecca slipped off the bed and picked up her discarded underclothes, rolling them into a tight ball. Her face heated with shame at the memory of Caleb's removing them from her willing body.

Willing. Maybe she should pack her things and move back to Kansas City. No doubt Lilah would welcome Kate's daughter to the Scarlet Garter with open arms.

She wouldn't be worth as much as before, of course. Men wouldn't pay as much for a used parcel as for an innocent virgin.

Rebecca covered her eyes in an attempt to dam the tears. She had been a virgin, all right, but never innocent. Her mother had seen to that.

Caleb's strong hands folded over her shoulders. She pulled away and headed for the door.

"Rebecca, wait."

She didn't. She grabbed for the doorknob, but Caleb stopped her, turning her to face him.

"Here," he said, pressing something into the palm of her hand.

She looked down, blinking hard several times to clear her vision. The money she'd taken earlier rested there, more wrinkled than before.

"You son of a bitch." Her shame melted into a fury that burned hotter than any blacksmith's forge. "I wasn't good enough for your money when I sewed a dress for your mistress, but now that you've bedded me, I am? Is that it?" She took a step toward him and held the cash in his face. "You can keep your money, Mr. Adams. I am not for sale. I have never been—nor will I ever be— a whore."

With that, she threw the money at him and quit the room, racing down the hotel stairs and across town as fast as her shaking legs would carry her.

She'd told Caleb she was no whore. The words reverberated through her mind again and again. And then a niggling doubt intruded, bringing her deepest fears to the surface.

The problem is, that voice warned, *maybe you are.*

Chapter Eight

A fierce pounding in her head woke Rebecca. It was only when she stumbled out of her room, barefoot and in her nightdress, toward the kitchen that she realized the noise was coming from the front door. When she opened it, Megan Adams swept into the house, her bright yellow skirt flashing.

"I can't tell you how much I love these dresses, Rebecca. They're so comfortable, I don't even want to take them off at bedtime. Where's the new one? I want to try it on."

Rebecca squeezed her eyes shut and tried to recall where she had put the new gowns. She could scarcely even remember making it. She shook her head in apology. "Would you mind joining me for a cup of tea? I'm not quite awake yet."

Megan followed her to the kitchen and crossed a leg under her as she sat in an unladylike fashion on one of the two chairs at the table. Her brows knit as she watched Rebecca.

"What is it?" Rebecca asked, noticing the odd way

Megan was looking at her. "Have I sprouted another head or something?"

"Something," Megan agreed. "Rebecca, you look horrible."

"Thank you very much," Rebecca replied sourly. "Just the thing to make a person feel special."

"No, I mean it. You look terrible. Are you all right?"

"I'm fine, why?"

"Well, first of all, it's nearly two in the afternoon, and you're obviously just getting up. Second, your face is as white as milk, and your eyes are as puffy and red as ripe tomatoes."

"Tell me my hair looks like a side of beef, and we'll be all set for a dinner party."

"What's wrong?" Megan asked worriedly.

"Nothing's wrong. I'm fine."

"Then why did you sleep past noon? You told me you're awake every morning at the crack of dawn."

Rebecca sighed and rubbed one bare foot over the other, partially to warm them, partially to stall for time. If her visitor had been anyone other than Megan, Rebecca would have excused herself and gone to dress, but she felt comfortable with the girl.

"I was up late last night. I finished your gown and then started reading a book. A very sad book, which is probably why my eyes are swollen. Didn't your mother ever warn you about crying before going to bed?"

Megan shook her head, and Rebecca began feeling guilty for her lie. In truth, it had already been midnight when she left Caleb's room and ran home. She'd spent the rest of the night—or wee hours of the morning— sobbing her heart out and chastising herself for being every kind of fool.

"What book was it?"

"Hmm?"

Megan sighed and propped her elbows on the table as Rebecca brought two cups and the tea kettle. "The book.

101

What's the title? If it was that good, I might like to read it."

"Oh, um, I . . . I can't recall the name." Rebecca scanned the room for something to take Megan's attention from the book. "It really wasn't good, just sad."

"But if you stayed up all night to—"

"Oh, look," Rebecca cried, spotting Megan's dress folded over the back of the rocking chair, right where she'd left it. "Why don't you go try it on while your tea cools?"

"But—"

"Go on, now. I know you're dying to see how it fits."

With much prompting and prodding, Rebecca finally got Megan into the bedroom. Holding the sides of her head as a sledgehammer began to pound at her temples, she gulped down three scalding hot cups of cinnamon tea before Megan reappeared in the moderately fancy smoke-gray dress.

"I think Papa will approve, don't you, Rebecca?" Megan twirled around, making the gown seem more exquisite than the color and fabric alone would have allowed. "He wants me to have one for Sunday services. Somehow he didn't think the others were appropriate, given their bright colors."

"I can understand that," Rebecca acquiesced.

"I'll wear it over to the Express right now and see what he and Caleb think."

At the mention of Caleb, Rebecca's head seemed to pound all the harder, and a small moan escaped her otherwise tight throat.

"Are you all right?" Megan asked, coming to her side with concern.

"Fine," Rebecca said, pushing herself up from the table. "Let me wrap the yellow dress so it doesn't get dirty." She moved to the other end of the house and got out the materials needed to protect the outfit. When she was finished, Rebecca handed the package to Megan.

"Here's the payment for the dress, Rebecca," she said. "And, you know, it's the strangest thing. Before I came, Caleb insisted I give this to you. He said he owed you for something but wouldn't say what. Funny, I thought he was all paid up for my things." Megan shrugged and handed Rebecca the money.

Her fingers closed over the bulge of cash. From the looks of it, these were the same bills he'd tried to foist on her last night. The son of a bitch.

For a moment Rebecca considered giving the wad back to Megan with explicit instructions to Caleb on where he could put his money if he was so eager to be rid of it. But she thought it best not to involve Megan in their battle. Although Caleb obviously didn't agree.

"Thank you." Rebecca forced a smile to her lips. "And thank your brother for me, too, please."

She held the stiff smile and politely wished Megan farewell. The minute the girl was out of hearing distance, Rebecca slammed the door and huffed in fury. If that bastard thought he could pay her for her favors, he had another thing coming. She was not a whore. She was not like her mother.

Once. It had only happened once, and Rebecca swore—to God, to the heavens, and to herself—that it would never, ever happen again. She would never let Caleb Adams or any other man seduce her into his bed.

And that was exactly what he'd done. He had taken advantage of her completely, grabbing her like that and kissing her senseless. What was that if not seduction? It wasn't as though she had undressed and climbed into Caleb's bed just waiting for him to walk in. She had gone there to collect her money, nothing else. Caleb Adams was entirely to blame. Rebecca wasn't innocent in the ways of men and women, but she'd hardly encouraged him to paw her the way he had.

Rebecca went to the parlor and dug through the Widow Fitzgerald's collection of old tea tins, settling on the one farthest in the back. She pried open the lid and stuffed Caleb's money inside. Oh, she would keep it, but she wouldn't touch it for anything other than the direst circumstances. She'd be damned if she would put that money toward her own comfort. For then she might as well admit she'd become a whore—just like her mother.

Replacing the tins, she walked into the bedroom and donned her oldest, ugliest, and most worn day dress. After all, why shouldn't her clothes match her mood?

A hot flood of pain rushed over Rebecca when Sabrina Leslie entered the shop later that day. The woman marched toward her, obviously having something to say. Rebecca made a show of putting aside her sewing, determined to hide her uneasiness from Caleb's mistress.

"May I help you, Miss Leslie?" she asked when the woman came to a halt before her. She looked up to find Sabrina glaring down at her, daggers shooting from her eyes.

"Stay away from him," she ordered without preamble.

"Excuse me?" Rebecca asked, though she knew perfectly well whom Sabrina meant.

"I take care of Caleb's needs," the woman continued, hands on her hips. "*All* of them. There is nothing he could possibly want from you. Except maybe the novelty of a quick roll in the hay with a hayseed."

Rebecca swallowed past the lump in her throat. She was painfully aware that Sabrina's words were true. Caleb was rich, handsome, and could have any woman he wished, any time he wished. Proof of that stood before her now.

Sabrina was beautiful, sophisticated. Even if the years were slightly dimming her physical perfection, she still knew how to make a man happy without even trying. Comparing herself to that, Rebecca had to wonder, what could Caleb possibly want from her?

Didn't she know better than anyone how men used women? Hadn't she told herself time and time again never to get involved with the opposite sex? How could she have let herself be lulled into such mindlessness last evening? How could she have let him touch her, make love to her?

"Don't think that your pathetic little act of innocence is going to work," Sabrina snapped. "I may be going back to New York, but that doesn't mean you can seduce him away from me. Caleb is only sending me ahead so that I can ready our apartments for his arrival. He'll be coming after me in a few weeks, and I'll have him all to myself again. He won't even remember your name."

Rebecca had no doubt that Sabrina was right.

She inhaled deeply, fighting back the tears that stung her eyes. "You needn't worry, Miss Leslie. Caleb Adams isn't the least bit interested in me." She forced the next words from her mouth, though they burned all the way up her throat. "Nor I in him."

Two Saturdays later, the entire town gathered for the annual Harvest Barn Dance and Good Eats, as the red-lettered banner boasted. Caleb Adams stood leaning against the open rear doors of the livery stable, his fingers drawing lazy patterns on his glass of punch as he watched couples dance in the bright lamplight. Each year at the end of July, the citizens of Leavenworth joined together to celebrate one last time before bringing in their crops.

Being the largest building in town, the livery had been cleared of any sign or scent of livestock and opened for the occasion. Bales of straw lined the inner walls for seating, and homemade streamers decorated with dried flowers adorned the rafters. A makeshift stage had been built in one corner for the musical group consisting of three fiddles, a banjo, and an off-key harmonica.

Caleb turned, somewhat surprised at the sound of his

companion's high giggle. She obviously found whatever she'd been saying very amusing. He allowed his mouth to lift in a false smile as he nodded, hoping she wouldn't realize he hadn't paid a whit of attention to her story. Nor had he heard a word she'd uttered throughout the two dances he'd been forced to share with her.

What was her name, anyway? He'd no sooner set the brake and stepped down from the wagon than the petite blonde had attached herself to his arm. Megan had introduced them, but he could no longer recall her name. She was pretty enough, Caleb thought, taking in her tiny form and small breasts, but she couldn't be more than seventeen, if that. A lovely young lady trying to sink her claws into a rich husband, like all the rest.

"Would you like another glass of punch, Miss . . ."

"Anabelle," she said, stroking his arm coyly. "I told you to call me Anabelle. And I'll call you Caleb."

"Very well," Caleb replied, looking down at eyelashes fluttering like the wings of a hummingbird. "I'll be right back." He took her cup and made his way around the dance floor.

Spotting his sister behind the refreshment table talking with another girl, he made a beeline for her and attacked. With a cold glare, he sent Megan's new friend skittering. "I don't know what you thought you were doing when you told that girl to keep me company, but you'd better get her off me—*fast*."

"Aren't you enjoying Miss Archer's company?" Megan asked, grinning wickedly. "Why, I thought for sure you'd find her to your liking."

Caleb grasped Megan's arm and squeezed. In a low voice he said, "I like her about as much as I would a mad dog. She grabbed on and won't let go. Get her away from me, Megan. I mean it."

Megan let out a martyred sigh. "I'll try. Why don't you make yourself scarce."

"I'll be outside." Caleb thrust the punch glasses into

her hands and turned for the double doors.

He took a deep breath of night air. Deciding to avoid the party for a while, Caleb stuck his hands into his pants pockets and moved down the deserted street of town, deliberately walking in the opposite direction of Rebecca's house. The music faded behind him, finally becoming almost pleasant, off-key harmonica and all.

He'd thought about Rebecca a lot over the past weeks. Hadn't been able to get her out of his head, in fact. Every time he closed his eyes, she was there, floating in front of his mind's eye like some silky, sultry apparition, exactly the way she had been that night more than two weeks ago. Writhing beneath him, setting his skin afire, her throaty little moans filling his ears.

And if the days were bad, the nights were pure hell. He would lie in bed for hours, tortured by the memory of her warm flesh, as smooth as satin, rubbing against his own. Rebecca's image would dance in front of him, and his traitorous body would react, swelling painfully—remaining that way until, in the early hours of morning, he could douse himself with cold water, hoping to ease his suffering somewhat and keep others from noticing his uncomfortable predicament.

She'd ruined him. Branded him. Mind, body, and soul.

Oh, he had tried to rid his memory of Rebecca—the feel of her tongue against his own, the spicy scent of each strand of her glorious hair, the tingle her touch sent to every part of his being. Even when he'd drunk himself into a stupor at the Dog Tick and taken one of its available women upstairs, Caleb hadn't been able to get Rebecca out of his brain. He'd ended up paying the redhead for her time and nothing more.

When Caleb reached the last building on Leavenworth's main street, he turned to slowly make his way back to the livery, kicking a small stone ahead of him.

He'd even thought about asking Rebecca to be his

mistress. He could ensure her financial security for a time and lavish her with fancy gifts from cities like New York and St. Louis. But if her parting words were any indication, she wouldn't be impressed by his offer.

He'd only meant to reimburse her for Sabrina's order, but he supposed immediately after sex was not the best time to be paying his debts. Giving it some thought, Caleb could see how Rebecca might think she was being paid for the sex itself. But even after her refusal to accept the money, he'd felt it necessary to pay for Sabrina's dress, since Rebecca had really had no way of knowing he'd put an end to his personal arrangement with Miss Leslie.

Caleb knew that ordering another gown at his expense was Sabrina's way of hitting back at him. At least she'd gotten the idea of revenge out of her system and then left town; he'd seen her board the stage less than a week after he'd told her to return to New York.

About to rejoin the festivities, Caleb raised his head and stuck a finger into his collar to loosen his tight tie.

He saw her immediately, coming from the house with a basket over her arm. A thick, braided chignon began at the back of her head and swept down to the nape of her neck, where the ribbons of a creamy lace bow fluttered in the evening breeze.

She looked even more beautiful than Caleb remembered. *Her dress must be new,* he thought, taking in the delicate trimmings that matched the lace in her hair. The deep wine color and diamond-cut bodice of the gown accentuated the light skin tone from her narrow throat to the generous swell of her breasts. He tried to convince his body not to react to the splendorous sight, but a heaviness grew in Caleb's loins, and his heart began to pound against his ribs.

He stopped a distance from the livery so she would be forced to pass him. He knew the moment she spotted him standing in her path, for her shoulders rose and her lips thinned. He took a step forward, striving for an arrogant demeanor to hide the way his blood raced through his veins.

"Finally decided to join the rest of the town, did you?" he asked, hooking a thumb in the pocket of his trousers. "The party started an hour ago."

Rebecca's chin rose a notch, and she pulled the basket closer in front of her. "Not that it's any concern of yours, Mr. Adams, but I was waiting to take pies out of the oven. I doubt anyone would appreciate my early arrival once they bit into an undercooked apple."

"Dad told me they always put you in charge of pies. Must be pretty damn good."

"You'll just have to taste for yourself, now won't you, Mr. Adams?"

She moved to pass him, but he put an arm out to stop her. He stood close enough for the scent of sweet brown sugar and cinnamon to swirl into his nostrils. Caleb wondered if anyone else would realize the spicy fragrance came from Rebecca and not the pastries.

"Don't you think we're past the formalities, Rebecca? After all, we do know one another . . . intimately."

Her face flushed, and she tried once again to get away. But Caleb grabbed her arm, trapping the wicker basket of warm pies between them.

"I must say I enjoyed myself immensely that night," he goaded her, impatient for some response to him. "Think we can do it again sometime?"

Caleb caught her hand in mid-air when she tried to slap him, gripping it tightly until her breath stilled. She bit her lip but uttered no sound.

Her reserve unaccountably maddened him, when he could feel so aroused simply by her presence. "What's the matter? Didn't I send enough money with Megan?" he taunted. He pushed still harder. "I haven't had a country whore for so long, I'm not sure what the going rate is. Especially for one who makes house calls."

Rebecca's eyes shot sparks. And, without warning, her knee came up, striking Caleb between the legs. The basket banged against his diaphragm. His hold on her loosened, and he doubled over, moaning.

He watched through half-closed, pain-filled eyes as a smile finally curved her lips.

"Have a nice evening, Mr. Adams," Rebecca said above his ear.

As she walked away, Caleb could have sworn he heard her laughing.

"Have you seen Caleb?"

Slicing and serving apple pie, Rebecca looked up into Megan's worried countenance. "I thought he'd be here with you," Rebecca evaded.

"He was. But Anabelle Archer attacked him, and he went out for a breath of air. That was hours ago. I haven't seen him since, and I'm beginning to worry."

"She attacked him?" Rebecca laughed. "That must have been fun to watch."

"It was, actually," Megan said with a chuckle. "But he should have returned by now."

"Don't fret, Megan. Caleb can take care of himself. I'm sure he'll show up any minute now."

Unless he's in the icehouse cooling off, Rebecca thought, turning so Megan wouldn't see her grin. She felt only the tiniest shred of guilt for kneeing Caleb. He deserved it. Not only for trying to physically detain her, but for his wretched, deplorable comments.

Her gleeful smile froze in place and her hackles rose as someone's hot breath dusted the back of her neck. She turned to find her eyes level with a broad male chest. Rebecca took a deep breath and struggled to raise her gaze, fear creeping along her spine like nails scraping a blackboard.

Caleb Adams towered over her, his gaze cold. "I'd like to speak with you, Miss Rebecca."

His words might have sounded polite and cultured to the people around them, but they didn't fool Rebecca. He was furious.

"I can't right now, sir," Rebecca choked out. "I'm quite busy serving dessert."

His fingers closed around her upper arm, making her wince. "Now."

As Caleb prodded her to walk in front of him through the crowd, Rebecca smiled and nodded to curious on-lookers. She wanted to scream for help—or at least warn Marshal Thompson that a murder was about to be committed—but she couldn't seem to find her voice.

He steered her out of the barn and into the dark, deserted night.

"Please, Mr. Adams—"

"Shut up. And it's Caleb."

"Caleb, I'm sorry, truly I am. It's just that you frightened me and—"

"Shut up."

The pressure on her arm increased, and Rebecca thought it best to do as he said. They moved down the empty street, and she closed her eyes, praying for Caleb to regain his sanity. When she stumbled up a set of wide steps and glanced around, she found herself being dragged into her own cabin.

Oh, the nerve! He's going to kill me in my own home.

Anger bubbled in her gut, and she balked, straining to get away from Caleb's fierce hold. "Let go of me, you bastard. I won't be treated like this. Do you hear me?" If he murdered her, she damn well intended to die fighting.

Caleb swung her in front of him, through the front door, and deposited her on a kitchen chair. "Sit there," he said menacingly, "and don't move one muscle. Do you hear me?" When she didn't answer, he leaned so close that their noses nearly touched. "Do you hear me?" he repeated.

She crossed her arms over her chest and slumped down on the seat. "Yes," she answered, grinding her teeth in frustration.

Caleb walked away to light an oil lamp. Then he began pacing the length of the parlor. "I didn't give much thought to the time you stormed into the Express office and upbraided me over Sabrina's first bill. Nor did your mistaken identification of my sister as some fornicating trollop bother me overly much. I even found myself moderately amused by the flush of your skin and the sparkle of your eyes when you held me hostage in a bathtub and ordered me to pay my debts." He paused to glare at her. "But I draw the line," he continued, "at being nearly emasculated by some willful, stubborn female."

"*Willful?*" Rebecca jumped to her feet. "I hardly call the act of protecting myself *willful.*"

"Protecting yourself from *what?*"

They stood toe-to-toe now, yelling.

"*You!*"

"I wasn't going to hurt you, and you damn well knew it!"

"How did I know? By your *friendly* words? Or the grip you had on my arm? I feared for my life," she announced dramatically.

Caleb remained silent for several seconds, as if thinking of a retort. "Damn," he said, running a hand through his hair and glancing around the room. He went to the rocker and dropped into it, propping his elbows on his knees. "Did I really scare you?" he asked quietly.

Rebecca rested a hip on the edge of the kitchen table. "I was more mad than frightened, I think," she admitted. "You called me a whore."

She had agonized over the possibility for two long weeks before coming to the conclusion that one small misfortune did not a whore make. Caleb's callous, hurtful comment had brought to the surface again all the fears she thought she'd buried.

Caleb raised his head and stared at her for a long moment. "That was cruel. I apologize. I didn't mean it. Truly."

He sounded sincere, but the last thing Rebecca wanted to do was trust a man, especially one who seemed able to lead her to temptation so easily. "Then why did you say it?" she challenged.

Caleb stood and walked toward her. "Hell, I don't know why. Because I was angry."

He stopped before her and lowered his voice. "Because I wanted to get back at you for leaving so quickly after we made love. For ignoring me ever since. For seeming to forget me so easily."

He wound a loose tendril of her hair around his finger. "Because I wanted to make love to you again."

He bent and teased her upper lip with his tongue. "Because even now, I want you."

Chapter Nine

Rebecca's lungs felt on fire from the breath she held. Caleb's feather-light touch danced over her face and neck, melting her resolve like warm butter.

"We can't," she said, pushing halfheartedly at his broad shoulders.

"Yes. We can." Caleb made quick work of the hidden hooks at the front of her gown.

"We shouldn't. It's not right." Her head fell back, and she moaned as the rough pads of his fingers brushed the tender tips of her breasts.

"You want this as much as I do. Feel it, Rebecca." He flicked one nipple with his thumb, sending a lightning-sharp bolt of pleasure down to curl her toes. "Let your passions guide you."

A thread of reason tugged at Rebecca's brain, but she pushed it aside and followed the dictates of her tingling flesh. She sank to her knees on the floor with Caleb, uncaring of the fate of the brand-new dress she'd spent so long making. It seemed to disappear magically, as did her shoes, stockings, and other underthings. How Caleb undressed, she had no notion, for his hands never halted in their intimate caress of her body.

"Aren't you sore? After I . . ."

"Never too sore for this," he answered in a husky voice, tugging at her nipple with his lips. "Not with you."

Caleb lay back on the rough plank floor and urged Rebecca to straddle him. With a leg on either side, she placed her palms on his chest and leaned forward to kiss him, taking his tongue into her mouth and gently sucking on it as he had her breast. He groaned, and she lifted her head, thinking she'd done something wrong.

"No, don't stop." He wrapped his hands around the thick braid of her hair, tugging her face back to his.

As their mouths plundered, Caleb's hands roamed down her sides, kneading their way to her waist. She felt his shaft pulsing at the opening of her throbbing chasm. With unbearable slowness, he rotated her hips, entering her slightly.

She moaned and tried to press closer. Caleb teased her for long moments, keeping her from what she wanted most before loosening his hold and allowing her to sheath him completely.

A raw moan escaped them both. She held herself still, savoring the feel of Caleb, hard and alive inside her. Soon the need to have more of him overtook her, and instinctively she began to move. Slowly at first, uncertain of what she was doing, and then faster, as his strong hands aided her progress. Her cry echoed through the room as she stiffened and then sank onto Caleb's chest with a contented sigh.

Rebecca didn't know how long she lay there before awareness descended upon her, filtering back in degrees. The sensation of floating fled, and she once again knew the weight of her own limbs. She felt a tender touch on her lower back as Caleb's fingers lightly caressed the ridges of her vertebrae.

He kissed her hair then, and she felt his smile. When Rebecca lifted her head, she saw the face of a very satisfied man.

She rested her cheek on his chest, her lips tickled by the tiny hairs when she spoke. "What are you grinning about?" The words sounded rough as she forced them past her dry throat.

"I was just thinking. Do you suppose the whole town will know what we're up to?"

That woke her. She sat up, trying to ignore the fact that Caleb was still inside her and becoming newly aroused. "How would they?"

His palms stroked her torso, sliding up to cup her breasts. "Oh, I don't know," he said. "Perhaps because they all saw us leave the dance together. Or because we still haven't returned." He stared at her for a minute, his thumbs brushing her nipples. "But I think your tangled hair and rosy cheeks will be what gives us away."

Rebecca's hands flew to her braid, and she tried to shove the errant strands back into their neat arrangement.

Caleb took hold of her wrists and brought them to his lips, feathering a light kiss on each. "Don't bother," he said, wrapping his arms around her waist and rolling her onto her back. His lips caressed the creamy silkiness of her neck as a tortured moan worked its way up from his throat. "I'll only muss it up again."

Rebecca stood in front of the small rectangular mirror in her bedroom, checking her freshly braided hair for loose tendrils.

"Perfect," Caleb said, coming up behind her and placing a warm, open kiss on the side of her neck. "You look nearly the same as when you left." He winked. "Just a bit rosier."

"What are we going to say if someone asks where we were?" she asked, brushing away Caleb's straying hands.

"We'll tell them we took a walk."

She cocked her head and gave him a doubtful glance. "Do you really think anybody will believe that?"

"No, but I doubt the good people of Leavenworth are crass enough to accuse us of lying."

He had a point. While the Wednesday Group would probably discuss the incident at great length and come to their own conclusions, not one would dare corner Rebecca to ask for the truth.

"What about your sister?"

"She won't find out. Even if she did, Megan would never tell a soul."

"I hope you're right."

She smoothed the front of her dress as she walked to the parlor. Caleb followed behind so closely that when she turned suddenly, they bumped into each other.

Rebecca gazed up into Caleb's bright eyes. They reminded her of a polished stone she had once seen as a little girl in the handle of a cane; amber, she believed it was called. Glowing, sparkling when the light hit it just so.

For the first time in as long as she could remember, the thought of something from her childhood didn't frighten her. Her heart didn't pound, and her fingers didn't turn numb.

Though she lowered her head to hide the gesture from Caleb, Rebecca smiled.

When she looked up, her armor was back in place, protecting her from all the world. "You mustn't breathe a word of what happened here tonight," she said, turning for the front door.

"I promise," Caleb answered. "But is it all right if I go over to the Dog Tick and tell them about that night at the hotel?" he teased.

"No!" Rebecca swung around, her eyes wide. The very thought mortified her. "You must never, *ever* let anyone know what happened between us."

A devilish grin lifted Caleb's mouth. "I love it when you're worked up. Your nose crinkles, and your breasts do the cutest little dance." He demonstrated with his hands in front of him.

Rebecca blushed, and he laughed. "Stop it," she said, halfheartedly brushing him away. "We have to get back to the dance."

Caleb touched her elbow. "I want to ask you something before we walk back into that crowded barn and have to pretend we're mere acquaintances."

She caught the serious edge to his voice, held her breath, and waited.

"I want you to let me take care of you, Rebecca. I'll see that you never want for anything."

She clenched her teeth. "What are you saying, Caleb?"

"You'll have the prettiest gowns and as many fancy baubles as you like. You'll never have to sew another stitch unless you want to."

Her mouth fell open. "You're asking me to be your mistress," she accused him.

"We belong together, Rebecca," he said.

She didn't answer, was too busy chastising herself. She should have known what was coming. Sabrina had gone back to New York, and now Caleb needed someone to take her place. Who would make a better candidate than the woman who had so eagerly spread her legs for him? Not once, not twice, but three times.

"No," she said quietly, hoping the short answer would be enough.

"Rebecca, I could make your life so much more comfortable. You wouldn't have to sew dresses just to keep food on the table."

Surprising herself, Rebecca didn't get angry. She spoke calmly as she made her way out onto the porch. The cool evening air smelled fresh and clean, clearing her lungs as well as her mind. "The answer is no, Caleb.

I've made enough mistakes in the past two weeks. I'm not going to make another."

Caleb's jaw tightened, his shoulders straightening with indignation. "It doesn't have to be a mistake. We're good together, Rebecca. You can't deny that."

She knew better than to tell him he was wrong. He could easily prove his point just by touching her. "I'm not denying anything. I'm simply saying that what happened was wrong, and it won't happen again."

Caleb loomed over her, his features taut with frustration. "If I kissed you now, we'd end up making love again, and you know it. Right here on this porch."

"But you won't kiss me. Because I'm asking you not to." She stepped from the house and started across the street. "I'm also asking you to make sure nothing happens in the future. I'll do my best to avoid you. Megan can come for fittings alone. You don't have to accompany her."

"So this is the way it's going to be?" Caleb walked beside her with long, angry strides. "You think you can just forget what's passed between us?"

She closed her eyes and bit the inside of her lip, trying to pretend his words didn't cut her to the quick.

"Well, let me tell you something. One of these days, you'll come to your senses. You'll lie awake at night, wishing you hadn't turned down my offer. I guarantee it."

Rebecca stopped dead in her tracks and watched as he stormed ahead. She stood there, in the middle of the dusty, deserted town, as the minutes ticked by. Until she could handle the curious stares of the townspeople. Until she didn't want to burst into tears at the thought of Caleb's dark, furious eyes.

Rebecca walked into the doctor's office, clutching her stomach and leaning against the wall for support. She had barely made it across town without fainting.

"Why, dear, you look terrible. Come in and sit down." Doc Meade took her arm and led her through a curtained doorway to the examining room.

"I'm dying, Dr. Meade."

The elderly man had the audacity to chuckle.

"It's true. I'm dying," she said, clutching at his arm.

The doctor helped her lie down on a waist-high table. The little hair he'd managed to keep was gray, shooting out in every direction. His white shirt bunched and wrinkled beneath his black suspenders. "Tell me what the trouble is, dear, and I'll try to help. You're much too young to die, I'm sure."

Rebecca shook a sweaty brow, sure of her diagnosis. "I've been ill for a week. Every morning I wake up sicker than the last. I can't keep anything down, and the slightest movement makes me light-headed."

"Calm yourself, my dear. We'll find out what's bothering you."

"I told you, you old coot," was Rebecca's surly reply. "I'm dying."

He laughed at that, too, while he poked and prodded and added to Rebecca's misery by asking the most embarrassing personal questions imaginable.

"You can sit up now," he said, holding out a hand to help her. "You're not dying, that's for sure."

Rebecca noticed that the man's wide smile had faded. "What is it?" she asked, bracing herself for the worst.

Still, she wasn't prepared for the impact when he told her. "That can't be. You must be mistaken." All her earlier symptoms seemed to vanish, replaced by the shock of his words.

"I've seen a lot of women carrying babies in my time, Miss Rebecca. Helped a few deliver, too. There's no mistake. You're expecting."

"But . . . but . . ."

"Now, I'm not one to tell you how to live your life, so I won't mention the fact that you're unattached. And

I won't go tellin' anybody, so your secret's safe with me. But I do suggest you think of something quick, 'cause near as I can figure, you're more'n a month along. 'Course, you'd probably know that better than I would.''

Rebecca sat in stunned silence, picking up bits and pieces of the doctor's speech. A child. She was going to have a baby. Her mind spun with the realization.

This couldn't be. She couldn't care for a baby when she barely had enough money to provide for herself. And who would come to her for dresses now? Not even the Wednesday Group would be able to overlook the sin of having a bastard child.

"The sickness in the morning ought to pass by the third month," the doctor was saying. "Try a little tea and crackers to settle your stomach."

Tears filled Rebecca's eyes as she hopped down from the table. "Thank you," she said, reaching into the pocket of her skirt for money. "How much do I owe you?"

"Now, you keep your money, dear." Doc Meade patted her hand in a fatherly fashion. "You'll be needing it for that little one."

She nodded and made her way out of the office. Tears coursed over her face as she ran, her steps echoing behind her on the wooden planks of the boardwalk. When she reached the house, she threw herself onto the sofa and sobbed. Her head whirled as she started thinking of ways to get out of this hopeless situation.

The first thing that popped into her head was the old woman who had come around the Scarlet Garter now and again for problems such as this. She had a potion she gave to the girls that sometimes ended unwanted pregnancies. Rebecca could surely find someone in town knowledgeable about such measures.

Even as she contemplated it, though, she knew she could never bring herself to kill her child.

She could give the baby away, turn it over to an orphanage. But she could hardly stand the thought of that, either.

Even if she did decide to give the child away, what would she do until it was born? She couldn't stay in Leavenworth if she ever expected to keep her business and her reputation.

The one thing that came to mind time after time seemed to be her only option. She would have a place to stay, perhaps even be able to raise the child herself. And in exchange . . . well, she wouldn't worry about that now.

Rebecca straightened from the couch, wiping her eyes, trying to compose herself long enough to pack. A change of clothes, her hidden stash of money . . .

She wouldn't need much to work at the Scarlet Garter.

Standing in the middle of the street, Caleb squinted, trying to make his vision clearer. From the corner of his eye, he had seen Rebecca stumble out of Doc Meade's office. He'd turned and watched her run home. She looked upset. He even thought he'd seen tears.

Caleb scoffed. He didn't know why he cared. Rebecca had kept her pledge; she hadn't been anywhere near him for the past month. She refused to even acknowledge him with more than a curt nod when they met in public, while he was almost always aroused now, wanting her.

His only hope was to get away from her. Far away. Where memories of her might cease to plague him. But here he was, still in Leavenworth, when he should have returned to New York weeks ago. For his father showed no signs of recovering from whatever ailed him. He still hacked and coughed and reminded Caleb that he needed someone to help run the Express.

"Look out, mister!"

Caleb moved just in time to miss being trampled by an oncoming feed wagon. He shook his head and continued toward his destination. He'd promised to post

Megan's letter—along with a short note of his own—to Mother. Veronica had written often of late, fretting over Megan's well-being and Caleb's extended absence. She'd even threatened to travel to Kansas herself, just to make sure Holbrook was handling everything properly.

When he left the post office, his head automatically turned in the direction of Rebecca's house. Why had she been to see Doc Meade? And what had upset her to the point of tears?

His feet began to move, stopping only when he found himself standing on her front porch. Slanting his head, he tried to spot her through the glass, to no avail. The curtain kept him from seeing inside.

He thought he heard movement through the open windows. Footsteps. Something clanging to the floor. Using the knuckles of two fingers, he tapped lightly. A second later the door opened with a harsh whoosh. Rebecca stared up at him with glossy, red-rimmed eyes. She made a sound deep in her throat and slammed the door in his face.

Before he could think, Caleb pushed open the door and walked into the house.

Rebecca turned, halfway to her bedroom. "Get out."

He ignored her demand. "Are you all right?"

"Get out," she repeated. Grabbing the nearest thing—one of many tea tins scattered across the floor—she drew back her arm and hurled it at his face.

Caleb ducked, and the object glanced off his shoulder. "Don't," he warned when she reached for another.

She paid him no mind. The second struck him in the jaw.

Tea tins rained down upon him, and he could do nothing but wait until she ran out of ammunition. When she did, Caleb looked up to see her grab the leg of a small end table. He stalked forward and captured her arms, tightening his grip until she released the piece of furniture.

She struggled and managed to get one arm loose. Snatching up a leather-bound book, Rebecca pulled back and smacked him over the head with the thick volume.

"That's enough!" Caleb bellowed. He shook Rebecca's hand until the book fell to the floor. Then he wrapped her in an iron grip, pinning her arms to her sides with one of his own, her back to his chest.

"Goddamn," Caleb swore, rubbing his head. "What's wrong with you?"

She kicked his shin with the heel of her shoe, making him yelp. He let go, and she staggered to the wall. She leaned against it for several seconds, her breathing ragged. Caleb kept her in sight, one hand on his stinging leg, the other massaging the bump on his skull.

"Would you like to tell me what the hell is going on?" he asked, his voice much calmer than he felt.

"I want you out of my house," Rebecca said.

"Yes, I gathered as much. My question is, why? I understand that we didn't part on friendly terms the night of the dance, but I hardly thought you would try to kill me the next time I set foot in your house."

"You thought wrong. Get out." Rebecca turned and disappeared into her bedroom.

Caleb wondered if she really expected him to leave. He had no intention of doing that, however. Not until he got some answers. He strode over to the curtain and yanked it aside. Rebecca stood at the bed, shoving garments and personal items into a faded carpetbag.

"What are you doing?" he asked.

She didn't spare him a glance. "Packing."

"Why?"

"I'm leaving Leavenworth."

He frowned. "Where are you going?"

Silence.

"*Why* are you going?"

Still no answer.

He tried another tack. "I thought you liked living here. You have this little house that you've decorated so nicely. I'm sure it took a lot of time to sew so many pretty curtains. I'll bet you made this, too." He ran a hand over the patchwork quilt on the bed.

He saw tears well in her eyes and knew she didn't want to leave. So why was she doing just that?

"And your business," Caleb pressed, his voice soft and encouraging. "You've become a successful seamstress with a loyal clientele. Why would you want to give all that up?"

"I don't," Rebecca cried. "I don't want to give up any of it." She grabbed the handles of her valise and tried to pass into the other room.

He caught her arm and turned her to face him. "Then why are you?" he asked quietly.

"I don't have a choice." Her voice grew louder with every word. "I can't stay."

Caleb lost his patience. "Why the hell not? Why all the goddamn secrecy, Rebecca? Are you rushing off to meet a lover?"

Rebecca's small hand felt like a two-by-four when it came in contact with his cheek. Caleb bit down on his tongue, resisting the urge to throttle her.

"What a cruel question," she said in a tone of voice that let him know she thought him despicable. "Do you want to know why I'm leaving? Do you really want to know?"

"Yes," he bit out, exasperated.

"All right, I'll tell you."

"Good." He exhaled a long, ragged breath.

"I'm going to have a baby."

Chapter Ten

The sting of Rebecca's slap was nothing compared to the burning Caleb now felt in his belly. Like flames igniting and climbing up through his chest. An annoying hum sounded in his ears, and he swayed slightly. "What did you say?"

"You heard me. I'm going to have a baby."

When he didn't respond, Rebecca turned and walked away. He watched as she passed through the flower-curtained doorway, sidestepped the clutter from their battle in the parlor, and moved on to the kitchen. She turned then, dropping the valise to the floor and crossing her arms over her chest.

Caleb thought she looked expectant in another way. As though she wanted something from him. And somehow, despite his earlier offers to give her whatever she desired, it disappointed him. Angered him, the more he thought about it. For maybe she'd found his initial offer too paltry for her tastes. And had invented a way to demand much more.

He caught a thumb in the pocket of his pants and smiled grimly. "Nice try, Rebecca."

Her lashes lowered, brows coming together in a frown.

"You're a good actress, I'll give you that. There for a minute, I almost believed you were actually pregnant."

"I am," she said softly.

"Oh, yes. And I'm supposed to do right by you, is that it? How long after the wedding will you come, teary-eyed, to tell me you lost the baby?"

A hand dropped to her stomach protectively.

She's quite convincing, he thought. If he hadn't seen the drama played out by some of the most skilled courtesans in New York City, he almost would have believed her. Almost.

"Better luck next time, sweetheart," he said in her ear as he passed.

The front door crashed back against its frame, and Caleb took the porch steps two at a time, heading for the Dog Tick. The saloon opened just as he arrived, and the barkeep showed a yellow-toothed smile as he handed Caleb a bottle of the establishment's finest bourbon.

Caleb sat at a corner table and poured three fingers of whiskey into a spotty glass. Knocking it back and pouring another, he balanced his chair on two legs but didn't drink again. An index finger circled the rim of the glass as he stared intently into the brown liquid.

A fire blazed in his gut. Not from the alcohol, but because, for all his doubts and vows to the contrary, he had begun to let Rebecca into his heart.

Oh, he didn't fancy himself in love with her. Nothing as poetic as all that. But he had begun to . . . care. He'd found himself thinking of her at the oddest times. And once—though Caleb was loathe to admit it—he had even envisioned coming home to her at the end of a long day, eating dinner with her, talking with her, making love with her.

He shook his head and emptied the glass.

She was trying to force him into marriage. Rebecca

127

hadn't said as much, but what other reason could she have to fake a pregnancy? The Adams name would bring her wealth and prestige, things she could never gain on her own.

But what if she really was pregnant, as she claimed?

The idea brought the front legs of his chair to the floor with a thump. If there was a child, Caleb had no doubt of its parentage. He'd accused Rebecca of having other lovers, but only out of anger and frustration. He was the first and only man she'd been with, of that he was certain.

With this new and disturbing thought racing through his brain, Caleb pushed back his chair and walked out of the saloon, the bottle of bourbon on the scarred tabletop forgotten.

He crossed the street to Doc Meade's office and pushed open the door. A plump young woman sat with a runny-nosed boy squirming on her lap, another playing at her feet. Caleb took a seat, tapping his foot impatiently as he waited for the doctor to examine the woman and her—three, it turned out—children.

When the sneezing, sniffling family left, Caleb leapt to his feet and met Doc Meade coming out of the examining room. The doctor's bushy gray eyebrows weaved together as he contemplated Caleb. "Caleb, is something wrong? It's not your father, is it?" He reached for his medical bag, ready to head out the door.

"No," Caleb said, stopping him. "Dad's the same."

"Not better yet?" he asked, dropping into one of the straightbacked chairs that lined the wall. "I tell you, I can't figure it out. Holbrook is as strong as an ox otherwise, but I don't know what's causing that blasted cough."

Caleb nodded distractedly. "I'm here about something else."

"Well, what is it?" Meade asked, pulling a chair away from the wall and motioning for Caleb to sit.

Caleb rested his arms on his knees as he leaned forward in his seat. "Did you see Rebecca this morning?"

The doctor sat back and shook his head. "You know better, young man. I'm not going to tell you about any of my patients."

"I understand that you wouldn't under normal circumstances, Doctor Meade, and that's very admirable of you. But in this case, I was hoping you'd see the importance of my knowing about the examination. You see, Rebecca says she's carrying a child."

The doctor crossed his arms over his chest but said nothing.

Caleb cleared his throat and continued, uncomfortable with what he was about to reveal. "If this is true, sir, then I deserve to know, because that would mean I am to be a father."

To his credit, Meade's face remained impassive.

"So I'm asking again. Did you tell Rebecca this morning that she's with child?"

The doctor pushed back his chair and stood. "If the young lady told you she's havin' a baby, and you're the father, why don't you believe her?"

Caleb shifted uncomfortably under the elderly man's intense scrutiny. "The young lady and I shared words, sir," he explained without elaboration. "I have reason to believe she may be telling me this only to . . . complicate matters."

"Yes, well . . ." The doctor cleared his throat. "I've known Rebecca for years. She's not the kind of a girl to tell lies. I suggest you two work things out." He walked toward the other room.

Caleb stood. "Yes, sir, I intend to. Sir, about the—"

"Child. Yes. Rebecca came to see me this morning, and I told her she's a little more than a month along. I hope you understand that I'm only telling you this because a child needs a father." The doctor looked pointedly at Caleb. "And Rebecca will be needing a husband."

Rebecca took one last look at the room that had been her home for the latter part of her life. The setting sun shone through a west window, casting a bright streak of light across the floor and rocking chair. She squeezed the handle of her valise and willed herself not to cry, thinking of all the evenings she had sat in that very spot to sew, basking in the warm glow. Now she was going back to the very place she'd run from as a girl, to the same sorry life her mother led. Soon she would have a child of her own to raise. That child would grow up in a whorehouse, too, and probably run away at the age of thirteen.

She sniffed and ran a hand across her face, surprised to find it wet with tears. Why did something like this have to happen? Just when she had begun to sleep through the night without fearing she would awake in the back room of a brothel.

The front door opened without warning, and Rebecca looked up to see Caleb standing there. Her jaw clenched, and she straightened her spine. "What are you doing here?"

"I came to take you home. Come on." He came forward and put a hand out for her bag.

She swung the valise behind her, out of his reach.

"Look," he said, running a hand through his hair. "I want you to come home with me tonight. I talked to Reverend Patterson, and he agreed to the necessity of a quick wedding. He'll be at the house in the morning to conduct the ceremony."

Rebecca retreated a step. She looked at Caleb in astonishment. First he accused her of trying to trap him into marriage; now he stood in the middle of her house, insisting they be wed. Her stomach began to roll, and she took a deep breath, fighting the need to run. She closed her eyes to keep the room from spinning.

"Absolutely not. You have no right to make plans for my life. Who do you think you are?" Her voice rose, and Rebecca could feel herself shaking.

"The baby's father," Caleb replied calmly.

"Two hours ago you didn't even believe I was pregnant," she reminded him, glaring.

He glanced at the floorboards and shifted, sticking his hands into his pockets. "How do you plan to provide for the child?"

Rebecca thought of the tiny, dark room at the Scarlet Garter that she had lived in for thirteen years. And the larger but not much nicer rooms Lilah provided for the girls. She could survive there, but what right did she have to consign an innocent child to that kind of hell? Or the hell of growing up in an orphanage, abandoned by those who were supposed to love him most of all?

She looked into Caleb's eyes, trying to see something there. That he cared, just a little, for her or the child they'd created together. She saw nothing but determination and . . . bitterness.

Rebecca certainly understood that. She was bitter, too. Since the moment Caleb Adams had brought his mistress to her for a dress, he had turned Rebecca's life upside down. Now he was trying to goad her into a loveless marriage. Ha! Love—or lack of it—was the least of their problems. She and Caleb couldn't be in the same room without wanting to do murder.

For the benefit of the child, could she take vows with him? *We don't even much like each other,* she thought.

"We don't have to," Caleb answered, and Rebecca realized she had said it aloud. "We just have to give this child a name."

The back of her eyes began to sting, and she blinked rapidly to keep the tears at bay. By marrying Caleb, she could give her child a name, something she had been denied.

"Come on." He took her hand lightly in his own and led her toward the door.

Rebecca thought she had put all doubts out of her mind, but the minute Caleb led her into the Adams home, she balked. She didn't belong in this fancy house, with these sophisticated people. She was only a seamstress, the daughter of a prostitute, for God's sake.

She turned and headed back out the door. "I can't," she mumbled.

He held her arm. "Yes, you can."

"No." She lifted her head, meeting Caleb's burning gaze. "I don't belong here." His fingers dug into the soft flesh of her upper arm, and she winced.

"We are going to sit down to a nice meal with my family, do you understand? All you have to do is smile. I'll explain it to them later."

She watched Caleb set her carpetbag at the foot of the stairs before following him into the dining room. Holbrook and Megan were seated at the table, awaiting the evening meal.

"Everyone," Caleb announced, "Rebecca is going to be staying with us for a while."

Megan jumped up from her chair, ran around the table, and hugged Rebecca. "Oh, that's wonderful. I'm so glad you're here. How long can you stay?"

"Let's just sit down and eat dinner, Megan. All right? I'll answer your questions later." He guided Rebecca to the seat across from his sister before taking his own place at the table.

The meal passed in relative silence. Megan tried several times to start a conversation, but each attempt was met by tense silence. Holbrook looked on with mild curiosity as Caleb brooded and Rebecca pushed the food around her plate nervously.

Finally, giving up the pretense of a quiet family gathering, Caleb stood, pulling Rebecca's chair out to help her stand.

"Now will you tell me what's going on?" Megan asked, joining them on the other side of the table.

"Later," Caleb said brusquely. "Why don't you show Rebecca upstairs and help her unpack. Her bag is by the steps."

Megan huffed about being left out yet again but led Rebecca away without a quarrel.

Caleb took one look at his father's face and sighed. "Perhaps we should talk in the study," he said, starting in that direction.

His father sat down behind his desk, sucking on a large cigar, while Caleb leaned back in a brown leather chair, resting an ankle on his knee. "Maybe your cough would get better if you stopped smoking those foul things."

"A man needs to relax at the end of a long day, Caleb."

He shrugged, knowing arguing was futile.

"So, are you going to tell me why you brought her here?"

"We're getting married."

Holbrook did cough then, exhaling a gray haze of smoke. When he regained his breath, he looked at Caleb with wide eyes and demanded an explanation.

Caleb thought about breaking the news gently but knew his father would rather hear it straight. "She's pregnant."

Caleb expected his father to start another round of coughing. He was more surprised when Holbrook didn't breathe at all for several seconds before speaking.

"Are you the father?"

"Yes." Caleb braced himself for a lecture, sure his father would have something to say about letting his member lead him in the wrong direction.

Instead, Holbrook nodded. "Then you're doing the right thing, son. Very good, very good."

"That's it?" he asked, surprised. "You're not going to tell me I'm getting what I deserve for dragging her into my bed? You're not even going to yell at me for compromising a lady's virtue?"

"Seems to me you've already thought of those things. At any rate, it's too late for those considerations now."

Caleb snorted and levered himself out of the chair. He picked a cigar out of the box Holbrook kept on his desk and bit off the end.

"I don't suppose you'll be going back to New York, then?" Holbrook asked.

"Doesn't look that way," he answered. "I don't think Rebecca would be very comfortable there."

Holbrook smiled. "Rebecca is a nice girl. She'll make you a fine wife."

"That woman doesn't know the meaning of the word *nice,*" he told his father as the older man held a match to the tip of the cigar. "Do you know what she did when I told her I was going to marry her and give the baby a name? She swore. She cursed me out and told me I had no right to interfere in her life."

"You *told* her you would marry her? To give the child a name?"

"It's my child. I won't let it be born a bastard." He pounded a fist on the mahogany desktop. "Rebecca is undoubtedly the most willful woman I've ever met."

"Your brother is the most boorish, insufferable oaf I have ever known! How can you live with him?" Rebecca pulled a rolled-up day dress out of her bag and threw it onto the bed.

Megan picked up the garment and shook it out, hanging it in the small wardrobe. "He's usually at the Express office, so I only see him in the evenings. Why are you so angry with him?"

Rebecca looked up, wondering how much to tell Caleb's sister. "We had an argument on the way here."

"Why are you staying with us, then?"

Straightening, she took a deep breath and considered how to answer Megan's question. "Caleb and I are getting married."

Megan's squeal hurt Rebecca's ears, and she expected every piece of glass in the house to shatter. Jumping up and down, the girl threw her arms around Rebecca. "This is wonderful! When? Oh, I'll wear my green dress. No, no, the yellow. Or maybe you can make me a new one. But, no, you'll be too busy sewing a gown for yourself. Oh, the yellow will be fine, don't you think? And I'll help with the preparations. I can write out invitations or—"

"Megan." Rebecca touched her arm and said her name three more times before the girl quieted. "There won't be any need for your help."

Megan looked crestfallen, and Rebecca hastened to explain. "The preacher is coming in the morning. At nine."

"So soon?" she asked, her head lifting. "But . . ." She seemed to change her mind about what she'd planned to say before hugging Rebecca again. "I still think it's wonderful. I'll finally have a sister!"

She stood in the morning sunlight, twisting her hands together, trying to convince her stomach not to empty itself on Reverend Patterson's spit-shined shoes. Holbrook had convinced them to hold the ceremony in the front yard to take advantage of the bright, beautiful day. With Caleb at her elbow and Megan and Holbrook on either side as witnesses, Rebecca felt boxed in and completely underdressed.

Earlier, when she'd realized she had nothing to wear except a few haggard-looking day dresses, Caleb drove into town to fetch her Harvest Festival gown. She hadn't packed it because it held memories—good and bad—that she didn't want tarnished by her new life at the Scarlet Garter.

But her plans had changed.

Even in her best dress, she felt out of place. Though she had to admit that the deep burgundy color did seem ironic perfection for the bride on her wedding day—far from white and virginal.

"I brought the marriage certificate with me," the reverend told Caleb. "After the ceremony, when we go inside, I'll fill in the names, and you and your wife can sign them."

"Fine," Caleb answered. "Let's get started."

"Do you have a ring?"

Caleb swore, then colored when the preacher frowned. "I'll get them later."

Patterson began to argue but thought better of it. "All right, let's begin. I'll need your full names."

"Caleb Zachariah Adams."

They all turned to Rebecca, waiting for her to answer. She kept her mouth closed.

"Miss," the reverend said, clearing his throat. "I'll need your full name."

"Rebecca . . ." She shifted uncomfortably, tugging at the front of her dress. "Fitzgerald."

"Wait a minute," Caleb said. "That's not your name. Widow Fitzgerald only took you in. She wasn't a blood relative, was she?"

"Of course not," Holbrook answered for her. "Octavia came here with her husband. She didn't have any other family."

"What's your real name, Rebecca?" Caleb asked, his brow beginning to furrow.

She cleared her throat. "I can't tell you."

"What do you mean, you can't tell me?" Caleb ground out, glancing briefly in the direction of the preacher.

"I can't tell you. I'm sorry."

"Well," Reverend Patterson blustered, "I'm afraid I cannot marry you without knowing your full name. It wouldn't be legal. I can't do it."

Caleb leaned close, his voice lowered harshly. "Do you hear that? We can't get married without it."

Rebecca stood statue-still, not backing down from Caleb's intimidating rancor. But she couldn't grant a wish she had no power over. Lifting her shoulders and holding his gaze, she said, "Then I guess we won't be married."

Chapter Eleven

"That's it." Caleb took Rebecca's arm and led her away from the group, up the front walk to the house. Once inside, he dragged her to the parlor and closed the sliding doors.

Rebecca watched, wondering why he bothered. The only person in the house besides themselves was Nina, and she had her hands full preparing the midday meal.

"I want to know what's going on, Rebecca. We have to be married, so why won't you tell me your name? You're not wanted by the law or something, are you?"

"No."

"Then what the hell is going on? And I want the truth."

"I've already told you the truth. I can't tell you my name." Caleb's face reddened, and she quickly explained. "Because I don't know what it is."

Caleb's open mouth closed by degrees. His eyes narrowed, and his rigid posture relaxed. "I'm not sure I catch your meaning."

"I really don't have a last name. Not one that I know

138

of, anyway. As I told you, I was . . . orphaned at a very young age and don't remember people calling me anything other than Rebecca."

"Did you ever think to ask? Someone surely knew your parents."

Rebecca shrugged and swallowed. "I never asked. I was just a girl. It didn't seem important."

"No, of course not." Caleb ran splayed fingers through the hair he'd groomed so perfectly for his wedding ceremony. "What do you propose we do?"

Rebecca's eyes widened in surprise. "I don't know," she said, following him with her eyes as he began pacing the length of the room.

"You've gone by Fitzgerald since the widow took you in, is that right?"

"Yes."

"Then that's the name you'll use." Caleb stopped his agitated movements and gave an affirmative nod.

Rebecca's fingers traced the seams at the sides of her skirt. "I don't think that's legal."

"Why not?" Caleb held up one hand and began ticking off reasons. "You don't know your parents' name. Widow Fitzgerald took you in when you were only . . ."

"Thirteen," she supplied.

"Thirteen," he said. "You lived with her until her death. She practically adopted you. You've lived in Leavenworth for . . . How many years?"

"Ten."

"Yes, ten. And whenever necessary, you've used the Fitzgerald name. Correct?"

Rebecca felt like a prisoner being interrogated in front of a firing squad. "Yes," she answered.

"Sounds legal to me." Arms crossed over his chest, one side of Caleb's mouth quirked up in a grin.

"I don't . . . I don't think so."

"Let's ask Reverend Patterson."

"No. Caleb, no." Rebecca followed after him, but it

was too late. He took the porch steps two at a time and came to stand at the preacher's side. After saying a few words in the man's ear, Caleb turned and led the reverend back to the house. Rebecca stood in the frame of the open front door, close enough to see Caleb wink at his father and sister, letting them know everything would be fine.

She stepped aside as Revered Patterson entered the house. Caleb ushered them both back to the parlor and once again closed the doors. Her heart beat three times faster than usual, and she clenched her fingers in the fabric of her dress.

"Reverend Patterson," Caleb began in a tone worthy of any courtroom lawyer, "we have encountered a small dilemma concerning the use of Rebecca's last name."

The reverend's bushy black eyebrows drew together, and his forehead puckered.

"You see, Rebecca was orphaned at a very young age and never really knew her parents. Isn't that right, my dear?" He turned, waiting for her to answer.

Rebecca drew a deep breath and stepped forward to stand at his side. "Yes, that's right."

"How dreadful," the reverend said, shaking his head sadly. "That must have been terribly difficult for you."

"Yes, it was." Lowering her head, she kept her sights on the toes of Reverend Patterson's black shoes and nearly jumped when a strong arm circled her shoulders. She raised her eyes to look at Caleb, who pulled her close to his side.

"She was too young to even remember her last name," he explained.

The reverend's eyes widened. "That does pose a problem."

"Yes. But we think we've found a solution."

"Oh?"

"When Rebecca was only thirteen, Octavia Fitzgerald—God rest her soul—took her in and gave her a home. She even allowed Rebecca to use the Fitzgerald name, though the widow never legally adopted her. Do you see what I'm getting at, reverend?"

"Yes, yes." Patterson nodded several times and then shook his head. "No."

Rebecca turned her face into Caleb's shoulder, stifling a laugh. She felt Caleb give her shoulders a squeeze.

"We feel that Rebecca should use the name Fitzgerald, since Octavia was like a mother to her for so many years. Our main concern is about the legality of such a decision." When the reverend didn't answer, Caleb continued. "Do you think it would be possible for Rebecca to use Fitzgerald on the wedding certificate?"

"You don't have any recollection of your true birth name?" Reverend Patterson asked Rebecca.

"No, sir."

"Well, if there's no other option . . ."

"None," Caleb said.

"Then I don't see why not."

A relieved sigh escaped her lungs as she leaned against Caleb. She would have fallen had he not tightened his arm around her and held her up.

"Let's go," the reverend said, sweeping out of the room. "We have a wedding to see to."

Reverend Patterson stayed for the reception, an early lunch of cold roast beef and a celebratory bottle of wine, which only Holbrook, Caleb, and the reverend chose to drink.

By noon, Rebecca was exhausted, nearly asleep on her feet. After waving good-bye to the reverend, she excused herself and went to her room to rest.

When she next opened her eyes, the room was dark. The curtains had been drawn, and only a scant blush of evening sun shone through. Rebecca sat up with a yawn, stretching and resisting the tiredness in her muscles that beckoned her to roll over and go back to sleep.

A gasp escaped her when she spotted a figure near the door. She jumped and pressed herself against the headboard.

"I didn't mean to scare you."

Caleb's low, textured voice reached her ears, and she put a palm to her chest, trying to slow the erratic hammering of her heart.

"Well, you did," she said, breathless.

"Sorry."

"What are you doing in here?" She pulled the edge of the quilted bedspread she was sitting on up to her neck, an unbidden reflex, since she was still fully clothed.

Caleb came to the opposite side of the bed, lifting the chimney of the lamp long enough to strike a match to the wick. A soft glow illuminated the room, and Rebecca turned away to slowly allow her pupils to adjust to the light.

"I thought I would move your things while you slept. That way you wouldn't have to bother."

"Move my things? Why? Where?" Rebecca now looked directly at Caleb.

"To my room."

He turned and went back to where he'd been taking articles out of a drawer and stuffing them into her valise. Then she noticed all her dresses had been moved from the closet to hang from a brass hook on the back of the bedroom door, obviously waiting to be transported.

"Wait a minute." She scooted out of bed, untangling her skirt and feet from the covers and hurrying to his side. She grabbed the camisole from his hand and hid it behind her back. The thought of Caleb seeing her underthings, much less *touching* them, made her blush. "I thought this was to be my room."

Paying no attention to the interruption, he simply went to her dresses and caught the wooden hangers on his thumb. "That was only for last night, to keep up pretenses. Now that we're husband and wife, we can share a room."

Rebecca shoved the camisole back into the dresser, along with the things Caleb had already put in her bag. "What if I don't want to share a room with you?"

"I don't remember bringing it up for discussion."

Rebecca bristled, clutching the carpetbag before her like a shield. "No, you didn't. Nevertheless, I think we should discuss it."

"You'll only end up packing them again," Caleb said, gesturing toward the clothes she had returned to their rightful places.

"I'd rather stay here. This room suits me perfectly."

"I'm sure it does. But how would it look to others if we didn't even reside in the same bedroom?"

"The same as being married so quickly, without inviting guests, I imagine."

Caleb chuckled. "Yes, I imagine. No sense in giving them more grist for the gossip mill, however. If you'd rather move your things into my room on your own, that's fine with me." He returned the dresses to the brass hook on the back of the door. "Just be sure it's done by suppertime." Checking his timepiece, he smiled. "Which happens to be in ten minutes. See you then, wife."

He quit the room before Rebecca had a chance to answer. But not before she decided the devil would be serving ice-cold lemonade in hell before she bent to Caleb's will.

"Dinner was delicious," Rebecca said, which was the truth, though she'd managed to eat little with an upset stomach. She followed Nina and Megan into the kitchen, all of them carrying handfuls of dirty dinnerware.

"Wasn't it, though?" Megan set down her pile of dishes and patted the young cook on the back. "Would you like some help washing them?"

"No, thank you." Nina reached for her apron, slipping

143

it over her head and tying the strings behind her back. "Peter will not be here for an hour. I need something to keep me busy."

"How is Peter?" Megan asked.

A rosy blush stained Nina's cheeks, and she turned away. "He is fine."

Megan smiled and turned to Rebecca. "They've been courting for almost a year. I really think Peter is going to propose any day now. Will you accept, Nina?"

"Of course." The woman turned, her face serious.

"Come on," Megan said, taking Rebecca's arm and giving a sly wink. "Let's leave Nina alone to the dishes. I'm sure she doesn't want us around while she daydreams of marrying and having pretty little babies with her beloved Peter."

Rebecca cleared her throat and averted her eyes. She didn't know if Caleb had told his family the real reason for their rush to wed, but she knew Megan was observant enough to figure it out before long.

They walked through the dining room and foyer as Megan led the way to the parlor. "I don't know where Caleb and Papa have gone. They're probably in the study." She wrinkled her nose in distaste. "I don't know why Papa insists on smoking those hideous cigars. And then he has the audacity to complain of a cough." She shook her head. "I will never understand men. Never."

Rebecca tried to smile. Neither would she. Especially one particular man. A man who had made it plain he had married her only because she was carrying his child, yet who insisted on sharing a bedroom. Rebecca mentally shook her head. No, she would never understand Caleb Adams.

Megan lifted her skirts slightly and crossed one leg under the other before plopping down on the settee. She patted the cushion, motioning Rebecca to join her.

Rebecca sat, smoothing her skirts modestly, unlike carefree Megan. Not that Rebecca was a prude, but a nervous jitter gnawed at her belly. She'd been comfortable in the Adams home before, when she came for Megan's fittings, but this time felt very different. This time she wasn't a visitor. She was Caleb's wife. This time she couldn't leave when her business was complete. There was no escape.

Rebecca's stomach lurched, and her fingers dug into the carved wooden arms of the sofa. She turned her head away, breathing deeply, trying to convince herself that she wasn't about to be sick.

"Are you all right, Rebecca?"

She nodded, keeping her eyes tightly shut.

A gentle hand touched her cheek and hair. "You don't look very well. Perhaps you ought to rest." Megan helped Rebecca to her feet and to the bottom of the steps. "Don't worry, it's probably just all the excitement of your wedding day. I'll tell Caleb where you are."

Rebecca forced a thank-you through drawn lips and clutched the bannister like a lifeline, dreading the trek upstairs.

Once she reached her room and lay down, the nausea seemed to pass. She sighed, counting in her head how much longer this morning sickness—which seemed to find perverse pleasure in striking throughout the day— would last. The doctor had told her it usually lasted through the first three months of pregnancy. That meant she would be miserable for at least another month. The thought did not cheer her.

She rolled over, moaning at the lurching discomfort it caused in her head. If only she could sleep for six weeks or so and wake up as healthy as she'd ever been.

Rebecca awoke to the sensation of floating. She opened her eyes and found herself hovering at least a foot off the bed. Her body stiffened, and she threw out her arms to catch herself. When she looked up, she found a set of brown eyes staring back at her.

Letting her head fall limply on Caleb's shoulder, she

groaned in frustration. "Can't a person get some sleep around here without you coming in to disturb her?"

She felt rather than heard his laugh, bouncing her lightly against the wall of his chest. "Not when that person is my new wife. A wife who *should* be sleeping in my bed."

"Put me down," Rebecca said, beginning to struggle. He ignored her. "Put me down, or I'll scream."

"And who will come to your rescue? My father? I doubt it. He tends to mind his own business. Or perhaps my sister, who thinks our one-day engagement and wedding is the most romantic thing since *Romeo and Juliet.*"

"Nina—"

"Left hours ago."

"There has to be someone in this house who will come to my rescue." Rebecca tried to pry Caleb's fingers away from her legs and waist, to no avail.

"No one would dare interfere. Not when I'm only moving my lovely wife where she can be closer to my side." He opened the door without loosening his hold.

Rebecca twisted back and forth, pushing at his chest. "Your side of hell, maybe. I swear, you're the spawn of Satan," she said through gritted teeth.

That seemed to amuse him. He laughed, then leaned forward to whisper in her ear as they entered the hallway. "Hush. You don't want to wake anybody, do you?"

She did want to wake someone. Not just Holbrook or Megan but the entire town of Leavenworth. She wanted to scream loud enough that every Ranger in Texas would hear and come running. But she kept her mouth shut while Caleb carried her two doors down and into his room.

The dark forest colors attested to the fact that this room definitely belonged to a man. A thick brown carpet that reminded Rebecca of tree bark covered the floor. The drapes and bedclothes were a deep pine-needle green. The effect was set off perfectly by the fine maple furniture. A heavy canopy covered the four-poster bed, its edges plain and straight with an air of masculinity.

Caleb walked toward the bed and deposited her in the middle of the wide mattress. Rebecca sat up, ready to bolt, when she noticed her silver-handled hairbrush, comb, and hand glass—a set that had once belonged to Octavia—resting on the hip-high bureau. She stilled, noticing how elegant they looked against the dark wood, their reflection shining in the mirror attached to the dresser. As if they belonged there amidst Caleb's personal items.

She turned her head and noticed the door of the wardrobe open a crack. Inside she saw a lacy cuff, the folds of a full skirt. And on the shelf below the dresses, her traveling bag. Rebecca looked at Caleb, who stood at the foot of the bed.

"I told you to be moved before dinner," he answered before she had a chance to speak.

"Yes, you did. But I had no intention of doing so."

A grin curved his full lips. "I know."

She hopped down from the bed—unable to locate the stool needed to climb onto the enormous berth—and went to the closet to remove her valise. "If you'll excuse me, I'll be going now. And I would appreciate it if you stopped packing and repacking my things. I don't want to share your room, thank you very much. I'd much rather be left alone."

"You should have thought of that before you trapped me into this marriage."

His words stopped her cold. When she lifted her gaze to meet his, she found all traces of a smile gone, his eyes cold and uncompromising. The bag fell from her hand to the floor with a soft swoosh. "I did not trap you."

"Then what would you call it?"

"*You* are the one who said we had to be married. If you'll recall, I was ready to leave town."

"Oh, yes. Quite a production you made of doing so. But you were still there when I returned. Did you deliberately give me the time to come back and propose?"

Her hands tightened into fists at her sides, crumpling the fine material of her gown. "If you are so opposed to this union, why did you insist upon it?"

"To give my child a name, of course. If indeed there is a child. For all I know, Doc Meade could be in on this little charade with you."

Rebecca clenched her teeth so hard, her jaw throbbed. "If you feel that way, I'll leave. There's no ring on this finger yet," she reminded him, displaying the digit in front of him. "I'm sure you can come up with a believable story for your family." She pushed past him, forgetting her clothes and other possessions in her desire to be free of this wretched beast and his razor-sharp tongue.

"You're not going anywhere, *wife*." Caleb took hold of her arm and pulled her back.

She started to struggle but thought better of it. They had been through this before, and she knew she would lose. If she fought, he would only increase his strength. If she screamed, Holbrook and Megan would discover that she and Caleb were not as well-matched as Caleb had led them to believe.

Instead, Rebecca let Caleb pull her against his chest, one arm around her waist. He heaved her onto the bed like a sack of potatoes and followed her down to the mattress.

She lay staring up into Caleb's tan face, small lines creasing the stubbly skin. At that moment, Rebecca realized she was not truly afraid of him. His temper could flare to the boiling point without warning, and his words often cut more sharply than a butcher's cleaver, but she knew instinctively, deep in her soul, that Caleb would never do her any real harm.

Caleb propped his head on one bent arm, his eyes

tracing the curve of her face, slowly caressing her neck and breast where he soon wanted his hands to be. "Is it always going to be like this between us?"

. Rebecca blinked but didn't answer.

"Are we always going to be at one another's throats?"

"You started it," she said softly like a petulant child.

Caleb laughed. He couldn't help it. He buried his face against Rebecca's collarbone, the bed shaking with the force of his mirth. When he finally lifted his head, Caleb saw Rebecca regarding him pensively. "Are we going to have a marriage in name only?" he asked.

No answer.

He cupped the lush swell of her breast, covered by the velvety texture of her wine-colored gown. His lips touched hers lightly, reverently. "Or are you going to let me make love to my beautiful new bride?"

When an arm came slowly around his neck, urging him closer, Caleb knew a swirling contradiction of emotions. He felt both happier and sadder than ever before in his life.

Chapter Twelve

Rebecca had never felt so uncomfortable in her life as when she walked into church that Sunday on Caleb's arm. Every member of the congregation from age three to one hundred stared at them openly. The ladies were polite enough to hide behind their hands to gossip, while the men discussed the shocking sight amongst themselves without concern for being socially correct.

Rebecca must have smoothed the front of her skirt at least two dozen times before Caleb took her hands and gave them a supportive squeeze. She raised her eyes to see him smiling at her as they walked down the aisle of the small house of worship to sit in the second pew from the front, next to Holbrook and Megan.

Her nervousness didn't stem from actually being in church. She and Octavia had attended services every Sunday, and Rebecca made a point of continuing the tradition even after the widow's passing. But being with Caleb, knowing Reverend Patterson would be introducing them as man and wife, made the butterflies in her stomach feel like a herd of stampeding buffalo.

The reverend's words seemed to rush around Rebecca, and she found herself unable to decipher their meaning or concentrate on her surroundings. She looked past her hymnal to where her hand still clasped Caleb's. Only when she saw the white tips of his fingers did she realize how hard her grip had become. She loosened her grasp slightly but kept her hand on his. She was rewarded with a wink as he flexed the stiff digits, restoring his circulation.

"And now," she heard the reverend say when the song ended, "I have an announcement."

Reverend Patterson nodded in their direction. Every head turned. Rebecca tried to smile as Caleb helped her to stand, her body feeling like a lead weight.

"Just yesterday," the reverend continued, "I had the distinct privilege of joining these two young people in holy matrimony." A congregational gasp echoed through the room. "It is with my warmest wishes for eternal happiness that I introduce to you Mr. and Mrs. Caleb Zachariah Adams."

Rebecca felt light-headed with relief when the entire room filled with the staccato rhythm of clapping, whooping, and cheers of good will. As they exited the building, a flock of townspeople shuffled around them, offering congratulations along with several invitations to dinner. Rebecca smiled, too overwhelmed by the group's acceptance to speak. Caleb shook hands with, and was slapped on the back by, what seemed like three thousand men, all wishing him luck.

When the crowd finally began to disperse, Rebecca expected Caleb to take the family home, where Nina would have dinner on the table. Instead, he left Holbrook and Megan at the church and drove the surrey across town, stopping in front of the mercantile.

"What are we doing here?" Rebecca asked as Caleb helped her down. She looked at the sign in the front window, clearly stating that the store was closed, as were all the businesses in Leavenworth on Sunday.

"You'll see," Caleb answered.

They stood on the sidewalk for a few minutes, shading their eyes from the sun and gazing across the street at other buildings, all dark and deserted. Rebecca waved a hand in front of her face, trying to alleviate some of the midday heat.

She was just about to question Caleb further when a latch rattled behind them. Rebecca spun around and saw the stoop-shouldered proprietor opening the double doors. When she looked at Caleb, she found him grinning like a boy with a brand-new Bowie knife. He placed a hand in the middle of her back and propelled her into the store.

"I really wish you'd tell me what's going on," Rebecca whispered so that Elbert, who was shuffling along in front of them, wouldn't hear. Going behind the counter, the old man bent forward and disappeared from Rebecca's vision.

"Hush," Caleb said, smiling. "You'll find out soon enough."

If Rebecca hated anything, it was surprises. Or rather the *not knowing* that preceded surprises.

Elbert straightened, a large, flat black case in his hands.

"I appreciate this, Elbert," Caleb said, resting an elbow on the high wooden surface.

"No problem, sonny boy." He set the box down on the counter and tinkered with the latch, which looked to be older than Elbert himself. "Zelda'll keep the potatoes hot," he said, speaking of his wife.

Caleb nodded and leaned forward eagerly.

Elbert popped open the lid of the case and turned it around so they could see. The red velvet lining inside sparkled with four rows of silver and gold rings, each glittering in the sunlight. A small breath escaped Rebecca as she took in all the bands and beautiful stones encased in elegant settings.

"Gotta keep this here locked up and hid, ya know. If I have 'em out on display, some thief is liable to come snatch 'em. I ain't so young no more, so's I couldn't catch the culprit and beat the tarnation outta him."

"What do you think?" Caleb asked, nudging Rebecca out of her mesmerized state.

She lifted her head and looked at Caleb, wondering what he expected of her.

"Best selection fer miles. Won't find anything better, lessin' you go to Kansas City er such."

"These will be fine, I think. Do you like them, Rebecca?"

"Hm?" She shook her head, trying to clear her mind, then turned back to the display of rings. "Oh, yes, they're lovely."

Did Caleb expect her to pick one? she wondered. She couldn't possibly be so presumptuous as to ask him to buy her one of these beautiful rings. Each must be worth a king's ransom. Any plain band would do, something to simply verify her status as a married woman.

"Which one do you like best?" he asked.

"I don't know," she answered truthfully. "They're all very . . . nice."

He chuckled. "Sorry. As much as I'd like to, I really can't afford them all."

He put an arm around her waist and pulled her close. Rebecca didn't know if she should interpret the affectionate gesture as being sincere or if it was put on for Elbert's aged but observant eyes.

"Tell you what," Caleb said, pressing his lips to her temple. "Pick one set now, and if I can, I'll buy you another for each of our anniversaries."

He can't be serious, she thought, weaving slightly in dismay. *He didn't want to marry me in the first place, and now he must be putting on an act for the benefit of the town.*

Rebecca pasted on her sweetest smile and studied the bands more closely. Some were absolutely stunning, and though she had often dreamed as a child of owning something that beautiful, she looked away and concentrated on the less impressive—and less expensive—rings.

"That one, I think." She pointed to a plain, thin circle of silver.

"This?" Caleb questioned, lifting it from its pocket in the soft lining. He turned it in his hand, studying the band closely.

She nodded.

"Not quite what I had in mind." He replaced the band and picked another. More costly by far than the one she'd chosen, for it was not only a wedding band of gold but came with a sparkling diamond ring to match. He held the set up to the window, where streams of sunlight brightened the room.

"These will do nicely."

Rebecca tried to argue with his decision. "No, I don't think—"

"I do," he cut her off. "And I am the one paying for them, after all." He lifted her left hand and slipped the rings onto her finger. "How do they feel?"

Rebecca flexed her hand, testing the size and fit of the jewelry. "Fine."

"Good. Now why don't you go outside. I'll be there in a minute."

She didn't move.

Caleb began reaching into the inside pocket of his suitcoat, then paused to give her a little push. "Go," he said. "I'll be right there."

She turned and walked out of the mercantile, her feet moving by habit alone. Her mind spun in a thousand directions at once, searching for a reason Caleb would insist upon such a set of rings. They had never been engaged, so she certainly shouldn't be wearing a diamond. And her marriage to Caleb was no more than a false union; she hardly felt worthy of even a wedding band. Perhaps he felt that his wife, however unloved, should wear jewelry befitting his family name.

When Caleb came up behind her, she jumped, startled. He didn't say a word as he helped her into the rig and turned the team back toward the churchyard.

Holbrook and Megan sat on the steps, waiting patiently. Megan immediately spotted the rings on Rebecca's curled fingers and began chattering up a storm that lasted the entire drive home.

Caleb pushed a pile of papers across the desk and leaned back in his chair. He rubbed his eyes and loosened the collar of his shirt, tossing the coffee-brown string tie in the direction of his earlier-discarded suit coat.

As his father had reminded him that morning, he had paperwork to get done. There were a hundred things to do—ticket sales to total, drivers to pay, schedules to chart—but Caleb couldn't seem to concentrate on even one.

It was this marriage thing that bothered him. Oh, he'd known it would be rough. He'd expected to be constantly fighting with Rebecca. He'd expected to fork out cartloads of money to keep her happy. He'd even expected to come home each day to find her in the parlor, doing nothing but drinking tea and eating sugar cookies. What grated on his nerves, though, was that none of them—these things he had braced himself to bear—ever happened.

Not only did Rebecca *not* argue with him, but she was warm and passionate in his bed. That was the one thing Caleb never would have counted on. Clawing and screaming he might have been able to handle. He wasn't so sure about the soft, willing woman he found in his room each night.

As for spending his money, Caleb practically had to beat Rebecca to get her to take even a small amount of cash for necessary items.

She did sit on the sofa most of the day, but Megan was more than eager to tell him why. She spent her time sewing. If she was not making something new for Megan, then she was mending her own dresses.

Yes, now that Caleb thought about it, Rebecca had seemed better outfitted lately. Even her oldest, most worn day dress looked prettier. She had patched loose lace around the cuffs or added a strip of new ribbon to hide the fraying hems. All in all, Rebecca was more beautiful than ever. She had time to take care of herself and her own clothes now rather than doting on customers.

Her frugality was almost enough to make Caleb rethink his low opinion of women. Almost.

"You ready to go home?"

Caleb raised his head to see his father standing in the doorway of the small back office. Caleb rose, the legs of the chair scraping across the floor.

"Did you get that work done?"

"Not yet. I'll take it with me to finish after dinner."

"Sure you will." Holbrook chuckled and turned away.

When they arrived home, Caleb sent his father in with the papers he was determined to work on that evening. He unhitched the horses, led them to their stalls, and rubbed down each thoroughly. After grabbing his jacket, which he had draped over a stack of hay bales, he walked around to the side of the house, where he intended to wash in the water trough before going inside.

Caleb rolled up his sleeves and scrubbed his hands and arms with the bar of lye soap left at the trough for just such a purpose. Then he gave his face a good splash, drying it with his now wrinkled and dirty coat. Slinging the garment over one shoulder, he headed for the rear entrance of the house.

Even before he rounded the corner, Caleb thought he heard the distinct sound of retching. Quickening his pace, he scanned the area.

He didn't see anyone, but the sound persisted as he looked all around the backyard, even circling the tiny toolshed located there. Just when he thought he must have imagined the noise, Caleb spotted Rebecca slumped over the stack of firewood piled against the house, her body trembling.

Caleb went to her, shaking out his coat and draping it over her shoulders. Her tremors seemed to stop as she leaned weakly against him. He hugged her close and brushed the hair back from her sweat-dampened face.

"Better?" He felt her head move affirmatively against his chest. Caleb knew the vomiting stemmed from her pregnancy; he'd helped her back to bed several mornings in a row after she'd frantically thrown off the covers and run for the chamber pot. What Caleb did not understand was why Rebecca was out back rather than inside.

He was still holding her close when Megan appeared, a damp cloth in her hand. "Is everything all right?" she asked, lightly wiping Rebecca's face.

Caleb nodded. Rebecca lifted her head and began to straighten. Her body shook a bit, and Caleb tucked the coat more securely around her shoulders. Her face was the color of chalk.

"Come on," he said. "Let's get you inside."

"Not that way," she said tiredly, clutching the front of his shirt.

Caleb frowned and looked at Megan.

"She was in the kitchen when she got sick," his sister explained. "The cooking smells nauseated her."

Finally understanding, he nodded and gently lifted Rebecca into his arms. He walked slowly and carefully to the front gate, worked the latch open with one hand,

and carried her up the porch steps. Megan ran ahead to open the door for them.

"I'm fine now, really," Rebecca argued, though her voice sounded weak.

Ignoring her, he carried her upstairs to bed, then unlaced her shoes and rolled down her stockings, watching as she tried valiantly to keep her eyes open. By the time he removed her dress and loosed the top two buttons of her camisole, Rebecca's eyelashes had fluttered closed, and her soft breathing filled the room, interrupted only by the occasional sound of a light snore.

Caleb awoke early the next morning. The fingers of his left hand tingled slightly with his movements, and he realized that he'd held Rebecca all through the night. Her head still rested on his shoulder, her face turned into his chest.

He allowed himself a moment to look at her. Rebecca was truly beautiful. Oh, not in the usual ways, and certainly not by cultured standards. Her skin was perhaps a shade too tan, her nails too short and uneven. Even the stubborn tilt of her chin seemed to defy society's norms.

Caleb scoffed to think that he had once counted himself lucky to have Sabrina Leslie as a mistress, the most beautiful, sought-after courtesan in New York. As far as Caleb was concerned, Sabrina didn't hold a candle to his Rebecca.

His Rebecca? Yes, she was his. He didn't completely trust her, didn't know if he ever could, but she was his wife and the mother of his child.

A hard tug tautened his heartstrings as his gaze slid to Rebecca's still-flat stomach. He brushed the area lightly with his fingers, wondering if she could feel the baby yet.

Rebecca mumbled something unintelligible at his touch and rolled away, snuggling into the pillow on the other side of the bed. He watched her a moment more before sliding his arm from beneath her shoulders and rising with a regretful sigh to dress for work.

It was still early, but he at least expected Nina to be in the kitchen preparing breakfast. Instead, he found the downstairs empty and dark. He built a fire in the stove and set a pot of coffee on to boil.

Then he made his way through the pitch-black hallway to the study. The folder of papers he'd brought home was in the middle of the desk, seeming to glare at him. Groaning, he sat in his father's office chair and opened the binder.

Caleb blinked at what he saw, thinking the hazy light of dawn was playing tricks on his eyes. He lit the nearby lamp and looked again. The handwriting and figures seemed real enough. He even rubbed at them with his thumb, just to be sure.

"Is everything all right?"

Caleb raised his head to see Megan, still in her nightgown and robe, standing in the doorway. Her voice sounded timid, not at all what he was used to from his impertinent, strong-willed sister.

"I think so." He hurriedly flipped through the rest of the papers to see if those, too, were finished. "Did Dad do these last night?" The possibility existed, but Caleb doubted his father would do the much-hated paperwork simply because his son had wanted to retire early with his new bride.

"No."

Caleb saw Megan straighten her spine and wondered what the devil was going on.

"I did them."

His eyes widened with surprise. *"You?"*

Her shoulders lost a bit of their stiffness, her voice softening. She even winced a little as she answered. "Yes."

He didn't say anything. Looking back at the papers,

he scanned each more carefully. By the time he finished, the first bright rays of sunlight had begun to shine through the large window at his back. Megan remained in the doorway, twisting her hands nervously.

"Everything seems to be in order. And all the figures look right." He heard his sister release a pent-up breath of relief.

"You're not angry, then?" she asked.

Angry? No, he was far from angry. Megan had saved him hours of mind-numbing work. He shook his head. "Why, though? How did you know what needed to be done?"

She came farther into the room, a smile brightening her girlish features. "They're monthly reports," she said, dropping into a leather-lined chair across from Caleb. "I simply added up the ticket sales and subtracted the drivers' pay. I get bored around here at night. You and Rebecca retire so early, I have to find something to do to keep busy."

Caleb felt a heated flush rise up from his neck at her mention of his and Rebecca's nightly disappearances. And from the wicked grin lighting her face, Megan knew exactly what went on in their bedroom after dinner.

He cleared his throat and changed the subject. An idea had come to him. A rather ingenious idea, if he did say so himself. "How would you like to make a little extra cash, sister dear?"

Megan shrugged one shoulder.

He supposed she didn't care much about money; anything she wanted or needed, Holbrook provided. But there was one thing she couldn't resist. Something Holbrook disliked and would not buy for his daughter.

"Let's make a deal," Caleb said, using the confident smile that had gotten so many stubborn businessmen to agree with him back in New York. "You do the paperwork for the Express, and I'll keep you supplied with reading material."

Get Four Books Totally
F R E E* —
A $21.96 Value!

(Tear Here and Mail Your FREE* Book Card Today!)

PLEASE RUSH
MY FOUR FREE*
BOOKS TO ME
RIGHT AWAY!

Leisure Historical Romance Book Club
P.O. Box 6613
Edison, NJ 08818-6613

AFFIX
STAMP
HERE

Megan sat up in her chair. "Really?"

Caleb nodded, knowing he had her in the palm of his hand.

Surprisingly, she shook her head. "No, the type of reading you would supply isn't what I'd like."

"Dime novels?" Caleb asked, hoping she would reconsider.

Her nose crinkled. "They're mostly stories about train robbers and outlaws. How boring."

"What would you like, then?" he asked, half afraid of her answer.

"I prefer romances. Papa refuses to let me read them."

Penny dreadfuls. If Holbrook ever found out he was supplying Megan with them, Caleb would be disowned. "Romances, then," he said, snorting at his sister's silly daydreams.

"Of course, they're much shorter than other stories. I'll need twice—no, three times as many."

"Fine," Caleb said in disgust. So much for getting the better of his little sister. She was an Adams through and through.

Megan started out of the room and was almost to the door before Caleb remembered something he'd wanted to ask her. "Megan, exactly what made Rebecca so sick yesterday?"

Megan looked at him for long seconds, disbelief written on every feature. "She's going to have a baby, silly. Didn't you know?"

"Of course I knew—know," he blustered. "How did you?" He and Holbrook had both agreed to keep Rebecca's condition a secret from Megan. At least until a proper amount of time had passed after the wedding.

"Let's see," she said, considering. "You rushed the wedding. She sleeps late every morning, comes downstairs looking pale, and usually excuses herself two or three times a day to be sick. Then there's the fact that she's started a few new dresses for herself, all with extra material at the seams so they can be let out to accommodate her expanding figure. Need I go on?"

"No."

Caleb tried to remember being sixteen. Had he been as knowledgeable at that age? Somehow he doubted it. Other than learning to run his maternal grandparents' newspaper, he had spent most of his time wooing Josephine. Lord, what a mistake that had been. The bitch had very nearly ruined his life. To this day, he still felt icy claws of hatred and distrust wrapped around his soul.

Caleb pushed the murderous thoughts out of his head. "So what made her ill yesterday evening?"

"Didn't she tell you? Rebecca and I cooked dinner."

His brows lifted.

"Your mind really must have been wandering at supper. Don't you remember? Nina quit. She and Peter are getting married next week, and then they're moving to Topeka."

"What does that have to do with Rebecca?"

Megan sighed, as though trying to explain something to a small child. "Rebecca decided to take over Nina's duties. With my help, of course. Until we can hire someone new." She clapped her hands in excitement. "She's going to teach me how to make an apple pie. Did you taste them the night of the dance? Oh, that's right, you were too busy avoiding Anabelle. Well, Rebecca's pies are divine, and she's going to show me how to make one."

Caleb nodded distractedly, and Megan left with a shake of her head and a small shrug.

Why would Rebecca be willing to cook meals for his family? Being dragged here against her will, he would have expected her to relish their dilemma. Instead, she rolled up her sleeves and pitched in, fighting a fit of nausea just to prepare dinner for his father and sister. He frowned, aiming to find out why Rebecca was being so helpful as soon as he had the time.

He decided to wait for his father in the dining room, but he ran into Megan again at the foot of the stairs. She'd changed into a powder-blue day dress and white kid slippers. Caleb bowed gallantly, knowing his sister's penchant for romantic gestures, and offered his arm. She took it, acting every inch the regal princess.

Caleb's laughter at one of Megan's high-handed comments died in his throat when they entered the dining room. The table was set, and heaping plates of food sent steam swirling into the air—oven-baked ham, boiled potatoes, and poached eggs, surrounded by shining china plates, silver utensils, and elegantly folded navy-blue napkins. Just then the kitchen door swung open, Rebecca's hands full with a tray of toast and a jar of elderberry jam.

She looked up, startled to see Caleb and Megan already there. Her eyes traveled to the table, and an apologetic smile lifted the sides of her mouth. "I'm sorry it's not more appetizing, but I was afraid the smell of anything else would make me ill." She looked warily in Caleb's direction, half expecting him to be upset.

"It looks wonderful," Megan said, taking her usual seat.

"It's fine," Caleb said, trying to overcome his initial shock at seeing all Rebecca had done in such a short amount of time.

Rebecca stood still, concerned that his short reply and statue-like stance meant he was angry. She held his gaze, the silence stifling. Then she noticed his brown eyes sparkling and curiosity sprouted in her brain. He didn't seem upset.

"You're sure?" she asked, hoping to figure out his puzzling reaction.

"More than fine," he clarified, and he pulled out a chair for her to be seated.

Chapter Thirteen

Rebecca looked up from her stitching, surprised by the voices that filtered in from the foyer. She put aside the length of fabric she was working on and opened the sliding parlor doors.

"Rebecca!"

"My dear, you look lovely."

"Marriage is treating you well, I hope."

Rebecca found herself crushed in the arms of Hariette Pickins. Then Thelma Wilkes. And finally Mary Archer.

"Please, come in and sit down," she said with a little laugh as she led them into the parlor.

"I'll make tea," Megan said and headed for the kitchen, returning several minutes later with a tray.

"Where's Anabelle?" Rebecca asked, noticing the girl's absence.

Mary shook her head. "She refused to come. Oh, Rebecca," she said, patting Rebecca's hand. "You know how taken Anabelle was with Caleb. I'm afraid she had it in her head that she would someday be his wife."

Thelma snorted. "A typical sixteen-year-old. She'll be

164

over it just as soon as some other handsome young man pays her a bit of attention."

"I suppose," Mary said with a motherly sigh and quickly turned the conversation in another direction. "We can't tell you how much we've missed seeing you on Wednesdays."

Rebecca smiled and refrained from reminding them that she had only been married for two weeks.

"Just look at this dress," Harlette said, standing and holding out the sides for inspection. "It's abominable. I don't know what I'll do without you. I suppose I'll have to order from Sears and Roebuck. Oh, but I dread buying clothes out of a catalogue."

"You wouldn't happen to be interested in continuing as our seamstress, would you, dear?" This from Mrs. Wilkes, who threw her a slanted glance.

Rebecca began to shake her head, knowing she could never be caretaker of the Adams household as well as continuing to sew for profit.

"Oh, do it, Rebecca," Megan urged. "You know you've missed your Wednesdays."

"But I don't have the time, not with—"

"Posh," her young sister-in-law spouted. "We're going to hire a new housekeeper soon, so you won't have to cook much longer, and you know I'm always here to help. I'm sure these ladies would be willing to keep your little business a secret. You could sew for them but not take on any new customers."

"Oh, yes," Hariette said. "We wouldn't tell a soul, would we?" she asked of the room in general.

The others shook their heads emphatically.

Megan leaned close to whisper in Rebecca's ear. "It will keep you busy. And happier."

She blushed, knowing how often she had complained before Nina left that there wasn't enough work around the house to keep her occupied. She'd mended all her own dresses and started a few new ones just to keep her hands from being idle. Megan was right. Another cook would be hired soon, and then what would she do with her time?

"All right," she gave in, causing a chorus of cheers to fill the room. "But I don't want too many people knowing, or I may get bogged down." She chuckled inwardly at the thought, knowing there had been many times when the Wednesday Group was the only thing that had kept her from starvation.

For the next hour, the ladies filled Rebecca in on the town's latest gossip. They agreed to keep their regular Wednesday appointments and promised to bring piles of work for her on their next visit.

After the women left, Megan took the serving tray back to the kitchen, leaving Rebecca to continue sewing together tiny patches for a baby quilt she'd decided to make.

A knock sounded at the door, and Rebecca went to answer it, smiling because she expected one of the Wednesday Group to be returning for something she'd forgotten.

Her smile vanished and her jaw nearly dropped to the floor at the sight of the woman standing on the porch. Her dress was a fiery orange-red, a color no decent woman would ever dare wear in public. Black lace edged the hem, sleeves, and low décolletage.

Rebecca raised her eyes to a rouged face surrounded by hundreds of tight sausage curls that very nearly matched the shade of the garish gown.

Rebecca grabbed the woman's arm and dragged her into the parlor. She slid the doors closed, ensuring minimal privacy. "What are you doing here?" she asked in a harsh whisper, praying Megan would stay in the kitchen a few minutes longer.

"Aren't you going to give Mummy a kiss?"

Rebecca crossed her arms over her chest, her whole body as taut as a tightrope. The heavy scent of Kate's perfume was smothering. "Drop the act. We both know you've never been a mother to me. Tell me why you're here, and then get the hell out."

Kate smoothed her skirts and sat primly on the settee, smiling up at her daughter through a thick layer of cheap makeup. "Is that any way to speak to your mother, darling?"

Rebecca felt bile rise in the back of her throat, and her eyes began to sting with the threat of tears. Why did her mother have to show up now, when Rebecca had finally begun to believe there was some hope of putting her past behind her? *Why?*

Her hands clenched until she felt the nails digging into the flesh of her palms. "I think you should leave."

"Before I meet my son-in-law? That wouldn't be polite, now would it, dear?"

The words stunned her. "How did you know?" she asked raggedly.

"News travels fast, especially through a crowded saloon."

"Whorehouse, you mean."

"Tut-tut," Kate admonished as her gaze traveled around the room, taking in the crystal tear-drop lamps, thick velvet draperies, and expensive silver and gold fixtures attesting to the wealth of its owners. "So where is this husband of yours? Caleb, isn't it?"

Rebecca didn't answer.

"I suppose he's at work running the Adams Express. Yes, he ought to be quite well-off after he inherits the business from his father. You'll have more money than the two of you could ever dream of spending."

"Is that why you came here? For money? Sorry to disappoint you, Red, but I don't have any." She took perverse pleasure in voicing the name she had so often heard customers use when addressing her mother.

"No, of course you don't. You've barely made enough to live on these past years as a seamstress. But your

167

husband is a wealthy man." She paused, as though adding emphasis to her next words. "Does he know? Does your fancy husband have any idea that the woman he married is the illegitimate daughter of one of the highest-paid prostitutes in Kansas City? How did you get him to marry you, Rebecca? Did he knock you up?"

A hand fell to her stomach before Rebecca could consciously stop the action.

"Ah, I see that he did." Kate cackled, putting Rebecca in mind of a wicked witch. "It seems you're no better than your mother, after all."

Kate got up from the sofa and sneered, causing Rebecca to retreat a step. There was a glow in her mother's eyes that she had never seen before, and it frightened her.

"And after you always acted as if you were so much better than me, you little bitch. Well, look at you now. It doesn't matter whether you spread your legs for one man or a hundred, Rebecca. When they pay you for it, it still makes you a whore. You're being paid with this house, the pretty clothes he buys you." She laughed. "If you want to see a hussy, take a good long look in the mirror. You're just like me, darling daughter. *Just like me!*"

Rebecca wished this were a dreadful nightmare that would evaporate when she awoke. She could feel tears brimming against her lashes, fighting to free themselves and run unabashedly down her cheeks. Would that her and her mother's lives could have been different. That, despite her circumstances, Kate had learned something about maternal love. But that had never happened, and Rebecca could afford no illusions that it ever would.

Gathering her strength, she took a deep breath, let her arms drop to her sides, and stepped toward her mother. She spoke slowly, her words so low they were almost menacing. "Get out of my house."

Kate backed up but made no move to gather her discarded gloves and leave. "I will. Just as soon as I get what I came for."

"What's that?" Rebecca asked, afraid she already knew the answer.

"Why, money, of course."

"I'm not giving you a dime."

Kate chuckled. "I think you will. Unless you want your husband and every other person in this town to find out who you really are. And who your mother is."

"You wouldn't dare." But Rebecca knew she would. "Why do you even need money if you're still the highest-paid prostitute in Kansas City?"

"Things have been slow lately."

Rebecca nodded grimly, trying not to care, trying to feel nothing for this woman before her. Feeling anything for Kate would only get her hurt, as it had her entire childhood. "You're getting older," she said quietly. "Once a girl gets wrinkles on her face and shadows under her eyes, men can't stand the sight of her anymore. That's why you need the money, isn't it?"

"Shut up! Shut up!" her mother screamed, lunging forward and slapping Rebecca hard across the face.

Rebecca put a hand to her throbbing cheek. The tears that had been dammed now spilled over, coursing in long, straight rivulets. The salty moisture stung the flesh that began to burn and swell from Kate's vicious attack.

Kate stood several feet away, breathing hard, her face flushed with fury. Rebecca watched her mother struggle for control of her emotions.

"I want the money," she said, "or I'll make sure everyone knows who I am. And that you tricked rich Mr. Adams into marrying you."

"I did no such thing."

"Maybe not, but you got the baby before the wedding. That's not the usual way of things, and I'm sure the townspeople would love to hear about it."

"It's not enough that you took my childhood, is it?"

Rebecca said quietly, unable to believe anyone's mother could be so deliberately cruel and hateful. "Now you want to ruin the rest of my life."

"Why should you have it any better than I did? Why should you be happy when I'm still working at the Scarlet Garter? I'm lucky to have even one man a night take a liking to me. So don't you preach to me about how horrible your life was."

Rebecca thought she saw a hint of remorse in her mother's eyes, but it quickly vanished. She tried to just as quickly dampen her own dangerous flash of compassion. "How much?" she asked.

Kate's head popped up as though Rebecca's response surprised her. "Five hundred dollars."

"Five hundred dollars? Are you crazy? I don't have that kind of money."

Plucking her snagged satin gloves from the table, Kate said, "No, but your husband does."

"He would never give me that much."

Kate took great care in aligning seams and smoothing the gloves over her arms. "He'd better, my dear, or your life will indeed be ruined. Bring the money to the alley behind the Dog Tick Saloon tomorrow at three." She moved to the double doors, sliding one open and stepping through the portal.

"Why do you hate me so much?" Rebecca whispered.

"I don't hate you, Rebecca," her mother answered, no emotion in her voice. "I simply need the five hundred dollars."

It was probably true. Kate had never seemed to waste any strong emotions on her daughter. Neither love nor hate. But the threat was there in her words. Rebecca had no doubt that Kate would expose her to Caleb and the whole town if she didn't pay up. Ruining her life—and her child's. And that Rebecca couldn't allow. But where was she supposed to get *five hundred dollars?* Though these were certainly desperate enough circumstances, her small tea-tin stash from Caleb's insulting payment wouldn't make even a dent in that amount.

Her fingers turning white on the doorknob, Rebecca watched her mother walk out of the house and down the front steps.

"Who was that?"

Rebecca jumped, startled to see Megan standing in the dining room entryway.

"No one."

"You look upset. Is everything all right?"

"Yes. Fine. I'm—" Rebecca stopped short as her stomach lurched. She just managed to reach the porch railing before losing both her breakfast and lunch.

After several long moments of gut-wrenching torment, she straightened and brushed a hand over her straggling hair. Megan offered a handkerchief and glass of water. Rebecca took both, rinsing her mouth and wiping the perspiration from her face.

"Come sit down." Megan led her to the swing and sat beside her. "Do you want to talk about it?"

Rebecca was amazed by the depth of young Megan's compassion. "No."

She felt a stab of regret that she couldn't talk to Megan about Kate. It would be nice to have someone to confide in. But no matter how much she trusted Megan, the girl was Caleb's sister. The risk was too great.

"We'd better go in," she said, rising carefully to keep her stomach from protesting. "It's about time to start supper." She had no idea how she could deal with preparing a meal on top of everything else that had happened today.

Rebecca tensed when Caleb entered the bedroom, not turning to face him. She had avoided meeting his gaze all through dinner, taken an extra-long time to clean up, and sneaked upstairs before he and his father had finished their nightly discussion in the study over a cigar for Holbrook and glass of brandy for Caleb.

He came up behind her and wrapped his arms around her waist, kissing the side of her neck.

"Something's different," he said, licking the lobe of her ear. "Flowers."

"Roses," she said, trying to keep her voice even. "Megan let me use her rose perfume."

"Mmm. Then why do you still smell so spicy?"

She leaned back against him, for a moment feeling safe and protected, as she had of late, in his arms. "Because I threw a cinnamon stick in my bath water, as usual."

He groaned and pulled her closer, if that was possible. "The combination is irresistible."

"I don't know if Megan will want me borrowing her perfume all the time, though." Her heart beat a little faster when Caleb's hand trailed down the outside of her thigh. It delighted and excited her that he'd not only noticed her new fragrance but also seemed to enjoy it.

"To hell with Megan," he said, cupping her breast in his hand. "I'll buy you your own. Damn. You keep smelling this good, and I'll buy you a bucket of the stuff."

She laughed. "You like it then?"

He growled and bit her collarbone, dragging the thin lawn nightgown up to bunch at her hips.

Rebecca sucked on her lower lip, knowing what she must do but dreading it all the same. She had to do it now, before Caleb made love to her and drifted off to sleep. Before she started feeling warm and tingly and guilty as sin.

"Caleb, I need to ask a favor."

"Hmm?"

"Caleb, this is serious." She turned in his arms, trying to distract him from an overly sensitive spot he'd discovered just below her right breast.

"I'm listening," he said, his lips moving against her throat.

"The Wednesday Group dropped by today, and—"

"Who?"

"The women who used to come to me for dresses. *Caleb!*" Rebecca swatted at his hand when it swept between her thighs.

"What about them?"

"I agreed to continue sewing for them."

"Good," he said, and she knew he was hardly paying attention to a word she said.

"Could I borrow some money? I have to buy supplies." The lie slipped past her lips a little too easily for her comfort.

Caleb put his hands behind her knees and lifted her legs around his waist, heading for the foot of the bed. "I'll leave you a bank draft in the morning. Take as much as you need."

"Thank you," she said, gasping as her buttocks rubbed against the cool wood of the bed frame.

"No. Thank *you*," he said, and let her fall back onto the mattress.

As he'd promised, Caleb left a blank bank draft on the desk in the study. When Rebecca walked in and saw it lying there, she sat down and cried. She tried to tell herself that she was just being emotional because of the baby, but even as her mind registered that excuse, she knew it wasn't true. She cried because things had been going so well, and because—damn it all!—she was starting to fall in love with Caleb.

When their marriage started they had been as ornery as two stallions fighting over a herd of mares, but since then things had calmed down considerably. They had come to something of an unspoken understanding, and Rebecca couldn't deny that she looked forward to watching the sun go down, knowing that in those dark hours of the night Caleb would make her feel things she had never thought possible, do things to her body that she had always considered taboo.

But it was more than the physical pleasure. It wasn't just that making love with Caleb didn't make her feel cheap and tawdry, as she'd always expected it would. It was that Caleb seemed to . . . care.

Each day when he returned home from work, he sought her out and asked about her day. He kissed her considerately on the cheek if they were not alone, passionately on the lips if they were. And how could she miss the way he rushed through the meetings with his father to retire early with her?

Caleb made her feel the way she'd always dreamt of feeling. Their wedding had been hurried, the joining far from idyllic, but somehow he made her happy to be his wife. And proud—so very proud—to be carrying his child. A child she would always love and cherish with all her heart and strength.

Rebecca spanned the slight swell of her abdomen with her hands, still utterly amazed that a life was growing there inside her. A life that she already loved and would risk all to protect. The reason behind what she was about to do.

In the long hours of the night, while Caleb dozed beside her, Rebecca had thought a lot about her own mother's threat. She didn't fear for herself. Not really. Caleb would surely be furious to discover her secret, and perhaps he would even send her away, opting to provide for his child from a distance. Or maybe he would want to protect the child by being rid of its mother completely. The thought of divorce hurt too much to even consider.

Still, she was not paying her mother off to protect her own reputation; she was doing it for her son or daughter. What child should have to deal with the taunts of others because of his mother's past, because she had grown up in a brothel?

Her child would not. If she had to lie, cheat, and steal, Rebecca swore that her child would never have to suffer even a fraction of the pain she had growing up.

With renewed determination, she dried her eyes and picked up the paper that held their entire future in the balance. She offered up a short, desperate prayer and tucked it into the pocket of her skirt.

"Mrs. Adams. How nice to see you." The bank clerk beamed at her from behind the counter.

She swallowed, uncomfortable at being called Mrs. Adams after so many years of being just plain Rebecca. She smiled nonetheless.

"Your husband said you would probably be stopping in today."

"Caleb was here?" Her throat became suddenly dry.

"Yes, ma'am. He came by to tell us you were allowed to draw money out of his account."

"Yes," she said. "He left me a bank draft."

The clerk nodded. "I know you're his wife an' all, but you couldn't have made use of his money without his written permission. Bank policy, you know."

"I see," Rebecca said. A trickle of perspiration was beginning to gather between her breasts, and it had nothing to do with the hot August sun.

"So then, what can I do for you?"

She removed the paper from her reticule and smoothed her hands over it before sliding the bank draft across the countertop. "You can show me how to fill this out for five hundred dollars."

Rebecca saw the clerk's mouth drop open and his eyes bulge. He reacted the same way she had, the same way she would expect of anyone within earshot of the huge figure.

"Fi—five hundred?"

Rebecca smiled as though she spent that amount every day of her life. She was, after all, an Adams now. Time to start thinking like one. She tried to incorporate some of the self-assurance Caleb always exuded into her demeanor.

"Yes. I'm planning many household improvements."

The clerk was still in a dazed state when Rebecca collected her money and waved good-bye. By then, her camisole was clinging to her damp skin, and her nerves were worn down to mere pinpricks racing the length of her spine.

The large grandfather clock in the bank showed it to be two-forty-eight, so Rebecca made her way along the boardwalk, smiling and nodding to everyone she passed. She avoided the Adams Express office altogether, afraid she would not be able to keep up her brave front with Caleb.

As inconspicuously as possible, she walked around the Dog Tick Saloon, careful not to step in broken glass or any of the foul-smelling puddles that lined the side of the building. Rebecca remembered only too clearly the number of visitors to the Scarlet Gastor who had slept off the evening's alcohol in alleys, along with the stench of urine that often accompanied them.

She raised her head, expecting her mother to emerge from the back door of the establishment. But she caught a movement out of the corner of her eye and saw Kate, dressed in one of her usual flashy dresses and stuffing a dangling lock of fire-red hair back into its arrangement, coming toward her from the opposite direction, a smug smile plastered to her face.

Chapter Fourteen

Kate's smile never wavered as she waltzed up to her daughter, hips swaying. "I knew you'd come," she said, gaily patting the bodice of her gaudy working-girl garb. "Just conducting a little business out back of the livery while I waited."

For one brief moment, Rebecca thought about running away and never looking back. But Kate's threat echoed in her mind, and she knew she had to appease her mother or risk having her child's life ruined by the bitter, hateful woman.

Rebecca knew her mother was waiting for a reaction to the remark—shock, aversion, indignation—but she remained silent, impassive, feeling only a deep sense of sadness and pity.

"Did you bring it?" Kate demanded.

Rebecca clutched her reticule more tightly and swallowed, her brain racing to find some other option, some other way to pacify her mother's resentment and greed.

"Did you bring the money?" Kate's voice remained low, but urgency edged her words this time.

"Yes."

Kate blinked but didn't move. "All of it?"

Rebecca nodded.

"Give it to me." Kate came forward with the speed of a raging tornado. She yanked the bag from Rebecca's hands and ripped it open, dragging out the packet of bills. She rubbed them between her fingers, even brought them to her nose to smell.

Rebecca stepped back, only too eager to be away. She tugged at the drawstrings of her bag and turned to leave.

"You got this awfully fast."

Rebecca stopped in her tracks. The blood in her veins seemed to chill.

"I'll bet you didn't have a wink of trouble, either."

Rebecca took another step, then another, hoping to get away from Kate before she said anything else.

"I want more."

That made Rebecca spin to face her mother once again. "What you have there is more than enough."

"I've changed my mind. I want a thousand."

Rebecca stared in shocked disbelief. "I can't possibly get another five hundred dollars."

"No, no." Kate laughed, fondling the money in her hands. "I want a thousand more. One thousand more U.S. dollar bills. Crisp, clean, and all mine. Bring them here tomorrow afternoon."

"Caleb would never let me have that much. I've already gotten five hundred. Don't you think he'll become a little suspicious if fifteen hundred dollars suddenly disappears from his bank account?"

"I don't care. That's not my problem. Just get it."

Rebecca closed her eyes and let her shoulders go slack. "I can't get it by tomorrow. I'll need more time."

"Tomorrow. Right here. One o'clock." Kate stuck a finger in her daughter's face. "Don't cross me, Rebecca. There are a lot of people right inside that saloon who would love to know who the new Mrs. Adams really is and where she came from. Just remember that if you start thinking I'll go away easily."

Kate strutted through the back entrance into the Dog Tick.

Rebecca headed for the buggy parked in front of the bank, then drove to her old house. She felt cold and disoriented, unconscious of her movements, unable to register the fact that she had to find so much more money for her mother. She only knew that she had to have extra sewing supplies when Caleb arrived home this evening, to help account for her bank withdrawal.

The first thing she noticed about her cabin was a thick layer of dust on the porch and steps, blown up from the street. A few barely visible footprints led to the door, but Rebecca thought nothing of it. Someone had probably come needing the craft of a needle, only to find the house empty.

She twisted the key in its hole, and the lock clicked open. Rebecca stepped into the house and gasped at what she saw.

The stove top looked like a mountain peak covered with thick white snow. Canisters had been upset and tossed to the floor—flour, salt, sugar, all her spices spilled. Rebecca could see a fine cloud of powder whirled about by the slight breeze drifting in from the open door.

The parlor was also in shambles, bolts of fabric strewn from one end to the other, every inch of material ripped and ruined. Strips of lace lay in tiny ragged pieces. Buttons, hooks, and needles were scattered across the floor. Spools of thread were unbound and left in clumps like tumbleweeds.

She took a step forward, her foot crunching on the shards of a broken tea cup. Rebecca bent to pick up the fragment of china. Half of a small, delicately painted blue flower filled her vision. Widow Fitzgerald's most prized tea service. In the years since Octavia's death,

Rebecca had only ever chipped the rim of one cup. It had taken her two hours to mend it properly, but after all that work, the nick had been nearly invisible. And now the china lay smashed into millions of tiny pieces, dust beneath her feet.

At the sound of someone behind her, Rebecca swung around, still in a crouch. When her legs twisted in the fabric of her petticoats, she put a hand out to catch herself, mindless of the broken china that would most certainly shred her palms to ribbons.

"Careful," Caleb warned, grabbing her upper arms and helping her to stand. "Christ. What the hell happened here?"

Rebecca's face had lost all color, and she weaved slightly.

"Are you all right? Did you cut yourself?" He grabbed her hands, searching for any sign of blood. Then he lifted her skirt, examining the folds for tears. He shook the hem to dislodge a few clinging china shavings, patting her legs and waist for any sign of injury.

"I'm fine," Rebecca said, pulling the fabric out of his hands. "Why are you here?"

Caleb straightened. He narrowed his eyes and studied her, curious to know why she was being so aloof toward him. Perhaps she was in shock over the damage to what used to be her home. "I was running an errand and saw the buggy here. I came to check on you," he said in a quiet, neutral tone. "Who did this, Rebecca?" he asked.

"I don't know," she answered. "Probably some drunken cowhands."

"They never bothered you before, did they?" His heart lurched in his breast as images suddenly filled his mind. He didn't think he could live with the knowledge that Rebecca had been harmed or even dangerously harassed.

"No. But they probably discovered the house empty and decided to have a little fun."

Caleb wanted to pull Rebecca into his arms and comfort her, but he didn't think she would welcome the gesture just now. Though her eyes were wide, he noticed the tight set of her jaw. Rebecca was no wilting lily, and he doubted she would appreciate his treating her as such.

"I wonder," he answered and stepped farther into the parlor. His boots grated over broken china. "Leavenworth men may get drunk, and they may get rowdy, but I've never known them to be purposely destructive. Especially to someone else's property."

He swept back a length of turquoise satin that had been draped over the settee. Stuffing poured out of the cushions like a frothy waterfall. Caleb let out a muffled curse and threw the fabric back over the ruined piece of furniture.

"Then who could have done this?" Rebecca asked.

"Was the door locked?"

"Of course," she snapped.

Pink began to seep back into her cheeks, and Caleb lowered his head to hide a smile. It would take more than a few torn pieces of fabric to keep his Rebecca down.

He stepped toward her, but as he did so, the toe of his boot sent some small object flying. It slid across the floor and clanged into the leg of the stove. Caleb leaned over to retrieve it and came up with a pair of shears.

"These yours?" The scissors swung back and forth on his index finger like a pendulum ticking away the time. The blades were nicked in several places, the tips bent.

She nodded. "My extra pair. I don't use them often. The good pair is at your house. Those I kept in a box under my bed."

Rebecca's face whitened. "Oh, God." She pushed past Caleb and ran for the bedroom. She held aside the curtain that separated it from the rest of the house and stared. Her quilt lay in shreds, taken apart almost piece by piece but by no means neatly.

Caleb saw the damage, his hands clenching into fists

at his sides. Who would have done something so destructive, so hurtful? Surely not someone who had stumbled in from the street. He could understand if things had been stolen, but whoever did this must have been truly demented.

"Come on," he said, taking her shoulders and turning her toward the door. "I'm sure this is all somebody's sick idea of fun. I'll report it to the marshal."

"Who would do this?" Rebecca asked. Her words were laced with fury.

He turned her face up to his. "Don't you worry about it, do you hear me? I'll see to everything." He put an arm around her shoulders and helped her through the house to the front door.

"Dammit!" Rebecca cursed for the hundredth time and stuck a stinging finger into her mouth to absorb the small bead of blood there. She was preparing a roast for dinner but slicing her fingers more than the carrots or potatoes.

Her mind was on other things, that was for certain. After everything that had happened already today, it was no wonder her head throbbed.

She probably should have been worried about who had destroyed her house, but that wasn't what caused the sledgehammer pounding in her brain. She had to come up with a way to explain her huge bank withdrawal to Caleb—and to get one thousand dollars more from him. If only she could sell her little cabin overnight and get some funds quickly. Now however, that would be more impossible than ever.

Replacing the ruined supplies from her house was one excuse to give Caleb, but what would she say if he finally started noticing there were never any new materials around? She couldn't pay off her mother and buy a huge new sewing stock.

The front door slammed, and Rebecca nearly dropped to her knees, sure her head was about to explode.

She heard heavy feet stomp up the stairs, still for a moment, then begin again. Through her headache she dimly wondered what Caleb seemed to be searching the house for.

She guided her paring knife over a large potato and watched the skin peel off onto the pile of other scraps. When the kitchen door crashed back against the wall behind her, she jumped. The blade of the knife slipped and hit the palm of her hand. It was a small cut, but it hurt nonetheless.

Rebecca whirled around, pressing her otherwise white apron to the wound. "Would you like to try again?" she asked, her voice sharp with her frayed nerves. "Maybe next time I can manage to sever my wrist."

Caleb stalked over and grasped her arm. He lifted the apron and dabbed away the blood. "It's going to be all right," he said.

"Well, it hurts like the devil," she told him, pulling her hand away and turning back to the counter. She didn't bother to mention the half dozen other pricks on her fingers.

"It'll heal. Rebecca, I need to talk to you."

Rebecca noticed a cold edge to his words and gripped the knife handle until her fingers turned white. "So talk," she said, trying to sound flippant. In truth her heart beat ten times faster than normal.

"In the study," he said, walking toward the door.

Rebecca stood at the counter, frozen in place.

Caleb came back and grabbed her elbow in a tight grip. "In the study. Now."

For a split second, she considered taking the paring knife with her, just in case. But logic soon broke through her fear, and she put down the would-be defensive weapon.

She went with Caleb, his grip never loosening. "Let go," she said, shaking her arm. When he didn't respond she stopped dead in her tracks, digging her heels as best she could into the hardwood floor. "I'll come with you, but let go."

He stopped and gazed at her for a long moment. Then, without a word, he dropped his hand from her elbow and continued on to the study. Rebecca followed more slowly, stopping just inside the door.

"Sit."

She raised an eyebrow. No matter how much trouble she was in, she had no intention of taking orders from some cold, rude, short-tempered barbarian. Even if he was her husband.

"You needn't order me around. I'm quite comfortable standing, thank you. And if you wish to discuss something with me, try speaking like a human being rather than a beast who's lived in a cave all its life. Complete sentences would be a good place to start." Her words were brave, but inside, Rebecca's stomach was trying to turn itself inside out.

Caleb inclined his head. "Very well. If the lady wishes for complete sentences, the lady shall get complete sentences." He strode to her side and propelled her forward, at the same time throwing the door closed behind them. "You may sit down of your own accord, or I will tie you into the chair. Is that understood?"

Rebecca pursed her lips primly, deciding not to call him on this particular bluff. "Quite." She moved in front of the leather armchair and smoothed her skirt before perching on the edge of the seat.

"What did you do this afternoon?"

Her heart thudded in her breast, but she kept her voice even. "Pardon me?"

"This afternoon. What did you do in town?"

She swallowed. "First I went to the bank, and then I went shopping for sewing supplies."

Caleb rested his hip on the desk, his arms crossed over his chest. "Didn't you have trouble carrying all those packages into the house?"

Rebecca felt the walls of the room closing in on her, cutting off her air. "No, I managed."

"Amazing." He shook his head and whistled through his teeth. "Just how many bolts of fabric and spools of thread can five hundred dollars buy? And where have you hidden this storehouse of supplies?"

Rebecca closed her eyes and collapsed against the back of the chair.

"I see you don't intend to deny it. Good." His voice became hard. "Now tell me why the hell you needed so much money."

She turned her face into the smooth leather, absorbing its coolness on her heated skin. "I'm sorry," was all she could manage.

"Sorry for what?" He threw up his hands and went around to the other side of the desk, kicking his father's chair with such force that it bounced off of the back wall. "Just what did you do with it, Rebecca?"

She opened her eyes and sat up, ready for Caleb's angry assault and more than willing to make amends. "I'll pay you back. I promise. I'll just need some time."

"I don't want the goddamn money!" he bellowed. "I want to know what the hell you did with it. Who did you meet behind the saloon?"

This time Rebecca's heart stopped altogether.

"That's right, I know all about it." Caleb ran a hand though his dark hair and sank into the desk chair. "I know that you took five hundred dollars out of my bank account. I know that you didn't do a stitch of shopping today. Marshal Thompson said he saw you out back of the Dog Tick with some painted whore. You're damned lucky he was the one who saw you. I'm pretty sure he can be trusted to keep this to himself. Otherwise the whole town would be talking about it by morning. What were you doing, Rebecca, looking for a job?"

Rebecca guessed she deserved Caleb's fury. She had, after all, stolen from him. "I would really rather not tell you. Just please trust me. I promise to pay back every cent as soon as I can."

"The *last* thing I'll ever do is trust you again."

His emotionless gaze and cold declaration caused Rebecca's eyes to brim with stinging tears.

"And I don't care whether you'd *rather* tell me or not. You damn well better if you want to see another sunrise."

"If I tell you," Rebecca said, wiping her running nose on the hem of her apron, "you'll hate me."

"It's too late to worry about that."

She lifted her head and stared at the stern lines of her husband's face. A muscle in his jaw jumped sporadically.

She cried harder at the thought that she had lost Caleb forever. They had just begun to get close, and now they were being torn apart. She saw in his eyes that he did indeed hate her for what she'd done. And he didn't even know about her past yet.

"The woman behind the saloon . . . She's my . . ."

"Your what?" Caleb asked when she didn't finish.

"She's my mother."

Caleb watched Rebecca's small shoulders tremble in an effort to hold back her sobs. He shook his head slightly, thinking he must have heard her wrong. There was no way the woman Thompson described could possibly be related to Rebecca.

"Your mother?" he asked quietly.

"Yes," she managed between shuddering breaths.

His muscles relaxed, all the anger and tension pouring out of his body. He brushed back a wave of hair that had fallen across one eye. Exhaling a lungful of air, he looked at Rebecca. Usually strong and self-assured, she now seemed frail and vulnerable.

"Maybe you should tell me more."

Rebecca raised wide eyes.

Caleb pushed back his chair and crossed the room to

the bar. He filled two glasses with brandy and returned to her side. He coaxed a drink into her hand and tapped the bottom to get her to put it to her lips. Then he leaned on the edge of the desk and emptied his in one shot.

"Tell me everything," he said. "From the beginning."

"I . . . grew up in a back room of the Scarlet Garter in Kansas City," Rebecca began haltingly. Then she went through the major happenings of her childhood.

"I overheard Lilah telling Mother I was old enough, at thirteen, to start working. Kate didn't argue. She seemed to agree quite readily. Said we could use the extra income. That's the night I ran away. I hid with the luggage on the back of a stagecoach until it stopped in Leavenworth. If Widow Fitzgerald hadn't taken me in, I probably would have ended up in an orphanage somewhere. Or back at the Scarlet Garter."

"And you never told Octavia Fitzgerald where you'd come from?"

"No. She probably would have understood, but if anyone else had found out, I would have been nothing more than the bastard daughter of a whore. Widow Fitzgerald taught me so much. When she died, I knew enough about sewing to continue with her business. It wasn't much, but I got by."

"I don't suppose it helped any when I refused to pay for Sabrina's dresses." Caleb frowned slightly, ashamed of himself for being so stingy, keeping money from Rebecca that she probably needed for food, treating her like an overly avaricious merchant.

Her mouth lifted in a small smile. "No, it didn't help."

"So all your life you've been afraid someone would find out about your past."

She nodded, averting her gaze.

"Didn't you realize that the people in this town like you for who you are? I doubt they'd give a fig about who your mother is or where you grew up. The important thing is that you got away from that life and made something of yourself."

A single tear welled on her eyelashes and slipped down her cheek. "It does matter. How will you feel when everyone in church stares at you because you married a prostitute's daughter?" She placed a hand over the mound of her stomach. "How will this child react when he finds out his grandmother is a whore?"

A streak of fury ran down Caleb's spine. Intense love filled his heart, and he knew he would do anything to protect his child from that stigma. And he would do anything to protect the mother of that child.

"Why did your mother come looking for you? Why now?"

"She found out I'd married you."

His brow creased. "What's so important about that?"

"You're rich, Caleb," she said softly. "Much richer than most people around here could ever hope to be."

The skin over his cheekbones tightened as he clenched his teeth. "I see. Yes, it stands to reason, then, that she would try to get money from you."

"She said if I didn't pay her five hundred dollars, she would make sure everyone in town heard about my past. And that I was with child before we married. Now she wants a thousand more to keep quiet."

"Son of a bitch!" He hit the top of the desk with his fist, then shook the hand to relieve some of the sting.

"I'm sorry, Caleb. I should have told you, but I was so afraid you wouldn't understand. I was so afraid you would hate me."

Caleb looked at his wife and felt a warm, niggling sensation in the pit of his stomach. He ran a hand over her soft hair. "Why don't you go upstairs and rest. You look exhausted."

She nodded and rose, keeping her head down. "What about supper?"

One side of his mouth lifted. "I'll think of something,"

he said and kissed her cheek. "Go get some sleep."

She walked to the door of the study and opened it, but before leaving she turned and fixed him with a concerned gaze. "Caleb. What are you going to do?"

He waved his hands, shooing her out of the room. "Don't worry," he said. "Go to bed."

Closing the door behind her, he rested his temple against the hardwood panel and took a deep breath. "I'll think of something."

Chapter Fifteen

Caleb snapped the lid of his watch closed and slipped it back into his coat pocket. He leaned against the dingy, splintered wood of the wall of the Dog Tick, the dusty heel of one boot digging a rut in the dry earth.

The back door of the saloon opened, and a red-haired, haggard-looking woman stepped out. She looked first to the right and then to the left, finally spotting Caleb. Voices filtered out of the saloon, mostly female, a few male. The front doors had opened only an hour earlier.

"Lookin' for something special, honey?" The woman ran a finger along the over-stuffed bodice of her bright red dress.

"You Kate?" he asked, intentionally keeping his eyes half closed, feigning disinterest.

"Sure am, sweetie. What can I do for you?"

She pressed against him, her heavy perfume invading his nostrils and almost choking off his next breath. Caleb pushed away from the side of the building, causing Kate to stagger back a few steps.

"For starters, you can leave my wife alone."

"I ain't never messed with no man's wife," the woman protested, waving her hands in denial. "It's not my style. If a man comes here, he's bound to get what he pays for, married or not. And I wouldn't be the only one to accommodate him."

"I don't think you understand," Caleb said, tapping the brim of his hat up to reveal his eyes. He kept them glued on the woman before him, "You've been making a nuisance of yourself, and I want it to stop. Leave Rebecca alone."

"Rebecca? Why, you must be my new son-in-law." Kate wiped a hand on her skirt and held it out for him to shake. "Pleased to meet you."

He ignored the offering. "Sorry I can't say the same. I didn't come to make small talk. I came to warn you. Stay away from my wife."

"Did Rebecca tell you about me? About her past?"

"I know everything, so you needn't bother trying to blackmail me the way you did your daughter." He wanted to spit just to clear his mouth of the vile taste the thought left. To blackmail your own flesh and blood, your own child. Despicable. And this was the woman who had raised Rebecca. It was a wonder she had turned out half decent, given the circumstances.

Kate twirled a length of hair between her thumb and forefinger. "So you wouldn't mind everyone in town knowing that your wife—your child's mother—is the daughter of a prostitute?"

"The truth? No, I wouldn't." Caleb took a step forward, rewarded by the widening of the woman's painted eyes. "But Rebecca would, and that's what matters."

She tugged at the small black bow at the center of her breasts. "Then maybe we can come to some sort of agreement to make sure no one finds out."

"Sounds good to me," Caleb said. He dug into his front pocket and removed several bills. "You take this money, and the money my wife gave you yesterday, and see if you can't find your way back to Kansas City. Got it?"

Kate grabbed the money and counted it. "There's only fifty dollars here."

"That's right. Which is more than you'd get for entertaining ten men a night. Take it and get out of Leavenworth."

"But I wanted—"

"A thousand dollars, I know. But this is all you're going to get, so I suggest you take it and make the best of a bad situation."

"What makes you think I still won't tell?"

"Oh, I just thought you might be partial to that pretty neck of yours. You try to ruin my wife's good name—now or ever—and I'll see you swing for the crime of blackmail. Understood?"

For a moment Rebecca's mother was silent, and he expected her to argue. He was prepared to give her the whole goddamn one thousand dollars—which he had in his pocket—if it meant she would leave Rebecca alone. But he didn't think he would have to go that far.

He was right.

Kate tucked the money into her bodice and walked toward him. "All right. I'll take the money. Five hundred and fifty dollars is enough to keep me happy—and quiet. For now."

"It better keep you happy until the day they put you in the ground." He spat at her feet and walked away.

Rebecca moved down the staircase, shamefully aware of her swollen, red-rimmed eyes and of the lateness of the hour. Though Caleb had claimed not to hold her past against her, he hadn't come to bed last night, leaving her to cry herself to sleep.

She tiptoed into the dining room, pulling her robe closed and tightening the sash. The breakfast dishes had already been cleared, and the sounds of someone washing plates drifted from the kitchen. She pushed the swinging door open and stepped in. Megan, face ruddy with exertion, was bent over a tub of soapy water, her white apron soaked through.

Rebecca walked to her side and picked up a dish towel. "Would you like some help?"

Megan spun around and pressed a dripping hand to her heart. "Oh, Rebecca, you startled me." She looked at her a bit oddly but simply said, "Yes, thank you."

Megan scrubbed clean an iron skillet and passed it to Rebecca to dry, saying, "I don't know how you cook breakfast every morning without going crazy."

"What do you mean?"

"Well, by the time the potatoes were brown, the eggs and ham were burned clean through. And then the food was cold before I could make coffee. Please don't leave me alone in here again." Water splattered on the floor as she waved a hand to encompass the room.

"I won't," Rebecca promised ashamed of having stayed abed so late. "But if I had to, you could always send your father and brother into town for breakfast. I'm sure Mrs. Wilkes would break her residents-only rule and give them a plate of bacon and eggs." She set the last frying pan aside and draped the towel on a hook to dry.

"Speaking of Caleb," Megan said, casting a curious glance in Rebecca's direction. "Did you and he have a fight?"

Rebecca flinched and turned away to straighten a set of linen napkins that was already perfectly neat. "No. Why do you ask?"

"Oh, he was all sullen and grumpy this morning, muttering something about bloodsuckers and gutter rats."

"And you thought he was talking about me?" Rebecca put her hands to her chest. "Oh, goodness, I'm flattered."

Megan's cheeks pinkened, and she gasped, "No, I didn't mean it that way. I just thought maybe you'd had an argument, and he was in a foul mood. I mean . . . oh, I'm sorry."

Rebecca had to chuckle. "Don't worry so. I didn't take offense."

"Oh, good. I have a bad habit of speaking before I consider how people will take what I have to say. The night of the Harvest Festival, I told Anabelle Archer that I thought she was being a little too flirtatious with Caleb, and she hasn't spoken to me since. I honestly didn't mean to upset her. I just thought she might find some-where to prop her breasts other than Caleb's arm."

"You're joking. Anabelle actually threw herself at Caleb?"

"She all but pranced around naked for him."

Rebecca chuckled again, imagining Caleb enduring such a show from the young woman. But then she began to wonder if Caleb had enjoyed Anabelle's attentions. And if so, just how much? "What did Caleb think of her?" she asked, a bit more seriously.

"He nearly killed me for having suggested that she ask him to dance. If I hadn't distracted her while he got away, I'm sure he would have strangled me."

"So he didn't seem interested in her?"

"Not at all. She's much too young and scatterbrained for him. Besides, he's got you now. What more could he want?"

A sweet, innocent young bride. A wife who doesn't have a past that could shame him. A woman who wouldn't embarrass him and his child. Unbidden, mois-ture gathered in her eyes.

"Rebecca, what's wrong?" Megan put an arm around her shoulders.

She tried to answer, but her throat clogged with tears. She let Megan lead her through the house and out onto the porch for a breath of fresh, mid-morning air. They sat on the swing, which afforded a view of the trees and fields that stretched the distance between the house and town, keeping the Adams home secluded.

In the long minutes that followed, Rebecca cried more than she had in years. Everything seemed so bleak that she didn't know how her life would ever get back to any semblance of order.

Her mother wanted to drag her reputation through the swamp. Her husband hadn't spoken to her since she'd told him the truth, and despite his initial gentleness, perhaps after some reflection he intended to send her packing. She was starting to show, and was still often sick and overtired, and she would never be able to find a job to raise money before the baby was born. And who in the future would ever want a dress made by a seamstress with a bastard child?

Megan kept urging her to talk out what was troubling her, and she haltingly began to pour out the secrets of her tortured soul. But between her sobs and trembling, her words were incomprehensible.

"Calm down," Megan said, rubbing Rebecca's back in a soothing circular motion. "I can't understand you."

Rebecca took several deep breaths, trying to calm herself and choose her words carefully. She finally told Megan about growing up in a brothel and about her mother's blackmail. About her many disagreements with Caleb and that they had married only because of the baby. She even admitted that their loveless marriage hurt, but that worse even than that was the fact that Caleb didn't seem to like her very much.

"What nonsense," Megan said, giving her leg a squeeze. "Caleb is wild about you."

Rebecca rolled her eyes and all but snorted her disbelief. "I hardly think so."

"No, it's true. Even a blind man could see that my brother is totally smitten with you. He never takes his eyes off you during dinner. And papa says he's as restless as a caged bobcat until he can excuse himself for the evening and go upstairs with you. And do I have to remind you of what goes on then?"

Rebecca felt her face flush ten shades of red.

"I didn't think so." Her sister-in-law grinned. "With all that evidence, how can you possibly think Caleb doesn't care about you?"

Rebecca turned her head and focused on a patch of blue and yellow wildflowers in the distance. When she answered, her words were soft and sad. "Caleb loves being in my bed, but he doesn't love me."

Megan reached over and took her hand, holding it firmly in her own. "Rebecca, you don't understand. To my brother, that's as close to love as he's ever gotten. Caleb doesn't know any other way of showing that he cares for you."

Rebecca frowned and faced Megan. "If he can only show his feelings in bed"—she blushed to so openly discuss such intimacies—"then he must have loved Sabrina Leslie, and all the other ladies he's kept for his pleasure."

"No, no." Megan tapped her foot on the porch restlessly. "I don't know how to explain it exactly, but despite his dalliances, Caleb has always been rather cold toward women. It's as if he's built a wall around his heart to keep them out. He's been that way for as long as I can remember. Ever since Josephine."

"Josephine?" Rebecca asked, her heart constricting at the sound of another woman's name, a woman from Caleb's past.

Megan shrugged. "I don't know her myself. I only know that anytime Mother or Father talk about Caleb's coldness toward women, they say it's because of Josephine." She gave Rebecca a look. "He might tell you about her, if you ask."

Rebecca averted her gaze. She didn't know if she had the courage to pry into Caleb's past when their present was about as stable as a raft made of straw.

"Give him a chance," Megan suggested, patting her hand in a sisterly gesture. "His heart may be buried deep right now, but it's still there."

Rebecca closed her eyes and called herself every kind of fool. She was the last person Caleb would ever trust after all the secrets she'd kept from him.

But maybe . . . maybe if she could get him to talk about this woman who'd hurt him, this Josephine, no matter how much it hurt her own heart to hear about his last love, it would help her understand him better. After all, he now knew all about her sordid past. What could be worse than being raised in a brothel?

Caleb reached to hang his hat just inside the front door. It missed the hook and fell to the floor. He ignored it and leaned back against the door, thoroughly exhausted.

If the confrontation with Rebecca's mother hadn't been enough to wear him out, he'd also gone to talk to the marshal about the mess at Rebecca's house. On top of that, the Express had been busier than usual. Caleb had sent his father home hours ago and stayed to finish the day's work. He would return the bay mare he'd rented to the livery in the morning.

All he wanted now was to drop into bed and sleep.

Rebecca came into the foyer from the dining room, an odd sparkle in her eyes. She bent to pick up his hat, placing it on the row of hooks.

"Your father said you'd be home late. He and Megan have already eaten and retired."

Caleb pushed himself away from the door and shrugged out of his suit coat. "I'm not that hungry, anyway."

"Oh, I hope you intend to eat something. I've kept a plate warm for you."

He raised an eyebrow curiously. She took his hand, leading him into the dining room before releasing him and disappearing into the kitchen. He fell onto a chair and rested his head against the back with a yawn. She returned a moment later with two plates of food left over from dinner. She set one in front of him and took her own seat directly across from him.

"Haven't you eaten yet?" he asked.

"I was waiting for you."

They ate in silence for several minutes before Rebecca set down her fork and cleared her throat. "Is everything all right?" she asked nervously.

Caleb ran a hand over his face and sighed. He must be even more tired than he thought. He should have known she would still be worrying about that sorry excuse for a mother.

"Your mother won't bother you again."

"How can you be sure? She wants a thousand dollars. If she doesn't get it, she'll tell everyone who I am."

"I took care of it, Rebecca. She won't be telling anybody anything."

She nodded, her eyes downcast. "Thank you."

Exhausted, he continued eating in silence.

"Caleb, may I ask you something?"

With a tired sigh, he said, "Go ahead."

She cleared her throat, as though buying time to think of just the right way to phrase her question. Finally she opened her mouth and spoke softly. "Who's Josephine?"

The fork all but fell from his hand. The chunk of potato he'd just eaten stuck in his throat like a burr. "What?" he croaked.

She raised her gaze to meet his and uttered the name again. "Who's Josephine?"

"Where did you hear about her?" he asked, slamming down his fork and wiping his mouth with the napkin from his lap.

Her fingers toyed nervously with her silverware, but she answered honestly. "Megan mentioned her today."

"Josephine is none of your business," he said sharply.

Rebecca stood, picked up her plate, and said softly,

"I see," before disappearing into the kitchen.

Why the hell would Rebecca ask about Josephine? Lord, he hadn't heard that name in more than ten years. And how had Megan found out about her?

When Rebecca returned to the dining room, she continued clearing the table, remaining so determinedly silent, he thought his head would explode with the tension. She moved into the kitchen again for a moment, then reappeared and started toward the hall.

"Rebecca," he said, rising from his chair to stop her. She turned to look at him, and he was struck by the hurt in her eyes. She didn't intend to press the issue, wouldn't nag him senseless as his sister was likely to do. And yet he felt the uncommon urge to explain it to her anyway.

"I was sixteen," he began, not quite sure how to go about divulging such a painful part of his past. He'd never spoken of it before to anyone. He was blunt now. "And Josephine was the love of my life."

He saw Rebecca flinch slightly at that declaration.

"Or so I thought at the time. She was the most beautiful thing I'd ever seen. She had long black hair that fell well past her hips, and skin as soft as satin. Every man in New York City wanted her. Including me."

His fingers clutched the back of his chair, the knuckles white against the dark mahogany. "Many men had her, I'm sure, but I was the only one who ever offered marriage. You see, Josephine's bloodlines weren't pure. No upstanding gentleman would take her as his wife, but every one of them wanted her as his mistress."

"Caleb," Rebecca whispered when he paused. "You don't have to tell me this."

He shook his head. "No, I do." He concentrated on loosening his grip on the chair back, then raised his eyes to hers. "I want to."

She stood not three feet from him, patiently waiting for him to continue at his own pace. For the first time in his life, he felt that he could talk about Josephine's deception, about the naivete of an adolescent boy.

"She didn't want to marry right away, but she was more than willing to take me to her bed. And then, after about a year of my proposing every month on bended knee, she said yes. My mother was furious, of course, considering Josephine's reputation, but I went ahead with the wedding arrangements."

He shifted uncomfortably, reliving it in his mind, once again seeing the coquettish Josephine with her painted, lying lips.

"About a month before the wedding," he continued, his voice growing harsher, "rumors started circulating that she was keeping company with another much older, much richer man." He gave a sharp bark of laughter. "I didn't believe it, of course. After all, Josephine had agreed to marry me. She was in love with me and would never be interested in another man."

He fixed Rebecca with a hot glare, telling her without words just how gullible he had been.

"That's what I believed. Silly me. Turns out the rumors were true. And I found out in the most convincing of manners. When I walked in on her in bed with the other man."

Rebecca's gasp cut to his heart, but he steeled himself against the emotions her reaction threatened to evoke. He'd be damned if he would let the memories hurt him after so long.

"What did you do?" Rebecca's soft voice questioned.

"I called off the wedding, of course. And I never let another scheming bitch take advantage of me again."

Chapter Sixteen

Caleb regretted the words the moment he saw Rebecca's lower lip begin to tremble. She thought he'd meant her. Considering their rocky relationship, he could have, but he hadn't.

"Rebecca, I—"

"Thank you for telling me, Caleb," she said, cutting him off. "I know it was difficult for you."

Head high, shoulders back, she strode from the room.

"Dammit," he muttered, giving the dining room chair a vicious shove. A perfect ending to a perfect day, he thought. Doubtless he should simply allow them both time to calm their agitation. But he turned and followed the sound of her footsteps on the stairs.

As soon as he opened the bedroom door, Caleb smelled the mixture of cinnamon and roses that always seemed to follow Rebecca. He expected to find her in a huff. Instead, she was curled up quietly in the over-stuffed armchair in one corner of the room.

When she heard the door close and saw Caleb, she jumped to her feet, wiping at the wet paths that coursed down her face. "I can be packed and out of your way by morning," she said, moving toward the wardrobe.

"Rebecca." He grabbed her wrist as she tried to pass by. "I don't want you to pack."

Her eyes widened for a minute before she took a deep breath and locked her jaw. "That's not how it sounded downstairs. You do consider me just another 'scheming bitch,' don't you?" She pulled out of his grasp and headed for her valise.

"Come here," he said, once again taking hold of her arm. He led her back to the armchair and sat down, pulling her onto his lap. She immediately began to struggle.

"Stop it, Rebecca," he said, holding her tight. "I just want to talk to you. When I'm finished, if you still want to leave, I'll let you, all right?" She stopped moving.

"Good."

He settled himself in the chair and arranged her more comfortably on his thighs. He tried to avoid being distracted by her sugar-and-spice scent and the way her breasts rose and fell with her exertion.

It didn't work, Caleb thought, shifting slightly.

"Now," he said, choosing his words carefully, "I apologize for what I said in the dining room." She opened her mouth to argue, but he placed a finger over her lips. "I realize how it must have sounded, but I was talking about Josephine, not you."

"Are you sure?" she asked, sniffing to clear her tear-clogged nose and throat.

"I'm sure," he said. "We've nearly gotten our lives back to normal here. Can't we enjoy it for a while before getting into another argument?"

"What about my mother?" she asked.

He sighed. Her mother. Another distasteful subject.

"Your mother won't be bothering you again," he assured her.

"How can you be so sure?" Her nose crinkled with her frown.

"Because I paid her. Not a thousand dollars, but enough to keep her quiet. And, I admit, I did a little threatening of my own to ensure her cooperation."

A smile as tentative as the dawn appeared on her face. "What did you say?"

Caleb chuckled at her expression. He ran a finger down her cheek. "I told her I didn't take kindly to anyone upsetting my wife."

"And what did she say?"

He looked away for a minute, not sure he wanted her to know. But she asked again, and he knew she wouldn't let it rest. "She said the money would keep her quiet—for now." He felt Rebecca go tense in his arms. "I said it would keep her quiet forever, or else. I said you're my wife, and you're going to stay that way."

Rebecca leaned back and held his gaze. "Really?"

Caleb watched emotions leap across her face. Her eyes were both eager and wary. Did she want to hear that he loved her, that he wanted to be with her until his dying day? Despite those very words seeming to claw at his gut, he could not say them. Especially when he wasn't sure he was capable of meaning them.

"I married you, didn't I?" Rising, he set her aside, loosening the buttons of his shirt as he moved to the dresser. If he didn't do something to put her at a distance, he was sure to take her to bed. And the way he was feeling, words of love and devotion might come pouring out of his mouth whether he meant them or not. He couldn't risk that.

"No matter what our personal preferences are, we took the vows. We're bound by them now." He shrugged out of his shirt and tossed it over the dressing screen.

Suddenly Rebecca was beside him. And when she brushed his chest tentatively with her fingertips, his breath caught.

"What are you doing?" His voice sounded gravelly and strained.

She lifted her face and pressed her lips to his. "Making love to my husband."

Caleb swallowed and stood perfectly still, unsure of this new side of his wife. A sensual, provocative side. As many times as they had been intimate, she had never initiated their lovemaking. Until now. He liked it.

"Come," she said and led him to the bed by hooking one finger in the waistband of his trousers.

He followed willingly. Sitting on the edge of the mattress, he watched as Rebecca turned her back to him to tug off his boots. Her bottom moved from side to side in her struggle, and she gave a groan of frustration when the boot stuck. Caleb smiled and at last uncurled his toes, the sudden release launching her forward.

She whirled around, hands on hips, one boot dangling from her fingers. "You held that on on purpose."

He gave a chuckle. "The view was so appealing, I wanted to make it last."

"Oooh!" She snorted and tossed the boot at his head.

He put up his hands, and the boot bounced harmlessly to the floor. Being so warned, he didn't give her a problem with the next one. She let it drop and turned to face him, slipping the buttons of his pants through their holes. Caleb lifted himself from the mattress enough to allow her to slip the trousers and cotton underwear down his legs. She pushed the clothing over the foot of the bed.

He drew her close, holding her face in his hands, drinking in the sweet warmth of her mouth. Then he pulled back, resting his hands on her shoulders. "Take your dress off," he said. "I want to look at you."

She straightened and began slipping loose the pearl-shaped buttons at the front of her bodice. With excruciating slowness, fabric fell away to reveal lush, flawless flesh.

Caleb closed his eyes for a moment to regain his equilibrium. When he opened them, Rebecca stood in her camisole and drawers, the dress pooled around her feet. White stockings sheathed her long, slim legs. Matching garters with tiny pink rosebuds kept the hosiery in place. She remained there, letting him look his fill, awaiting his next command.

He stared at her, memorizing every angle and curve of her. The way her flowing chestnut hair fell over one shoulder, curling just below her right breast. The smooth planes of her face and slight flare of her hips. She began to fidget, twisting the hem of her camisole between her fingers, too long under his scrutiny.

He held out a hand. "Come here."

She did so, putting her palm in his and balancing on her knees on the bed. Her hair cascading like a silken curtain about them, she began to kiss him. First his mouth, then the lobe of his ear, the bridge of his nose. Back to his lips.

He caught the nape of her neck, bringing her closer. His hand slid down the length of her body to cup the roundness of one buttock. His tongue delved between her lips, and he moaned at the honeyed heat he found there.

Rebecca pulled away, sitting back on her heels. He tried to bring her back, desperate to taste more.

"Wait. Caleb, let me," she said, her voice a bit breathless.

Levering herself from his chest with her hands, she proceeded to kiss his jawline, the dip of his throat, the Adam's apple that bobbed when he swallowed. She giggled, then kissed it again. Then her lips moved lower, caressing his collarbone and chest. Her tongue darted across one taut male nipple, and Caleb shuddered with the shock that ripped through his body.

She smiled wickedly and kissed a path to its twin, teasing, taunting, rolling it into a small pebble of acutely sensitive nerve endings. Then the devastating touch of her mouth moved lower, her hands at his waist. When she came to within inches of his straining manhood, she stopped.

Caleb held his breath, waiting to see what she would do. He half hoped she would continue her sensual journey but he didn't know if he could handle that much pleasure.

She lifted her head. Her eyes were filled with trepidation, and she licked her lips nervously.

He smiled and tugged at her elbow, bringing her body atop his. He reminded himself that Rebecca was not as advanced in sexual prowess as his past women had been. And he was strangely glad.

Caleb kissed the tip of her nose and hugged her tighter until her breasts flattened between them. He spread his hands across her bottom, drawing one leg up to his side. His thumb ran in circles over her thigh as he focused on her mouth.

His need grew to a fever pitch, and he quickly relieved his wife of her camisole and drawers, leaving only the stockings. He enjoyed the feel of the garters and hosiery against his legs and found the sight of her making love with them on erotic. He urged her to straddle him, her long hair tickling his sweat-dampened chest and driving him to the brink of insanity.

She welcomed him with a breathy sigh, sinking down on his full, rigid length. Caleb groaned and held her still for a moment, dragging deep gulps of air into his lungs to keep from reaching a climax too soon. He wanted this to last.

Rebecca whimpered softly and nipped at his chin, her teeth running roughly along his skin.

He bucked upward, gasping at the friction the movement caused. His mind spun away, reality somersaulting into pure sensation.

Rebecca was so hot, so wet and ready for him, and so damn willing. Her body moved above him, her low moans mingling with his. Caleb thought he might die from the desperate, animal release that lingered only moments away. It spiraled through his veins, roiled in his stomach.

He clasped Rebecca close and took her mouth with a frenzied kiss, rolling her beneath him. With a final thrust, Caleb buried his face in the hollow of her neck and felt his life flood into her. Her muscles contracted around him as she came, her cries of ecstasy echoing in his ear.

When he was once again able to move, he tucked his wife's limp body into the curve of his arm, her head resting on his shoulder. Her even breathing soon told him she had drifted into spent silent sleep. Caleb's mouth turned up in a grin, and he closed his eyes, ready to float off to slumber himself.

But sleep didn't come. He lay awake late into the night, wondering what fate sent this amazing, troubling woman his way.

"I talked to the marshal," Caleb said the next morning at the family breakfast table.

Rebecca abruptly raised her head to meet his eyes. He winked to assure her he would not reveal things she would rather leave unsaid in front of Holbrook. She looked down at her scrambled eggs and tried not to blush.

"He said he'd go to your place and take a look, but he hadn't heard any commotion over that way. He'll keep an eye out."

"Thank you."

Caleb nodded, swallowing a gulp of coffee. "Probably just some dumb, rough types looking for something to do after a couple of drinks at the Dog Tick, and your cabin happened to be empty."

In truth, she hadn't given her house much thought, not when there had been more important things to worry about. But Caleb had assured her that her mother was gone, and for now, at least, her reputation was safe, and that was what mattered.

"There was a young girl in town yesterday inquiring about work. I told her we needed a housekeeper and cook. She ought to be out sometime within the next few days." Caleb pushed back his chair and finished the last of his coffee. "You and Megan can interview her and decide whether or not she gets hired. It's up to you. You know what we need better than I do."

"Can I go into town with you this morning, Caleb?" Megan dabbed the corners of her mouth with her napkin and began to stand. "I want to get a few things at the mercantile."

"I can pick them up for you, if you'd like."

"No. I'd much rather go myself. You'll be all right by yourself, won't you, Rebecca?"

She gave a little laugh. "I will as long as these dirty dishes don't decide to band together and rebel."

Caleb put his hands on her shoulders from behind while he kissed her cheek and whispered, "I'll be home early tonight."

She ducked her head in embarrassment, glad that Megan and Holbrook had already left the room. A grin spread across his face as he sauntered out. She was beginning to suspect that Caleb enjoyed making her blush. He seemed to do it often enough.

As the lumbering sound of the buckboard began to fade in the distance, Rebecca cleared the table and put a pot of water on the stove to boil. While she waited, she decided to go through her sewing basket. The Wednesday Group would be stopping by tomorrow, and she might need more supplies to fill their orders. If so, she should have sent a list with Megan, but it was too late for that. Perhaps Caleb would take her back to town tonight if need be.

Unless he had another idea of how to spend the evening hours. Her blood heated at the very thought. She buried her face in the patch of soft, cool satin in her hands and waited for the uncontrollable leap of passion to die down.

"That bastard! First he fucks her, then he marries her."

Sabrina Leslie paced back and forth across the dirty cabin. Mud, dust, and mouse droppings covered the floor, discoloring the hem of her pink taffeta gown. She gave no notice to the conditions around her, her mind too set on revenge.

"Word is, she's got him wrapped around her little finger. The whole town's talkin' about the rings he bought her. Most expensive set they had."

Sabrina stopped and fixed her gaze on the man speaking. He was leaning back on two legs of his chair, a big chaw of tobacco bulging his lower lip. He moved his head only a fraction of an inch to spit and didn't seem to notice the long line of saliva dripping down his chin.

She reminded herself that she needed to keep him around only until Rebecca Adams was good and dead. Then she would be back in Caleb's arms, able to have the finest of everything.

No longer would she have to reside in this hovel. No more beans and bacon for breakfast, lunch, and dinner. Soon Rebecca would be gone, and she could once again seduce Caleb into her bed.

She, not that mousy Rebecca, deserved to be taken care of by such a prestigious, wealthy man. Not to mention such an attractive, virile one, perhaps the best lover she'd ever had.

True, she hated Leavenworth. Kansas was swelteringly hot, especially at the end of August. And there was nothing here, only dust and heat and vulgar cowhands. She would have to convince Caleb to go back to New York City, ill father or no. She couldn't possibly survive out here much longer.

A bead of sweat ran between her breasts, adding to her discomfort. She tugged at her bodice and ran a hand over the pile of tangled hair atop her head. There wasn't even a mirror in this hellhole, so she couldn't curl and arrange her tresses properly. She had to take Bart's word that the walnut coloring hadn't begun to wash out.

With her light blond hair now as black as coal and her usual style of makeup redone, nobody would ever suspect that she was still in town, simply in hiding. She'd even been brave enough to walk down the street a few afternoons ago, and no one had recognized her. Oh, she'd gotten a dozen lustful looks from the men—had even considered ducking behind a building with one of them for a few gold pieces—but they hadn't actually known she was Sabrina Leslie from New York City. Next week she would go to the boarding house and rent a room. That way she would be better able to keep an ear bent to the local gossip. And it would get her off Bart's flea-ridden bedroll onto a real mattress.

A real bed. A clean room. Oh, what she wouldn't do for those things. The thought made her groan aloud.

The front legs of Bart's chair hit the floor with a thump. He looked at her with what passed for a smile on his lips, brown tobacco juice soaking his teeth. "You wantin' somethin' over there, honey? 'Cause old Bart here would be happy to give it to you."

Sabrina almost snapped. She nearly told him that she didn't want his filthy, callused hands on her body, didn't want the stench of his breath stinging her eyes and nostrils. But if she did that, he would never help her. And it was imperative that she have someone to do her dirty work for her.

Bart wrapped his arms around her and pulled her close. She could feel his hardness pressing against her, straining against the confines of his trousers. She turned her head away from his seeking mouth, still filled with chaw.

"Wait. You have to promise to do something for me."

"Oh, I'm gonna do somethin' for ya, honey."

"I want you to get rid of her."

"Aw, I already got ya your damn information."

"But I want you to get rid of her." Sabrina ran a long, red fingernail down his unshaved cheek, speaking in a caressing tone. "She has to be gone, Bart. And when she is, I'll make it worth your while." She moaned in his ear, long and breathless. "It will be so good. So good."

Bart swore and lowered her to the hard plank floor, pushing her skirt up with one hand, fumbling to open his pants with the other. His throbbing length popped free, and he held it for a moment, still trying to get through the layers of her gown.

"Promise me," Sabrina cried, frenzy and desperation beginning to pulsate through her body. Now she wanted it, too. But Bart had to promise first. "Caleb and his father will be at work, Rebecca will be at home. You can go there and kill her. Kill her, Bart. Kill her!"

"Kill her," Bart repeated mindlessly, driving into her, his movements fast and furious.

"Promise me!" Sabrina screamed, the waves of orgasm washing over her.

Bart's thrusts became even more hurried, his mouth dripping discolored saliva. His breathing was quick, but he managed one word before stiffening and spilling inside her. "Promise."

Chapter Seventeen

When no one showed up at five o'clock for dinner, Rebecca began taking peeks out the front window between stitches in a seam of Mary Archer's dress. By seven she was pacing the length of the parlor and going out on the porch every few minutes to search the horizon for some sign of Caleb. And at nine, she went for her coat, ready to ride into town and get the marshal.

She had just fumbled with the first button when she heard an approaching wagon in the distance. Reaching for a lantern, she ran to the porch and held the light high over her head. For a long time she saw nothing, but then the faint outline of a buckboard came into view.

She held her breath until she could see Caleb's form clearly on the seat. Holbrook had the reins, though. And where was Megan? It was unusual for her not to be kneeling in the back, chattering away.

Rebecca hung the lantern from a hook on one of the porch supports and ran down into the yard. She threw open the gate and waited until Holbrook brought the wagon to a halt beside her.

Caleb turned and leapt awkwardly to the ground. That was when she noticed the thick white bandage around his wrist.

"What happened? And where's Megan?" she asked, worriedly clutching the side of the buckboard. "Oh, my God."

Megan lay in the back, wrapped like a baby in layers of blankets and quilts. A wide band of gauze was wound around her head. Even in the darkness, Rebecca could see the ghostly pallor of her face.

"What happened?" she asked again.

Caleb dropped the tailgate and climbed up. He lifted Megan gently in his arms and hopped back down to the ground. "We had a little trouble on the way into town this morning."

A million questions swirled through Rebecca's brain, but she knew Caleb would tell her the whole story in due time. The most important thing was to get Megan inside.

She followed Caleb to Megan's room and helped him tuck his sister safely into bed. She touched the back of her hand to the girl's forehead, glad to feel no sign of fever. She still had no idea what had occurred or what condition Megan was really in. Finally Caleb took her arm and guided her downstairs.

Holbrook sat behind his desk in the study, a glass of brandy in his hand. His skin seemed whiter than usual, and his hands shook.

The clink of glass against glass was the only sound in the room as Caleb poured himself a drink. Rebecca noticed that he, too, was shaking.

Her stomach clenched. Caleb was a strong man who could remain as unemotional as a plaster statue even in the direst of circumstances. Seeing him like this, she knew that whatever had happened must have been very serious.

"Will you please tell me what happened now?" she insisted.

"Megan was shot."

Rebecca's heart stopped. Her mouth fell open, and she staggered a few steps. A chair bumped the back of her knees, and she dropped into it, glad to have something to support her.

Caleb tossed back his brandy and poured another. "About two miles outside of town. We heard a crack, and the horses went wild."

"We were all thrown," Holbrook added.

"It took me a few minutes to realize Megan wasn't up and brushing herself off. Then I saw the blood. It was running down her face, soaking the front of her dress. I thought for sure she was dead."

Rebecca noticed the lines of worry and fatigue around her husband's eyes. She wanted to wrap her arms around him and comfort him, but she couldn't seem to move. Shock still raced through her veins.

"Turns out the blood was from her arm, not her chest," Holbrook clarified.

"But her head . . ."

Caleb nodded. "The bullet grazed her above the temple. If she hadn't put her arm up to shade her eyes from the glare of the sun . . ."

His words tapered off, and Rebecca saw a muscle in his jaw convulse. "If her arm hadn't been there, Megan could have been killed. As it is, the doctor says she has to be watched for a few days to make sure the injury didn't do more damage than we think."

Caleb swallowed, and Rebecca thought he might be about to cry. Instead, he chuckled. "Boy, when she woke up in Doc Meade's office, she was fit to be tied. She nearly brought down the roof, yelling for the marshal to catch the weasely bastard who shot her."

Holbrook laughed, too, and Rebecca's terror began to wane.

"She's exhausted now, though, poor girl." Holbrook stood and came around his desk. "And I'd best be getting to bed, too. Wake me if there's any change."

Caleb nodded to his father and gulped down another three fingers of the strongest liquor in the house.

When they were alone, Rebecca went to his side and squeezed his arm. His fingers were white against the glass in his hand. She wrapped her arms around his waist and laid her cheek on his back.

"She'll be all right, Caleb. Otherwise Doc Meade wouldn't have let you bring her home."

His body remained rigid, every muscle tense. She felt the uneven rhythm of his breathing and knew it echoed the erratic beat of his heart.

"She could have died," he said. The words were low and choked.

"But she didn't." She turned him to face her. The brown of his eyes shimmered with a mist of unshed tears. "Caleb, she's going to be fine. I know she is."

"Sure she can be a pain," he said, his voice strained and ragged, "but she's my sister, and I love her. God, Rebecca, I don't know what I'd do if I lost her."

His arms closed around her like a vise, and her toes barely touched the floor.

She kissed his cheek and ran her fingers through the hair at the back of his neck. "You won't lose her. She's going to be fine."

She whispered words of comfort, anything she could think of that might relieve his tortured mind. She ran her hands over his back and hugged his neck. His grip never loosened.

They stood in the middle of the study, holding tight to each other, until the oil lamps burned low and cast them into darkness. Then they slowly made their way upstairs, arm in arm, and held each other through the rest of the night.

* * *

Rebecca pushed open the door with her hip. She turned around, ready to deposit the large serving tray on the trunk at the foot of the bed, when she spotted Megan trying to escape.

"You get back in that bed this instant."

Megan looked sheepish and tucked her dangling leg back under the covers. "I feel fine," she whined.

"The doctor said you needed rest. And Caleb insists you stay in bed for at least another day."

Megan punched the mattress and gave a tortured sigh. "I wish Caleb had conked his head when he fell out of the wagon. Then he would have to stay in bed, too."

Rebecca handed her a glass of milk and plate of buttered toast. "If it will make you feel better, I can tell you that Caleb's wrist is giving him no end of trouble. He can't even lift a cup of coffee without filling the room with expletives."

"Good." Megan smiled and took a sip of milk. "Have they found the person yet who tried to kill us?"

Rebecca's muscles tensed at the blunt question. She still hadn't quite recovered from the idea that someone might actually want to do Megan or one of the other Adamses harm.

"Not yet. The marshal really doesn't have much to go on. But he's keeping his ears open in case someone comes into town bragging about the incident."

Megan snorted. "Not bloody likely."

Rebecca nodded in agreement.

"Can't I please get up?" Megan pleaded. "I'm going to become permanently attached to this mattress if I don't walk around soon. My bottom is already numb."

"No." Rebecca shook her head. "But I do have a bit of a surprise for you."

Megan sat up, her face lighting with anticipation.

Rebecca reached under the serving tray. "Caleb told me to bring these for you. But you have to hide them from your father."

"Oh." She clutched the flimsy paper magazines to her chest. "I can't wait to read them. The heroes are so wonderful."

"Caleb thought you'd enjoy them." Rebecca picked up the tray and went to the door. "Now be sure to finish your breakfast."

Megan nodded, but Rebecca knew she was already caught up in her newest romantic adventure. She smiled and made her way downstairs.

Caleb had decided not to go to work, leaving Holbrook alone at the Express. She filled a cup with coffee and took it to him in the study.

He looked up from the papers on the desk. "How is she?"

"Bored and impatient, as usual. She was half out of bed when I walked in."

"If I have to sit on her, that girl is going to stay in bed."

"Caleb, the doctor examined her yesterday and said she was just fine. You're the one making her rest an extra day."

"What if she just thinks she feels all right? The minute she takes a step, she could fall flat on her face."

Rebecca laughed. "I hardly think so. And it's not as if she's threatening to race you to town. She just wants to get dressed and maybe have dinner with the family for a change."

He took a sip of steaming black coffee. His brows knit together, and he asked, "Do you think she's well enough for that?"

"I think she's going to jump out the window if you don't let her move around a bit."

"All right. But keep an eye on her. If she looks pale or sways on her feet or—"

"Caleb!" She crossed her arms over her chest and glared at him.

"All right, all right." He waved his hands in surrender.

"Tell her she can come down for supper. But it's right back to bed after that."

Rebecca dropped into the chair behind her and leaned back, relaxed now in this male environment. "Have you heard anything yet from Marshal Thompson?"

He shook his head. "They're never going to catch the bastard."

"Who would want to hurt Megan? She's a sweet, innocent young girl. Besides, she's only been here for three months, and she seldom even goes into town. Who could possibly hate her enough to shoot at her?"

"I don't know. The more I think about it, the more I wonder if they might have hit Megan by accident."

She straightened in the chair, leaning forward a bit. "What do you mean?"

"I think the bullet was meant for me. Or Dad."

"You? Why would anyone want to hurt you or your father?"

"I don't know. Dad never angered anyone but Mother. It's much more likely that I offended someone."

"That's true enough," Rebecca said teasingly. "I've considered shooting you myself." Then she gasped, realizing that she had indeed had the opportunity to sneak out of the house and try to kill him and wondering if he, with his untrusting heart, might suspect that.

Caleb chuckled. "Don't look so worried. I know you've damned my worthless hide more than a few times. I hardly think you were the one to ambush us, however." He took another drink and ran his fingers through his uncombed hair. "Even if you were angry enough to hurt me—and had the guts to do it—you'd never endanger Dad or Megan."

Rebecca was glad he trusted her at least that much.

"Besides," he continued, "you'd choose something much more appropriate. Perhaps you'd put a pillow over my face and leave me dead in my own bed."

"Hmph." She turned her face and pretended to be preoccupied with the sunlight glinting off the row of finely etched crystal decanters.

Caleb rose and came around the desk, pulling her up from her chair. "Now, if you would be so kind as to tell Megan she will be expected for dinner, I think I'll go into town and help my father. I'm feeling much better than I did this morning."

And with that he leaned over and kissed Rebecca for so long that her knees grew weak, and she was glad of the chair beneath her.

With her head cocked to one side, Sabrina Leslie pretended to be studying a display of fabrics near the door of the mercantile. The best place to get information, she'd learned, was at the general store. And she couldn't wait to hear about the discovery of Rebecca's mutilated body.

Bart was supposed to have done the deed yesterday. She could almost picture it in her mind. Rebecca alone in that big, fancy house. Bart sneaking up from behind and putting a knife to her throat. Making her suffer before delivering the final, deadly blow.

The image made Sabrina draw a sharp breath. The thought aroused her almost unbearably, and she clenched her thighs together. As soon as she heard today's gossip, she would have to visit Bart. He wasn't her first choice, but he was the easiest to find. And until she had Caleb back, he would have to do.

Inside the store, the ladies gathered. Outside, the town's oldest male residents sat on a worn bench to discuss the latest happenings. While the women whispered behind their hands, too polite to spread rumors outright, the men quite loudly passed the time jawing. So rather than risk trying to infiltrate the tight knot of ladies at the back of the store, Sabrina preferred to listen to the tall tales out front.

A puff of cherry-wood tobacco filtered in through the

open double doors. Sabrina fought not to cough, fearing it would attract attention to herself and her eavesdropping.

"Poor girl," one of the old timers was saying.

"Yup. I'm surprised Caleb hasn't already formed a posse to go after the bastard. Leastwise, he was threatenin' to do it yesterday."

"Poor, poor Holbrook," a lady at the back of the room said in a loud, pitying voice. "First he comes down with that dreadfully mysterious cough, and now this. The Lord is surely testing him."

Sabrina gritted her teeth, struggling to listen to the outside conversation, yet wanting to hear the inside one as well.

"String 'im up, that's what I'd do to the man who hurt my daughter."

Daughter? Sabrina frowned. She didn't know Rebecca had a father in Leavenworth, or any family at all. She was almost sure she'd heard that Rebecca was an orphan.

Oh, well, she thought, mentally shaking away the unease that skittered down her spine. As long as Rebecca was good and dead, she didn't care if the devil himself decided to reap revenge; they would never trace the shooting back to her. Even if Bart somehow got caught, who cared? Surely no one would take such a ruffian's word over that of a gentle woman like herself. As far as she was concerned, if Bart swung for the crime, the world would be rid of one more mean, filthy beast.

"Who would want to hurt sweet young Megan, though? The girl hasn't been in town long enough to make enemies."

Megan? Why were they talking about Caleb's *sister?* Sabrina held her breath, waiting to hear more.

"Doc says she'll be okay, though. The bullet only grazed her."

Bullet? No, no. Bart was to have cut Rebecca, sliced her to ribbons.

"A few days of rest and she'll be right as rain. And Rebecca will take good care of her. Sweet girl, Rebecca. Glad Caleb was smart enough to marry her. There'll be wee ones crawling around that place before you know it."

Sabrina's fury boiled low in her belly. A snarl escaped her as she ran from the mercantile, oblivious to the pyramid of tinned goods she knocked over on her way out.

Less than half an hour later, Sabrina burst into Bart's shack and slammed the door behind her. She stood with hands on hips, her chest heaving. It took a moment for her eyes to adjust to the dimness of the room.

Bart balanced on two legs of his chair, a game of solitaire spread out in front of him on the table.

"You worthless son of a bitch!" Sabrina screamed and sent the cards flying in every direction. "Can't you do anything right?"

Bart was on his feet in less than a second. He pressed Sabrina back against the door and glared down at her with cold gray eyes. He turned his head to the side and spat a stream of brown tobacco juice across the floor.

"I did what you wanted, honey. I killed the bitch."

"No, you didn't, you stupid bastard." She put her hands to his chest and pushed him away. "The bullet only grazed the girl. And you didn't even shoot the right one!" She pummeled his shoulders and face with her fists.

Bart grabbed her wrists, but she only kicked him instead. He pressed her to the floor and covered her with the weight of his body.

Sabrina struggled. "You were supposed to go to the house. She was there. You were supposed to go to the house and kill Rebecca." Tears of frustration filled her eyes. "Beat her, rape her, do whatever you liked, but she

221

was supposed to be dead!" Finally she closed her eyes and went limp.

Bart moved to the side and got to his feet, leaving her on the floor and going back to his chair. "I was on my way through the woods to the house when I saw the wagon leavin' it. Two men and a woman. How was I s'posed to know it weren't the right one? You didn't never tell me there was two females livin' there."

Because I didn't know, Sabrina thought, chastising herself for sending Bart to get facts rather than finding things out on her own. She had known Caleb's sister had come to Leavenworth from New York, but she'd also remembered that Caleb had wanted to send her back. How was she supposed to know the little baggage was still here?

You were too caught up in learning about Rebecca, her mind chided. *You should have paid more attention. You should have found out every detail about the Adams family—their relatives, their routine, their likes and dislikes. But you were too eager to be rid of Rebecca. From now on, you must be more careful.*

Yes, she had to be more careful.

Sabrina glanced at Bart, who was busy gathering up the scattered deck of cards. He would never be able to help her. He acted without thinking, which could get her in trouble.

No, she had to find another way to murder Rebecca. The shooting had attracted too much attention. She needed something more subtle. But what?

She shook her head. No hurry. It would come to her. And when it did, it would be perfect.

But first, she had to convince Bart to leave town. She couldn't trust him to keep his mouth shut or not be a bother to her. She dug into the bodice of her gown and pulled out a fairly thick fold of bills. She set it on the table in front of him.

"I want you to go as far away as this will take you."

"Why, honey?" he asked, eyeing the money and then her breasts. "You gettin' tired of me already?"

"Of course not, darling. Things are getting too dangerous here. I heard some men in town talking about forming a posse and hunting down the man who shot Megan Adams. They'll find you, Bart, and they'll hurt you. The Adams family is very rich and important; they aren't going to let something like this pass. It's best for you to leave."

"What're you gonna do?"

"I'm staying here. No one has recognized me yet, so I'm still safe. Oh, darling," Sabrina cried, throwing herself against a startled Bart, "you must leave. I couldn't bear it if they were to catch you."

"You that stuck on me, huh?" Bart asked, squeezing her buttocks.

Sabrina swallowed and forced herself to smile. "Oh, yes."

"Then I'll go," he said and tucked the bills into his vest pocket.

Sabrina sighed with relief and started to straighten up.

"Not so fast there, honey. I'll go, but not 'fore I get another roll outta ya." He winked. "Somethin' ta remember ya by."

Chapter Eighteen

"Would you like thum more tea, ma'am?"

"Yes, please, Bessie." Rebecca swallowed the last drops of tepid tea and held out her cup for more.

She smiled at Bess, thinking the new girl they had hired to cook and clean was working out wonderfully. She had been wary at the beginning, realizing Bess was below average in intelligence. And for the first two days everyone thought her name was Bethie until they figured out that it only sounded that way because of her lisp. Bessie had finally, painstakingly, written her name for them in big, childlike letters.

Rebecca liked Bessie. She was a bit slow and sometimes had to be instructed several times before doing a task correctly, but she was more than eager to please and beamed when given even the tiniest word of praise.

Rebecca had taken time out the past few days to sit down and help Bessie better learn her numbers and letters. And Megan simply adored the girl. She had taken Bessie outside to gather flowers or investigate animal tracks in the woods, causing meals to be late on more than one occasion.

The fact was, with Bessie, Rebecca often found herself doing more work than she had when there was no housekeeper about. But she truly enjoyed having Bessie around and was willing to give a new definition to the term "hired help."

"Anything elth?"

"No, thank you, Bessie. I'm expecting some visitors soon. When they arrive, will you please bring them in here?"

Bessie's eyebrows drew together in confusion.

"When the women come to the door," she explained slowly, "bring them in here to me."

Bessie smiled brightly and nodded.

Rebecca smiled back, wondering if Bessie had really understood her. No matter. She or Megan could answer the door if Bessie forgot.

Within a quarter hour, the Wednesday Group piled into the parlor, Anabelle Archer most unhappily in tow. Her mother gave her a stern look and pointed to a chair in the corner. The young girl stomped over and dropped into the seat to sulk.

Rebecca welcomed them all, and Bessie stood in the doorway, bobbing up and down merrily because she'd done well at what she was told.

"Very good, Bessie. Thank you," Rebecca said. Bessie bobbed some more. "Would you please bring the ladies some tea now?"

"Yeth, ma'am." She nodded and turned toward the kitchen.

After serving the group of women steaming cups of Rebecca's special cinnamon tea, Bessie ran off to find Megan. Rebecca wondered if the girl would remember to put the roast in the oven for dinner and then made a mental note to check within the hour.

"You're such a dear to take in that young lady," Thelma Wilkes commented. "Octavia would be proud of you. That poor thing has been wandering around town

225

for a week now. I felt so sorry for her, I started feeding her dinner out back of the hotel kitchen."

"She's quite sweet," Rebecca said.

"Oh, I'm sure," Hariette agreed. "A mite slow, but an angel."

"How is she doing here? Is she helpful?"

Rebecca chuckled. "At times, she's a godsend. At others, I find myself cleaning up after her."

"Get used to it," Mary said, cocking her head at Anabelle. "It will prepare you for motherhood."

The room filled with the tinkle of knowing feminine laughter.

Rebecca glanced at Anabelle and felt nearly frozen by the icy daggers being cast in her direction.

"Don't mind her," Mary said, patting Rebecca's hand. "She's acting spoiled, and you know very well why. She's been pouting like this for months. I tell you, I can hardly stand it. Her pa and I are about ready to send her off to boarding school."

Rebecca noticed the girl's eyes narrow at that statement, but they both knew full well that Mr. and Mrs. Archer would do no such thing.

"My, my, Rebecca!" Hariette squealed, pulling her off the settee to her feet. "You're filling out beautifully. I knew you and Caleb would start your very own brood soon enough."

Rebecca placed a hand on her belly, turning away in embarrassment. She certainly had gotten larger of late. It now looked as if she was hiding a small throw pillow beneath her skirt and blouse. She only hoped no one was counting back to the time of her wedding. She would surely melt into the hardwood floor if someone accused her of being with child before the nuptials.

Seeing the brilliant smiles on the ladies' faces, she breathed a sigh of relief, deciding they weren't going to say anything, even if they did suspect.

She returned to her spot on the sofa and took up a

day dress one of the women had brought. She put on her spectacles and tried to determine what work would need to be done.

Thelma quickly explained that the hem needed to be lengthened, but there was no hurry. Hariette ordered a calico bonnet, and Mary asked Rebecca to make a set of embroidered handkerchiefs for Anabelle, with her initials, of course.

With all that settled, the ladies seemed much more interested in hearing about Rebecca's life.

"Have you and Caleb discussed names for the little tyke yet?"

"No, not—"

"Oh, you must. You have to have them ready. One for a boy and one for a girl."

"Then you simply use whichever applies."

"Well—" she tried again.

"I always preferred names from the Gospel," Hariette said. "Simon, Andrew, James, John, Philip, Bartholomew, Thomas, Matthew, Thaddeus."

"Or you could use old family names. I'm sure Holbrook would be happy to tell you about Caleb's ancestors."

"Yes, well. Caleb and I haven't discussed it yet, but I'm sure we will before long," Rebecca said. In truth, she didn't know how her husband truly felt about the child. He didn't seem averse to becoming a father, but he didn't seem overly excited, either.

With her increasing girth, she was beginning to wonder if Caleb even found her desirable. She hadn't missed the fact that he now turned down the light each night before climbing into bed with her. Nor did it escape her attention that he seemed to be staying in town longer and longer of late.

Suddenly, Rebecca was overwhelmed by insecurities. What if Caleb found her body repulsive? What if he felt trapped, having a wife and a baby on the way? What if

. . . dear God, what if he'd taken to visiting the Dog Tick for more than a drink? Or what if he was keeping another mistress at the hotel? He'd done it with Sabrina Leslie, so Rebecca shouldn't be foolish enough to put it past him.

No, Caleb couldn't have a mistress staying at the Wilkes Hotel. If he did, Thelma would certainly have informed her of her husband's licentious behavior by now. And none of the ladies would be bubbling with happiness over her marriage and pregnancy.

Her muscles relaxed, and she forced herself to listen as the Wednesday Group suggested more baby names. Still, she couldn't dismiss the idea of Caleb's infidelity. It was more than plausible; it was distinctly possible.

Oh, why had she ever allowed herself to get into this blasted situation? She had been much more content living in her tiny cabin, sewing her fingers raw for just enough money to get by. Now she lived in a beautiful house, didn't have to do a lick of work if she didn't want to, and she was miserable.

The baby chose that exact moment to tickle the inside of her womb, and she smiled. He'd been doing that a lot lately, reminding her that things weren't as terrible as they sometimes seemed. She couldn't feel the movements from the outside yet, but inside it felt as though he was doing flip-flops.

"Yes, yes, she likes that idea."

Hariette clapped her hands together in delight, and Rebecca realized they thought she was smiling at one of their names.

"What *is* Caleb's middle name, by the way?"

"Caleb's middle name?" Rebecca searched her brain for a moment. "Zachariah, I believe." Yes, she distinctly remembered a large, fancy Z on the hotel register the long-ago night she'd gone to collect her money. Her cheeks heated a bit at the memory of what had happened there. And when they had wed in such haste as a result,

Reverend Patterson had surely said Zachariah.

"Oh, yes, I knew that," Thelma chimed in. "Zachariah is a perfectly wonderful name for a little boy."

"Zachariah Adams. Hmm. Yes, I like it," Mary said.

"And it's a Gospel name," Hariette put in. "I like it very much, indeed."

Rebecca held back a chuckle, amused by the decision the Wednesday Group had made. Of course, if the baby was a boy, and if she and Caleb chose a different name, they would be very cross. Very cross, indeed.

"I hate you."

The harsh whisper came from the corner of the parlor and startled Rebecca. Everyone turned to stare at Anabelle Archer, who stood panting, her face beet red, the pulse at her throat pounding fiercely.

"Anabelle! Sit down!" Mary ordered.

But the girl didn't heed her mother's words. "I was going to marry Caleb when I got old enough, and you stole him from me. You seduced him away from me and ruined my life, and I hate you for it." Anabelle ran out of the house, leaving a roomful of gaping, astonished women.

Rebecca felt a viselike grip around her hand and looked to see Mary Archer's face streaked with tears. "I'm so sorry," she said, her voice quiet and ragged. "I'm so sorry she said those things. She didn't mean it, I'm sure."

Rebecca nodded but knew that in her sixteen-year-old mind, Anabelle truly felt that Rebecca had ruined her life.

Mary rose somewhat unsteadily and made her way to the door. The other ladies soon followed. Rebecca hoped the incident would blow over quickly and things could return to normal before their next visit. She wished each visitor a fond farewell.

"What was that all about?" Megan said, coming up

behind her. "I heard screaming and saw Anabelle run across the yard."

"She's upset with me," Rebecca said vaguely.

"Very upset, I'd say. Why?"

"She's in love with Caleb. And she thinks I stole him from her."

"Oh, posh." Megan waved away such a notion. "Caleb couldn't stand that clinging vine. He practically had to dig a hole in the ground to get away from her at the Harvest Festival."

Rebecca closed the front door and leaned against it, feeling tired all of a sudden. "I didn't say Caleb was in love with her," she clarified. "I said Anabelle was in love with him. There's quite a difference. She seems to believe that I've done an admirable job of destroying her life."

"Oh, she'll recover," Megan said, totally unbothered. She took Rebecca's arm. "Come into the kitchen. I'm teaching Bessie to make biscuits. She'll love for you to watch."

Rebecca lay awake in bed late that evening, feigning sleep when she heard the bedroom door squeak open. She had decided to stay awake until Caleb got home. She saw no reason not to get to the bottom of his late nights.

The minute the door closed, albeit silently, she bolted upright. She sat there, waiting for him to discover her. She almost chuckled when he did, for he jumped a good three inches off the floor.

"What are you doing up?" he asked, shrugging out of his suit coat.

"Waiting for you."

"Oh?" His eyes twinkled in the low lamplight. "Eager for me, are you?"

She would have flushed at his teasing if her mind had

not been burning with angering images. "Hardly," she said, her voice cold as chipped ice.

His brow furrowed, fingers stilling on the buttons of his shirt as he came forward a step. "Is everything all right? Are you ill?"

"Not at all." She flipped back the covers and set her feet on the floor. "I simply have a question for you."

Caleb continued undressing. "What's that?" he asked.

Rebecca crossed the room and picked up his jacket. She brought it to her nose and took a sniff. Exactly as she'd expected. It smelled of smoke and stale beer. However, she could detect no traces of cheap perfume and so lost some of her ammunition.

"What were you doing at the Dog Tick?"

He shrugged. "Having a drink. What else?"

"Oh, I don't know. I thought maybe you'd been keeping some harlot company." She hurled the piece of clothing at his chest, but he caught it.

And laughed. He actually let out a long, rather loud laugh. "What a vivid imagination you have."

"Perhaps," she said, grinding her teeth. "But then, what is a bride of only three months to think when her husband seems to enjoy the company of drunken cowboys to that of his own wife?"

"Now, Rebecca," Caleb said with a hint of amusement in his voice. "I hardly think I have to answer to you for my every action. I had a few beers before coming home, that's all."

"And I suppose you just happened to have those beers with a tall blonde."

"Yep. Come to think of it, I did."

"Oh!" She threw an arm out, hoping to catch him on the jaw even from nearly three feet away.

Caleb caught her by the wrist and brought her hard against his chest. He held her tight and nibbled on the lobe of her ear. "His name was Charlie."

She froze, letting her head fall back to look up into his soft brown eyes. "What?"

"The tall blonde. His name was Charlie."

"Oh, you . . . you . . ."

"Yes?"

She shook off his arms and backed away from him. "What were you doing there in the first place?" she asked.

"I told you. Having a drink."

"I certainly don't believe you spent the last six hours in a saloon just because you wanted a drink when you have a whole bar of perfectly good liquor down in the study."

Caleb shrugged and gave her his back while he threw his shirt over the dressing screen.

"What is it, Caleb?" she asked. Her eyes filled with tears, and her voice became scratchy. "Do I disgust you so much that you can't bear to look at me in the light of day?"

He turned around, an odd expression on his face. "What the hell are you talking about?"

"Look at me!" Rebecca cried. She could see herself in the dressing mirror and wanted to cry all the more. Where her stomach had once been flat as an iron skillet, there was now a bulge that caused her nightgown to puff out. She more resembled a hot-air balloon than a human being.

"I look as if my bellybutton blew a bubble."

Caleb threw back his head and laughed.

Tears poured down Rebecca's face until she could no longer see the mirror image or her husband through the haze. Caleb was still bent over with laughter when she recovered herself and dried her eyes.

"I'm—" Caleb held his side and wiped the moisture from his cheeks. "I'm sorry."

He chuckled again, which made her strongly doubt the sincerity of his apology.

"I'm sorry. It's just that, well . . ." Another spasm of laughter. "You do sort of look as if your bellybutton blew a bubble."

Her mouth dropped open at his rudeness.

"No, no. Don't start to cry again. That's not a bad thing." Caleb took her hand and drew her over to the bed, patting the mattress for her to lie down. He kicked off his half-gaiters and lay down beside her. He kept his trousers on, open at the waist.

"Now," he said, tucking her head against his shoulder. "What caused all this hysterical female behavior?"

Rebecca stiffened and started to pull away.

"Come back here." He tugged her over and wrapped an arm under her breasts. "Tell me."

"Well, you haven't come home for dinner in more than a week."

"Yes. And?"

"And I'm starting to get fat, so I could understand it if you wanted to spend your time with someone pretty. But everyone thinks we're so happy, and I couldn't bear it if they found out you didn't even want to share my bed anymore."

"I take it that group of old biddies was here today."

"They are not old biddies. They're my friends. And they keep a very close eye on things like this. I would just die if they found out you were paying some woman at the Dog Tick for something you should be getting at home."

"Something I have been getting at home," Caleb said, and he gave her breast a little squeeze.

"Well, yes, but they wouldn't know that. They would see you coming out of the saloon and think you had to relieve yourself of some kind of primal male urges or whatnot."

"Right about now, I have a very distinct male urge to throttle you."

Rebecca raised her eyes and stared at him.

"Well, there are a few other urges I'd like to take care of, but first things first. Number one, I was not relieving my male urges, or anything else. I had a drink or two and played a few hands of cards."

"But—"

Caleb put a finger to her lips. "And I only did that because I was hoping to hear something about the shooting. I thought a few swigs of whiskey might loosen some tongues. But it hasn't in the past week, so I won't bother to go back. I also admit I was keeping an eye out for your mother. But I didn't see her, either, so I trust she left town like she was supposed to.

"Number two. You are not, and never have been, unattractive to me. Okay, so I thought you were a bit mousy the first time I saw you in your shop, but the minute you came charging into the Express office all hellfire and damnation, my body turned hot." He leaned close to her ear. "I haven't cooled down since."

A bolt of excitement ran down her spine. She snuggled closer to his warmth.

"I love how round you're getting. I love falling asleep with my hand on your stomach, knowing our child is resting peacefully inside. So don't ever think you repulse me. Far from it. I can barely keep my hands to myself when you're around."

"You'll come home for dinner from now on?"

"I'll come home for dinner from now on," he said with a nod. "Even if it's not quite cooked all the way through. Maybe you should hire someone to help Bessie."

"I might just do that. And if you do have to stay out late for some reason, you'll tell me, won't you?"

"I promise."

"Good."

"Good," Caleb said, grinning. "Now that that's all settled, how about helping me to relieve some of my primal male urges?"

"What kind of urges do you have?" she asked innocently.

"Well, there's this one, where my wife . . ." His words trailed to a soft whisper in her ear.

"Caleb!"

Chapter Nineteen

"I don't know about this."

Sabrina shifted her feet on the last crooked step leading out of the back of the boarding house. "There's nothing to worry about, Dolores. No real harm will come of it, and no one will find out, I promise."

"But Mrs. Adams is paying me good money. It just don't seem right to be foolin' her this way."

"Listen," Sabrina said sharply. "I hired you first, and I'm giving you half again what they pay you a week. All you have to do is put a little of this in her tea."

"But what if someone sees me? I ain't the only one they got working for them, you know."

Sabrina took a breath to calm her growing irritation. "Yes, I know. But the other one's an idiot, isn't that right?"

"Bessie ain't none too smart, I'll grant you that. Nice gal, she is, though. Loves them folks like they was her own."

"Well, then, if she happens to see you putting this in Rebecca's tea, tell her it's to keep her healthy until the baby is born. She ought to believe you."

"Yes'm. I suppose she would."

"Good. Then there won't be a problem."

"I still don't like it."

"You don't have to like it," Sabrina hissed. "You just have to do it. Now, listen carefully. You sprinkle a good amount of this in the bottom of Rebecca's cup before pouring her tea. *Every time,* do you hear? If you don't do it every time, it won't work."

"Won't she taste it?"

"I hope not. Make sure it isn't bitter before serving it to her."

Dolores's eyes widened, and she took a step back. "I ain't gonna taste it."

"Don't be silly," Sabrina said. "Just a sip won't hurt you a bit. It has to be taken in large doses to have its desired effect. That's why you must put it in *every* cup, *every* day."

The graying woman still didn't look convinced but nodded and took the palm-sized bottle of herbs. "What is it, ma'am? If you don't mind my asking."

"Pennyroyal," Sabrina answered.

She knew the name would mean nothing to the old housekeeper. It had taken her a month to come up with the bud of an idea and even longer to put it into motion. Once she had decided to poison Rebecca, she'd had to find someone to supply her with the herbs. And the best she could do was an old whorehouse remedy for unwanted pregnancies. Pretending to be a woman in trouble, Sabrina had gone to the Dog Tick, crying and pleading with the madam for help. It hadn't been easy, but she'd finally gotten a bottle of pennyroyal out of the stingy bitch. She'd listened carefully to the madam's instructions on how to use the herbs safely, and then she'd come up with her own directions on how to use their full potential to poison Rebecca.

"When you run out," Sabrina told Dolores, "come back to the boarding house, and I'll give you more."

Dolores grabbed the money Sabrina held out to her and disappeared into the night.

Caleb and Holbrook arrived home from work looking for all the world like two little boys who'd just lost their puppy. Holbrook headed straight for his study, but Caleb remained in the hallway with Rebecca. When she inquired about their solemn mood, he handed her an ivory envelope, already torn open at the top.

"This came in the afternoon mail."

She unfolded the enclosed sheet of paper, reading the large, feminine script. The letter was from Caleb and Megan's mother and got straight to the point. She wanted Megan sent back. Now.

"What are you going to do?" Rebecca asked.

He took the letter. "I don't know. I don't think Dad knows, either."

"What's going on?" Megan asked, skipping down the stairs, a bright smile on her face.

Caleb cleared his throat, reluctant to tell Megan of her mother's message. But Rebecca knew they couldn't keep it a secret. She nudged him in the ribs, urging him to show his sister the letter.

He scowled at her but turned over the letter nonetheless. "This came today," he told Megan.

Rebecca watched as the girl read her mother's missive. Her bright smile faded little by little, and her face fell. Until, at the very end, tears ran down her cheeks.

She crumpled the paper in a tight fist. "I won't go back," she said, shaking her head. "I won't." With that, she threw the balled-up letter to the floor and ran to her room.

That was where Rebecca found her a few minutes later. She was lying on her side, clutching a pillow in her arms. The wet lines of tears streaked her cheeks. Rebecca sat on the edge of the bed and stroked her fingers through the damp hair at Megan's temples.

Her eyelashes fluttered a moment before opening. "I don't want to go back to New York, Rebecca."

"I know you don't, sweetie." She didn't know what else to say. She didn't want Megan to leave, either, but she could hardly do anything about it.

"Please don't let them send me back," Megan said, her eyes once again turning liquid with tears.

The plea nearly broke Rebecca's heart. "I don't know what I can do to stop them, Megan."

With a sudden surge of energy, Megan sat up. "You can talk to Papa. He likes you so very much, I'm sure he'd listen to you."

"Megan—"

"And Caleb. You can ask him to help convince Papa. Oh, please, Rebecca. Please help me. I don't want to go back there. I want to stay here with you so I can take care of the baby when it arrives."

Rebecca considered it only a moment before hugging Megan close and promising to do the best she could.

"What do you want me to do, Rebecca?"

"I don't know." She sat on a cushioned stool in front of the dressing mirror, running a brush through her hair. "But you should have seen her, Caleb. She's usually so strong and proud, but those sheets were soaked with tears. I've never seen her so unhappy. Do you really think she'll survive for long in New York?"

"Survive?" he asked incredulously, coming to stand behind her. He put his hands on her shoulders and rubbed a few strands of her silken chestnut hair through his fingers. "She survived the long trip out here—by herself, I might add—without a lick of trouble. You expect me to believe she'll be worse off in a big city with a string of beaus and a gaggle of servants to fulfill her every whim?"

Rebecca set the brush none too gently on the mahogany dresser top and turned to face him. "Oh, Caleb, you don't understand. She'll die there. If your mother insists she go back and live like a caged circus lion, she'll wither and die."

"You're being melodramatic."

"I'm not," she said, going to the bed and tossing back the covers. "She may put on a happy face and prance around like the belle of the ball, but her anger and misery will eat at her from the inside."

"So I'll ask again, what am I supposed to do?"

"You could talk to your father."

"Are you kidding?" Caleb asked with a harsh laugh. "If Dad tells her he wants Megan to stay, Mother will come here herself and drag Megan back bodily."

"Well, I think that if you and your father sit down over a glass of brandy, you'll surely be able to come up with some sort of strategy to win over your mother."

She climbed into bed and pulled the quilt over the mound of her stomach. Caleb soon followed.

"Who could resist two utterly charming Adams men?" she added sweetly.

Caleb propped himself on one elbow and stared down at his wife. "You'll be the death of me, do you know that?"

"I hope not," she said, grinning cheekily. "Then Megan and I would have to deal with our mothers all on our own. And I'm not sure I'd be up to that big a challenge."

"Do you feel all right?"

Rebecca brushed the back of her hand over her damp forehead, closing her eyes against a sudden wave of dizziness. She'd been having the spells for about a week now and wasn't sure what could be causing them. Most likely it was the heat of September rolling into the chill of October. That and the beginning of her sixth month of pregnancy.

"You look a little pale."

She looked up at Caleb. "I'm fine. It's just the heat."

"It's really not that warm," he said, a frown wrinkling his brow.

She forced a smile and nodded in Holbrook's direction. "Have you talked to him yet?"

"Not yet. But I will."

Holbrook sat on the front seat of the surrey, reins gripped severely in his hands.

"Why did you bring your sewing basket?" Megan asked from where she sat beside her father.

Rebecca toed her basket with the tip of her shoe. "I need to buy a length of ribbon to match the fabric Mrs. Pickens brought me, and a bolt of fabric to match the ribbon Mrs. Wilkes brought."

Caleb chuckled. "Sounds like a well-organized group you have there."

"Not very," Rebecca said and then clutched the seat as the surrey hit a deep rut. A wave of nausea swept over her, and she had to bite her lip to keep from crying out.

Caleb grasped her arm and helped her right herself. "All right?"

She nodded, though a flicker of doubt flared in her mind. When the morning sickness had passed after her third month, she hadn't expected it to come back. But from time to time she felt herself become dizzy, and her stomach seemed to roil without provocation.

She had considered telling Caleb but decided against it, thinking the strange illness would go away on its own. Now she wasn't so sure.

They spent a good hour at the mercantile, the men on one side of the store looking at saddles and carpentry tools, the women on the other, trying to decide about sewing supplies. Then they left their purchases in the surrey and walked to the Express office so Caleb could pick up some paperwork.

When they arrived home, just before dusk, Caleb piled

her purchases in the crook of one arm and followed her into the house.

"I talked to my father," he said as they entered the parlor.

"When? While you were deciding which saddle soap to buy?"

He nodded.

"Well, what did he say?" she asked, hope rising in her breast.

"He doesn't want Megan to leave, either. And when I told him how upset she was, that she cried herself to sleep after reading Mother's letter, he said he would take care of it."

"What does that mean?"

"I think he intends to write to Mother and tell her firmly that Megan is staying in Leavenworth a while."

She winced. "Your mother won't like that."

"Hardly," he agreed with a chuckle. "But then, she hasn't liked anything about my father in quite a while. At the very least, this will buy Megan a little more time."

"I hope it works."

Caleb only nodded as he set her packages on the sofa.

"Speaking of your father," she said, "have you noticed that his cough seems to have all but disappeared?" She gave him a knowing glance.

"Now that you mention it, yes. I don't think I've heard him cough in . . . oh, a long time." He looked back at her with a distinct twinkle in his eyes. "You know, I never quite believed he needed me to come here because of his health. He tried awfully hard to convince me that he wanted me to learn the family business before he passed on."

"So how is it that he's suddenly made a full recovery?"

"Oh, I think it has something to do with the fact that I told him I'd be staying in Leavenworth. Indefinitely."

"It's a good thing. He'll need all his strength to deal with your mother."

He laughed. "I think you're right. I'll go unhitch the horses."

As soon as Caleb had left the room, Rebecca's mind turned back to her original concern. *Poor Megan,* she thought. It really would kill her to go back to New York, as surely as a bout of consumption. She could only hope that Megan's mother wouldn't put up too much of a fuss in response to Holbrook's soon-to-be-sent letter.

Rebecca settled on the sofa and reached for the wicker basket. If she started now, she could probably get a basic bodice basted together by dinner.

She lifted the lid and reached in without looking, wrapping her hand around the nearest parcel. Her fingers came in contact with something wet and sticky. And then something . . . fuzzy.

She lowered her eyes and gave a high, piercing scream.

Chapter Twenty

She leapt to her feet and threw the basket as far as she could. It landed beneath one of the windows, and the contents toppled out. Material, ribbon, brown-paper-and-string wrapped packages—and a tiny, blood-spattered animal. Blood covered her fingertips, matted with something else. Small brown bits of fur or feathers.

All of a sudden Caleb burst through the doorway. The rest of the household soon followed.

"What's wrong?" Caleb asked, gasping for breath. He ran to her side and gripped her shoulders. "Are you all right?" His eyes darted to her belly. "Is it the baby?"

She shook her head and opened her mouth to speak, but no words came out. She held her hand up.

"What the hell . . ." He touched the blood on her fingers and smeared it between his own.

"The basket," she managed.

He gave her one last once-over before releasing her and going to where her sewing basket lay dumped on the hardwood floor. He poked at the dead animal, rolling it to figure out just what it was.

"Looks like a bird," he said, finally finding the head with a small yellow blood-covered beak.

"How did it get in your sewing basket?" Megan asked.

"I . . . I don't know." Rebecca felt herself shaking and clamped her teeth together to curb the shivers running through her body.

"Megan," Caleb said, "would you please get a cloth to wash Rebecca's hand? And a cup of tea to calm her nerves."

Megan and Bessie and Dolores all headed for the kitchen without further prodding.

"Is there anything I can do?" Holbrook asked, shifting uncertainly.

"Yes. Would you mind getting rid of that, please?" Caleb tilted his head toward the lifeless bird.

Holbrook quickly stooped and swept everything back into the basket, carrying it out of the room.

Caleb put an arm around Rebecca's waist and helped her to the sofa. He took her hands in his own, heedless of the sticky fluid there. Her face was as white as chalk, her lips tightly pressed together. He could feel the tremors racing through her body, and he pulled her against his chest.

"Are you all right?" he asked. He felt her head move up and down but didn't believe her for a minute.

Megan came into the room with a warm, damp washrag, and he gently wiped Rebecca's fingers, careful to get every spot of blood off. Then he cleaned his own hands and balled up the cloth, sure to fold the dark stains on the inside. He handed it back to his sister, who held it away from her with thumb and forefinger, a frown of distaste drawing down her mouth as she raced toward the kitchen. She returned a moment later with a cup of hurriedly brewed tea in her hands. Caleb took it and urged Rebecca to drink.

She sat up straighter and swallowed the entire serving

before pushing the cup and saucer away. "I'm fine now. Truly."

He could still feel her body shaking and knew she wasn't completely recovered from the shock. But he sat back and held her gaze.

"Do you have any idea how it got in there?" He refrained from actually naming what she'd found.

She shook her head. "It wasn't there when you took the basket out to the carriage."

"Then someone must have thrown it in when we were at the Express," Megan said, eager to help.

But who? That was what Caleb wanted to know. Who would have done something like that to Rebecca? She had never harmed anyone in her life, he was certain. So who would want to hurt her?

Jesus! Caleb thought suddenly. What if the person who had thrown the bird into Rebecca's basket was the same person who had destroyed her house four months ago? What if that person decided to try to hurt Rebecca directly next time?

And what if Megan's accident had nothing at all to do with Megan? Or with him or Holbrook? What if that bullet had been meant for Rebecca?

His heart lurched at the thought. No, surely he was imagining things. Surely all these things were purely coincidental.

"Would you mind leaving us alone for a few minutes?" he said to his family. Their concern was obvious, but reluctantly they shuffled out, closing the doors behind them.

He turned back to Rebecca, trying to think of the best way to broach the subject of who might want to see harm befall her.

He took her hand and began rubbing his thumb in lazy circles over her palm. "Rebecca, I don't want to scare you, but—"

"You think this has something to do with my cabin, don't you?"

Her eyes were wide and tinged with just a hint of fear. "Why would you say that?" he asked, feeling her out.

"Whoever was in my house wanted to hurt me. If not physically, at least emotionally. Otherwise they would have simply stolen my things, perhaps tried to sell them. But this person destroyed everything. They went through every cupboard, every dresser drawer, every nook and cranny of that place."

He nodded in agreement.

"And whoever put that poor baby bird in my sewing basket wanted to hurt me, too. Or at least scare me half to death. They knew the basket was mine and that I would probably be the only one to get into it. I would be the one to find the bird.

"But it doesn't make any sense, Caleb. I don't have any enemies. I've never done anything to make someone mad enough to do this kind of thing. Except . . ."

"Except? Except what?" he urged.

"Well, the other day, Anabelle Archer came with her mother and the others." She hesitated.

"And?"

"She sat in the corner and sulked. I knew she'd been upset when we married, but I didn't think much of it."

"Why would she be upset?" he asked, completely confused.

"Oh, Caleb, surely you knew she was in love with you."

His eyes nearly popped out of his head. "No, I didn't know. I only ever talked to the girl once."

"Yes, but she's sixteen years old. Sixteen-year-old girls fall in love very quickly. And she wanted you to love her back. When she found out about the wedding, she was crushed."

"I still don't see what this has to do with anything."

"Well, Anabelle just sat there sulking the whole time.

I figured her mother had forced her to come and she was pouting because she really didn't want to be here. But when we began talking about the baby, she suddenly blew up. She started screaming that she hated me and that I'd ruined her life."

Rebecca lowered her eyes, a little embarrassed at repeating the story.

"And you didn't see fit to tell me this before now?"

"I didn't take the words to heart, Caleb. My goodness, she's just a distraught young girl, trying to get someone to believe that her feelings are as strong as she claims."

"Do you think she could have had anything to do with the bird?"

"Anabelle? Risk getting blood on her dress? You must be joking."

"It sounds like she was awfully mad. She could be the one who was in your cabin. And she could have gotten someone else to kill the bird and throw it in there."

"I suppose that's possible, but—"

"We'll talk to Anabelle and see what she has to say, but until we get to the bottom of this, I don't want you going out of the house unless I'm with you, all right?"

"Caleb, it was only a dead bird. I—"

"I don't want you going out by yourself, Rebecca. I mean it. What if it's not just some stranger who broke into your house, or some angry teenager who wanted to frighten you with the bird as some kind of sick revenge?" He gave her fingers a light squeeze. "What if the person who did those things is the same person who shot Megan?"

She gasped. "No! That can't be. Why—"

"I've spent months trying to figure out who shot at us. I can't think of anyone. Can you?"

"No, of course not. I can't think of a soul who would want to hurt Megan."

"Right. And I'd like to think that anyone who wanted

to hurt me or my father would do it face-to-face. That leaves you."

"Oh, Caleb, that's ridiculous."

Her words dismissed the possibility, but her brow knit, and he knew the idea frightened her. He wanted her to be afraid. At least enough to listen to him when he told her to keep to the house.

"I don't think so. I think you're in danger, Rebecca, and I don't want to take any chances."

"But why would someone shoot Megan if they were after me?"

"Maybe they thought it was you in the wagon. The sun was bright. Megan had her hand up to shade her eyes. Maybe her face was covered. Or maybe the shooter was too far away and simply assumed it was you. Hell, Rebecca, I don't know."

He got to his feet and went to the window, pulling aside the draperies to look out. "I don't know what the hell is going on or who would want to hurt you."

Turning back to her, he fixed her with a stern glare. "What I do know is that I'm not going to stand by and do nothing while some son of a bitch kills my wife. Do you understand?"

She nodded.

"Good. Then from now on you stay in the house. If you need anything, I'll bring it home from town or take you in for it in the evening."

"All right, but—"

Caleb reached her in three long, purposeful strides and gripped her shoulders, bringing her off the sofa. "No *buts*, dammit. I don't intend to lose you to some lunatic."

Rebecca stared at him, and her heart did a little somersault. His eyes were dark with concern, the lines of his face more pronounced from fear. He'd never said he loved her, but he did seem to care a little.

She smiled and put a hand to his cheek. "I was only going to say that I want you to be careful, too. If there really is someone out there intent on doing harm, he may not be too particular about his victims."

Rebecca shifted her position on the hard pew. Caleb could tell her back was bothering her. If Reverend Patterson didn't soon conclude his sermon, he imagined his wife would curl up and fall asleep. That ought to show the reverend how riveting his sermons were.

He nudged her arm and mouthed the words, "Wake up."

She gave him a dirty look before turning to face the front of the church once again.

After another half hour of fire and brimstone, mixed with pleas to follow the Lord's word to the letter, the reverend finally brought the service to a close and blessed the congregation for another week.

Caleb helped Rebecca stand and tucked her arm through his to lead her out of the church. The procession moved slowly while everyone stopped to shake Reverend Patterson's hand and compliment him on his wise words.

"Do you see the Archers?" Caleb asked above Rebecca's ear.

She looked around for a moment and tilted her head toward where Mary Archer stood talking with Thelma Wilkes. Then she pointed across the churchyard to Anabelle, who was digging at the dirt with the heel of her shoe. They started in her direction.

"Anabelle," Caleb said.

The girl lifted her head. A smile lit her face—until she saw Rebecca at his side. Her smile turned upside down.

"Anabelle," Caleb repeated. "I'd like to speak with you."

He let go of Rebecca's arm and took a step closer to the girl, lowering his voice so only the three of them would be privy to the conversation. "I have a couple of

questions to ask you, Anabelle, and I'd like you to answer me honestly, all right?"

She remained silent.

"I want the truth, Anabelle." His voice was calm but
firm. "Do you know anything about the break-in at Rebecca's cabin?"

She shook her head quickly. Too quickly.

Caleb narrowed his eyes. "All right, then. Do you
know anything about what we found in Rebecca's sewing basket?"

Her eyes grew round, and she began to tremble.

"You put it there, didn't you?" Caleb said grimly.

"I didn't kill it, I swear. It must have fallen out of its
nest or something."

"But you put the bird in there?"

"Yes." Tears began to form in the corners of her eyes.
"I waited until no one was looking, and I threw it in. I
wanted to scare her."

Anabelle's mother had come up behind her daughter,
catching the direction of the conversation.

"What about all the ripped fabrics and broken china
at the cabin?" Caleb asked.

Anabelle finally nodded. "I was so angry," she said,
an edge to her voice. "After you danced with me at the
festival, I thought for sure you liked me a little. And
then you went and married *her*."

"You destroyed my house?" Rebecca asked. "Oh, Anabelle, how could you do such a thing?"

"I'm sorry." Two fat, wet tears rolled down her
cheeks. "I didn't really mean to hurt you, Rebecca. I
didn't even mean to ruin your cabin. I was just mad at
you, and I sneaked in to look around, and I guess . . . I
guess I got carried away."

Mary put a shaking hand on Anabelle's shoulder, her
face flushed with mortification. "How could you do
this?" she whispered harshly.

Anabelle didn't answer. She kept her head down, the

front of her dress becoming wet and splotched with her flood of tears.

"I am so sorry, Rebecca," Mary said, clasping Rebecca's hand. Her own eyes glistened with unshed tears. "I had no idea Anabelle had done those things. I would never have thought her capable. Of course we'll make good on all the damage she's done."

"It's all right, Mary. You're not to blame."

"Yes. Yes, I am. I should have been stricter with her when she was a child. Her father and I have been much too lenient. I should have—"

"There's no sense dwelling on the past, Mary. It's the present I think you should worry about."

"Yes, you're right." She straightened her spine and took a firm hold on her daughter's arm. "We're going home, young lady. And don't think you'll be hearing the end of this any time soon."

Caleb let Mary and Anabelle go, even though doubt niggled at his conscience. Something just didn't add up.

Rebecca turned to him, eyes narrowed. "What is it?" she asked. "You got the answer you were looking for."

He shook his head. "Later" was all he said as he guided her to the surrey.

When they arrived home, they all sat down to a quiet dinner. After the meal, Rebecca pleaded exhaustion and escaped to her room.

Caleb followed her several minutes later. The door clicked closed behind him, and Rebecca raised her head.

"Tired?" he asked.

"A little."

"It's been quite a day."

"What is it, Caleb?" She sat up a bit. "Something's been bothering you all afternoon."

"I don't know," he answered honestly, removing his suit coat and loosening his tie. "I just have a feeling this isn't over yet."

"Anabelle won't be playing any more horrible tricks,

that's for sure," she said, lying back once again. "I'd be surprised if Mary didn't cane her to within an inch of her life."

Caleb couldn't argue with that. Mary Archer had been furious. But something still didn't add up.

"Okay," he said. "So Anabelle put the dead bird in your basket and tore your house apart. But I have a hard time believing she would want revenge badly enough to shoot at someone."

"Caleb," Rebecca said with a sigh. "Anabelle admitted that she's responsible for the other events, no one has tried again to shoot anyone, and that's good enough for me. Maybe what happened to Megan was an accident. Maybe someone was hunting too close to the road, and a bullet went wild."

"Is that what you think?" he asked, a hard edge to his voice.

"I don't know," she admitted, plumping the pillow beneath her head. "But I think that if someone wanted to hurt me—or Megan, or you, or anyone else—they would be a little more forward about it. It's been months since Megan was shot. Do you really think that if the bullet was meant to kill her—or me, as you suspect— the person would let me live this much longer without trying something else?"

She snuggled farther under the bedspread and covered a yawn with the back of her hand. "I think you're reading more into it than there is. Can't we just forget about it?"

Caleb tossed his boots aside and came to the bed, staying above the covers. "You really think that's all there is to it, hm?"

"Mm-hmm."

Her eyelashes fluttered and grew heavy.

"All right," he said quietly. "Then I'll let it go. But if anything else happens . . ." His words trailed off, and he rolled to his side, wrapping an arm around Rebecca. He held her tightly until sleep claimed his worried mind.

Chapter Twenty-one

"I have good news," Caleb said with a smile, closing the bedroom door behind him.

Rebecca sat up, stretching after her long afternoon nap.

"Mother has agreed to let Megan stay."

Her eyes widened. To her knowledge, Holbrook had sent his letter only a little over a week ago. "You heard back from her already? So soon?" she asked, holding the covers over her breasts, though she still wore her camisole and stockings.

He nodded, loosening his black string tie and the top button of his shirt. "We got a wire from New York this morning."

"Well, what did she say?" Rebecca asked, shimmying to the edge of the bed.

"She's not happy, but she agreed to Dad's suggestion of letting Megan stay until spring. She'll want her back in time for school in the fall, but Dad says we can cross that bridge when we come to it."

"Oh, Caleb, that's wonderful." Her eyes burned with

the threat of tears as she moved to give him a hug. "Have you told Megan yet?"

"Dad wanted to do the honors." His arms came around her waist. "He's talking to her now."

"I think we should celebrate," she said, tipping her head back to meet his eyes. "Help me dress for dinner."

She searched the wardrobe for a proper dress, then held the bodice of the gown to her chest while Caleb finished closing the row of hooks at the back. The fit wasn't quite perfect, but it would do.

"There," he said. He pressed his lips to the side of her neck. "I think I like being a ladies' maid."

"Oh, really? Then how would you like to arrange my hair?"

He gave a chuckle. "I don't think I'm up to that. But call me when you want out of this thing." He tugged at the back of her dress and gave her a lascivious grin. "I'd be happy to help."

He took one last look in the mirror, rearranged his tie and collar, and moved to the door. "Are you ready to go down?"

"I'll be along in a minute," she said, sitting down at her dressing table and reaching for her toiletries. "Go congratulate Megan."

"All right. See you downstairs."

Rebecca lifted the brush and ran it through her hair. When she raised an arm over her head to stroke the hair back from her other temple, though, a wave of dizziness washed over her. She dropped the brush and gripped the edge of the table, keeping her eyes closed until the sensation passed.

She took a deep breath and watched her reflection in the mirror. Her hair looked a duller brown than usual, and her skin was a bit pale. But that was to be expected when one had been nauseated for the past two weeks.

What did worry her was the cramping she'd begun to feel in her belly. Not the stabs of pain she expected would alert her to labor—though she wasn't due for more than two months—but long, throbbing spasms that wrapped around her abdomen.

She supposed she should have told someone. Caleb, perhaps. Or maybe it would have been a good idea to stop in at Doc Meade's one day while she was in town. But she hadn't done either yet, and she was beginning to regret it.

She ran the brush quickly through the rest of her hair and tied a wide emerald ribbon in a bow at the top of her head.

The illness would pass, she told herself for the hundredth time. Surely any number of women had suffered the same annoying sickness while with child. She simply wasn't sure. She'd seen too many females in the act of making babies and too few actually having them.

She got up, leaning against the dresser for a moment to allow her queasy stomach to settle. Then she made her way across the room and into the hall, keeping a hand to the wall to guide her heavy footsteps.

Was the house exceptionally hot this evening, or was it her? And why had she never before noticed how long this hallway was? It seemed to take her forever to reach the staircase and slowly falter her way down the difficult decline.

Once she reached the parlor, she took one last second to gain her equilibrium and entered the room where everyone was gathered for a drink before dinner.

"Here she is," Caleb said and came over to her. He kissed her forehead and handed her a sherry, then returned to his father's side.

She tried to concentrate on the happy conversation but soon found that even that small task caused a fine sheen of perspiration to gather on her brow. She moved behind one of the medallion-backed armchairs and gripped the mahogany rim, swaying slightly and biting the inside of her lip to keep an anguished moan silent.

Then the room began to spin, and Rebecca felt herself falling. The sound of breaking glass filled her ears a moment before darkness claimed her.

"Rebecca!"

Caleb turned at his sister's cry to see Rebecca weaving back and forth unsteadily. He started toward her as the sherry glass rolled past her fingertips and to the floor, spraying sharp pieces of crystal in every direction. He knelt at her side and picked her up in his arms.

"Somebody go for the doctor. Get him out here now."

He stalked out of the room, taking the stairs two at a time. He pushed the bedroom door open with his shoulder, letting it crash back against the wall. Throwing the covers aside with a fierce tug, he laid Rebecca carefully on the bed.

Her skin felt hot and sticky to his touch. He turned to his father and sister, who stood at the foot of the bed, and began to issue orders. "Get cold water and cloths. I have to bring her fever down. Megan, find a fresh gown for her, and then go downstairs to wait for Doc Meade. Send him up the minute he arrives."

Megan rummaged through several dresser drawers before pulling out a thin cotton nightdress and handing it to Caleb. Then she ran out of the room to help her father.

"All right, sweetheart," Caleb said softly, practically tearing her clothes off. "Everything's going to be all right." He flung the heavy satin gown to the floor and began removing her underclothes.

Megan brought a bowl of water and went back downstairs to watch for the doctor. Caleb soaked a cloth in the chilly water and bathed Rebecca's face and neck. Then he slipped the nightdress over her head and straightened it over her body.

"Jesus," he breathed. His hands stilled, and he stared for a moment. "Oh, Christ." Spots of bright red and dark-purple blood dotted her inner thighs. Without conscious thought, he grabbed the towels from beside the water basin and pressed them between her legs.

A moment of panic seized him. His ribcage seemed to tighten around his heart, and he struggled to get air into his lungs. What if she lost the baby? Dear Lord, she was already so far along. The child couldn't be taken from them now. Not when he'd just begun to think of it as real, as a little person they would soon be able to see and touch and hold in their arms. Tears sprang to his eyes. No! No, God couldn't be so cruel.

He crouched beside the bed and increased the pressure on the towels until his arms ached. He rested his forehead against the mattress and smoothed his thumb over the back of Rebecca's hand. "Stay with me, sweetheart," he said. The words were muffled, but he repeated them over and over.

Twenty minutes later, pounding footsteps sounded on the stairs, and Doc Meade ran into the room. Caleb lifted his head and stood, moving aside to give the doctor room to work but keeping pressure on the cloths between Rebecca's legs.

Megan and Holbrook stood in the doorway, looking on anxiously. Caleb cocked his head and asked them to give him a moment alone with the doctor and Rebecca.

"She's bleeding," he said desperately.

The doctor put a hand to Rebecca's forehead and dug in his bag for a stethoscope. He put the instrument around his neck, ready to continue his examination.

"Why don't you wait outside, son."

"No," Caleb said sternly.

"Caleb, I know this isn't easy for you, but you can't do her any more good in here than you could downstairs. Get yourself a glass of the strongest liquor you've got and wait. I'll be down in a few minutes. Go, son."

Caleb reluctantly released Rebecca's hand and the towels, moved away from the bed, and left the room.

* * *

Megan helped Bessie arrange cups and saucers on the silver serving tray. She knew tea would be the last thing on Caleb's or her father's mind, but staying busy in the kitchen helped to keep her from imagining all the horrible things that could be wrong with Rebecca.

For some reason, Dolores had disappeared after summoning Doc Meade. Megan imagined the older woman had stayed in town to see someone; she seemed to go in quite often of late, and always after dark. Bessie managed as best she could without assistance at those times.

"Mith 'Becca gonna have thum?" Bessie asked with her usual lisp.

"No," Megan said softly. "Miss Rebecca is ill. The doctor is with her now."

"Thee be all right?"

"I don't know." Megan looked away as her vision became misty. Rebecca was such a part of their lives now. She was like an older sister, full of stories and eager to teach Megan new things. Megan didn't even want to think about what life would be like without her.

"Don't need it then," Bessie said, pouring steaming water from the stove into the china teapot.

Megan watched Bessie with interest. "You don't need what?" she asked.

"The medithin."

"Medicine?" Megan's eyebrows rose. "What kind of medicine?"

Bessie shrugged her shoulders. " 'Lores put it in Mith 'Becca'th tea. It good for baby."

Megan's hackles rose in alarm. "Could you show me this medicine, please, Bessie?"

Bessie turned and dug around in a clutter of herbs and spices. She picked up the only brown glass bottle in the lot and handed it to Megan.

Megan pulled out the cork stopper and brought it to her nose. It didn't smell all that odd, she thought. But neither did it have a label to tell what it was.

"You've been putting this in Rebecca's tea?"

" 'Lores," Bessie corrected.

"Dolores has been putting this in Rebecca's tea," she said.

The girl nodded.

"Has Dolores put it in anyone else's tea?"

She shook her head. "Only Mith 'Becca. It for baby."

"How long has Dolores been giving this to her?" Megan asked.

"Long time," Bessie said, stretching her arms out to indicate the passage of time. "Sinth thee came."

"Since she came," Megan repeated under her breath.

Bessie began to lift the tray to take it to the parlor.

"I'll get it," Megan said, placing the bottle of herbs beside one of the cups. She picked up the serving tray and headed for the other room.

Chapter Twenty-two

A loud rapping awakened Sabrina from her early-evening nap, and it took her a minute to realize that someone was banging on the door. She got up, put on a wrapper, and went to answer it. A flushed Dolores, breathing hard from overexertion, stood before her.

"What do you want?" Sabrina snapped, annoyed at having been awakened during a rather erotic dream.

"Miss Rebecca . . . she's sick. . . ." The woman's words were choppy as she struggled for oxygen.

At the mention of Rebecca, Sabrina brightened. "How sick?" she asked.

"Bad. She fainted . . . husband carried her . . . upstairs. They sent for the doctor."

Sabrina caught herself a moment before an excited giggle bubbled up from her throat. She coughed and regained control of her emotions. "You've been using the herb as I instructed, correct?"

"Yes'm. Is that what done it?"

"Oh, very unlikely," Sabrina lied. "But why are you here?"

"To tell you," the woman said, leaning against the doorjamb as her breathing began to return to normal.

"Stupid woman," Sabrina spat, grabbing a dark-colored dress and boots out of the wardrobe. "You should have stayed there and found out what was wrong. You'll have to go back."

Dolores shook her head adamantly. "Uh-uh. I ain't never goin' back there. They'll know, I tell ya. They'll know I done it, and they'll kill me."

"How will they know?" Sabrina asked, hoping to calm the woman's fears.

"I don't know, but they'll know."

Sabrina threw off her wrapper and sat to lace her shoes. "Oh, very well, blast it all. Run away if you must. I'll do the rest myself."

"But I want the resta that money you promised me," Dolores stated.

Sabrina huffed but got up and went to the bureau. She pulled out several wrinkled bills and thrust them into wrinkled hands. "There," she said. "Take it and go away."

"Yes'm." Dolores turned to leave but then stopped. "Mrs. Adams. She ain't gonna die or nothin', is she?"

"Of course not," Sabrina said. "She'll be just fine, I'm sure."

Sabrina closed the door behind the old woman and finished dressing. She no longer had anyone inside the Adams house who could give her information, so she would have to get it herself.

She pulled her long black hair away from her face and tied it back with a thin brown ribbon that matched the dress she wore. It was dark enough that no one would see her. And everyone inside the house would be too preoccupied to even notice someone lurking outside the windows.

*   *   *

Caleb threw back his third glass of Kentucky bourbon and rested his head against the leather chair.

What the hell was taking that doctor so long?

His father stood at the window, smoking a cigar and staring out into the night. Megan was off somewhere doing whatever. Fixing more tea. Begging God to save Rebecca's life.

That's what he should be doing, Caleb thought, somewhat ashamed that he hadn't considered it sooner. He should be down on his knees praying for his wife and child to be all right. But all he could seem to concentrate on was the fact that his life would feel utterly empty without them.

Rebecca was the most important part of his world now. He fell asleep beside her at night and woke up beside her in the morning. They had arguments—which amused him no end—and intellectually stimulating conversations. Once she had even gotten him into a discussion about the merits of using horse manure in vegetable gardens.

He smiled at the memory and took another gulp of whiskey. Setting the glass on the table before him, he put his head in his hands, his elbows on his knees.

Maybe it was time to pray. There was nothing else he could do. And he felt so damned helpless.

But where did he begin when he had long ago given up on believing that someone on high might actually care about a cad like him? It had been so long since he'd bowed his head in prayer, other than ritualistically, impersonally, in church, he wasn't sure he remembered how it was done. And who was he to think God would listen to him after all these years of angry silence?

Still, he tried.

The back of Caleb's eyes began to sting, and he blinked several times, astonished to see drops of moisture fall to the floor at his feet. *Just don't take her from me,* he pleaded, grinding his teeth. *Not when I've only just learned to love her.*

His head snapped up. He wiped his face dry with the sleeve of his shirt and tried to grasp the last words of his silent plea.

Yes, he realized in a flash. *Yes, I love her.* By Jesus, he really did love Rebecca. And he wouldn't be able to go on without her in his life. He bolted to his feet with a surge of newfound determination. He couldn't let her die. He wouldn't.

Just then Megan came into the room with a tray of tea.

Caleb headed for the door, but she touched his arm. "Caleb, I need to talk to you."

"Not now, Megan, I have to see Rebecca."

"Caleb, it's important."

Something in her voice warned him not to leave yet. "What is it?" he asked, turning from the doorway, hands on hips.

"I don't know if this has anything to do with Rebecca becoming ill, but—"

"Spit it out, Megan."

She took up a small brown bottle from the tray and handed it to him. "Bessie told me that Dolores has been putting this into Rebecca's tea."

He uncorked it and sniffed. "What is it?" he asked.

"I don't know what it is. Dolores told Bessie it was to keep Rebecca and the baby healthy. But I don't think that's what it's for at all."

Caleb's fingers tightened around the bottle, and he pulled Megan into a swift, fierce embrace. "Thanks, little sister," he said before running out of the room and racing up the stairs to the doctor.

Sabrina crouched beneath one of the lighted windows, assuming the family was gathered inside. Another light shone from one of the upstairs rooms, but there was no way she could ever climb that high to sneak a peek.

She pushed aside the scratchy branches of the shrubs that grew alongside the house, trying to get closer. A sharp piece of brush pierced her flesh, and she let out a stream of muttered curses. A plan that had started so simply was rapidly becoming a dangerous mission. She had to find out what was going on inside and then hurry back to town.

Once again she pushed the bushes out of her way and grabbed hold of the windowsill. Her fingernails dug into the wood as she struggled to get a good grip. She used the shrubbery as a stepladder, climbing onto the narrow branches for support.

Her nose just reached the glass as she fought to keep her balance and see inside at the same time. Caleb sat in a chair with his back to her. She would know him anywhere just from his full head of ebony hair. Holbrook Adams stood across the room, staring out a parlor window. Sabrina gave a sigh of relief that she had decided against sneaking up onto the porch to spy inside. He surely would have seen her had she done that.

So the newly smitten Caleb wasn't upstairs at his wife's bedside. Sabrina smiled. Maybe this wasn't going to be as hard as she'd begun to think. Oh, Caleb was putting on a good show for the townspeople, but here he was, sitting in the parlor with his family as if it were any other day of the week, while poor, sweet Rebecca was upstairs deathly ill.

Even if the pennyroyal only caused Rebecca to lose the brat, Sabrina was sure everything would work out. Without the child, Caleb would have no use for Rebecca any longer. He could seek a divorce or annulment, and Sabrina would be free to move back into his life.

Yes, things were working out beautifully. All because of her careful planning.

She readjusted her grip on the windowsill and rose on her tiptoes. She watched as Caleb bowed his head, holding it in his hands. If she didn't know better, she would think he was a grieving husband. But of course that was ridiculous. He was simply putting on an act for his family.

Then a girl came into the room. At first Sabrina thought her a servant, but she so resembled Caleb that Sabrina knew instinctively it had to be Megan, the sister Bart had been asinine enough to shoot.

The sister laid a tray on the low table in front of the sofa and stopped Caleb before he could leave the room. He turned to her, and they exchanged words. Sabrina strained to hear, but it was no use.

Dammit! Megan handed Caleb the bottle of pennyroyal, and he looked at it suspiciously. Why the hell hadn't Dolores taken it with her? Now they would find out what was wrong with Rebecca all the sooner.

Oh, well, it really didn't matter. There was nothing they could do to stop the effects of the herb, was there? She hadn't thought to ask the madam about such things.

Caleb hugged his sister, turned, and rushed out of the room.

Why did he look so happy to have found the herb? Perhaps he was glad to know Rebecca's illness wasn't just something passing, that it was indeed serious.

Sabrina extended a foot, searching for support before letting go of the sill. She landed on the ground with a thump and a low groan. For a split second she wished she could have sent Bart to do this but then realized he would only have gotten himself caught. He really had been a bumbling idiot.

She yanked her skirts out of the clawing bushes and ran across the yard, retracing her tracks back to town.

When Caleb threw open the bedroom door, he saw Doc Meade bent over his still-unconscious wife. Beads of perspiration dotted the elder man's brow.

"Dammit, Caleb, I told you to stay downstairs."

Rebecca looked so pale and fragile that fear constricted Caleb's heart. He watched as the doctor ran his hands over the slope of her stomach.

"Is she going to be all right?" he asked.

"Damned if I know," the doctor said. He shook his head and apologized for the sharp words. "I just can't figure out what's wrong with her. Has anybody else in the family been ill?"

"No," Caleb said and moved forward. "But this could have something to do with it." He handed the bottle to the doctor.

"What is it?" he asked, holding it up to the lamp.

"I have no idea, but Megan found out from Bessie that Dolores has been putting it in Rebecca's tea."

Doc Meade squinted through the bottle, then poured some of the contents into the palm of his hand. "I'll be damned," he said softly. "How long has she been giving this to your wife?"

"I have no idea. What is it?" Caleb asked, clenching and unclenching his hands.

"Pennyroyal. Looks like ol' Chloe over at the Dog Tick has been giving it out again."

"What the hell does Chloe have to do with anything?" Caleb asked anxiously, becoming even more worried about Rebecca's condition.

"She gives it to her girls when they miss a flux. If given in large enough doses right away for three or four days, it can cause a spontaneous miscarriage."

"Sweet Jesus," Caleb swore, running splayed fingers through his hair in agitation. "What will it do to Rebecca this far along?"

"I'm not sure," the doctor replied, thinking.

Fury began to build in Caleb's belly. "You're not sure? You're a doctor, for Christ's sake. How can you not know what this stuff will do?"

Doc Meade turned tired eyes to Caleb, then poured the herbs back, recorking the bottle. "I don't give pennyroyal to my patients, Caleb. And Chloe knows what she's doing, so I don't get many of her girls in who are sick from it. The best I can tell you is to let it work its way out of her system. Give her plenty of fluids. Maybe even help her sweat it out.

"I'll pay Chloe a visit," Doc Meade continued. "She ought to know a little about it." He wiped his face with the back of his arm. "The bleeding has been minimal, just spotting, so I don't think we need to worry about the baby. Not yet, at least. I'll come by again tomorrow to check on her. And be sure to send for me if there's any change."

Caleb watched as the doctor packed up his medical bag and put on his jacket. He thanked the physician stiffly, still upset that there was nothing the man could do for Rebecca. He felt helpless enough; he didn't need to hear that a medical professional didn't know what to do, either.

After the doctor's departure, Caleb pulled a chair up to the side of the bed and lifted Rebecca's limp hand in his own. He had an overwhelming urge to tell her about his revelation, to confess his love. But he held back, deciding that when he told Rebecca how much he loved her, she would be wide awake. He would never give her cause to suspect that his words had been only a dream.

Chapter Twenty-three

Soft voices drifted through her consciousness. She blinked several times and tried to clear her vision. A moan passed her parched lips, and the voices grew silent.

Rebecca opened her eyes and saw Caleb's handsome countenance before her. A dark shadow across his chin hinted for a much-needed shave, but she couldn't help finding him attractive. His thumb was rubbing her hand in the most delicate, delightful, circular pattern. A dull pounding started in her head as she drifted back toward darkness.

"How are you feeling?" he asked gently.

She groaned, hoping that would suffice as an answer to his question.

"You gave us quite a scare, young lady."

Rebecca opened one eye and focused on the source of the other masculine voice. Holbrook stood behind his son, looking on with a small smile. She tried to smile back before letting her eyes drift closed.

"Rebecca," Caleb called, shaking her hand. "Sweetheart, wake up."

She shook her head, wanting to relax on the soft cushion of blackness surrounding her.

"Come on, darling, stay with me. You've slept long enough."

Oh, but they couldn't know. They couldn't know how very comfortable the darkness was. How free of worry and pain.

At the thought of pain, the throbbing in her head began again.

"Megan, could you get some tea for her, please? You have to wake up now, Rebecca."

She opened her eyes and looked around the room, only to find that she and Caleb were alone. She tried to speak, but the words came out garbled. Her lips and throat felt dry and sore.

"Here, take a sip of this."

Caleb helped her to sit up, and she took several swallows of tepid water. He fluffed the pillows behind her and propped her into an upright position.

"What happened?" she asked, searching her mind but recalling nothing. The last thing she remembered was walking downstairs for dinner. Only they had met in the parlor first, and . . . oh, yes, it was a special dinner for Megan, to celebrate her mother's allowing her to stay in Leavenworth until fall.

"You don't remember?"

She shook her head. "We were having a special dinner for your sister."

"That's right. But you got jealous and decided to become the guest of honor."

Her eyes widened. She hadn't. Oh, Lord, she was feeling dizzy again. "I—"

"You didn't mean to, actually. You fainted."

She leaned her head back and closed her eyes. "I hadn't been feeling very well, but I never expected to pass out."

"You were sick, and you didn't tell me?" His voice held an edge of anger.

Rebecca looked at him and shrugged. "I didn't think much of it. I thought it was just the heat—and my condition."

Caleb stormed to his feet, nearly toppling the armchair, pacing to the opposite side of the room. "You didn't even bother to tell me you weren't feeling well? How stupid could you be?"

She watched him with astonishment. His movements were sleek, like those of a stalking panther. The muscles rippled beneath his wrinkled white shirt. A flame of passion leapt within her, and she wondered at the desires he could evoke from her even now.

"Remind me never to ask you to sit at my deathbed. Your compassion would surely kill me right off."

He turned to her and stood perfectly still. "Do you have any idea how scared I was?"

"Caleb—"

He returned to her side, dropping into the armchair. "I thought you were going to die. And when I saw the blood, I thought you were going to lose the baby."

Rebecca's breath caught, her hands going automatically to her belly.

"No." He took both her hands in his own. "The doctor was just here and said you and the baby seem to be fine. But we're to send for him if anything changes. That means you're to tell me if you don't feel well. No matter what. Do you understand?"

"Of course," she answered quickly. "Caleb, you have to know that I would have told you if I'd thought something was really wrong. I just thought it was the weather. I thought it was normal to feel out-of-sorts in my condition. I don't know much about bearing children, but I would never take a chance with our baby, Caleb. You have to believe me."

"I know, I know," he soothed her. "And there's no

way you could have known that you were slowly being poisoned."

"What?"

"Dolores has been tainting your tea. For as long as she's been here, we suspect."

"But why? With what?"

"We don't know why. Not yet, anyway. But I intend to find out. It was pennyroyal. An herb used by—"

"Prostitutes to prevent children," she said softly.

He gave her an odd look, and she explained. "Lilah at the Scarlet Garter used to serve it to her girls each month . . . in hot tea. At first I didn't know exactly what it was. It was to clean them out, Lilah said. In case they'd gotten . . ." She cleared her throat. "Um, 'knocked up.' "

Caleb nodded. "Doc Meade thinks it may have come from the Dog Tick. He says the madam there uses it for the same purpose."

"But why would Dolores want to give it to me? Especially when I'm already so far along?"

Caleb's eyes narrowed. "I'm not so sure Dolores came up with the idea herself."

"You think someone made her do it?"

"Paid her to do it is more likely, yes."

"But why?"

"I don't know. Even Doc Meade didn't know what effect the herb would have on you. It's usually used very early in a pregnancy, not later. He wasn't sure what, if anything, would happen. We didn't know how much you'd been given or for how long."

"But I'm all right now? And the baby is going to be okay?"

Caleb cocked up his lips in a grin and squeezed her fingers. "You both seem to be fine. The doctor will stop by to check on you now and again, though, just to be sure."

"Good." Rebecca smiled and pressed back into the

soft pillows. She felt exhausted even though she had just awakened. Yawning, she let her eyes fall closed.

Caleb watched as Rebecca's eyelid's grew heavy. She snuggled into the pillows and fell back to sleep. A low, rhythmic snore began, and he smiled, knowing her sleep to be a comfortable, natural, safe rest.

He sighed and tucked the covers more securely around her, then made his way quietly across the floor and closed the door with a soft click behind him. He had meant to tell Rebecca that he loved her. He was fairly bursting at the seams with his newfound knowledge of an emotion he'd thought too long buried to be resurrected.

But she'd looked so tired. And the rest would do her good. It also gave him a chance to get out of the house and start searching for the answers to a few questions.

He met Megan coming out of the dining room with a silver tray of tea and sugar cookies.

"I thought Rebecca might like a little something to eat when she wakes up," she said. "How is she feeling?"

"Better. But she's asleep again. I'm sorry."

"She needs the rest to build up her strength."

"That's what I thought. I'm going into town for a while. I'll be back in time for supper."

"What's in town?" she asked, her curiosity piqued.

"None of your business," he said, giving her nose a tweak. Then he bent and kissed her cheek. "Keep an eye on that wife of mine. She's liable to get herself into a heap of trouble while I'm gone."

Caleb leaned an elbow on the scarred bar of the Dog Tick Saloon and waited for the barkeep to finish pouring drinks at the other end.

"Whiskey, Mr. Adams?"

"None today, Luther. I'm looking to talk to Chloe."

The bartender's Adam's apple bobbed in his throat as he swallowed. "Chloe, sir?"

Caleb wondered how long it would take for the rumor that he was cheating on Rebecca to run rampant through town. "That's right," he said. "Is she around?"

"She ought to be up by now. But her girls don't start working till later."

"I'm not here to see one of the girls," he said, straightening. "I'm here to see Chloe. Where is she?"

Luther inclined his head. "Last door on the right."

Caleb started toward the stairs in long, smooth strides. He could feel every eye in the room on his back as he climbed to the second story. Some of the cowboys put up a fuss and tried to follow, but a few wall-shaking bellows from the barrel-chested Luther settled them down.

He rapped on the door and heard a muffled reply from within. He turned the knob and walked into the room.

A half-dressed, shapely young brunette lay sprawled across a wide mattress. She rolled over and brushed tangles of hair away from her face. When she opened her eyes and saw Caleb standing inside the door, she gave a yelp of surprise.

"Who the hell are you?" she asked, sitting up. The twisted sheets slid over the mound of her breasts to gather at her waist. She didn't seem to notice. "What are you doing here? Luther never lets anybody upstairs this early."

"Well, he did," Caleb said.

The woman licked her lips and shook the cascade of hair back from her shoulders. "You pay the right price, honey, and I'll forget it's only noon," she drawled.

Caleb withdrew his watch from his jacket pocket and flipped open the lid. "It's past three," he said. "And I'm only here to talk."

Chloe gave a snort. "That's a new one. What is it with you men, lately? The doc's already been here to talk. Talkin' don't make money, so it'll cost ya."

"Tell you what," Caleb said, coming close enough to

reach out and touch her. "I'll pay you your usual rate if you tell me what I want to know."

"And if I don't?" She thrust her breasts forward and turned her lips down in a pout.

"Then I'll make sure you're put in jail for trying to kill my wife."

"Now, wait a minute," she said in a panic, waving her hands in the air. "I've never done anything like that in my life. Ask Luther, he'll vouch for me. I don't even leave the Dog Tick but about once a month."

"I know that," Caleb said leisurely, leaning against a bedpost.

She let out a long breath and relaxed. "Then what are ya burnin' my butt for?"

"My wife was poisoned this week—with pennyroyal." He noticed a spark of recognition in the madam's eyes. "Now, as I understand it, you use that herb quite often on your girls."

"That's common enough," she replied, pulling the sheet farther up her body, trying to avoid looking directly at him.

He gave a nod. "What I want to know is who, outside the saloon, you gave it to."

She didn't answer and didn't look as if she was going to.

"Come on," he said. "You tell me who came to you to buy some pennyroyal, and I'll try to convince Marshal Thompson not to arrest you for attempted murder."

"I don't know who she was."

Caleb narrowed his eyes, fixing her with a determined stare.

"I'm telling you the truth," she hurried to explain. "Some woman came to the back door one night, and Luther sent her up to me. She started crying about how much trouble she would be in if her limp-cocked husband found out she was breeding. He would kill her and

275

what not. I've heard the story before. So I gave her some pennyroyal to take care of the problem."

Her brow wrinkled. "Come to think of it, she did ask an awful lot of questions. More than just how to take it. She wanted to know how much and how often would make it dangerous or even lethal. Said she didn't want to make herself sick. And she insisted I sell her a full bottle instead of the amount that would have taken care of things for her. She said it was in case she got in trouble again, 'cause she knew she wouldn't be able to stay away from the guy who was giving it to her."

"Did she tell you her name?"

"Nope. Don't suppose she wanted me to know."

"No, I don't suppose she did," Caleb said, more than a little disgusted. "What did she look like?"

"Real dark hair. Darker than yours, even. She looked to be getting up in years, but I couldn't be sure, she was wearing so much face powder. She looked like a lady. Held herself real proper-like. 'Course she couldn't have been all that proper if she was spreading her legs for someone other than her husband, right?" Chloe laughed. "I think it's a real hoot how these ladies walk around with their noses up in the air, pretending to be so much better than me and my girls. Truth is, most of them are doing the same thing we are, they just ain't getting paid."

Caleb brushed off her final comment, wanting to get more information about the mysterious woman. Chloe's description didn't bring anyone to mind, and he wanted to see if there was any other detail that might ring a bell.

"What else can you tell me about her?"

"That's it. Nice clothes, real proper speech. But I haven't seen her since, so I don't know where she is or what she's been doing. You ain't going to send the marshal over here, are you? We've been real good about keeping trouble to a minimum, and he hasn't made any rounds for the last couple months."

Caleb dug in his jacket and handed her a couple of bills. "Don't worry. I appreciate your help."

"No problem, honey," she said, leaning over to stuff the money into the toe of an abandoned slipper on the floor. "You ever need more than just information, pay me a visit. And if I'm not the kind of gal who catches your fancy, I'm sure I can find one who will."

"I'll remember that," Caleb said as he moved to the door.

Caleb stepped into the jailhouse and looked around the front office. Marshal Thompson was either out or in back with a prisoner. Caleb sat down in an available chair, balanced on two legs, and propped his boots on the desk, crossing them at the ankles.

Within ten minutes, Thompson walked in the door. "Caleb," he said, holding out his hand. "Hope you haven't been waiting long."

"Not at all, Marshal," he answered, shaking the man's hand.

Thompson brushed down his mustache and went around to the other side of the desk. "What can I do for you?"

"Have you heard about Rebecca?"

"Sure have. I'm real sorry, Caleb. Doc says she's gonna be all right, though. Thank the good Lord for that."

"Then you haven't heard the rest?"

The marshal leaned forward in his chair. "Well, now, I have heard a thing or two, but you know how gossip runs rampant in this town. I don't pay it much never-mind anymore." He took off his hat and set it on the desktop. "Rumor has it that Doc Meade was over at the Dog Tick after he left your place. The ladies are all in a lather, thinkin' he's consorting with those kind of folks, but Doc swears he was only talking to Chloe. About a medical matter."

"That's true," Caleb said. "I just came from there myself."

Thompson's bushy eyebrows rose.

"To talk, Marshal. My wife is sick in bed. What kind of man do you think I am?"

"I didn't say anything, Caleb. But I've seen better men than you go over there for an hour or so. 'Specially when their wives are too far along to keep them happy."

"I'm happy, Marshal. Except for the fact that someone is trying to murder my wife."

"Murder! That's quite an accusation to be tossing around, don't you think? You want to be sure before you make those sorts of charges."

"Oh, I'm sure. And I think the bullet that hit Megan was meant for Rebecca, too."

"Now, Caleb—"

"Marshal, my wife was poisoned with an herb called pennyroyal. She nearly died, and she almost lost our child. I consider this very serious. If you talk to Chloe down at the Dog Tick, she can give you a description of the woman she sold a bottle of the herb to. I suspect that woman employed one of our housekeepers to put it in my wife's tea."

"Can you prove it wasn't just another prank Anabelle Archer cooked up?"

Caleb raised an eyebrow. Gossip traveled fast if the sheriff knew about that already. Only he, Rebecca, Anabelle, and her mother had been involved in that conversation about Anabella's mischief-making. "If this was a prank, it wasn't a very funny one. Rebecca almost died. Besides, Chloe said the woman was dark, not blond."

"Still, everyone knows about Anabelle's confession in the churchyard. Her mother's been bawling around about it ever since. How do you know it's not just another one of her vengeful tricks?"

"I don't," Caleb said reluctantly. "So let's go ask her."

Chapter Twenty-four

Caleb wasn't too happy about having to ride out to the Archer home and waste time better used looking for the real culprit, but if that was what it would take to convince Marshal Thompson that there was someone trying to kill Rebecca, so be it. They would find Anabelle, ask her some questions, and ease the marshal's mind, as well as his own. Then he would make sure Thompson got down to business tracking down the black-haired woman Chloe had told him about.

They found Anabelle outside, shaking a rug over the front porch railing. She looked at them warily and glanced behind her, and Caleb suspected she didn't want her parents to know they had company.

"Marshal Thompson. Mr. Adams," she said softly, coming down the front steps and draping the small rag rug over the banister. "Can I help you?"

Caleb didn't bother to dismount, and Thompson only shifted in his saddle.

"Seems there's been more trouble with Rebecca Adams," the marshal said.

"What?" Anabelle exclaimed in a hushed voice. "I swear I haven't done anything to her. Honestly, Mr. Adams. Ma has punished me something fierce for mistreating Rebecca before. I haven't been allowed to leave the house since."

"Then you don't know anything about the poisoning?" Caleb asked.

"Poisoning! Oh, no! Nothing! I swear it on a stack of Holy Bibles. Is she all right?"

"Far as we know," Caleb said. "I hope you're being truthful with us, Anabelle."

"I am. Oh, I am, Mr. Adams."

"Good enough. But if we find out you lied—"

"No, no. I would never do that again. I'm real sorry about how I acted before." Her face flushed in embarrassment. "It wasn't very grown-up of me."

Caleb inclined his head. "Then if you hear anything, you'll let us know?"

"Yes, sir. I'll tell Ma and Pa, too."

"I didn't think she had anything to do with it," Caleb said as they rode away.

"You understand why I had to be sure, don't you? I mean, I can't very well go chasing after some imaginary murderer if there's the chance it's just a childish prank."

"Well, now that you know, I hope you'll help me find the woman Chloe described."

"You know I will, Caleb. Just tell me what she looks like, and I'll get the word out."

"Good. And I want you to look for our housekeeper, Dolores, too. She was the one giving Rebecca the herbs in her tea. She may be able to lead us to the other woman."

It was after dark when Caleb finally made his way wearily into the house. He left his coat on a hook inside the front door and headed immediately up the stairs.

His father and sister were crowded around Rebecca,

each offering to do some good deed to aid in her recovery.

"You might think of letting her rest," Caleb suggested from the doorway.

"Oh, Caleb, you're home." Megan rose from the chair beside the bed. "We were beginning to worry."

"No need."

"Well, now that you're here, we'll leave you and Rebecca alone. Supper will be ready whenever you are."

"I'll be down in a while," he said.

On their way out, Megan stopped beside him and stood on tiptoe. "She's doing much better," she whispered in his ear. "She'll be up and around in no time."

"Is Megan right?" he asked once his sister and Holbrook had left the room. "Are you feeling better?"

"Oh, much," Rebecca said. "I've been awake almost all evening. Where were you?"

"I had some business in town."

"Important business, I hope. Otherwise I would feel terribly neglected."

He went to her side, balanced on the edge of the mattress, and cupped her cheek in his palm. "It was very important." He lightly touched her lips with his own. "And I would never dream of neglecting you."

"I should think not," she said with a slight smile. "I hear you took excellent care of me while I was sick."

"And where did you hear that, my dear?"

"From your father and your sister and Doc Meade . . ."

"Liars, every last one of them."

"I doubt it," she said quietly. "Your face was the first thing I saw when I opened my eyes. That meant a lot to me."

"Did it?" His voice was just as soft.

She only nodded.

Caleb swallowed and moved closer, taking her hands in his own. "There's something I've been meaning to tell you. I just never found the right time."

"What's that?" she asked.

"I love you," he said without hesitation.

Caleb thought for a moment that her eyes would pop out of her head. Then he realized she wasn't breathing, and he became concerned. "Rebecca? Rebecca?" he said, giving her hands a little shake.

"What did you say?"

"You heard me." He brought her fingers to his mouth. He couldn't help but smile. "I love you."

"You're just saying that because—"

He gripped her hands tightly. "I am not just saying it. When you were unconscious and the doctor sent me out while he examined you, I spent a lot of time thinking. And trying to pray."

"You? Pray?" she asked incredulously.

"Yes, me," he said with a chuckle. "I know it's not an everyday occurrence—at least it wasn't—but I didn't know what else to do. I couldn't help you, and I was going crazy with worry. I didn't see any harm in trying my hand at prayer."

His voice lowered. "I don't think I did a very good job, though. All I could think was that I didn't want to lose you." His hold on her hands loosened while he threaded his fingers between her own. "I love you, Rebecca. I love holding you in my arms at night and waking up beside you in the morning. I love your spirit, your intelligence—even your stubbornness. My whole life has turned brighter since the day you blew into the Express office in a flurry of peach skirts and petticoats, with a tongue as sharp as a razor."

Rebecca flushed prettily and ducked her head. He tapped her under the chin with a knuckle until she was once again looking him in the eye. "I don't even think I realized it until you were nearly taken from me. I don't know how or when it happened, but you burrowed your way into my stone-cold heart and curled up just like you belonged there."

Rebecca threw her arms around his neck and held him close. At first she had thought herself delusional, imagining the words coming from Caleb's lips rather than actually hearing them. But the more he spoke, the more she believed. And the naked vulnerability that shone in his eyes couldn't be anything but real.

"Oh, Caleb," she whispered. "I love you, too."

Caleb pulled away and gave her a giddy, astonished look. "Well, why the hell didn't you say so sooner?"

She wiped at the tears gathering in the corners of her eyes. "I couldn't. It would have hurt too much to have you laugh in my face."

"Sweetheart, you say a lot of things that amuse me, but 'I love you' could never be one of them."

"I can't believe it," Rebecca said softly. "For so long, I thought you hated me for trapping you into this marriage. I never thought you would grow to even like me, let alone love me. And now you do. Or at least you say you do."

He brushed the moisture from her cheeks with his thumbs. "I do. I'll never give you reason to doubt it again. Besides, do you really believe someone could force me, Caleb Zachariah Adams, to do anything I didn't want to? Come now, Rebecca, I'm a bit more determined than that, aren't I?"

She nodded. "It's true that your stubbornness is about the size of Kansas itself."

"Don't be so eager to agree, sweetheart," he said with a chuckle. "I could point out a few of your shortcomings, as well."

"Such as?" she asked, feigning defensiveness.

He closed one eye and pretended to concentrate. "Your temper. But I already said that, didn't I? Well, you're also stubborn, willful, mulish—"

"Those are all the same thing," she pointed out.

"Oh. In that case, I guess you only have one character flaw. It just happens to be a very large one," he teased.

She snorted. "And here I thought that's what you loved best about me."

"It is. If it hadn't been for your temper and bullheadedness, you never would have stormed into my office that afternoon. And if you hadn't bent my ear about that bill, I never would have noticed your pert breasts or sashaying hips. And if I hadn't noticed your figure, I never would have wanted you so badly. And if I hadn't wanted you so badly, we never would have made love. And if we hadn't made love, we never would have made this little one." He put a hand on her belly. "And you never would have married me."

"So what you're saying is that my stubbornness is a good thing?"

"A very good thing. As long as you don't use it too often. At least not with me."

"Oh, well," Rebecca said haughtily, "if you're going to tie my hands . . ."

A wicked light came to his eyes, and he gave her a conspiratorial wink. "We'll try that later. After the baby is born."

She flushed to the roots of her hair. "If anyone gets tied up, Caleb Adams, it will be you."

He gave a deep belly laugh. "A hellion, that's what you are. How did I ever end up with such a hellion for a wife?"

Rebecca opened her mouth to answer.

He held up a hand to stop her. "No, don't remind me. But rest assured, my dearest Rebecca, that I never hated you. Perhaps I wasn't the most gracious of husbands to start, but I never hated you. And even though I don't think I knew it then, I was glad to have the baby as an excuse to make you mine."

"Really?"

"Absolutely. Now, wife," he said, straightening, "tell

me once more that you love me before I go downstairs for our meals."

"I love you," Rebecca whispered, her heart completely light for the first time since she had met this infuriating man.

"You aren't leaving again, are you?" Rebecca asked, finally allowed out of bed. She sat in the comfortable green armchair, a book in her lap, watching Caleb adjust his tie.

"I shouldn't be long," he answered. He came to her side and pressed a light kiss to her cheek.

"What will you be doing?" she asked. He had gone into town the past three evenings in a row, and she was beginning to suspect that something was not quite right.

"I have some business to take care of."

"That's what you said last night. And the night before that."

"Then it must be true."

Caleb heard her teeth click together and saw the sparks in her eyes. She probably thought he was up to no good, though he didn't know how she could even imagine such a thing after the intimate discussion they'd had. Hadn't he told her that he loved her? Didn't she believe him?

"All right," he said. "I didn't want to tell you this because I thought it might upset you, but I've been out with Marshal Thompson the past few nights looking for Dolores and the woman who gave her the pennyroyal to give you."

"Oh, Caleb," Rebecca cried, letting her book fall shut.

"Now don't fret. We've only been questioning some people in town, sweetheart. It's not like we're forming a posse to hunt them down."

"Still, it's so dangerous."

"Which is exactly why I didn't tell you. But I don't want you worrying, all right? I'll be fine." He winked.

"I'm letting Thompson do all the dangerous work, anyway."

"You will be careful, won't you?"

"Of course I will. I'm not going to let myself get hurt now that I've got a woman at home who loves me."

Caleb found Marshal Thompson with his spurs on the desk, the same as every other night he'd come to town. This time, however, Thompson's face lit up at his arrival.

" 'Bout time you got here, son. I have something I think you'll like."

He waited while the marshal jingled a ring of keys and unlocked the door to the cells, leading him to the end of the row. On a small cot in the corner of the cell sat the big-boned Dolores. Her gray hair fell in greasy strands about her face.

"Someone here to see you, ma'am," the marshal said.

Dolores lifted her head and looked at Caleb. When she realized who it was, she came to her feet, hurriedly trying to improve her appearance. "Mr. Adams, sir."

Caleb felt a twinge of pity for the old woman. Then he remembered that she had helped poison his wife, and he strengthened his resolve to get to the bottom of this.

"Dolores," he said with a brief nod. "I think you know why you're here."

"Yes, sir. I did something I oughtn't. I feared it was wrong, but she said no real harm would come of it, and she paid me so much. I'm real sorry, sir."

"Who's *she?*" Caleb demanded.

"I don't know, sir. She was a stranger, and I—"

"There's going to be a trial," Caleb said matter-of-factly. "You'll be charged with trying to murder Rebecca."

"But it weren't my idea, Mr. Adams! Honest to God, it weren't. She said she'd pay me good money if I could get a job at your place. Then she made me give that stuff to your wife. I worried at what it might do, but she said nothin' serious, and she paid me so good. Enough to go back to Lansing and take care of my sister. She's real sick, she is, sir."

Caleb showed no sign that her words affected him. "I hope the woman paid you extremely well, and I hope you sent the money to your sister, because you won't be getting out of prison any time soon. Unless they hang you, of course."

"Oh, no, sir," she said, wringing her hands. "You can't let them do that to me. It weren't my idea. I only did what I was told."

"You'll forgive me if your story doesn't tug at my heartstrings, but my wife and child nearly died. It certainly doesn't matter to me what they do to you."

"Get me out of this, sir, and I'll do anything to make it up to you and your family. Anything at all."

Caleb shared a glance with Marshal Thompson and shrugged his shoulders in an uncaring gesture. "Since it was my family you tried to *murder*"—he stressed the word—"I suppose the judge would listen to me. He might even go easy on you . . . if I gave him good reason."

Dolores's eyes pleaded with him, but she made no sound.

"You would have to tell me quite a bit, though, to make it worth my while."

"Oh, yes, sir. I'll tell you anything you want to know."

"Good." Caleb turned from uninterested bystander to a man intent on getting answers. "Let's start with who gave you the herb to hide in my wife's tea."

"Don't know her name, Mr. Adams, and that's the God's honest truth. I never seen her before she hired me. But she had the blackest hair I ever seen. Black as the bottom of my shoe, it was." She lifted her foot and showed him the sole. "Cold woman, she was, too. Perty,

I guess, for a woman gettin' on a bit in years. She covered it real good with all that face paint and such. Dressed nice, too. Real fancy-like."

"What else?"

Her eyes darted from Caleb to the marshal. "You're gonna get me off, right?"

"I'll do my best," he said. And he would, if she gave him the information he needed.

"Don't know if she's still there, but she always had me come to the boardin' house. After dark, o' course, so's no one would see us talkin'. Sometimes she come out back, but other times I went to her room."

"Where is it?"

"Very back corner of the first floor. It's right easy to sneak in and out without being seen."

Caleb turned without another word and left the building. His boot heels echoed on the planks of the boardwalk as he made his way down the street to Alwilda Herring's boarding house.

Chapter Twenty-five

Caleb and the marshal sneaked around the side of the boarding house, not wanting the woman they were after alerted to their presence. Though the sun had set, the curtains at the window of the corner room hadn't been drawn yet, and they could see lamplight glowing within.

A shapely figure crossed in front of the window, and both men crouched lower. The woman seemed agitated, quickly pacing back the way she had come. Caleb tried to get a look at the woman's face, but the angle of his view only allowed him to see a torso wrapped snugly in bright yellow material.

He waved a hand, signaling Marshal Thompson to follow him to the back of the building, where a door would gain them entrance. When he saw the crooked, rickety steps up to the door, he cautioned the marshal to move stealthily. Any sound might scare off their prey.

Thompson insisted on going in first, gun drawn. Caleb wanted to barrel past the older man; he believed his fury would be much more deadly than even a gun.

Thompson moved forward, and Caleb winced when

the floorboards gave a loud creak. An instant later they heard a door open and close.

"Dammit!" Caleb yelled. "She heard us coming!"

He ran out of the building and around to the front in time to see a flutter of yellow disappear down the street. He raced after it but found only darkness. A lone horse tethered nearby snorted at being awakened from his nap. If only the animal could tell him where the woman had gone.

Caleb cursed as the marshal caught up to him.

"I lost her," he said, smacking his fist against his thigh. "Dammit! She probably saw us, knows we're on to her. She'll never come back here now."

"Let's go back and search the room. Maybe we'll find something that will tell us who she is and where else she might hide."

Caleb nodded and followed Thompson. He felt like a failure. The person he was after was a woman, for God's sake. How hard could it be to catch her? Then he remembered his sister—and his wife—and their single-minded determination, and he admitted that if a woman wanted to hide badly enough, she damn well might not be found until the turn of the millennium.

This time they knocked on the front door of the boarding house. Alwilda Herring took a long while to answer. She opened the door only a crack and squinted through her spectacles at Marshal Thompson, taking her time to confirm his identity. Finally she let him in, only grudgingly allowing Caleb to follow at the lawman's behest.

Thompson explained, without giving away any details, that they needed to speak with the woman who occupied the first-floor corner room. Both men feigned disappointment when no one answered Alwilda's knocks. Thompson smiled and said he'd need to take a look around the room.

The elderly Alwilda stood in the doorway while they searched, her hands propped on her hips as she tapped her foot impatiently. "That girl better not have taken off for good. She still owes me a month's rent. I never should have given her a room. Didn't trust her from the very start. Too bloody secretive, she was, insisting on her privacy. Hmph! Up to no good, I tell you. And she didn't think I knew about her late-night visitors. Caught her once, I did. Was about to throw her out, too, till I saw it was a woman. I won't have any lascivious business going on under my roof. No, sir."

Caleb clenched his jaw to help him endure Alwilda's long list of complaints against the black-haired woman, wishing she had something useful to offer. But Alwilda wasn't even sure of her mysterious boarder's name.

Thompson was rooting through the dresser drawers, so Caleb went to the closet and absently flipped through the dresses there.

He was about to turn away and look elsewhere when a fluff of scarlet fabric caught his attention. He pushed aside the other dresses and moved in for a better look, lifting the gown and bringing it out into the light of the room.

The material and style seemed familiar. He had seen this dress before. But where? What kind of woman would wear a gown this shade of red? With this outrageous cut? And then he remembered.

"Christ!" he swore aloud.

The marshal turned around and gave Caleb a look. "What is it, son? Did you find something?"

Caleb threw the dress onto the bed and ran out of the room.

Thompson followed close on his heels.

"It's Sabrina," he called back. "She's the one trying to hurt Rebecca. She's probably on her way to the house right now."

Rebecca set her stitching on the cushion beside her and gave a little stretch. The baby quilt was coming along nicely.

"Would you like some tea?" Megan asked, hopping

up from her seat on the settee, where she was happily reviewing some of the paperwork she did for Caleb and the Express office. "I'd be happy to make some for you, since Bessie has already gone to bed."

"I'd love some tea," Rebecca answered. "As long as you promise not to put anything but tea leaves and a cinnamon stick in. No strange herbs, mind you."

Megan looked shocked that Rebecca could joke about such a thing.

"I'm fine now," Rebecca pointed out. "In fact, I think I'll help."

"I don't think that's a good idea." Her sister-in-law chewed on the inside of her bottom lip. "Caleb would be furious if he knew I even let you come downstairs. You're still supposed to be in bed."

"I told you, I feel fine. I couldn't stand being cooped up in that room another minute. I'll sit perfectly still and watch you do all the work. All right?"

"All right," Megan agreed. "But you can't tell Caleb. He'll come after me with a switch if he ever finds out."

"It will be our secret. I promise."

Megan went ahead, letting Rebecca follow at her own, much slower pace.

In truth, Rebecca felt marvelous. All signs of the pennyroyal poisoning had long since disappeared, and she was back to her usual self. She smiled. Knowing Caleb loved her had something to do with her quick recovery, she was sure.

She sat at the kitchen table and watched as Megan put on the water to boil and began to set the serving tray. She was about to ask Megan to run upstairs for her shawl when shouts sounded outside, followed by several loud animal screams. Megan dropped the rag in her hand and ran toward the parlor.

She flew back into the room before Rebecca, heavy with child, could even struggle from her chair. "The barn's on fire!" she panted. "Frank and Papa are trying to put it out."

"Dear Lord!"

"You stay here. I'll go help."

Rebecca had never felt so helpless in all her life. She comforted herself with the thought that, even if she hadn't recently recovered from a brush with death, her present condition still wouldn't have allowed her to do much. Her huge girth would have been more of a hindrance than a help. But she couldn't just sit there. She had to know what was going on.

It took her a long minute to lever herself up from the chair. Then she took the tea kettle off its burner before leaving the kitchen. She walked through the dining room and hallway and into the parlor, where she would be able to see the barn from the side window.

She pulled back the draperies and stared at the orange flames licking at the corner of the barn. Holbrook and Megan were busy throwing buckets of water on the blaze, as well as slapping at it with horse blankets. Rebecca began to wonder where Frank was, until she saw the horses charge out of the barn. He soon followed and took up fighting the fire.

"Beautiful, isn't it?"

She whirled around. In the doorway of the parlor stood a tall woman dressed in a gown the color of sunflowers. Rebecca noticed sprigs of hay hanging at its hem, as well as several dirty smudges and a tear just below the waist. She raised her eyes and stared at the woman's face. Loose tendrils of midnight-black hair hung around her cheeks from a lopsided arrangement of curls. Her expression was hard, her blue eyes cold.

"I wasn't sure what I would do to get you alone until I got here. The fire was a nice touch, I think. It ought to keep them occupied for a while."

Even if Rebecca hadn't found a single feature familiar, she would have recognized that hard, grating voice in a minute. "You look . . . different, Sabrina," she said.

Sabrina laughed. "Yes. I couldn't very well stay in town without changing my appearance. You'd be amazed at what coloring your hair can do. No one knew who I was. No one."

Rebecca cleared her throat, unsure what to do. She wasn't even sure why Sabrina had come. "I didn't realize you'd stayed in Leavenworth."

"Of course not. Everyone thought Caleb sent me away." Her voice held a sharp edge. "But he couldn't get rid of me that easily. I will not be pushed aside for some homely, no-account seamstress. Caleb thought he could give me a little money and send me on my way, but he was wrong. *I* decide when to call it quits. *I* decide! Caleb should be with me. And if you hadn't tricked him into marrying you, he would have come back to me."

A chill ran down Rebecca's spine. For the first time since she had turned around to see Sabrina across the room, she felt a real shiver of fear.

"I didn't trick Caleb, Sabrina," she tried to reason. "Truly, I didn't. I really didn't even want to marry him. In fact, you can have him."

Sabrina squinted, confused.

"Yes," she hurried on. "Why, all we have to do is file for divorce. As soon as that's taken care of, he'll be all yours."

While Rebecca didn't mean a word of it, she decided to say whatever she must to mollify Sabrina. If only she could get Sabrina away from the door. It was her only means of escape.

Rebecca began to move away from the window. Little by little she rounded the room. She gave a sigh of relief when Sabrina took the bait and started to move also, keeping parallel to her.

"Caleb would never leave you now. Not with the brat." She waved a shaky hand at Rebecca's stomach.

Rebecca settled a hand on the mound of her belly. "Caleb won't care about me once the baby is born. I didn't really want it anyway. I'd be happy to leave it here and go away."

Sabrina took a moment to digest that piece of information. Then she seemed to come out of her stupor. She shook her head and took several strides toward Rebecca.

Rebecca moved quickly aside until she stood at the opening of the parlor. Her breathing became shallow, her nerves taut.

"You would never do that. Caleb would never let you. No, I have to get you out of the picture—for good."

Hearing that, Rebecca turned and raced for the front door. She yanked it open just as Sabrina grabbed hold of her hair and jerked her backward.

"You're going to die, Rebecca," Sabrina said in a singsong voice. "How would you like to go? I could take you out to the barn and burn you alive, but there might be witnesses." She twisted her fist in Rebecca's hair and steered her into the dining room.

"No, I think I'll use a knife. You have a sharp knife in the kitchen, don't you, Rebecca?" She kicked open the door and pushed Rebecca into the room ahead of her. "Let's see, where would the longest, sharpest knife be? I planned to cut you all along, you know. Only things didn't go as perfectly as I'd planned. No matter, I'll fix it right now."

Rebecca turned her head slightly and found herself pressed against the counter. She spotted the tea kettle almost immediately and prayed for a chance to reach it.

Sabrina searched cupboards and drawers for the perfect murder weapon. She swung around, a helpless Rebecca in tow, and released a sigh of pleasure. "There's one," she said happily. "Right next to the cutting board. Now, how could I have missed that?"

Rebecca saw the cutting board and the glittering silver blade. She closed her eyes and took a deep breath. If only she could turn a fraction of an inch . . .

Sabrina loosened her hold as she moved toward the knife. Rebecca pulled away the necessary inch, ignoring the stinging at her scalp, and reached for the kettle. In a flash of movement, she dumped it over her shoulder, spilling the hot water onto Sabrina's arm.

Sabrina screamed and let go of her hair. Rebecca fell back against the stove, her shoulder burning where the water soaked through her clothes. But she was free.

When Sabrina righted herself, Rebecca threw the pot at her, remaining water and all. She didn't take her eyes off the woman as she began moving toward the back door. If she could get outside, where Holbrook and Megan and Frank were, she would be safe.

Sabrina raised her head. Her hair lay in wet tangles over her shoulders, the black coloring staining her face and clothes. Her eyes were ice-cold with fury. She let out a banshee-like howl and lunged forward.

Rebecca grabbed the heaviest object she could find and swung it with all her might at Sabrina. The woman's eyes rolled back in her head, and she slumped to the floor in a heap of yellow taffeta. A spot of blood oozed from her temple and ran down her cheek.

Rebecca still clutched the large black skillet tightly. When the door behind her flew open, she pivoted and held her weapon at the ready. She sighed with relief when she saw that it was Caleb. The frying pan fell to the floor with a clang as she closed her eyes and slumped forward into his open, waiting arms.

"You really flattened her with an iron skillet?" Megan asked, her eyes wide with excitement.

"She really did," Caleb answered. He grinned and kissed the top of Rebecca's head.

They all sat around the parlor, Holbrook and Megan covered with soot from their battle to save the barn. It had been well worth it, though, for only the door and one corner were scorched. The rest of the building was fine and could be cleaned and repaired with little effort.

Rebecca looked up at her husband, who sat balanced on the arm of the settee, and gave him a weak smile. She still couldn't believe all that had happened that evening. One minute she was being warned to take it easy, and the next she was fighting for her life against a madwoman. It was no wonder she'd swooned. At least Caleb had been there to keep her from falling flat on her face.

That was the most wonderful thing about becoming Rebecca Adams, she decided. There would always be someone there to catch her. The nameless little girl from the Scarlet Garter had finally found a home. Found a family. Found love enough to give and receive. And she reveled in the knowledge that her child—their child—would feel the warmth and wonder of that life from its very first day.

"I'm going to take Rebecca upstairs," Caleb said, rising. "She must be exhausted."

"Oh, but I wanted to hear the story again." Megan hopped up and down on her chair.

"You can hear it again tomorrow. Rebecca needs at least eighteen hours of sleep."

Still inwardly marveling at the many small miracles that had carried her from her cold Kansas City existence into the loving light of the Adams family, Rebecca gazed with deep fondness at Holbrook and Megan as she allowed Caleb to help her to her feet. "Good-night, everyone," she said, "and thank you all."

"Good-night," they chimed in.

Caleb put an arm around Rebecca and helped her up the stairs.

"I'm glad you came home when you did," she said when they got to the bedroom.

"You had the situation pretty much under control by the time I got here," he reminded her. "All the marshal had to do was haul Sabrina away." He lifted her long, silky hair and draped it over one shoulder, then started loosening the hooks at the back of her dress.

She stood so still, Caleb thought she might have fallen asleep on her feet. But a low moan of pleasure escaped her when the pads of his fingers ran over her skin as he pushed the dress down her body to pool at her feet. He swept her up in his arms, and she snuggled against his chest, letting out another contented sigh.

Placing her on the bed, he stripped out of his own clothes before joining her, then drew the covers up over both of them. He pulled her against him so that they were cuddled together, her back to his chest. His arms rested beneath her breasts, over the roundness of her stomach.

He kissed and nuzzled her ear. "I love you, Rebecca," he whispered.

"I love you, too," she said, sounding a bit groggy already. "All of you. Every last infuriating Adams—and every Adams to come."

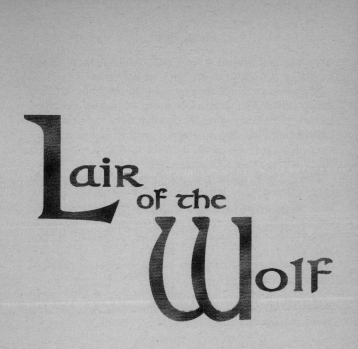

Lair of the Wolf

CHAPTER TWO

Bobbi Smith

Lair of the Wolf also appears in these *Leisure* books:

COMPULSION by Elaine Fox includes
Chapter One by Constance O'Banyon

On January 1, 1997, *Romance Communications*, the Romance Magazine for the 21st century, made its Internet debut. One year later, it was named a Lycos Top 5% site on the Web in terms of both content and graphics!

One of *Romance Communications*' most popular features is The Romantic Relay, an original romance novel divided into twelve monthly installments, with each chapter written by a different author. Our first offering was *Lair of the Wolf*, a tale of medieval Wales, created by, in alphabetical order, celebrated authors Emily Carmichael, Debra Dier, Madeline George, Martha Hix, Deana James, Elizabeth Mayne, Constance O'Banyon, Evelyn Rogers, Sharon Schulze, June Lund Shiplett, and Bobbi Smith.

We put no restrictions on the authors, letting each pick up the tale where the previous author had left off and going forward as she wished. The authors tell us they had a lot of fun, each trying to write her successor into a corner!

Now, preserving the fun and suspense of our month-by-month installments, Leisure Books presents, in print, one chapter a month of *Lair of the Wolf.* In addition to the entire online story, the authors have added some brand-new material to their existing chapters. So if you think you've read *Lair of the Wolf* already, you may find a few surprises. Please enjoy this unique offering, watch for each new monthly installment in the back of your Leisure Books, and make sure you visit our Web site, where another romantic relay is already in progress.

Romance Communications

http://www.romcom.com

Pamela Monck, Editor-in-Chief

Mary D. Pinto, Senior Editor

S. Lee Meyer, Web Mistress

Last month, in Chapter One of *Lair of the Wolf* Lady Meredyth watches the approach of a troop of English soldiers under the command of Sir Garon Saunders, known as Longshanks' Wolf, whom she has been ordered to wed. Refusing to flee the castle and leave behind the people who depend on her, and equally determined that she will not wed Sir Garon, Lady Meredyth disguises herself as a boy to escape detection. Her plan works only too well. Or does it? Sir Garon drafts her to serve him as a squire, and her first duties—to see to his armor . . . and then assist him at his bath!

Chapter Two
by Bobbi Smith

Lady Meredyth fought desperately to control her temper as she carried Sir Garon's armor away. How dare he come into her home and order her about as if she were a servant? He was naught but an Englishman, and she would serve no English master. Her fury quickly faded, replaced by fear as she remembered the look of hardness in his eyes. The Wolf was a warrior, her enemy, and she was completely at his mercy. She had thought herself clever to pose as a boy. But instead she found herself trapped, and trapped well indeed, for he had commanded that she attend his bath.

Meredyth made her way through the castle, lugging the heavy armor as best she could. Dame Allison had told the servants of the need for her disguise, yet they were still startled to see their lady so garbed and with her hair cut as short as a lad's. Meredyth tried to reassure them, but it was difficult, for she, too, was afraid of what the future held.

Stopping to catch her breath before climbing the winding stone stairs that led to the bedchambers, she tried to think of a way to defeat the Wolf and his king, but it seemed so hopeless. What could mere women and children, who were already suffering from the deprivations of war, do against their mighty conquerors? She would have despaired completely had not the memory of her father's praises crept into her thoughts.

"Daughter, you are as bright as your brothers. Sometimes, I think perhaps more so," he had told her. Pride had shone in his eyes that day. "You may not have their physical strength, but you do have intelligence. Always use your wits, my child. They will serve you well."

Blinking back tears, Meredyth tried to concentrate on her father's words. She had to find a way to outsmart and ultimately defeat this invader of her lands.

An idea came to her as she spied a hound sleeping near the hearth. Leaving the armor, she sought out Dame Allison, the only person who could help her with what she needed.

Meredyth found the older woman in the kitchen overseeing the preparation of the meal the Wolf had ordered. Dame Allison looked up as she entered, relief showing plainly on her features.

"Thank God, you're safe!" she said as she rushed to Meredyth's side. "The Wolf didn't recognize you, did he, my lady?" she asked urgently, lowering her voice even though none of the English soldiers were anywhere near the kitchen area.

"No, he quite believed I was who I claimed to be—plain John, formerly squire to the late lord of this castle. In fact," Meredyth said, disgust in her voice, "Sir Garon was so taken in by my claim that he wants me to be his squire and has ordered me to assist him with his bath."

"You cannot!" Dame Allison cried out in horror. "What can the beast be thinking? Why, that would mean that you would have to . . . to . . ."

"I would rather tend to the needs of a real wolf than him," Meredyth complained. "Perhaps, though, as his squire, I will be privy to his more private conversations." She drew in a deep breath, and her chin tilted in defiance. "Then I shall discover his weakness and use it against him."

"But what of his bath?" Dame Allison fretted. "That is the immediate problem."

"That's why I sought you out. I have an idea, but I need your help."

"What would you have me do, my lady?"

"I need one of your sleeping potions—highly potent and quick-acting."

Dame Allison's eyes shone in anticipation. "You would drug him?"

Meredyth nodded. "We will slip the potion into his mead, then see that he is served his meal long before I go to him. By the time I attend him, he will be too sleepy to bathe tonight."

"What of the morrow, my lady?"

Meredyth was silent for a moment. "I must see to this day first."

Dame Allison led her young charge to a bench by the kitchen fire. "Sit you there, my lady, and have some of this stew," she said, scooping up the bowl that had been prepared for Sir Garon's meal and handing it to Lady Meredyth with a chunk of dark bread.

"I will hurry to mix the herbs while you rest yourself a bit," the older woman said, rushing across the room and taking several crockery jars from a high shelf. She lifted the lids off one and then another and another, sniffing each in turn before she found what she wanted. Then she moved a small pot of boiling water from the fire and crumbled a handful of dried herbs into the steaming liquid. After stirring the brew a moment, she added a few more leaves for good measure. "We want our new lord to have a long rest," she said with vigor.

And for the first time that day, Lady Meredyth smiled.

A short time later, a servant was sent to the Wolf's chamber with food and drink. When two serving maids went off to set up his bath, Meredyth knew that the time was nearing for her to go to him. When they returned, she knew she could delay no longer.

"Did Sir Garon drink his mead?" she asked.

The young girls looked frightened. "W-W-We d-don't know," one of the maids said nervously. "W-We were t-too afraid to look."

Grimly, Meredyth knew that she would have to dare entering the chamber alone and pray that he had partaken of the drugged brew. Girding herself, she ventured to the rooms that had once belonged to her parents and now were the quarters of their English conqueror. What

306

had once been a haven of love, this hour threatened to be a torture chamber.

Fervently, Meredith prayed that Dame Allison's potion had worked and that the Wolf was asleep, for she did not know how long she could continue her charade. The Wolf was known for his brilliance and resourcefulness in battle. She would not be able to fool him for long.

Reaching the chamber door, she paused to gather her courage. Her heart was pounding in her breast, and her hands were cold and shaking. Then, bravely, she knocked on the closed portal and waited.

Meredyth's hopes were dashed as the Wolf's call rang out.

"Come."

Her spirits sank. The only hope she could cling to was that he had just begun to drink and would soon drift off. That thought was what gave her the strength to open the door and face the man the king had decreed would be her husband.

Garon looked up as John entered. "It took you long enough, boy. Come. My water grows as cold as my meal," he growled.

"We had thought you would eat right away since you were hungry from your travels this day," she said, trying to keep her voice steady.

"Had I but someone to taste for me, I would have partaken of the fare."

"Taste for you?" Meredyth tried to keep her nervousness from her tone.

"Yes, of course," the Wolf said impatiently, "to make certain that the enemy hasn't poisoned my food."

"You have no enemies here, sire," she said quickly, but the words sounded unconvincing, even to her.

"Are you so sure, young John?" he asked mockingly as he stripped off his shirt and stood before her, naked to the waist.

307

Her expression faltered as she stared at his broad shoulders and powerful, darkly furred chest. He was a fine specimen of manhood, but she could not appreciate his male beauty. He was the enemy. He was English. She swallowed nervously and looked away as she mumbled, "Yes, lord."

He gave the youth a hard look. "Well, I am not. Since you are so certain of everyone's loyalty, you shall taste of the mead for me. It doesn't smell quite right."

"The mead, lord?" Meredyth was trapped. To refuse would indicate guilt.

"Well?" He lifted one eyebrow as he waited.

"Yes, lord." She moved to the table and lifted the heavy mug. She took a sip and replaced the vessel on the tray.

"Come, John," Garon taunted, watching her with a knowing gaze. "You're a hardy young fellow. You can do better than that. Take a deep drink."

With all the inner strength she could muster, Meredyth lifted the mug to her lips and drank deeply. She did not know how long she would be able to fight off the effects of the potion, since Dame Allison had made it as strong as possible to fell the Wolf for the entire night.

Sir Garon turned away to shed the rest of his clothes. "Well, John, how does it sit?" he asked conversationally.

"Fine, my lord, although I rarely drink mead and have little knowledge of it." Meredyth had not looked up until then, and when she did, her eyes widened. He had intimidated her before, but now as he stood before her nearly naked, he was even more compelling. There was no denying that the name they'd given him suited—the Wolf. This English knight was strong. There was no spare flesh upon his powerful, manly form. Every inch of his body was solid muscle. As their gazes met, she saw the keen intelligence in his eyes and knew that it would be dangerous, possibly even deadly, to underestimate him. She would not make that mistake again.

"Bring what soap you have and cloths for washing. Attend me as I bathe, John. I want to hear more from you about Lady Meredyth. You say she is taller than I am, has blackened teeth, and the temper of a shrew?"

"Yes, sire," she said, finding that she had to concentrate carefully in order to say even those simple words.

Garon turned to face her as he removed the last of his clothes. Then he stepped into the tub of hot water the servants had set near the fire and settled in for his bath.

At the sight of him so revealed, Meredyth quickly looked away, but not before she had seen his entire manly physique. For all of her life, her virtue and innocence had been fiercely guarded by her father and brothers. But no longer. She had no protector now. She was alone, and she was afraid. She began to tremble, but she had to be brave, for herself and for her people.

Garon seemed unaware of the effect he was having on his squire. His voice was contemplative as he spoke. "The king has commanded that I wed your lady, and he looks upon me with favor. Yet if what you say is true, why do you suppose he would see me married to such a hag?"

Meredyth was approaching the tub from behind, glad that she only had to look at his bare back and shoulders. His words infuriated her, and she almost lost her temper. He'd called her a hag! The urge to hit him was almost overwhelming, but she caught herself in time. She had created the lie, and now she had to live with it.

"Those of us who love Lady Meredyth do not think of her as such," she said in her own defense, wondering if the words sounded as shrill and high-pitched to the Wolf as they did to her.

Sir Garon's eyes narrowed thoughtfully. "How do you think of her, John?"

"Why, she is . . . she is kind to those in need. And she cares for the sick and loves little children. It is injustice and violence that she hates." Meredyth began a recitation of her own finer points. "Had she been born a man, she would have taken up the sword like her father and brothers. She would have fought and died beside them, rather than live on to face this."

"This?" Sir Garon taunted.

"English on our lands . . ." Meredyth was suddenly light-headed, and she realized that the potion was taking effect.

"You think the English are monsters?"

"They are . . . You are . . ." Her words were slurring, and she found herself swaying on her feet.

"A monster, my lady?"

His voice seemed to come to her from a great distance, and the words *my lady* echoed eerily in her mind. She was vaguely aware that he had risen and stepped from the tub. He stood before her, a shimmering giant.

She knew she should be afraid of him, that she should flee and save herself. The last thing she saw as darkness overtook her were his eyes, dark and gleaming, and his feral smile as he closed the distance between them.

Meredyth's head was aching, and she wondered why she felt so awful. She supposed she must have taken ill. Her thoughts were fuzzy and disjointed as she tried to recall when she had been stricken.

And then her memory returned.

Her eyes flew open as she remembered that she had been forced to drink the drugged mead she had intended for the Wolf.

Meredyth was shocked to find herself in bed in the master chamber. She started to sit up, wanting to get out of there, needing to escape, but the sudden movement intensified the pain in her head, and she groaned out loud. Bracing herself, she tried to get her bearings. Only then did she realize that she was naked beneath the covers. Shame colored her cheeks as she clutched the blanket to her breast. How had she come to this?

She tried frantically to recall exactly what had happened. All she could remember was calling the Wolf a monster . . . and him standing naked before her. . . .

"So, you're finally awake?"

Meredyth saw him standing before her now, albeit in clothing, and her anger cleared her befuddled mind. "You!" she exclaimed. "I demand to know what happened here. How did I come to this?"

"You *demand?*" His dark eyebrows arched, and his tone was mocking. "By your own words, you are but a squire. Or could it be that you were deliberately trying to deceive me? Have I the honor of speaking to my future bride, Lady Meredyth?"

Her trickery exposed, high color stained her cheeks. She wanted to freeze him with an icy, regal glare, but her head was hurting too badly. She managed only to look more bedraggled than outraged. "I am Lady Meredyth," she said with what little dignity she could muster.

"And I am your intended, Sir Garon Saunders. Rumor had it that you were tall and ugly, with a terrible disposition, but events of the night just past have proven otherwise." His gaze went over her with a knowing look.

Meredyth's blush deepened. She had no actual knowledge of what intimacy transpired between a man and a woman, so how could she know if . . . "You didn't dare!"

"I would dare much to claim what it is rightfully mine." His tone was fierce, as was his expression. "I do not look kindly on those who would betray me."

Panic seized Meredyth as she saw for the first time the fury that Garon's enemies faced when they met him in mortal combat. And this was combat. She was fighting for her very soul.

Watch for Chapter Three of Lair of the Wolf *by Evelyn Rogers, appearing in February 2000 in* Sweet Revenge *by Lynsay Sands.*

Lair of the Wolf

Constance O'Banyon, Bobbi Smith, Evelyn Rogers, Emily Carmichael, Martha Hix, Deana James, Sharon Schulze, June Lund Shiplett, Elizabeth Mayne, Debra Dier, and Madeline George

Be sure not to miss a single installment of Leisure Books's star-studded new serialized romance, *Lair of the Wolf*! A tale of medieval Wales, *Lair of the Wolf* was originally featured in *Romance Communications*, the popular romance magazine on the Internet. Each author picked up the tale where the previous chapter had left it and moved forward with the story as she wished. Preserving the fun and suspense of the month-by-month installments, Leisure presents one chapter a month of the entire on-line story, including some brand new material the authors have added to their existing chapters. Watch for a new installment of *Lair of the Wolf* every month in the back of select Leisure books!

Previous chapters of *Lair of the Wolf* can be found in:

___4648-2   *Compulsion* by Elaine Fox $5.99 US/$6.99 CAN
which includes Chapter One by Constance O'Banyon

NEXT MONTH: Chapter Three by Evelyn Rogers can be found in:
___4680-6 *Sweet Revenge* by Lynsay Sands $5.99 US/$6.99 CAN

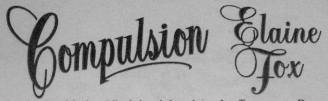

Compulsion Elaine Fox

On the smoldering Virginia night when she first meets Ryan St. James, Catra Meredyth knows nothing can douse the fire that the infuriating Yankee has ignited within her. With one caress the handsome seducer has kindled a passion that threatens to turn the Southern belle's reputation to ashes—and with one torrid kiss she consigns herself to the flames. Ryan has supped at the table of sin, but on Catra's lips he has tasted heaven. A dedicated bachelor, Ryan finds that the feisty beauty tempts even his strongest resolve. In the heat of their love is a lesson to be learned: The needs of the flesh cannot be denied, but the call of the heart is stronger by far.

Also includes the first installment of *Lair of the Wolf*, a serialized romance set in medieval Wales. Be sure to look for future chapters of this exciting story featured in Leisure books and written by the industry's top authors.

___4648-2 $5.99 US/$6.99 CAN

Dorchester Publishing Co., Inc.
P.O. Box 6640
Wayne, PA 19087-8640

Please add $1.75 for shipping and handling for the first book and $.50 for each book thereafter. NY, NYC, and PA residents, please add appropriate sales tax. No cash, stamps, or C.O.D.s. All orders shipped within 6 weeks via postal service book rate. Canadian orders require $2.00 extra postage and must be paid in U.S. dollars through a U.S. banking facility.

Name_____
Address_____
City_____State_____Zip_____
I have enclosed $_____ in payment for the checked book(s).
Payment <u>must</u> accompany all orders. ❑ Please send a free catalog.
CHECK OUT OUR WEBSITE! www.dorchesterpub.com

The Snow Queen
ANNE AVERY

When Boston-bred Hetty Malone arrives at the Colorado Springs train station, she is full of hope that she will soon marry her childhood sweetheart and live happily ever after. Yet life amid the ice-capped Rockies has changed Michael Ryan. No longer the hot-blooded suitor Hetty remembers, the young doctor has grown as cold and distant as the snowy mountain peaks. Determined to revive Michael's passionate longing, Hetty quickly realizes that no modern medicine can cure what ails him. But in the enchanted splendor of her new home, she dares to administer the only remedy that might melt his frozen heart: a dose of good old-fashioned loving.

_52151-2 $5.99 US/$6.99 CAN

HAWK

ELAINE BARBIERI

"How can you stand to let him touch you, Eden? He's an *injun!*" Young and idealistic, Eden believes passion will overcome the obstacle of her lover's Kiowa heritage; instead, the hatred and prejudice of two cultures at war force them apart. "Her arms cling to you and your heart answers, but the woman will never by yours." Such is the shaman's prediction about the beautiful girl he once adored, but Iron Hawk refuses to believe it. Eden's betrayal might have sent him to the white man's jail, but her smooth, pale body will still be his. A hardened warrior now, he believes her capture will satisfy his need for revenge; instead, her love will heal their hearts and bring a lasting peace to their people.

___4646-6 $5.99 US/$6.99 CAN

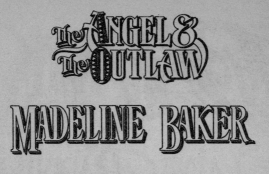

THE ANGEL & THE OUTLAW

MADELINE BAKER

Bestselling Author Of *Lakota Renegade*

An outlaw, a horse thief, a man killer, J.T. Cutter isn't surprised when he is strung up for his crimes. What amazes him is the heavenly being who grants him one year to change his wicked ways. Yet when he returns to his old life, he hopes to cram a whole lot of hell-raising into those twelve months no matter what the future holds.

But even as J.T. heads back down the trail to damnation, a sharp-tongued beauty is making other plans for him. With the body of a temptress and the heart of a saint, Brandy is the only woman who can save J.T. And no matter what it takes, she'll prove to him that the road to redemption can lead to rapturous bliss.

_3931-1 $5.99 US/$7.99 CAN

Dorchester Publishing Co., Inc.
P.O. Box 6640
Wayne, PA 19087-8640

Archer's Crossing — **JEAN BARRETT**

Crossing Archer Owen seems like the last thing anybody would want to do, or so Margaret Sheridan thinks. Bringing dinner to the convicted murderer is terrifying—for though he is nothing like her affluent fiancé, he stirs a hunger in her she has never known. Then the condemned prisoner uses her to make his getaway. In the clutches of the handsome felon, Margaret races into the untamed West—chasing a man Owen claims could clear his name. Margaret wonders if there is anything Archer won't do. And then he kisses her, and she prays there isn't. For if this bitter steamboat captain is half the man she suspects, she'd ride to Hell itself to clear his name and win his captive heart.

___4502-8 $5.99 US/$6.99 CAN

SONYA BIRMINGHAM

Song of the Lark

When the beautiful wisp of a mountain girl walks through his front door, Stephen Wentworth knows there is some kind of mistake. The flame-haired beauty in trousers is not the nanny he envisions for his mute son Tad. But one glance from Jubilee Jones's emerald eyes, and the widower's icy heart melts and his blood warms. Can her mountain magic soften Stephen's hardened heart, or will their love be lost in the breeze, like the song of the lark?

___4393-9 $5.50 US/$6.50 CAN

Love, Cherish Me
Rebecca Brandewyne

The man in black shows his hand: five black spades. Storm Lesconflair knows what this means—she now belongs to him. The close heat of the saloon flushes her skin as she feels the half-breed's eyes travel over her body. Her father's plantation house in New Orleans suddenly seems but a dream, while the handsome stranger before her is all too real. Dawn is breaking outside as the man who won her rises and walks through the swinging doors. She follows him out into the growing light, only vaguely aware that she has become his forever, never guessing that he has also become hers.

__52302-7 $5.99 US/$6.99 CAN

Dorchester Publishing Co., Inc.
P.O. Box 6640
Wayne, PA 19087-8640

Please add $1.75 for shipping and handling for the first book and $.50 for each book thereafter. NY, NYC, and PA residents, please add appropriate sales tax. No cash, stamps, or C.O.D.s. All orders shipped within 6 weeks via postal service book rate. Canadian orders require $2.00 extra postage and must be paid in U.S. dollars through a U.S. banking facility.

Name_____
Address_____
City_____State_____Zip_____
I have enclosed $_____ in payment for the checked book(s).
Payment <u>must</u> accompany all orders. ❑ Please send a free catalog.
      CHECK OUT OUR WEBSITE! www.dorchesterpub.com

ATTENTION ROMANCE CUSTOMERS!

SPECIAL TOLL-FREE NUMBER
1-800-481-9191

Call Monday through Friday
10 a.m. to 9 p.m.
Eastern Time
*Get a free catalogue,
join the Romance Book Club,
and order books using your
Visa, MasterCard,
or Discover®*

Leisure
Books